WALKING HAWK

Crazy Horse gazed through the open tipi flap upon the distant walls of the Black Hills. "You must be given rank," he said. "Tonight you shall receive Canounye Kicicupi."

My heart rabbited up within me at these words. I was to receive the Giving-of-War-Weapons, among the highest of Sioux ceremonies. By its ancient rites, I would become forever Oglala.

To the tribe it meant the birth of a new warrior, Walking Hawk, into the band. To me it meant the death of Col. John Clayton, Confederate States Army officer, southern gentleman, white man.

To all other white men, wheresoever I should meet them, it would mean one deadly unforgiven thing —Indian lover.

NO SURVIVORS
WILL HENRY

BANTAM BOOKS
TORONTO · NEW YORK · LONDON · SYDNEY

While the character of Colonel Clayton and his journal, which constitutes the book, are purely fictional, all references to historical characters both white and Indian, battles, Indian campaigns and other recorded incidents of the Indian warfare are true to the history of the period.

NO SURVIVORS
*A Bantam Book / published by arrangement with
Random House, Inc.*

PRINTING HISTORY
*Random House edition published October 1950
2nd printing . . . January 1951
Doubleday Adventure Book Club edition published June 1951
Serialization syndicated by NEA Service, Inc., September 1951
Bantam edition / December 1951
2nd printing . . December 1951   3rd printing . . . . January 1952
New Bantam edition / November 1953
New Bantam edition / September 1965
2nd printing . . . . . . July 1969   3rd printing . . . . . . June 1978
4th printing . . . September 1983*

ISBN 0-553-23698-9

Published simultaneously in the United States and Canada

". . . What happened to Custer that 25th day of June, 1876, from the time he disappeared with his 225 troopers into the twisted hills which flanked and straddled Sitting Bull's great war camp on the Little Big Horn, has preoccupied historians ever since.

"It is at best an endless riddle, for the tongue of silence is the language of the dead, and the only living thing found on the field forty-eight hours later, was Captain Keogh's horse Comanche . . ."

Battle of the Little Big Horn

PART ONE

Chapter 1

HISTORY talks with many tongues and they are not all straight. Captain Keogh's horse Comanche may indeed have been the only living thing found on the banks of the Little Big Horn "forty-eight hours" (as the books say) after Custer's last battle, but the implication that the horse was the only survivor of the general's immediate command is not true. There was another survivor, though, to be sure, "forty-eight hours later" found him riding far out and away from the stark windrows of tongueless dead. And riding far out and away from the remembered pages of history. I was that survivor.

It is not the purpose of this journal to dim the memory which General George A. Custer enjoys among our people as a hero. But I saw him die, and the tragic knowledge of the detail of that final hour will not rest in me. I write with the hope the heroes may stay alive in legend, while their dead rest in peace.

I was sixteen when the War between the States burst into bright flame. Within the year I was brevetted a captain, and, following Chickamauga, one year to the month later, I was promoted to field grade. I spent the next eight months under J. E. B. Stuart, and was again brevetted, this time at Spottsylvania, to full colonel. My age at the time: nineteen years, seven months.

I was twenty-one, a full Colonel of Confederate Cavalry,

Transcribed from the personal journal of Colonel John Buell Clayton, C.S.A. (1844-1878). Colonel Clayton's documentary of his life on the frontier from the spring of '66 to late winter '78, including his strange part in the Custer Massacre, exists in fact today, among the papers of the Clayton family of La Grange, Georgia.

In working from the original it has been necessary to abbreviate and rephrase in part, and even to furnish some connective continuity where the colonel's original was illegible. However, no essential detail has been deleted or altered.

the night Lee called his last war council in the wood outside Appomattox.

As these words fall onto paper they appear all too simple. But I had found the war a fierce crucible, it being my fortune to be continually in its highest heats. As a result, if I wasn't the hardest of the forgings dropped from its metal, I wasn't the softest, either.

This statement will appear immodest. Well, to one who hasn't ground his teeth on a pistol barrel while a dirty-fingered army surgeon digs a .50-caliber Yankee slug out of his groin, it may. Or again, if one hasn't enjoyed the pleasures of biting his own arm to keep from screaming like a woman while an orderly pours fuming nitric acid into a saber cut across the great muscles of the back, he too, may be excused his dubiety.

But to a boy who experienced such things at an age when most youths are pondering school sums or giggling with girls over a church supper, the accounting seems bare enough.

At the time I would have thought I could take Appomattox without the quiver of a face-muscle, yet to watch Lee that night, as he read the requiem mass of the Confederacy, would have broken the heart of a rock.

Our forces were chopped to pieces. Yet they were fighting furiously when at 3:00 A.M. General Lee sent to know what progress we were making. I was with General Gordon as cavalry liaison officer when the message came to our front. I heard his reply.

"Tell General Lee," he stated, quietly, "that my command has been fought to a frazzle and unless Longstreet can unite in the movement, I cannot long go forward."

Colonel Venable, Lee's aide, later told me that when he delivered his message, the old warrior stared into the morning blackness, soundless for a full minute, then slowly announced, "There is nothing left for me but to go see General Grant, and I had rather die a thousand deaths."

In the following reaction on our immediate front I had my first contact with the man who was to prove such a fateful factor in my later life, and who was to furnish by his strange death, one of the greatest military mysteries of all time. My first sight of him was as he came riding into our lines from the Union side in company with our Confederate truce officer, Colonel Green Peyton.

Our message to the Union commander had read: "General Gordon has received notice from General Lee of a flag of truce, stopping the battle." The Union commander opposite was the hated Sheridan. Hence, all of us on Gordon's staff were prepared for the awkward task of responding gracefully to "Little Phil's" approach.

Imagine our feelings when we saw, not Sheridan, returning with Peyton, but an unknown Union general whose appearance was so remarkable as to keep us all in silence as he drew up.

The man's posture and motion in saddle were faultless. Accustomed as were all us Southerners to fine horsemanship, none of us had beheld a more thrilling rider.

He was a thin man, as gracefully slender as a woman, yet with the impression of whipcord in that slenderness. He wore his hair falling in great flat curls to his shoulders, and in the coming sun of that funeral day, it gleamed with the brightness of yellow-gold.

A nervous private, standing close to me in ranks, muttered aloud, "Look at his hair. Yellower'n field-corn in August."

This compelling officer galloped up to General Gordon, halting his charger with a beautiful flourish of horsemanship a scant foot from the nose of the general's mount. Presenting his saber in salute, he announced: "General Gordon, sir, I am General Custer and bear a message to you from General Sheridan. The General desires me to present you his compliments, and to demand the immediate and unconditional surrender of all the troops under your command."

Gordon, white-lipped, replied, "You will please, General, return my compliments to General Sheridan, and say to him that I shall not surrender my command."

Unperturbed, the Union officer concluded, "General Sheridan directs me to say to you, sir, that if there is any hesitation about your surrender, he has you surrounded and can annihilate your command in an hour."

General Gordon remained adamant, saying his position was perhaps better known to him than to Sheridan, and that if the latter wished the responsibility for further slaughter, it was his.

Custer now saluted, wheeling his horse as if to depart, but instead edging the nervous beast along our lines until he halted him in front of me. Looking intently at me, he saluted. Puzzled, I returned the salute and we both sat looking at one another.

My mind raced in search of an explanation of his singling-out of me. Then, even before he spoke, I had it.

When Custer had approached our command, while he was still seventy-five yards out, an ungallant Confederate private had half-raised his musket as though to fire at him. Guessing the fellow's intent, I had struck his piece from his hand, ordering his arrest in a back-flung sentence without taking my eyes off the approaching Union officer. The private was a hill man from Tennessee, one of the deadliest shots in the company. I was satisfied Custer had been a trigger-finger twitch from death; the honor of the Confederate Army equally close to lasting disgrace.

But the action had been so swift, so completely trivial to the major drama, that men in our own company had not noticed its occurrence. That Custer might have seen this by-play seemed incredible.

"Colonel"—his voice had a disturbing depth—"my compliments. You have doubtless saved my life. Should our paths cross again, I shall remember you."

Turning to go, he gestured toward the soldier who would have shot him. With a nod to me, he queried, "May I issue an order, Colonel?" I nodded back, perfunctorily, and he immediately called to the corporal whose detail stood guard over my glowering trooper. "Corporal. Release your prisoner, please. Give him back his rifle." Then, wheeling his horse in a sharp, near-foot spin, he presented his saber to the entire line. His parting words were all the more memorable for the deep hush in which they were delivered.

"My compliments to the incomparable Confederate Army." He was gone in an instant, dashing off to his own lines.

Chapter 2

I SHALL recount nothing further of the death of the Confederacy at Appomattox. Such accounting as has been given, may be regarded as the preface to the real saga of my life, its westward course following my abortive attempt to "go home" after the surrender.

My sole assets at the outset of the journey west, beyond a personal hardihood already described, were my horse and an old Colt Dragoon revolver. I assume the three of us made something less than a reassuring picture.

Hussein, as the foundation of this dilapidated trio, contributed his full share to our appearance of villainy. A magnificent bay stallion, reputed to carry in his veins, undiluted, the blood of the original Barb, he had been presented to me by my troops after Chickamauga.

He had somehow miraculously survived the last two years of the war, but at what price! A Union Minié ball had ploughed a crooked furrow aslant the last five ribs of his near-side. To balance this, he bore half a dozen foot-long, saber scars on the off-side, these diligently appliquéd there by various Yankee students in sundry cavalry-crocheting bees. His off-ear had been inletted by a charge of Union grape, that I believe was looking for me, and, as a result, it flopped down with all the elan of a Georgia jackass's. His winter coat half shed out, his mane and tail splintered alike by bullet and bramble, his numerous battle wounds and picket scars grown-in a ghostly white, his general condition that of a coondog fed on creekwater, he was indeed as lordly a Rosinante as ever Confederate Quixote bestrode. Withal, he was so thin his shadow had holes in it.

Nor was his appearance alone wicked. Hussein's happiness of spirit lay somewhere between that of a wounded grizzly and a rutting elk. He hated mankind in general, womenkind in particular, would kill another horse quicker than look at him. Two things were sound about him: his lungs and heart. The former had never known exhaustion, the latter was as big and strong as a nailkeg, containing in all its iron-bound stavings, one sentiment only—an abiding love for me.

I was fit companion to this beast. My outfit was not gray simply from the colors of my beloved cause. Over all my person, from the crown of the rim-crimped stetson to the worn-open toes of the high cavalry boots, lay a film of powdery dust. This deposit did nothing to enhance my features, none too graced by nature in the first place. I once overheard a private of my command describe me to a courier.

"Yew'll find Cunnel Clayton on the left front up ahaid. Look fer where the Minié balls is thickest and the most Rebel yells comin' from. He'll be the one 'bout three ax-handles tall and one broad acrost the shoulders. If yew cain't find him from that, look fer a face like a Cherokee's standin' ahint a mustache black as a Yankee's heart and stiffer'n a bobcat's whiskers in squattin' time. If yew still cain't spot him, give a Johnny-yell. The fust officer which hollers, 'Forward, men!' is him."

This sketch of my charms, while florid, need not be greatly footnoted. A union of black Irish and deep Creole blood in my ancestry had conspired to leave me with a face and complexion more designed for a murdering aborigine than a Georgia gentleman.

One would not think a mere gun could claim a personality warranting description. But the Colt Dragoon which had hung at my side since First Manassas, defying all replacements by later models, had earned that distinction.

Dubbed "Ol' Cottonmouth" by some forgotten soldier, it had gained that title in my command because of the number of Yankee visitors it had welcomed with true Southern courtesy. It was credited with having struck down more Yanks than the dysentery.

It was this tender trio which favored Market Square in Kansas City with its appearance in the spring of '66, a little over a year after Appomattox. It had taken me that long in the South to learn that the Yankees spelled reconstruction and destruction the same way.

First, I had found the Clayton plantation effectively dedicated by Sheridan to Sherman's proposition that war was hell. My mother had died: my two sisters "gone Nawth."

I hung around below the Line, working the cribs and card games from Macon to Mobile, from Augusta to Austin. I went up the Mississippi on a river boat, gambling. I got shot in Memphis, losing my roll and thirty pounds of good weight. I drifted back home, crowding twenty-three, a border-tough, cardsharp, bordello client, general all-around ruffian. I'd been out to Texas and hadn't liked it. But I'd been "up the river" and heard talk of Kansas City, the Oregon Road, and California.

Kansas City of the late '60's was the head kettle of the frontier fleshpots. And Market Square was the raw heart of the red meat in that kettle. Here came the off-season scourings of the frontier to "simmer in the sun and summer in the sin." Here were the cowmen, traders, trappers and buffalo hunters of the West, in town for a hot summer before another hard winter. Here were the emigrants, teamsters, scouts and wagon captains, drawing a last safe breath before sailing their prairie schooners out into the perilous Indian sea, beyond.

Here were all the refinements of the effete East laid out for sale to the grimy buckskin brigade whose members were following spring down the Missouri from Montana, and up the Red from Texas. Here a buffalo hunter could buy one of the new Henry rifles for $100 or seventy-five prime robes. Here a horn-fisted trapper from the Upper Snake could sell fifty winter beaver for $200 and buy a woman for one dollar. Here cowmen picked up herd-delivery checks of $85,000, following sixty- or ninety-day drives from the Staked Plains, and left half or all the money scattered around Market Square and its sub-arteries of sin, in less than twenty-four hours.

My problem was where and how to get an outfit. A pressing problem, too, but in the interests of candor I must admit an ace-in-the-hole.

The day after Appomattox I had sold my saber to a souvenir-hunting Union lieutenant for twenty dollars. This precious blade was, I informed my benefactor, General Gordon's personal property, given me by him in gratitude for my faithful service. The fact I had taken it no earlier than the day before, from a luckless Yankee officer in no way diseased my conscience. All's fair in peace as well as war. Caveat emptor.

The money still held lonely vigil in the breast pocket of my tattered army jacket. It must be admitted, too, the thought had crossed my mind that should this golden ace need a blue-steel "kicker," such a card hung low and handy in the worn holster at my side.

Thus, the old Colt, the lieutenant's goldpiece and I set out from Market Square to improve our fortunes.

I dropped the reins on Hussein, leaving him standing amidst the teeming activity of the square. I had no worry he would not be there on my return. It would have been worth any man's broken bones to touch him, much less take him off.

I shall always maintain it is the "s" of Southern to partake properly of spirits, and the "g" of Gentleman to know the spots on a pasteboard. My education in cards and whiskey had begun early and run late. I fancied that among other of the little polishes of self-preservation, I could take care of myself in a poker game. My first thoughts of multiplying the twenty-dollar goldpiece turned around visions of straights, flushes and fours-of-a-kind. I thought I was old enough to know a bust from a bobtail when the chips were down.

It did not take long to locate as chancy a game as a man would care to buy into. Even from ten feet away, the deck looked as cold as a clam in an ice-cake.

Five men, all hard cases, had a saddle blanket spread on the ground in the shade alongside a livery barn. The play was table stakes and, as in all camp games, the stakes were running high. A gallery of frontier riff-raff circled around the players. Elbowing my way forward, I watched the play for several minutes.

Chief of the camp scavengers who preyed upon the free-spending buffalo hunters were the deliberate cardsharpers. These airy-fingered gentry ran a pose of being honest trappers or prospectors but in reality were on the range for one purpose: to sweat the spendable suet off the hard-fatted calves of the frontier. They worked in pairs, a skillful team making enormous profits in a good season; a good season being any one they happened to survive.

Still, by the very nature of their profession and of the rawhide gentility of the clientele upon which they practised it, these sharps were nearly always gunfighters and killers. Their routine never varied: build a game to a point where they were losing, then set in to fleece the honest player unmercifully. The answer to any and all objections to the style of play from this point on, was the six-gun. The clean player who opened his mouth to question any deal would be summarily shot out from behind his hand. Few were those who cared to declare for sweet fairness under such rules.

Three hands were enough to let me know where the spots were on this leopard. The game was crooked as a hound's hind leg and twice as dirty.

Stepping out of the circle of onlookers, I slid the old Dragoon out of the holster, spun the cylinder, flexed the hammer, eased the gun gently back into its worn resting place. When I had made my way back into the circle, one player, white-faced and shaking, had just risen and left the game. I stepped into his place, dropped to one knee, asked for cards. As these were being dealt me, I gave my holster just a suggestion of a forward shift, observing calmly, "If no one has any objections, we'll play honest poker."

Not a word interrupted the soft fall of the cards. The two men who had been rigging the game, and opposite to whom I had been careful to place myself, looked across the blanket at me for a brief moment after the last card fell. Then, not troubling to regard me again, they picked up their cards and the play continued.

In a few hands, with a luck not inherent in an honest deck, I had won a considerable amount. Now came the hand for which I had been waiting. From the betting it was evident everyone had been dealt a big hand. The man on my right opened; I raised. The man on my left, a small, simian-eyed prospector, raised. The first of the two riggers did likewise and his partner raised him. The last man dropped.

The game getting where it was, it was time to take a last sizing of the opposition.

The man on my left front, the smaller of the two sharps, was exceedingly thin, shallow-eyed, nervous and quick, with a mouth almost lipless, above a sallow, weedy goatee. His clothing was stylish, of good quality. It would be fatally easy to underrate his hypersensitive type in a gunplay.

The other man was big, quiet, compelling, not quite the picture of the conventional cardman. I got the feeling, watching him make his lazy, slow moves handling cards and money, there was in him some animal strain of vitality. In the entire play he had not said a word, making his bets and requests with monosyllabic grunts.

It would be a hazard to fix his age, but it was probably no less than thirty-five. His dress was that of a buffalo hunter. Two late-model Colts hung low and far forward on his massive thighs. At variance with the custom, he wore his mustache trimmed close and was otherwise smooth-shaven, while his hair, which was the most singular hue of ashen-gray, escaped in thick growth from beneath his black slouch hat. His skin was prairie-burned almost mahogany. This, with his strange, pale eyes and silver hair, presented an unforgettable contrast. In build he was heavy, yet one knew before he moved just how he would be; light, easy, deceptive, blindingly fast.

We now all took cards. The man called Slate was dealing.

I held three queens, drawing the fourth and a jack. The only sounds came from the watchers, an occasional cough, the nervous clearing of a throat, the sibilant movements of many feet in thick dust. I knew, without looking, that those behind me were drawing back and away.

"How much left in your pile?" My words, directed to Slate, broke the richest silence I'd ever paid to listen to.

Without moving his head, which was bent in study of his hand, he raised his pale eyes until they met and held mine. This was the first time our glances had met directly. I confess to a momentary nervousness and, had wishes been wings, I would have been soaring far away from there. The feeling passed and, since under the rules of a table-stake game, a player must answer the question, Slate told me what I wanted to know.

"Three hundred." His voice was as flat as the click of a cocked trigger.

"All right, my friend." I hoped my voice wasn't shaking any worse than a wet hound in a hailstrom. "I'll tap you."

In a moment, every dollar in sight was in the middle of the blanket. The little man looked repeatedly at Slate, but the latter's field of vision never wavered from my mid-person, a field which included, very nicely, my cards, my hands, my gun.

The play had now reached the point of no return. To the crowd it must have seemed I was playing squarely into the hands of the crooked gamblers. I had built up a big pot, betting into their combined hands, and had cleaned the table on the last raise after the draw.

"You're called." The big man's deep-grunted phrase had all the salutary effect of a tumbler of ice water thrown into the small of the back. Let no one tell you the hairs at the nape of the neck cannot rise; human hackles literally lift.

"Queens. Four of them." The cards accompanied my words.

"Full," said the smaller man. "Tens over jacks."

The big man seemed to hesitate. My whole body was singing-tight. Then his cards came down. "Four aces."

My left hand was on the ground in front of me, my right free, carried lightly across my right knee. "I reckon you didn't hear me when I said we'd play honest poker." I scarcely recognized my own voice.

Slate's hand froze in mid-reach for the pot.

In gentler times and places the charge of cheating at cards has proven the most reliable percussion for the cap of gun-play. Both my men wore double pistols. I made no move for my own.

The little man went for his and I shot him in the stomach. He had his guns out, though their muzzles never pointed higher than groundward. From the tail of my eye, my gaze and gun now covering Slate, I saw the other gambler slide slowly forward, eyes wide, his body following his guns down into the dirt of the stableyard. He rolled partly on his right side, started to say something, hemorrhaged and died.

Slate's hand remained in mid air.

"Any more bets?" My voice rasped with tension.

Slate's hand drew back. His eyes on mine, as they had been from the onset, he grunted very softly, "I'll pass."

With that he was on his feet in a motion which defied any definition of starting and stopping. No further word or glance did I get. He simply turned and vanished, the crowd drawing back to admit him, closing again to swallow him.

Chapter 3

I SHALL never know why Slate threw in and backed down. Even at the time I knew it was not from fear. Later, when I learned from events then undreamed, that he always played his string deadout, I could guess he made his decision with characteristic coolness. I had him outgunned, his partner was out of the play. The cards, for that deal, were stacked against him. At the time, as well as now, I can only guess that he weighed the stakes, found them light and tossed in accordingly. My humbling of him, pridewise, meant nothing. He proved the only man I ever went up against who carried not an ounce of the fat of human weakness on his spiritual frame.

But there on the blanket in front of me were nine hundred hard Yankee dollars. All mine by Colt-induced default.

Rising to go, I felt a hand on my shoulder. Tensing, I glanced at it, finding it more nearly resembled the paw of an old boar grizzly, than any human member. The owner of the hand redeemed the note of its bearlike promise.

He was not over five and a half feet tall, weighing I would say, two hundred pounds, yet his voice was oddly soft, almost womanlike. "Son, I thought for a minute there you was gonna be weighed down by your boots when you made the big jump."

"Friend," I agreed, anxious to talk now that the tension was broken, "I was never so scared in my life."

"Wouldn't be surprised." There was a chuckle in the soft voice. "You looked cool as a cucumber and twice as green. Any idee who that was you was buckin'?"

Reaction to the string-up of the game was setting in hard. My esophagus wrestled manfully to see if it couldn't keep my stomach pinned down. Apparently it could, at least long enough for me to answer. "No, none at all. His partner called him 'Slate,' I think."

"Yep. That's right. Name's Slatemeyer. John Slatemeyer. Slate to his friends, of which there ain't none. Leastaways, there ain't now that you slung your gun on his partner."

My new friend went cheerfully on. "He's got another brand on him in this here range's tally books, though. Folks out there," gesturing vaguely off toward the west, "call him 'Arapahoe Jack.' "

I thought it best to find a building to lean on. My knees had abruptly turned to pure gelatin, while my gullet threatened anew to loose its hammerlock on my stomach.

If I had made an enemy, I had done no piker's job of it. Arapahoe Jack was almost a latter-day Simon Girty. I knew at once why the onlookers at our little game paid me such respect of distance following Slate's departure. Arapahoe Jack! I had indeed raised hell and put a chunk under it.

Perhaps the moment's fright fathered an undue modesty in me though, for my squat friend's next words pulled the bridle on my galloping imagination. "I will say, I never seen a slicker hand with a gun. You come into that draw like chain lightnin' with a link snapped. Still, you caught Slatemeyer asleep. Elsewise you'd be nine hundred dollars poorer and not worryin' none about it, neither. Ever done much gun-slingin'?"

I told him I didn't figure I had. And a bit more about myself, as well.

"If you're bound west," he offered, after hearing my story, "and can handle yourself like you can your Colt, I can hire you on."

"Where you heading and what's the work?" I was not too impressed.

"Headin' for Montana Territory. Takin' a wagon train through. Twenty hook-ups. Mostly the people are headin' out for the goldfields. That ain't so much interestin' as the fact they're aimin' to go across the Powder River country to get there.

"The Sioux got a off-the-record Gov'mint guarantee, protectin' that country last year. They're not figurin' on forgettin' it. At the same time the new Montana road—the Bozeman Trail, that is—runs right through them guarantee lands. There's big strikes in Last Chance, Confederate and Alder Gulches. The whites is gonna get through to that gold no matter what, and the Army is garrisonin' a whole string of forts from Laramie clear to Virginia City. Now them Injuns ain't got a signed treaty, yet. But they got the Gov'mint's promise to keep settlers and trains outa that country. If you don't give an Injun nothin' it's no trick to take it away from him. But once you've handed him a present, it don't pay to go tryin' to grab it back.

"Old Red Cloud ain't gonna put up with this here new Bozeman Road. If he has his way, our wagons nor nobody else's, is gonna get to Montana across Powder River country.

"Still, gold is gold, white people is white people, politics is politics, graft is graft, the Injun Bureau is crooked, the Army is stoopid, and I'm guidin' for this train."

"Where do I fit in?"

"Scouts is scarce. There's more trains than there is of us to guide 'em. I need help and I figger four years of sneakin' around in them southern woods, pot-shootin' Yankees, nominates you."

"Mister," the impulse to accept came on me suddenly, "you've got yourself an apprentice. My name's John Clayton and west is my direction."

Cocking his big head speculatively, his eyes gleaming, my self-appointed employer acknowledged the introduction. Squeezing my hand in a grip that would have made a bench-vise hang its handle in shame, he announced, "I'm Ed Geary."

My jaw must have hung as open as a dog's mouth in July, for he squinted at me quizzically and added, "Oh, you needn't let it throw you. Bridger's a better scout. Carson's a better guide. Cody's a better shot."

I stammered some pointless reply but my imagination was already saddled and running full-out again, spurred into a hand-gallop by the magic of my companion's name. Ed Geary—scout, Indian fighter, great plainsman. True, Jim Bridger and Kit Carson ran one-two in the frontier-worshipping presses of the East, while "Buffalo Bill" Cody was the unchallenged champion of the Ned Buntline penny dreadfuls.

Yet, on the prairies, up the rivers, in the mountains; with emigrant, Army and Indian alike, no scout headed Ed Geary. It began to look as though my morning's purchases had not been too poor. If I had bought a Simon Girty for nine hundred dollars, I had also got a Lew Wetzel in the bargain.

A man is very apt to sneeze at the pepper sprinkled at the banquet of fame. I thought I had done handsomely meeting Arapahoe Jack and Ed Geary in the same hour, but within another I had heard so many heralded names and seen so many famous faces that I was panting like a lizard on a hot rock.

Geary was now guiding me across Market Square, having issued a flowery set of instructions, to wit: "Come on."

The Marshal of Kansas City was an old frontiersman named Tom Speers. He held forth with his court of Indian scouts and buffalo hunters in front of the jail. I soon learned this was our destination.

Geary stopped where a considerable group lounged before a building whose lean, gray flank bore the legend, "City Police Dept." He was greeted by several of the crowd, then found a seat on the outer fringe of the group, motioning me to join him. "We'll just keep quiet and listen. You've elected yourself into a business where gun-handlin' puts you at the head of the canoe or the bottom of the river. These men are all experts."

In that amazing gathering that morning, were Kirk Jordan, Emmanuel Dubbs, Bermuda Carlisle, Billy Dixon, Jack Gallagher and James B. Hickok. These were all men of reputation but for me they each lost face and form when I realized I was looking at the fabulous "Wild Bill."

Hickok was a big man, graceful as an antelope, richly and immaculately dressed, of a lionlike bearing distinguished even among such a group. He wore two ivory-handled Colts, very low, slung far forward. His tall boots were a mirror of polish, his fancy frockcoat, handmade, with rolled collar-facings of green velvet. A shirt of spotless Irish linen underlay a splendid vest of white buckskin, literally ablaze with Indian bead and quillwork. His shirt collar was of the stylish, turndown cut, with a perfectly knotted black string bow tie. Black broadcloth trousers, fitted snugly down over the boottops, and the widest of black sombreros, creased mathematically in the center, completed his outfit.

He carried a superlative new Winchester repeating rifle, heavily engraved and richly stocked. This, I learned later, was a gift from Ned Buntline, whose hair-raising stories owed no little debt of gratitude to the real-life adventures of "Wild Bill."

It was a great surprise to me to see such dress on the most famous of frontier gunfighters. One would expect buckskin, hickory wool and fringed leather on such a figure. But I found most of the plainsmen adopted this dandified attire while in Kansas City, many of the wildest of them affecting silk shirts, brocaded vests, and even fancy derbies and top-hats.

Where the appearance and dress of this group were fascinating, their talk was doubly so. The sole topic of conversation was firearms and killing of Indians, buffalo and one's fellow white men, not necessarily in such order.

In the hour I spent listening, I learned more than would be possible in a lifetime of personal activity.

Pistols were worn in any position convenient to the user but were generally carried in open holsters, slightly forward and low in "hang," two being the favored number. Colts were the favored short arm, the models being the later ones of the war, quite advanced over my old Dragoon. The new models had a jointless frame with top straps to which the barrel was firmly attached and in which the cylinder was enclosed. Some of the men of reputation carried unique guns known as derringers—short, all-metal, single-barreled pistols, firing a .41-caliber slug. These were considered very efficient as the sixth card in a poor poker hand.

In rifles, the new Winchester was due to replace the old Henry. This short, wicked, saddle gun, brought out within the year, had a wonderful feature in a spring plate in the right side of the receiver, through which the magazine could be loaded with great speed.

The armament some of these fighting men carried with them, was astounding. Two pistols, a rifle and shotgun, one or more derringers, with belts of ammunition for all, constituted the riding arsenal a lot of them wore. Some, particularly the oldtimers, carried a sheathed bowie knife back of their right hip, or slung on a buckskin thong around their necks, inside their hunting shirts.

Until this moment, as I sat with Ed Geary, listening to the frontier fighters of the day hold forth, I had thought myself a good hand with a rifle, pistol or shotgun. Just one of these demonstrations was sufficient to poke the cold barrel of reality into the belly of any such idea.

Hickok was sitting on Marshal Speer's bench with others of the crowd. They were all looking over a brace of ivory-handled six-guns some senator had given Hickok in appreciation of his services as a guide through the Indian country. The marshal was riding Hickok, as only a very old friend might do, about his legendary marksmanship. Earlier in the day the famous gunman had performed his two favorite trick shots: driving a cork through the neck of a bottle with a bullet, and splitting a bullet against the edge of a dime. Since these two feats were done at about twenty-five paces, Speers was chiding Hickok about being a "short range" artist. There was also some question of the worth of the fancy new guns.

Before anyone in the group had time to guess his intent, Hickok had the new guns smoking.

Across Market Square stood a large drygoods establishment, the Boston House, distant at least eighty yards. Hickok fired with his right-hand gun, five shots; shifted guns, fired the left-hand gun, five more shots. He held his guns slightly forward above the waist level, elbows crooked to the sides.

When the tenth shot was off, the sequence taking about three seconds, Hickok suggested, "Tom, send one of the boys over to look at those *o's* in *Boston*." Several men went across the square, returning with a tale I have heard a hundred times and ways, since. There were five shots centered in each *o,* both groups in a hand-spread.

After this lesson, Geary thought I had seen enough to make a wise selection of shooting outfit. I had. An hour later we were outbound, I riding with Geary at the head of the train, feeling a surge of eagerness for the coming venture, no whit burdened by the hang of the two blue-steel Colts on my thighs, or the snug feel of the new Winchester under my knee.

Our route lay up the Oregon Road as far as a point fifty miles beyond Fort Laramie, where Geary planned turning north up the Bozeman Trail for the Montana gold fields. The journey was quiet, our train encountering no hostiles, though several bands were seen far off, scouting us. From my first sight of them, these wild plains Indians fascinated me.

Chapter 4

THE YEAR before my advent into the Powder River country, the Indians had asked for and been given the guarantee Geary had told me of. This in effect promised the Sioux, Arapahoe and Cheyenne all those lands lying between the Yellowstone River, the Rocky Mountains and the Black Hills, extending from the foothills of the mountains eastward to the Little Missouri. This was the best buffalo pasture in all the northern plains. It had always belonged to the Indians, they had a promise deeding it to them, and they intended to see that promise kept.

Geary had repeatedly stressed the dangers we faced once we left the Platte and headed north. Our trail led squarely across guarantee lands. Between us and the end of the Bozeman Trail at Virginia City, lay hundreds of miles and thousands of Indians. The Sioux chiefs, Red Cloud, Man-Afraid-of-His-Horses, and a swiftly arising Hunkpapa medicine man named Sitting Bull, were all out. Dull Knife of the Cheyenne, Black Shield of the Minniconjou, were with them. Behind these great chiefs, shrouded in mystery and legend, stood the solitary figure of Crazy Horse, leader of the Oglala band of Bad Faces, and, according to Geary, the greatest Indian of them all.

As we approached Fort Laramie, an event took place which shook even Geary to the soles of his moccasins.

It was just twilight, our camp having been made earlier than usual to allow for an early start on the remaining day's journey to Laramie. With our wagons in a tight circle, good high ground under us, our guards on post, plenty of wood and water in camp, we felt reasonably secure, particularly so because of the proximity of Fort Laramie. In five minutes this pleasant prospect burgeoned into a nightmare of apprehension.

Geary called me to him shortly after sunset, saying he had spotted smoke from many fires to our north. We squatted out of earshot of the others, under the bed of the lead wagon.

"Colonel," he continued (he always called me by rank, over my objections), "if those fires are what I think they are, we're in for a hotter time than hell with the draft open."

"Indians?"

"No. Worse." He kept his voice low, talking fast. "You remember the trapper that rode through, headin' down-river when we was noon-halted?"

"Yes. He appeared to be in a hurry to get where he was going."

"He was. And where he was goin' was away from here."

"Where'd he come from?"

"He come from Laramie. Big man from Washington is in Laramie. Name's Taylor. Head of the Injun Bureau, I think. Red Cloud, Crazy Horse, and purty nigh the whole Sioux Nation has come into the fort to talk treaty on this new Bozeman Trail, which the Army is aimin' to lay a string of forts along and which we're aimin' to take our train up. That's right, smackdab acrost Powder River country, Colonel. The self-spittin' land the Injuns got that guarantee on last year.

"Them Sioux ain't agency Injuns. Red Cloud is ugly and his people is with him. Council's called for tomorrow mornin'. This here trapper smelled big Injun trouble and headed out. Said there was maybe better'n two thousand warriors camped around Laramie."

I had learned much from Geary about the Indians and their country in the twenty-eight days from Kansas City, but this knowledge didn't give significance to what he was now saying.

"Where does that put us, Ed?" I asked. "If they're all in Laramie, what are those fires to the north?"

"Only one answer to that." His tones were so low I scarcely caught the words. " 'Fraid I know what it is, but I'm ridin' north right now to make sure. You want to come along?"

We saddled and slipped out of camp unnoticed, though by this time it was black-dark and the whole camp was aware of the nightfire-glow to the north.

In an hour we were working our way to the crest of the last ridge between us and the fires, Geary seeming to have no more trouble finding his way than in daylight. We tethered our horses and crept the last few yards on our bellies. Not knowing what to expect, I parted the last scrubgrowth, peering down into the valley below. Geary made no sound, but the intake of my breath was as sharp as an arrow's whisper.

Below us, spreading along both banks of a beautiful stream, stretching for half a mile, dotted by dozens of campfires and ghost-white against the moonless night, lay scores of evenly spaced tents; a scene which at once brought nostalgia to an ex-officer of the Confederacy.

"It's an Army camp, Ed. Infantry. Must be a thousand men."

"That makes it perfect," said Geary, his voice as calm as water in a horse trough. "Not enough of them to do any good, too damn many not to cause trouble. Colonel, we've got to mosey down there and find out what they're doin' here. God help us if they're headin' for Laramie."

It was a nervous half-hour which saw us finally on our bellies a hundred yards out from the pickets. Just as Ed was about to rise up and call out our identity, I felt him tense in the darkness and heard him mutter, "Well, I'll be damned if it isn't old Big Throat."

"What was that?" I whispered.

"Never mind, Colonel. We won't have to go into that camp, after all. You see that man in the buckskins? The one sittin' just outside the firelight in front of the command tent?" I finally made out the figure he referred to. "Well, you watch him."

As I followed his instructions, Geary cupped his hands tightly to his mouth, emitting such a marvelous series of fox barks that ten inches away I could not believe they came from a human throat. I actually looked around for the fox. For a moment the man by the faraway fire didn't move. Presently, he arose, left the circle of firelight. Three minutes later, a fox barked off to our right.

"There's the real thing," I whispered. "And it's no better than yours."

"That's better than the real thing," Geary answered. "That's Bridger."

Another minute, another fox bark, brought the man in buckskins to our side. He grew right out of the ground in front of us.

" 'Lo, Ed."

" 'Lo, Jim."

"What's in the wind?"

"That's what we want to know," Geary said, "We got twenty wagons over the hill yonder and we hear Red Cloud's primed to flash his pan."

"Who you got along, there?"

"This here's Colonel Clayton, Jim. Scoutin' with me. Colonel, Jim Bridger."

We acknowledged each other with nods, I too taken with viewing the great scout to respond to his friendly grin. My memory of him shall always be unreal, for the darkness was such that only general impressions could be gained. Still, I could make out enough to see he had a large goiter, recalling Geary's reference to "Big Throat." I learned this was his Indian name.

But now Bridger was talking, his words compelling attention. "This outfit's under Colonel Carrington, a sure enough garrison officer. Never been out in Injun country, a engineer, good man fer barracks drillin'. The troops is all green. There ain't a thousand of 'em, countin' a whole passel of musicians. They ain't got a round of ammunition, and are aheadin' into Laramie to draw a hundred thousand rounds." Here a slight pause, then the dry conclusion. "I'd say jist the kind of outfit which ought to be roamin' around in the neighborhood where the Sioux raised sich particular Ned with Gen'ril Connor last summer."

"Yep. And him with three thousand veteran cavalry, too." Geary's agreement was equally dry, but his next words rose in pitch. "My God, Jim! Do you know there's two thousand Sioux and Cheyenne sittin' around Laramie right now, tryin'

19

to set up a treaty with the Injun Bureau on the Bozeman Road?"

"I knowed there was somethin' more than drawin' ammunition in Carrington's orders, and by God, that's it."

"Lord." Geary lingered on the word, then, softly, "They're goin' in there with a barracks engineer and a few hundred green boys, to run a bluff on two thousand mounted warriors."

"Oh, thet ain't all, Ed. These boys is got nothin' but muzzle-loaders."

Geary's only answer was a groan.

"Ed, you figurin' to take your train through, tonight?"

"Got to. Any livin' thing left on this prairie twenty-four hours after Carrington brings them troops into Laramie won't be white and two-legged."

We shook hands and parted, Bridger with the promise to try once more to dissuade Carrington from entering Laramie while the treaty was in progress, failing that, to hold off the entry of the troops long enough to allow us to get our train into the fort well ahead of them. Every hour had become suddenly precious.

Back at the wagon camp, Geary ordered a forced night march. The people were in a panic until the burly scout sobered them up with the threat, "If you don't work like devils and drive like hell, your hair will be dryin' over a Sioux lodge smoke-hole before the sun is two hours up tomorrow." Everyone, children included, pitched into the loading and harnessing. The spirit of fear blew his convincing breath on their heels and the train was moving twenty minutes after our return.

We had no trouble. Our wagons being all mule-drawn, the trail broad and clear this close in to the fort, daybreak found us rattling into Laramie through the largest Indian encampment I'd ever seen.

Geary pointed out the lodges of five of the seven Teton Sioux tribes, Brule, Minniconjou, Oglala, Two Kettles, and Hunkpapa, the latter the fiercest of all red warriors and the people of Sitting Bull. Absent, were the Sans Arc of the south, the Blackfoot Sioux of the far northwest. Many of the distinctive, sixteen-pole lodges of the Cheyenne were to be seen, with a scattering of the simpler structures of the lordly Arapahoe.

The confusion, noise, stark glittering panoply of this vast concourse were unbelievable.

Multitudes of yelping Indian curs followed our train, lunging and snapping at our mules. streaming in and out among our wagons like a horde of canine locusts. Everywhere were groups of blanketed squaws and beady-eyed children, the doeskin costumes of the former covering everything save their slitted eyes, the clothing of the latter consisting generally of a toy bow, eaglebone whistle, or other plaything.

Their vast pony herds stretched for five miles along the river opposite the fort. The constant neighing, wheeling, fighting and stampeding among these herds added a mixture of red dust and ceaseless uproar to the already wild scene.

Before every lodge was a sun-stinking pile of fresh buffalo meat, swarming black with flies and adding the engaging odor of decomposing flesh to the already high quality of the camp's general stench. Strangely absent from the camp as we rode through, were the warriors. Only women, children and old men lined our route through the lodges.

As we forded the river, a group of about fifty mounted braves swept around one corner of the fort. In their lead rode a magnificent chief, tall, statuesque, his naked skin gleaming copper-red in the morning sun, a battle chief's full eagle-feather war bonnet shadowing his dark face and streaming far down his muscular back. To my surprise, Ed and this splendid warrior greeted each other like long lost brothers, exchanging the palm-out sign of peace, handshakes, back-slappings, and the full treatment of men glad to see one another after long separation.

After a moment's conversation in a language I thought was Cheyenne, the chief and his warriors rode off. I had the uncomfortable feeling the chief had taken too long a look at me while talking to Ed, but dismissed the thought as unlikely.

"That was Dull Knife, the Cheyenne. He is my brother."

I looked sharply at Geary to see if he were serious. He grinned at the earnestness of my expression and, as off-handedly as though speaking of the weather, told me he was half Cheyenne, his mother and the mother of Dull Knife being sisters. Strange, the tricks of heredity. Looking at the two of us, one might very well take me for a blood Sioux, while my companion could be nothing but the typical white plainsman.

As if reading my thoughts, Geary at this moment remarked smilingly, "The chief wanted to know what tribe you were from. I told him I didn't know, that you came from far to the south of the Father of Waters, but that you were mighty in war, making big *hmunha* with the little guns."

"What the hell is *hmunha?*" I asked, my curiosity aroused by Dull Knife's interest in me, with its supposition I was an Indian.

"Strong medicine," Geary replied. "The chief was impressed. He paid you an Indian compliment."

"How so?"

"Said you were unquestionably a chief among your own people. That you had the 'eyes and beak of the hawk.' "

"Is that last a part of the compliment, too?"

"You bet. The hawk is one of their big symbols. In a kind of a simple way it stands for speed and fierceness and power in the chase. But it's got a mite more to it than that. The hawk is a medicine bird with them. You've made a good start."

I would have carried on the discussion, having no great resistance to flattery, but we were in the shadows of the fort now. Camp was made, Geary then leaving me in charge of the wagons, to disappear in the direction of the Cheyenne lodges. "I'm goin' on a scout-see," was his sole explanation.

He was back in an hour with disturbing news.

"Colonel, we've got it. Big trouble. Red Cloud and Man-Afraid aren't here yet, though they know the council's set for this mornin'. They're the key chiefs, exceptin' Crazy Horse. How they act is goin' to swing the hatchet on this pow-wow. If they don't show, or don't like what they hear when and if they do show, there goes the gopher. Everything will be down the hole, and all hell to pay with no credit till Christmas."

"Suppose they ride out on the council or don't come in. Will the others join them?"

"Yep. They're itchin' and don't know where to scratch. Even I didn't want to stay too long over there"—indicating the Indian camp—"and I was brung up with them Cheyenne."

"What about our train? Can we get the wagons into the fort in case of an attack?"

"I talked to Captain Fetterman, in command here till Carrington shows up. He's a fool. Said if he had fifty good men he could ride through the whole Sioux Nation.

"When I told him Carrington was a day's march out, he said, 'Good! I'm goin' to ask him if I can take two troops and teach the red devils a lesson!' He didn't have no idee at all about what effect Carrington showin' up with them troops would have on the Injuns.

"I tell you, Colonel, there ain't ten men on this frontier, in the Army, that is, knows how a Injun's mind works. If there was, we wouldn't be havin' these damn massacrees all the time."

"But we can get our outfit into the fort?"

"Oh, sure. But that won't mean anything. Injuns won't try to take the fort. We're safe right here. Trouble is where the fool Army tries ridin' out into Injun country and teachin' lessons. God help them if they try it."

"What are we going to do, meantime?"

"That council's gatherin' right now on the grass south of the fort." In truth, I could now see a seemingly endless procession of gorgeously caparisoned Indians and horses filing out of the camp, crossing the stream, disappearing beyond the walls of the fort.

"Reckon you and me had better have a listen-in. Leave your horse, bring your gun," he instructed me, as I started for Hussein.

The sight of the now gathering council was enough to gallop a turtle's pulse. The ground chosen for the meeting sloped up and away from the fort. Mr. Taylor, the agent, had his tent pitched close in under the fort's walls. In front of the tent were seated the parleying chiefs, in exact order of rank, row on row of them. Behind them, crowding on the hill and scattering back a quarter of a mile, were the warriors, all mounted and armed. There must have been nearly a thousand of them. The sun, now high, flashed and glittered from countless lance points, knives and war-ax heads, while the splashing color of the snow-white eagle feathers, myriad-hued beads, quills, and smeared face markings of vermilion or ochre, backdropped by the harsh blue of the Wyoming sky and the endless variety of dappling and spotting among the Indian ponies, made a sight of the utmost wild beauty.

Geary and I seated ourselves with the Army scouts, alongside Taylor's tent, a privilege arranged earlier through Captain Fetterman. Looking over the vast, restless panorama of savagery, I was struck with the queer feeling that something was unnatural about the whole picture.

I turned to Geary. "What is it, Ed, that's wrong with this crowd? There's something queer but I can't put my finger on it."

"It's the silence," he said, at once. "You find it only in Indian gatherings. Always dumfounds a white man first time he locks horns with it."

I knew he was right. There were a thousand Indians within earshot of us, yet not one word or sound of human exchange reached us. It was eerie. All to be heard was the shuffle of ponies' feet, their snuffling or whickering, the occasional clank of some metallic arm or harness. This was a peculiarity of Indian concourses which I was to encounter many times but to which I never grew accustomed.

Its odd impact on me proved but the first of that June 16th morning's shocks.

Scarcely had the negotiations opened, when the outermost ranks of warriors opened with a great shout. Down the hill, through the corridor thus opened, rode two chiefs, bedizened in such manner as to leave no doubt of their exalted rank. The larger wore a blanket of blood-red, topped by a war bonnet of pure white eagle feathers. He was a very large man, clothed to the waist in leggings of doeskin beadwork, bearing himself with the simple elegance of an hereditary king. The other, an older man, was trapped in white elkskin and quillwork, his face so hideously splattered with ochre and cobalt as to appear totally inhuman. Red Cloud and Man-Afraid-of-His-Horses had come to the council.

They had hardly taken their places, one to the right, one to the left of the foremost row of chiefs, when a third figure made a notably different entry.

This time the ranks on the hill uttered no shout, but through them ran a deep-welling, *"Hum-hun-he!"* a guttural, thrilling sound that lifted every hair on my head. Once more those ranks parted, this time in a diagonal path, down and across the hill. There was a pause during which not even the wind breathed. Then, over the hill and down the slanting path to the council tent, rode a lone horseman.

He was slender, of medium yet superb build. He rode stark naked, save for moccasins and breech-clout of black wolfskin. His skin-color was very dark, almost mahogany, his face, one of the handsomest I have ever seen on a man of any race—thin, aquiline nose, high-bridged; wide mouth, eyes set far apart and slanting; small, flat ears, shapely head, with the cheekbones high, the chin beautifully chiseled and square.

If Red Cloud had ridden like a king, this man rode like an emperor. His faultless stallion was jet-black as the warrior's own waist-long braids. In his hair was a single black eagle feather, worn at the rear of the head, Dacotah-fashion, aslant from right to left. Not a glance of his glittering eye was given any man as he dismounted and took his place exactly between and one foot ahead of Red Cloud and Man-Afraid.

There could be but one man in the Indian hierarchy who

would dare this position. I had guessed his identity when Geary, his voice for once excited, whispered in my ear, "Tashunka Witko! Crazy Horse!"

Here was the mightiest Sioux warrior of them all, perhaps the greatest man of his race and time. Crazy Horse, the ferocious fighter; Crazy Horse, the fearless. And yet, among his people, wise, kind and gentle. Here was a great man, red or white. I felt it then; later I was to know it.

The council began. Well into the afternoon it ran. Taylor was skillful in debate and had the Indians' confidence. Red Cloud and Man-Afraid, with many minor chiefs, were coming to a point of agreement. Only Crazy Horse remained to be converted.

Here, with success in view, the thing which Geary dreaded and against which he had warned Captain Fetterman, happened.

Down the long valley of the Platte, guidons streaming, band playing, ammunition and field wagons rumbling, men shouting a lusty, "Hep! Hep!" as they swung along, came Carrington's command. And in the dead hush that followed his appearance, he marched the troops squarely up to the council grounds.

A long sound ran through the assembled savages, like nothing so much as the harsh intaking of breath which precedes any angry dog's snarl. Man-Afraid and Red Cloud were on their feet immediately. Behind them, the serried ranks of sub-chiefs began coming to their feet with the spreading action of a water-ripple moving out from a cast stone. Only Crazy Horse remained seated.

Yet, when he spoke, all were still and Carrington listened.

"Where goes the Little White Chief with the troops?"

Colonel Henry B. Carrington was a man totally unversed in Indian dealing, moreover a man of frank and honorable character. In so many words he told Crazy Horse exactly what his mission was.

"My orders are to march into the Powder River country, there to build forts and garrison them. The forts and soldiers are to guard the new road to Montana, the Bozeman Trail."

At this, Red Cloud burst out, his voice shaking with fury. "The Great Father sends us presents and wants a new road, but the Little White Chief goes with soldiers to 'steal' that road before the Indians say yes or no!"

Man-Afraid ominously announced, "Within two moons you will not have one hoof left."

Said Crazy Horse, the warrior. *"Hopo,* let's go!"

In a matter of minutes there wasn't an Indian in sight. Within the hour the encamped thousands were streaming up the trail, north. If the white man came north of the Powder, there would be war.

Tashunka Witko had said it.

Chapter 5

BY THE MIDDLE of July, Carrington had garrisoned Fort Reno, just south of the Powder. Then, with attention to orders but little to sanity, he began building his new post, Fort Phil Kearney, seventy miles further *north*.

I had long since parted company with Ed Geary, he going on up the Bozeman Trail with our train, I staying on as a civil scout and meat hunter for Carrington's command at Fort Kearney. By this time I had fully given in to the peculiar fascination the Indians held for me. A yoke of bull buffalo couldn't have dragged me away from the Powder River country.

While the fort was abuilding, we lost men almost daily.

A work crew would be in the timber felling logs. The day would be hot; the guard detail might relax. The noon air would be split with war whoops and a dozen or more mounted Sioux or Cheyenne would sweep through the work camp, firing their squat war bows with incredible speed, continuing on their way, pace unabated, to disappear as rapidly as they had sprung up. Invariably, such slashes left one or more dead, several wounded.

More ominous actions were pending.

The fort was finished; proving to be one of the finest in the West, and the general tension had somewhat abated. But then, come December, Captain Fetterman played the prelude to his final symphony of tragedy at Fort Phil Kearney. And with the playing I got my first real brush with the Indian military mind at work.

I was lounging in quarters, having been in the field the entire night previous, scouting a rumor of a giant war camp on the Tongue, when word came the captain wanted to see me "on the double."

I was immediately apprehensive. Fetterman was the one who had told Geary, "With fifty good men I could ride through the whole Sioux Nation." Not just Fetterman but the whole personnel at Phil Kearney was desperately ignorant of the ways and warfare of the plains Indians. Earlier in the same day, one of the young officers had shown me a notebook kept by a private of his company, in which the latter had filed a list of game taken in the vicinity of the fort. Numbered carelessly among the elk, bear, antelope, and buffalo, were "five common Indians." This regarding of red warriors as "game" was accepted. None of the men saw anything grim in such a listing.

How grim it actually was, they were soon to know.

Almost daily I overheard wagers being made among the cock-sure young officers, many of whom had served dashingly in the War between the States, as to who would take Red Cloud's scalp, how they would divvy-up Black Shield's squaws, or who was going to get Crazy Horse's black war pony. And this at a time when my own scouting had shown me no less than five thousand Indians camped along the Tongue River, forty miles north.

It was with these thoughts I reported to Captain Fetterman, quickly learning my fears had been conservative.

"Clayton, we've got a wood train stuck over on the Tongue. Ambushed and surrounded. Report came in while you were away up the river last night. This is the chance I've been waiting for. We'll give these red scuts a lesson they'll not soon forget. Care to scout the action for me?"

You're a gay blade, I thought to myself. Not every man would be so delighted at the prospect of having his brains puréed by a tomahawk. Aloud, I said, "I'll go. How many men are we taking?"

This was not presumptuous of me. I was a civilian scout. It was understood I had the right to refuse service, to question tactics. Of course such an attitude persevered in was not conducive to long employment. Especially with an officer like Fetterman. He was a small man, red-bearded, imagining himself, I always believed, a second coming of "Little Phil" Sheridan.

"Forty," he went on, in reply to my question. "Colonel Carrington insisted. 'Taking no chances, you know.'" His tones neatly imitated the thin voice of his superior. "I could do the job with ten. Particularly with 'The-Eye-and-Beak-of-the-Hawk' along." This with a short laugh. It was the first I knew that this nonsense had gone beyond Geary. Apparently some of his enlisted Crow scouts had told Fetterman of my unearned Indian reputation.

I looked at the man, thinking what a fool he was and what a fool's policy he was implementing.

"How far up on the Tongue is the wood party?"

Awaiting his answer, I could hear, outside, the sergeants bawling orders, the clank of arms and accoutrements, the always exciting snaffling, stomping, and whickering, of the cavalry horses. I never fail to wonder at the response to "Boots and Saddles" shown by seasoned campaign mounts. They love a fight and have the nose and guts for one just like any good soldier.

Fetterman was pulling on his gloves, hitching up his saber, heading for the door. His answer trailed behind him. "Way up!" His voice was cheery. "On the slopes of the Wolves."

This was bad news. The Wolf Mountains were twenty miles away, through very rough country, just as close to the Sioux war camp as to the fort. Sending forty green men and a raw, rash officer into such a field was like dropping a cat clutching a sirloin into a barrel of bulldogs.

Nevertheless, off we went; Fetterman, a young lieutenant named Wands, two sergeants, thirty-eight raw troopers and I. The sum total of Indian knowledge represented in the force was my thirty-day course from Ed Geary on the trail out from Kansas City, plus what I had picked up for myself around the fort.

I had to smile stiffly at that. Geary had sold me to Carrington as a competent scout. (Which I honestly think he thought I was.) I, blessed with nothing if not a handsome respect for my own abilities, had said not a word to disabuse the colonel. So far, too, I had had pretty good luck. The area around Phil Kearney swarmed with game. I had done well as post hunter, thanks largely to my new Winchester, the only one of its kind, incidentally, I had seen north of Laramie.

In the few light brushes with small raiding bands of hostiles around the fort, I had found occasion to warm up the brace of late-model Colts. However I did nothing with them to enhance the reputation Geary had established for me in his talk with Dull Knife. Now, heading into my first reconnaissance-in-force against the red warriors, I wondered if Geary had not done a bit too well with his "Big medicine with the little guns" fiction.

There was little time for such doubts. Two hours hard riding brought us within sound of the firing. Lieutenant

Wands and I went in ahead, scouting. We brought Fetterman back what appeared to be good news. The train, which I now knew had a guard of twenty soldiers, was in excellent defensive position, the five wagons half-circled up against an overhanging bluff, two hundred yards from the river on their front. There was a steady rifle fire pouring from the wagons. Twelve men were visible, on their feet and fighting.

The Indians were acting strangely coy, riding back and forth across the train's front, shouting insults and firing what few muzzle-loaders they possessed, with apparent carelessness. I recognized a minor chief, Walking Rabbit, but saw no other Indian of rank.

I must admit, with ready shame, I shared Fetterman's rash confidence over this news, a confidence which, before sunset that day, cost the lives of eight of the grinning boys so eagerly crowding their mounts behind us now.

On Fetterman's command we went cowboying down into the river valley, our troops yelling, brandishing sabers, recklessly discharging side arms; this latter action again illustrating the ignorance of certain frontier officers, Fetterman not having troubled to issue rifles for this lively frolic, surmising it was a short-range, revolver-and-saber job.

At any rate, our appearance greatly heartened the defenders of the wood wagons and apparently demoralized the hostiles for with echoing whoops they scattered off up the valley. In the van of their gallant pursuers galloped the eager Hussein, fat from six months of Army oats, while in his rocking saddle went Civilian Scout J. B. Clayton, for that moment and action quite as fat as his frisky mount, notably in certain regions bounded by the hair and ears.

As official scout for the expedition I have got to share responsibility for what followed. The blame, historically, cannot all be Fetterman's.

Yes, we were ambushed. As neatly and professionally as you please, and a lot more so than most of us pleased.

Past the wagons we went, pell-mell, on up the valley after the "cowardly redskins." No sooner had the last of our troops cleared rifle-range of the wagons than the hills on both sides of the shallow Tongue disgorged such a lively number of interested friends and relatives of our intended victims as shortly to put in our rear, and between us and the wagons, no less than a hundred Sioux and Cheyennes.

Now, from up-valley where they had disappeared but moments before, the original group of about forty warriors reappeared. With them rode another hundred or so red partisans, who undoubtedly owed their presence there at such an opportune moment to sheer luck—the kind of sheer luck which keeps red chiefs-of-staff, like Crazy Horse, up late, burning the midnight pitch-pine.

It was a beautiful trap. Well laid. Prettily sprung. As with most good traps, it wound up with a little blood on its jaws.

Fetterman—God forgive his judgment—actually gave a shout of pleasure when he saw our predicament. Splitting his command, he sent Lieutenant Wands and thirty men in a pistol-charge back at the Indians in our rear. Then, with a joyous yell to me, "Come on, Hawk-beak! Let's give 'em hell," he led the remaining eight troopers on a wild dash toward the one hundred and fifty savages above us.

Hussein, the ugly beast, brought me within reach of the captain's coattails in twenty jumps.

There was no time to think what was happening. The red ranks in front of us opened up like a great scarlet maw, swallowing Fetterman and his eight troopers whole. By some miracle I won through, breaking out behind the seething mass of warriors into the clear. By the time I could check Hussein, I beheld an equal miracle. Fetterman was still mounted, though the length of his future at that minute could have been counted in seconds on the fingers of one hand. The futures of his eight men were behind them.

I do not account myself a paragon of bravery; my actions at the moment were those of battle-hysteria, a familiar enough insanity to any old soldier. Besides, I was mounted on a crazy beast who would rather be in a cannonading than in a quiet stall. Hussein had me back into that yelling mass before I could think what he was about. Given another second I would surely have been spurring him up the valley in a desperate bid toward saving my own skin, but the mad bay devil had me alongside Fetterman before any such sensible plan could be put in motion.

Once in the stomach of the savage body, there was but one thing to do, try a bit of Colt surgery to cut our way out. Such had been the momentum of Hussein's original dash through the Indians, I had not fired a shot.

"I'm going to drill a hole through!" I shouted at Fetterman. "When I say ride, *ride!*"

The Indians, checked momentarily by my unexpected return and kept from slaughtering us with arrow-fire by the fact they couldn't shoot without hitting each other, now swept forward to finish us off with lances. As they came, I fired the Winchester as rapidly as I could lever it. At such close quarters the effect was devastating. A path literally did open in the direction of my fire, the Indians pulling their charging ponies aside to get out of the way of the spewing lead. Fetterman's mount was through the opening a neck ahead of Hussein.

Behind us the Indians reformed, streaming after us in a wave. Their bows were busy now, the air around us hissing with arrows.

Before us lay no apparent escape. I had thought to try and join the survivors of the thirty troopers, should there be any, but on all the field not one showed, while between us and the wagons lay a sea of red warriors. At least a hundred rode at us from the front, the remaining scores of them closing in on the wagons for the kill. I can remember, an instant before we hit them, hearing a great cheer go up from the wagons. Our men had seen us.

I recall the foolish phrase flashing through my mind, "Well, Eyes-and-Beak-of-the-Hawk, you will never have a better audience for your Magic-with-the-little-guns performance." Then the Colts were in my hands. The buck of them, hard and clean against my gripping palms, brought the thrill it always does to the dedicated gunman.

In the short seconds of our gallop down the valley, Fetterman had come out of his shock. A stream of shots from his Henry repeater joined with my Colt fire to make a river of lead which impacted on the red ranks before us with the suddenness of water from a burst dam. Again the Indians broke and once more, unbelievably, we were through them.

Now our string was clear out. Fetterman and I were both without loaded weapons. There were still a couple of hundred savages howling on us, front and rear.

Fetterman laughed hysterically. "Come on, Hawk! We're almost there!" At the same time he swerved his horse for the wagons, threw his empty rifle in the faces of the oncoming Indians, and drew his saber. I clubbed my rifle, put Hussein alongside his mount, and in a stirrup-locked charge we headed for death.

For the third time that day the Indian forces split open to make a path for us. But this time they got the wedge in their red rears, an unprotected, tender quarter. Charging toward us through the opening, rode Fetterman's thirty troopers led by Lieutenant Wands, in a lightning stroke out from the cover of the wagons. We slammed into their midst, the whole group wheeling with us and heading back for the wagons. The Indians followed but their hearts were bad. They'd been out-maneuvered.

Once inside the wagon circle, we learned Wands in his pistol-charge had carried clear through his section of Indians. Looking around for us at the other end of the valley, he could see nothing but hostiles, assumed we were wiped out and headed his command for the wagons. He hadn't suffered a casualty, man or horse, and when he saw us break clear had organized his remarkable charge. Out beyond, the Indians had settled into the wooded area on the far side of the river, having had enough of us for the moment.

"What do you make of it, Clayton?" Fetterman was at my side, joining me in peering through a wagon wheel. "Think we should rush them again? We've got the devils backing up now!"

"Captain," my voice was flat with anger, "I think you've done enough rushing for today. There are eight boys out there now, dead from rushing. We've got forty able men here, the Indians, over two hundred. I saw Wild Hog, Black Moccasin, American Horse and Wolf-Lying-Down out there. Those are fighting chiefs, not agency Indians. If there's any more rushing done, it won't be by us."

In support of my sentiments the hostiles now came swarming across the river to renew the attack. For thirty minutes nobody talked. We lost four more men, wounded, before the assault lost strength and ebbed. Wands and I, with our repeating rifles, had arranged for mourning in sixteen Sioux and Cheyenne lodges that night. In the lull, Fetterman came to me.

"Clayton, I'm writing a dispatch for you to get through to Carrington. Use your own judgment on when and how to leave. You can make it, of course?"

"I'll never know whether I could or not, Captain, because I'm not going to try."

"How's that?" His face was colorless. "Look here, man. You saved my life today. I'm not forgetting that. But this is an order. If you're afraid—"

"Yes, Captain, I'm afraid. Also I'm using my head, not losing my hair. And you're suffering shock. Better go lie down someplace."

At that he purpled. I talked on to cool him. "We're overdue at the fort now. Carrington will be coming out with relief. There's only an hour of daylight left. The Indians will make one more stab while there's light, then we're safe for the night. Carrington will be here before daylight."

"He's right," young Wands broke in, earnestly. "It would be murder to send a man out now. And he wouldn't get to the fort before Carrington started, no matter what."

The obviousness of this made Fetterman furious.

"I believe I'm senior here, Wands. Any question of that?"

"None at all, Captain. Just giving my opinion."

"When I want that I'll ask for it. Get back to your post." Wands went, without a word.

"That boy saved our lives," I began, my voice edged with nerve-wear.

"Don't you think I know that, damn you, Clayton!"

"You'll not damn me, Captain. Now or any time."

Fetterman looked at me, his face gray with fatigue. "All right," he said. "All right."

"Here they come!" yelled Wands.

And come they did, wave after wave, with about fifty to the wave, each group dashing a little closer before breaking and washing back, the last bunch breaching our wagon line, fifteen or twenty of them riding their squealing ponies into our midst. Had the others followed in, another massacre would have been official.

Thank God, Indians don't fight that way.

I was beginning to learn. Of the seventeen who got into the wagon circle, one rode his way out, perhaps living to boast of his exploit, but I take leave to doubt it. I got him twice in the body with revolver shots on his way out. I might have known more of his fate but for the fact that he rode me down going out. I woke up in Fort Phil Kearney, not much the worse for all the excitement, save a respectable scalp-wound which mercifully spared me the jolting details of the ride back in one of Carrington's mule-drawn ambulances.

As soon as I could stand I went to see Carrington. "Colonel, I want to resign," I told him.

"Now, Clayton, slow down. I know Fetterman and you had a little fuss, but—"

"He's a fool," I interrupted.

"—but," Carrington went on, not acknowledging my speech, "we need scouts here badly. I have Fetterman's report mentioning your refusal to carry a message. I think you were right and I so informed Fetterman. In the same paper he compliments your daring, details your rescue of him, and puts Lieutenant Wands on report for insubordination."

33

"I don't care a shot-canteen what—" I began, but Carrington's nervous voice kept on.

"He also requests your discharge, which I refused. Now, Clayton, I want you to stay on. I'll back you up when you're right. The report on Wands won't go in. Fair enough?"

"Sure, Colonel. It's fair. You're a fair man. But that's neither here nor there. Any more than it's here or there that Fetterman is an incompetent. Neither fact has anything to do with my resignation."

"Well, what's eating you, man?"

"Maybe just a bum hunch. I don't know. But I learned something out there yesterday that bothers me. Something which looks to me like it might be big. A hell of a lot bigger than Fetterman, anyway."

"Let's have it, Clayton. I respect your judgment."

"Well, it's just this. Six of the hostiles who got into the wagon circle, took a little time dying. Three of them were pretty drunk. Their breaths would have broken a polecat's heart."

"So—?"

"Colonel, it's Ed Geary's opinion, and mine through him, that the whiskey running that goes on out here has more than a little to do with the hostile outbreaks. Not with the attitudes of the big chiefs like Red Cloud and Crazy Horse, you understand. They are honestly convinced of their rights and there's no question of liquor influencing their actions. But you know that for every raid led by one of their rank, there's a dozen wagon train burnings and settler-scalpings with which they have nothing to do and which are, in fact, expressly against their orders. It's these minor, constant outbreaks, which Geary thinks are fomented by the whiskey runners."

"Well, what of it?" The colonel's question showed impatience. "You know an Indian will do anything when he's drunk. We can't help that."

"I think you can," I disagreed, "and I'm willing to help you. Back in Kansas City I had a little buck-up against the man who Geary says is the big wheel in these whiskey operations. I know this man, I know he's out here, operating, and I want to go after him. If you'll give me thirty days and a few men, I can—"

"Good Lord, Clayton"—Carrington's words revealed his idea of the preposterousness of my suggestion—"if you want to go chasing after whiskey runners, I can't stop you. But I can't give you any men. We know all about whiskey and Indians. And we know all about the men who run the whiskey. I assume, in this case, you mean Arapahoe Jack Slatemeyer.

"My God, man. We have laws against the importation of spirits into the Territories, and we try to uphold them. But, damn it all, you can't enforce laws like that. Sure, trade whiskey has floated off more than one scalp, and will float off more. But it is not the Army's opinion, nor mine, that liquor is a major factor in this situation. You talk like an Indian Bureau agent. That's their lament. 'Lo, the poor red man and demon rum!' I'm sorry, Clayton."

"Colonel, I know you can't do anything officially. I've been in the Army, sir. But anyone with half a glass eye can see there's another Indian war building up on the frontier. Any least thing that can be done to stop it—"

"Just what did you have in mind?" His question lacked interest.

"Give me ten men, out of uniform of course; horses and supplies for a month. I can break this whiskey ring. I'm convinced of it. Cut off a snake's head and the body dies. I know where the head is."

"Out of the question, absolutely. I'm sorry."

"No need to be, Colonel. I'll ride my trail the way I read its signs, anyway."

"Does that mean you're still going to resign?"

"No. I did that before I came in here."

"Well, I regret your attitude. Though perhaps it's just as well. You've been listening to Geary too hard. He's half Cheyenne. I think you've 'gone Injun,' on us, Clayton, and when a scout gets soft on Indians his usefulness to the Army is questionable."

I thought of Bridger, Grouard, Carson, the whole roll of great scouts, all "soft" on Indians.

"If there's anything else I can do for you, Clayton—"

I started to say there wasn't, when I remembered a forgotten voice. . . . "Colonel, my compliments. Should our paths cross again. . . ."

I turned to Carrington. "There is something you could do, Colonel. I'd like to know where General Custer is now." I didn't know yet what I intended doing or how Custer would fit into my plans, but I knew he had a record among the Indians of scrupulous fairness and intelligent understanding, and a thought was growing.

"Do you mean George Custer, Fifth Cavalry?"

"I believe so. Though it was the Third, then."

"Then? Where did you know him?"

"I surrendered to him at Appomattox."

"Did you now! I knew there was something more to you than thirty days with Ed Geary. A Johnny field officer, I'll bet. No infantryman, either. Right? Well, no matter. We'll get you your information. . . . Orderly!"

An orderly stepped in, saluting.

"Bring me those files on regimental distribution, the new ones. No, the hell with that. Have Sergeant Kelly look it up. I want to know where General George A. Custer is. Fifth Cavalry."

"Yes, sir."

While the orderly was gone, Carrington tried drawing me out, his professional interest aroused by my knowledge of Custer. I told him it was useless, that the past for me had ceased at Appomattox.

"There's a Lieutenant Colonel Custer in the T. O. of the Seventh, sir. Would that be him?" The orderly had returned.

"Yes, of course. So Custer's finally been busted back, eh? He had a long ride. Last I heard he was still coasting on his war brevet, two stars, I think. And a new regiment, too. Well, that's the cavalry for you. All the cream, the blue-john's left for the damn infantry."

"Beg pardon, Colonel," I suggested. "I didn't get the location."

"Of course you didn't. Speak up, Simpson. Where is he?"

"Fort Riley, sir, Kansas."

"All right. That's all."

As the post commander and I parted, I requested permission to rest two days at the fort before leaving to seek out Custer, also permission to leave my spare horses there.

"Naturally. What the devil. Do anything you like. We're friends, you know. The sutler should be glad to have the horses." We shook hands, the feeling on my part genuine. For all his faults, Colonel Carrington was a good man.

A word here about my "spare horses." At Fort Laramie, with the remainder of my Kansas City poker-game funds, I had culled a herd of fifteen hundred Cheyenne ponies, purchasing three mares to breed to Hussein. When it came time to sell or geld the old devil, I could bear neither to part with him nor to see his evil blood die out.

So the mares, all carefully picked for Arab characteristics, were obtained and bred to Hussein. They were beautiful things, two copper chestnuts and a bright blood-bay, all showing clearly the dished faces, short backs, and trim bone of the Spanish Turks, Barbs and Arabs, whose blood stood behind all the vast Indian pony herds.

It had gone very much against my spirit to destroy Hussein's stallionhood, but Geary had convinced me that either stallion or mare were poor mounts for scouting in Indian country, both being prone to neigh, as the sex might indicate, a challenge or an invitation to any passing horse. At any rate, I now arranged for the care of my mares, took one of my requested two days' rest, packed up and set forth to scout Yellow Hair.

Once out of sight of the fort, I suffered a twinge of that "Indian prescience" which was rapidly becoming a part of my frontier character. I turned north, cutting across country for the Tongue valley. As an excuse, not wanting to admit I was becoming addicted to the drug of hunches, I told myself I wanted one last look at that big war camp before heading south. I traveled all day, keeping to a small valley that paralleled the Tongue, and all day the thought would not leave my mind that disaster hung over Fort Phil Kearney.

By nightfall, I was fifty miles north of the fort, five due east of the string of camps along the Tongue. Leaving Hussein tethered in a thick alder copse, I struck out westward on foot, over the Wolf Mountains. I had little fear the horse would whicker even if mounted Indians passed close. Old Hussein was so used to having his nose pinched to keep him from betraying me on scouts into the Union lines, that I constantly expected him to beat me to it, reaching hooves up to grab his own nose when the occasion warranted. I felt doubtly certain of him now that he was gelded.

Of such is the confidence of fools.

Four hours brought me to a ridge overlooking the lodges of the Oglala Sioux. It was now midnight. To the south of the Oglala, down river, ran the lodges of the Arapahoe and Cheyenne; to the north, up river, those of the Minniconjou, Hunkpapa, and Brule. The Oglala lodges were pitched in a *dopa*, or group of four villages, each village forming a corner of a large, open square. Within this square an enormous bonfire was burning, throwing its light back onto the flanks of the hills in which I hid, a distance of two hundred yards. The whole of this square was alive with twisting, stomping, whooping Indians.

In a second, I had my old draw-tube, pocket scope on the scene, starting involuntarily as the figures came into focus. I broke into a clammy sweat a moment later, despite the fact I lay on frozen ground in snow-heavy scrub.

A dance was in progress, probably had been for two days. This was not what shook me. But in the center of the ring of crazily wheeling figures was a tall pole, painted a vivid scarlet. From the top of this, sticks radiated in the manner of wheel spokes, a buckskin thong hanging from each of these spokes to within about eight feet of the ground. On each thong dangled a small, knotted object which at first lacked definition in the glass. The circling warriors gestured and jabbed at these objects with their lances, making them dance and jump wildly in the blazing firelight. Perhaps it was this motion which delayed me in identifying them, but suddenly my glance froze on one particular thong, drawn by the color of its burden, different from the rest.

It was bright red, not from paint or blood, but from nature, and it had once been the hair of Private James Halloran, Troop G, Fourth Cavalry.

I did not need to count the other thongs to know their number.

The manner of the dancing was changing rapidly, causing me to concentrate on the movements and hand signals of the performers below. Individual orators were coming forward, making talks. I recognized Black Shield, Iron Moccasin, Crazy Horse, Little Wolf, Dull Knife and others.

In two hours I learned enough to put a price of five hundred ponies on my scalp. The sign language of the plains Indian is simple. I knew enough of it to pick up and translate the pantomime and gestures coming to me through my glass. . . .

There would be war . . . It would begin with the next sun . . . The warrior societies would all choose new leaders before the moon sank . . . They would move on the fort laying a trap for the pony-soldiers and walk-a-heaps to come out into . . . The order of march would be Cheyenne, Arapahoe, Minniconjou, Oglala. . . . The war chiefs would be Dull Knife and Crazy Horse . . . They would travel fast, make their last camp ten miles from the fort . . . With the sun they would attack . . . Final plans would be made in council in the last camp. . . .

I could have learned more but there was no time. The moon, cold and blue as a cake of river ice, was already down; dawn, two hours away.

As I was about to pocket the glass, a commotion arose on the outskirts of the dancers. Three lathered ponies dashed through the ranks, scattering squaws and yelping dogs in every direction. The warriors, Oglala Bad Faces, stopped in front of Crazy Horse.

Their report was patently urgent. I waited, to try to get its gist. Who says, "He who hesitates is lost"? Had I not done so that night, a ninth scalp would have festooned that scarlet pole.

Translating the hand wavings of the three scouts, the skin under my hair shrank like a squeezed sponge . . .

Riding up a valley, east of the Tongue, returning from a scout of the fort, the fresh trail of an iron-foot horse . . . Following trail, a pony calls out from the trees . . . He was tethered there, the trail of a toes-out man, leading away . . . This way . . . Short Dog claimed the pony, walked in to cut the tie-rope . . . The horse is a *sunke hmunha*, an evil one . . . He screams and breaks the rope, lunges at Short Dog . . . Short Dog is dead . . . The horse had eyes of fire . . . We ran away . . . We are here. . . .

This was already more than I wanted to know. Apparently Hussein's gelding had not sugared the bitter pull of his temper. I cursed him and loved him, and would have flayed him alive had I had him to hand.

Tactically, my position was interesting. A mounted group was forming below to take the trail. Chance was they would not ride swiftly, knowing their quarry to be afoot, fifty miles from "home." My gamble was that Hussein would not abandon me, waiting rather in the vicinity in which he had been left. I had now but to backtrail with all speed, keep from bumping into the search party, slip around the trailing warriors, find Hussein, mount up and make a run for it; all in two hours of darkness!

Chapter 6

I RAN the five miles at a slogging dogtrot, my moccasins beating a crunching rhythm in the crusted snow.

Dawn was fingering the east when I cut Hussein's trail a mile south of the spot I'd left him. I quartered this trail, finding no return tracks, hence figured he'd hung around his tie-out. No sooner had this hope been fulfilled than a scattering of shots rang out in the timber to the north. These were followed by Indian whoops and the challenging neighs of an excited horse.

Hussein! I knew his voice like a mother would her child's.

They had shot, or tried to shoot, the vicious devil, a possibility which disturbed me since I hadn't counted on it; an Indian usually being ready to abandon any pursuit or halt any battle to capture a valuable horse.

I could now try for the fort on foot, or whistle up Hussein, chancing his having escaped the fusillade. With snow on every foot of the ground between Phil Kearney and me the first course was suicide. I hesitated, confused, as two more shots echoed from up-valley.

Thrusting fingers in mouth, I blasted a whistle in the three high notes of a nighthawk's cry, my call for Hussein. From the north, wild and thrilling, much nearer than I'd hoped, came his answer. The old devil had heard me.

Now—was he wounded, possibly down, or could he get to me? I had no thought the Indians would not detect the spuriousness of my nighthawk. No human sound, save that from another Indian, could fool the ear of the red hunter.

There was no time to twist on the spirit of uncertainty. Two hundred yards to my right, a bay bombshell burst from the pine timber, spraying snow and ice in every direction.

"Hussein!" Shouting and waving, I leaped into the open meadow between us.

He didn't see me at once but came at a fast rack, up-meadow, his evil head swinging in the wind, thin nostrils flaring wide, ear flicking and pointing, eagerly searching out my position.

Though dawn was now upon us, the light was not good enough for him to see me yet. Just then a group of twenty gaudily-feathered Sioux cascaded out of the timber on his trail. Now, either Hussein saw me or I was done for, for the Sioux spotted us both, coming up-meadow in a joyous, yelping swoop. I ran thirty yards toward Hussein before he saw me and broke into a gallop in my direction. Swinging onto his back, I gave him his head. Behind us, the Sioux burst into renewed howls, the three or four who had muskets firing them haphazardly, the others showering us with arrows. All were beating their ponies to greater speed.

In a lean way that run back to Fort Phil Kearney was enjoyable.

As we began it, the frost-blue of the Wyoming winter dawn

lit our way. Some pale stars were still winking in the west and north. The cold was intense, the air as still as though holding its breath against the winning or losing of the race. Hussein's drumming hoofbeats echoed from the black haunches of the flanking hills, while the Sioux war cries bounced back and forth in such eerie fashion as to fill the whole valley with the hi-eeing and screaming of a thousand warriors.

The winter-thin Indian ponies had no chance once Hussein settled into his stride. The snow-sheathed miles fell away beneath his reaching feet like loose white pages flicked into the wind. Halfway to the fort, the Sioux quit, allowing me to slow Hussein first to a hand-gallop, finally to his space-eating single-foot.

In this way we came to Phil Kearney about nine o'clock in the morning. Riding in, I levered the Winchester into the air in the steady cadence of timed fire: one, two, three shots, a pause, then four, five.

It was the scout signal for an Indian alert.

Carrington had me in to see him at once. Fetterman was with him. I gave my information without embellishment. The post commander's reaction was logical, Fetterman's typical.

"Fetterman, take every precaution to withstand assault. I want the powder magazine stocked with rations for the women and children. They are to retire there when the attack begins. Mine the magazine so that it may be blown up if the Indians get over the stockade. Hold Phillips in readiness to carry a dispatch to Fort Laramie." (Portugee Phillips was the scout who had replaced me.)

Fetterman acknowledged the orders, leaving at once to effect them.

I followed him, listening to him rap out the colonel's order to Sergeants Kelly and Fairchild. When they had gone, he turned on me, snapping, "Well, what the hell do you want?"

"I saw another wood train hitching up outside. You forgot to tell Kelly to stop them."

"I forgot nothing. They're going. It's the last train of the season, we need the wood, they're only going six miles out and it's none of your damn business. Satisfied, General Clayton?"

I ignored his remark, answering briefly, "No. Sending that train out will cost lives. The hills are crawling with hostiles."

"Clayton, I don't like you. To me you're an Indian-lover and a rotten scout. But we'll pass that. You, yourself, reported those Indians fifty miles up the Tongue. Even if they're

41

coming, they won't be on us for twelve hours. I can have that train back here in six. And I mean to have that wood."

"Reckon I'll ride along with the train then, Captain, if you don't object."

"Like hell you will—" he began. At this point Carrington stepped out of his office, wanting to know what the verbal firing was about. Fetterman told him, making the journey of the wood train sound as simple as going to the latrine. Carrington backed him up.

"We do need the wood and there should be plenty of time to get it in. It's all cut, just needs stacking in the wagons."

Smiling my unctuous greasiest (and four years in the Army had taught me the full value of the professional boot-licker's disarming charm) I cooed as sweetly as a sub-baritone may, "I was just asking Captain Fetterman if I might go along with the train, just in case—" I deliberately left the statement up in the air.

"Of course, of course! Good idea. Thank you, Clayton. Good man. Come along, Fetterman. I want to see to that powder-magazine work."

Fetterman shot me a dirty look. "Good luck, Daniel Boone. Thank God we've got you at Phil Kearney. I'm sure we'd never make it with just the Army, alone." I threw him a five-fingered salute, being satisfied to see him take it and go white in the face.

Hussein was blown, so I asked the stable sergeant to bring me Sheba, my favorite of the three mares. Saddling, I joined the wood train, already heading out.

We jogged up the Bozeman Trail for two hours, drew off a mile to one side and began loading the wood, having seen no hostile sign whatever. The sergeant in charge of the detail, a bright chap named Schuler, put his men to work at the double, posting double lookouts, obviously edgy about the situation. After a bit, I rode over to him.

"Schuler, I don't like this quiet. Too thick."

"Me neither, Mr. Clayton. Mr. Geary always said, 'When you don't see 'em, is when you're lookin' at 'em.'"

"Mr. Geary was most usually right. I'm going to ride around. Better have your guard posts run a patch through their muskets. They'll have something else running through them shortly."

I put the mare in a shuffling trail gait, starting down a long draw that ran behind the wood location, quartering north from it and toward the Bozeman Trail.

A mile out I ran, head-on, into a war party of two dozen Cheyenne.

We exchanged insults, mine being admittedly a sort of back-hand variety, since Sheba was stretching her belly back toward the wood camp.

There was no use trying to decoy them out, there being only one reason for their quiet approach. I fired my rifle into the air as I topped the rise behind the camp, shouting and waving frantically to the men below. Schuler had the wagons circled-up before I reached them.

"Here they come, Schuler! I'm heading for the fort."

He heard me, though his only answer was a wave of his cap. Sheba already had me out of earshot. The ragged fire of Army muzzle-loaders began behind me as I hit the Bozeman.

Carrington received my news with agitation. He was something of an old hen of a man, inclined to flutter and squawk a lot when cornered, but a cautious, sensible soldier, nonetheless. After a bit of cackling and flopping around, he managed to ask, "How many of them were there, for God's sake?"

"I saw twenty, but you know Indians. There's always a bunch sneaks out ahead of the war party to grab the first scalps and count the first coups. I believe you're up against the main body."

"How in the devil could we be?" snorted Fetterman, who had brushed into the room in time to hear the last remark. "It's only been six hours since you got here. Mean to say two thousand warriors made the ride in the same time?"

"Possibly. They might have started sooner than I thought they would, ridden faster and not stopped as they planned. After all, they did know I got here. They may easily have assumed I knew of their attack plan. Anyway, I think the main bunch is not an hour behind the outfit that jumped the wood train."

"Fetterman, he may be right. We'll suppose he is. My plan—" At that moment Sergeant Kelly burst into the room without benefit of buttoned jacket or proper salute.

"Jist got a flag from the lookout on Signal Hill, Colonel."

"Well, what is it? What did he say?"

"Jist, 'Many Injuns!' " gasped Kelly. "He kept flaggin' it over and over again. Jaysus! There must be a million of 'em. That's Hollihan on the hill and he ain't the man to overrate the haythan!"

"Kelly! Button your jacket. And put yourself on report

43

for improper dress and conduct." This from Carrington, the martinet.

"And get the hell outside and blow a call," yelled Fetterman. "Or they'll be over the wall while you're standing there!"

"Fetterman, take a big detail. Forty mounted, forty foot. Go out and get that wood train. And, Fetterman! Don't go beyond Lodge Trail Ridge. I don't give a damn what happens, you're not to go beyond Lodge Trail Ridge. I just want that wood train brought in. Is that clear?"

"Right!" shouted Fetterman, already out of the room.

Within minutes the stockade gates swung open and Captain W. J. Fetterman rode out at the head of his eighty men to keep his date with destruction.

He disobeyed his orders before he was out of sight of the fort. Ten Indian decoys showed themselves in the brush along Big Piney Creek. They were so close to the fort Carrington actually threw a couple of cannon shots at them. Feigning panic, the decoys cut and ran for the hills to the north—away from the wood train. Fetterman swung his command after them.

That was the last any white man, myself excepted, saw of Fetterman and his eighty troopers, *alive*.

Seeing him make this idiotic move (he had refused point-blank to have me scout for him) I ran to Carrington. For once the colonel was ahead of me. "Clayton," he called, as I came up "a relief column is going out at once. Fetterman may get into real trouble. Captain Ten Eyck will go after him with the rest of the infantry. I want you to go with him."

I'd had no sleep for thirty-six hours but a man doesn't get yawny in the middle of an Indian fight. "Colonel, I'll do better than that. Let me go out ahead of him. I'll go right now, scout Fetterman's position, report back to Ten Eyck on the march."

"Good. That's right. Go on, and good luck."

"One other thing, Colonel. I'll try to get Fetterman and turn him back. He's heading into a trap. But if I miss him and that relief doesn't get up to him within an hour, he won't need it. I can tell you that without scouting him."

I ran to the stable, saddled Hussein, stretched out of the fort on a belly-flat gallop after the ill-fated column. In the distance, scattered firing could be heard. Good old Fetterman. Really giving those decoys hell.

I had in mind the most likely spot for an Indian ambush.

To the north, a small stream called Peno Creek, forked off in east and west branches. From the crotch of the fork, which pointed southeast, a long, narrow ridge rose in the direction of the fort. This was Lodge Trail Ridge, down which Fetterman had been ordered not to go, and down which, also, ran the Bozeman Trail to Montana.

I figured the little band of decoys to lead Fetterman down this ridge. When he neared the bottom, the ridge would suddenly swarm with Indians. These would close the slope behind him, sealing him off from the fort. He could then only go down the sides of the ridge, where hundreds more waited, or on down the trail to the creek flats. If he stayed on the ridge when the trap sprung, he had one chance in a thousand to fight his way back to the fort. If he went ahead to the creek flats or down the roof-steep sides of the ridge, he would be swallowed up. *

If I could reach him in time to warn him back . . .

History didn't have it plotted that way. No man reached Fetterman in time.

When I started up the east fork of Peno Creek to try and head him, I ran into a literal wasp's nest of hostiles. The woods were alive with them. Only the fact some of the warriors were chanting a last-minute war prayer, saved me from blundering into their arms. I grabbed Hussein's nose, tied it tight with a piggin' string, snubbed him short-up in a dense clump of birch, began snaking down-creek on my belly for a view of the ridge.

All around me was an unearthly quiet now. I saw two parties of warriors, one Minniconjou, one Hunkpapa. That would put the Oglala and Cheyenne on the west side of the ridge. Before I could think more of this, an opening in the cover loomed up and I could see the ridge. My breath came sucking in with a stab.

Far down the ridge, almost to the bottom, rode Fetterman with his forty pony-soldiers. Behind him, halfway down, came the remaining group of walk-a-heaps, the whole command being already deep within the jaws of the waiting trap. I had time to see the decoys riding back and forth down on the creek flats, still drawing Fetterman's fire, before both sides of the ridge seemed to vomit Indians. They came rabbiting out of every conceivable cover, armed to the teeth.

"Hookahey! Hookahey! Hopo! Let's go!"

The fierce cry echoed from two thousand red throats, the Indian horsemen surging like a flood up the ridge, engulfing the bluecoats on every front. It seemed to me the very ground under me shook with the thunder of eight thousand pony hooves.

The Minniconjou, under Thunder Hawk, struck the mounted troops first, driving them back through the foot soldiers and a hundred yards up the ridge beyond them. Here the pony soldiers dug in. Below them, the walk-a-heaps took to a cluster of small rocks on the otherwise naked ridge. Their forty muzzle-loaders began a serrated, hopeless volley.

Forty men and muzzle-loaders against a thousand Indians. Arrows filled the air like swarming locusts. Suddenly a lone Minniconjou warrior drove his pony clear through the pitiful group, bursting out the far side of it, sliding his pony on its haunches, wheeling, splitting the air with the Sioux cry, "*Hopo!* Let's go!" His feat had breached the dam of soldier invincibility; his command loosed a flood of death through it. Directly into the muzzles of the forty rifles, the Sioux charged their frantic ponies. There were moments then of furious action with knife and war club and ax. A scattering of the high screams of dying men.

And then an utter silence on the lower ridge.

Above, the tumult of shots and cries continued. But below, stark on the raw back of Lodge Trail Ridge, the red warriors prowled and snarled in triumph among the dead. In the time a man might take to speak a hundred words, forty white men had died like butchered hogs, their sightless, staring eyes the only mirrors of a terror none had lived to tell.

The action could not have exceeded fifteen minutes so far. Now, the warriors released by the massacre of the infantry went whooping up the hill to join their allies. Apparently at command, every bluecoat in the ranks released his horse. The animals broke back for the fort with a rush. For a moment my heart leaped. If the Indians went after the horses the troops might reach the top of the ridge, where a circle of waist-high boulders offered some chance to stand off the attackers. The ruse worked and I cheered Fetterman, silently.

The whole pack of savages went yelling off after the big, valuable horses of the white men. With the minutes of respite thus gained, Fetterman worked his command up into the boulders atop the ridge. At this point the Indians came racing back, the attack resuming, full fury.

If Fetterman had found a place to make a stand, he had also found one from which there was no escape. The ridge at this spot was no more than fifty feet wide, falling away in dizzy ice-patched slopes in three directions, with a gently rising slope behind. This slope was covered with savages, while at the bottoms of the other three declines waited the remainder of the horde. My own position was in the exact middle of the left wing of the attackers. I hardly dared to breathe and that with painful lightness.

One branch-crack or audible movement would have brought me swift and vicious death.

The Indians, forced to hesitate by the breechloading carbines of the pony soldiers, contented themselves momentarily with firing showers of arrows into Fetterman's position. But all the while they were working up closer and closer under the rim of the ridge.

I now heard them calling back and forth to one another over the heads of Fetterman's men, asking, "Is all ready over there?" And being answered, "All is ready. Our hearts are brave!"

Like lightning then, a Minniconjou chief, Long Fox, leaped from cover, exposing himself to the rifles of the soldiers, shouting exultantly, *"Hopo!* Let's go."

Go they went, like released red arrows, flying in among the high boulders, stabbing, braining, lancing their enemies at hand's length. I think I breathed no more than twenty times before all was quiet.

The last white man to die was an officer, whom I believed to be Fetterman, who broke clear of the slaughter, backing up the ridge, swinging his carbine and firing crazily, shouting aloud as he went. White Bull rode him down, driving a war arrow squarely through his chest.

Then there was no sound except that of the Indians quarreling over the trophies among the dead.

The stripping and scalping had already begun and here and there the Cheyenne were marking their victims with their brand, the severing of the left hand or whole left arm; the Sioux following suit with their specialty, slitting the throat from ear to ear or amputating the whole head. Others were mutilating, "marking" as they call it, after their own customs: slitting the thigh to the bone, mashing the forepart of the skull with a stone ax, excising the genitals, driving a war lance through the throat, scarifying the face.

It was a sight to turn any white man's stomach. I buried my face in the frozen mud and snow where I lay, and was sick again and again.

I was aroused from this retching by the far-off clarion of an Army bugle. A few minutes and Captain Ten Eyck appeared at the top of a high hill overlooking the battlefield.

He had taken over an hour to arrive. Fetterman did not need his relief.

I raged then, there in my hiding place; at Ten Eyck, at Fetterman, at myself. We were all wrong. This whole thing was wicked, wasteful, unnecessary. There was no sense in it, no victory for anyone. It would bring no one any glory, no one any spoils, no one any peace. I cursed an endless chain of Army stupidity, white greed, race pride and prejudice. There was no justice in this crazy hatred of Indians. No logic in a great nation hurling armed forces against a people who never at any time could put more than a couple of thousand troops in the field. Oh, yes, there was some logic. Power logic. White logic. These men were red. They ate with their fingers. They called God Wakan Tanka, and worshipped animals. They were heathen. Alien. Dark. Inferior.

It was too bad they didn't know they were all this. For not knowing it, they had just done something an Indian can't do: defeated white troops in open, fair, regular warfare.

The Indians shouted insults and challenges at the new soldiers, but Ten Eyck, seeing no bluecoats and hearing no firing wisely held his ground.

I believe the lives of this new command were spared by one of those weather changes which scourge the northern plains. In fifteen minutes the temperature plummeted twenty degrees; a bitter wind full of icy snow rode swiftly in to blanket the dead with a merciful sheet of white. The Indians picked up their own dead, departed for the war camp on the Tongue. Their medicine men had promised them a hundred white men slain. They had slain a hundred. It was time to go.

Now there were scalps to be danced over. Besides, Wanitu, the Winter Giant, was breathing heavily. Frost was growing on the ponies' flanks and ice in their eyes and noses. *Hopo! Hookahey!*

Sickened by the carnage on the hill, frozen to the marrow by the intense cold, stiff from not moving for an hour, half a mile from my horse, surrounded by battle-drunk hostiles, I found myself in but temporarily better position than my dead fellows. I suppose I was in shock and didn't know it. Dazed by what I had seen, I did not yet believe it.

My mind, for the few seconds necessary for what followed, must have been functioning under an incubus of unreality.

A single file of mounted warriors loomed out of the swirling snows on my left. In the lead came a dozen braves, then a string of led-ponies bearing the corpses of the fallen. Not knowing why, I dully counted these: sixteen Sioux, two Cheyenne. While tabulating this as a lean price for victory, a more piercing fact knifed into my thickening senses. Progressing as it was, this ghost parade of the quick and the dead, would trample me underfoot in ten seconds.

I exploded out of that snowy cover like a stepped-on cottontail. The lead pony in that file reared and whinnied, throwing the ones immediately following into confusion. This gave me a start. Pursuit developed with a rush however and I ran knowing that seconds separated me from the final swift kiss of arrow or lance. And as I ran, I beat my hands upon my body, swung my arms in great arcs, filled my lungs to bursting with huge gulps of air; anything to set the sluggish blood in my frozen veins to galloping. Behind me the ponies of my pursuers crashed and plunged through the thick brush, the denseness of which, preventing arrow fire, momentarily stayed my execution.

I had that day worn an outer coat of wolfskin against the cold. Now I tore this from me to clear the two guns I wore beneath it. My hands were bleeding and ripped by brush and thorns but were at last flexible, free from the paralyzing cold. It might yet cost these warriors a good price for my fine black scalp.

For a fleeting instant I lost my pursuers. Hope jumped within me at the thought of possible escape. Then, a second later I burst into a clearing full of dismounted Oglala Bad Faces.

It would be hard to say which force was the more surprised but I got in my introductions first. The right-hand Colt opened for me. Somehow I missed one of them, but five were down with their bellies shot out before the fight started. Just as the others rushed me, I thought I saw a new figure join their ranks, a bolt upright chief in black wolfskin, riding a black horse. My thought was, "Crazy Horse. Where did he come from . . . ?" Then my left-hand gun, three shots unfired, was knocked out of my hand by a war club, an arrow drove through my shoulder, another through my thigh, a stone ax crashed into the side of my skull and I knew no more.

Chapter 7

THE PHANTOM face would come and go, as lovely and luminous as a dawn star on a misty morning. At first it was just the face, the kind of unreasonably beautiful face which haunts a dream. When it came to me out of the black east of unconsciousness, it brought light. For a brief spell it would hover somewhere over me, seeming to offer guidance in a darkness which was endless. Then the interminable blackness would descend again.

Presently, these stygian nights became shorter. The star face shone with greater clarity, remained longer in its gentle orbit. I felt its presence now even when I could not see its light. An ease pervaded all the blackness around me, where before an almost panic force had possessed me.

There came long pauses when the star hung over me, ceasing to move in its orbit, and for the first time what had been a disordered vision of loveliness, became edged with the focus of reality. Clouds and mist and whirling nebulae pulled away. Darkness withdrew. There was no star, only a face. A face which, if I were to spend ten thousand years in blackness would never lose its least lineament in my memory.

It was oval in outline, as true and sure in its form as a master's sketch. The skin was waxy and petal-clear, the hue of a virgin copper vein broken asunder in subterranean darkness, glowing with its own dusky inner fires, carrying within its velvet self a living bloom of copper-gold. The eyes were long, lashed with charcoal blackness and set ever so slightly aslant by the high-curving line of the cheekbones. Their color a clear, depthless green, at once as cold as north sea ice and hot as the fire in an emerald's heart.

The nose and chin, straight and cleanly chiseled. The mouth, full and wide and wild-cherry red, with that hint of curving half-smile which has set men mad ever since the first woman parted her lips and beckoned.

Around this face and above it, held in restraint only by two copper ornaments, one above each tiny, close-lying ear, tumbled a profusion of hair, jet-hued as onyx yet alive with vitality.

No man has loved a woman who could not, with eyes unseeing, detect her presence, know her nearness, by the indescribable thrill of her personal perfume; and this not the artful scent of earthly cosmetic, but the God-instilled smell of her own warm body. A man who has really loved will know this excitement.

To me it came but once, lasting forever. And this once-and-always fragrance of mine came with the star of my dream face. It came with all the indefinable softness and mystery of forest air; of clear lakes, sparkling streams, golden sunlight and black aromatic night; of winter snow and summer grass, of woodsmoke, cedar, pine, and balsam boughs; of doeskin, fresh earth in the rain, of north wind whistling over mountain ice, and of south wind wandering over prairie flowers. It came to me with the smell of naked rocks warm in the sun. Of prairie grass nodding in the west wind. Of heat lightning in a summer shower. Of sand and starlight and spring rain.

I would remember that face and that fragrance so long as breath stirred in me, and then forever after. Yet, when I awoke, it was gone. In its place crouched a squat, ugly Sioux woman, close-wrapped in a dull black blanket.

"I am far from home," I said, using the Sioux expression for "lost."

"You have been on a long journey. Thirty suns," she answered gravely.

"Where have I been?"

"Walking in the evening," she replied, employing the poetic Sioux phrase for unconsciousness.

I lay back then, wondering if it were possible. Thirty days out of my head, still alive, lying in a Sioux tipi, apparently having been given careful nursing the entire time.

"Why am I here, who should be dead?" I queried.

"*H'g-un! H'g-un!*" She intoned the Sioux warrior's courage shout. "*Hmunha, hmunha,* magic power to hurt. *Tahunsa.*" This last, after pointing first to herself, then me.

I was alive because I had shown great courage and a mighty power to hurt. Also because we were *tahunsa,* cousins. My mind was still not functioning with normal clarity but I could gather that Ed Geary's nonsense with Dull Knife about my being a great chief had become accepted by these people. I knew that often in their own battles among tribes, if a warrior of the enemy showed extreme courage, being

51

subsequently taken alive, he was carried off to the lodges of the conquerors, feted and served in every way, in no sense a captive but an honored guest.

That this treatment had been, or was to be, afforded to me was conjectural. But since the Sioux, contrary to white lies, do not torture their captives and in fact scarcely ever take an adult white male captive, the conclusion was not illogical.

The Sioux regarded me as of their blood and mighty in war.

I would have questioned her further, but the woman indicated I was to drink out of a buffalo horn spoon she held to my lips. I drank the liquid, bitter and soapy tasting, and almost immediately the night came up around me.

When I awoke again, it was to an empty tipi. My head was clear and for the first time I was aware of strength in my body. I sat up cautiously, feeling no ill effects save a slight dizziness which passed at once. The wounds I remembered receiving, arrows in thigh and shoulder, tomahawk blow on the head, proved upon gingerly examination to be nearly healed, evidence positive I had lain a long time in recovery, for they had been grievous injuries. The miracle was I had lived at all, let alone healed so completely.

As I sat there, feeling of my wounds, trying to make some pattern of my predicament, I was aware of a figure standing just inside the tipi's entrance flap. It had not been there a moment before, yet I had seen no one enter. I looked up, seeing an Indian of medium size, straight as a lodge pole, garbed with simplicity, wearing no ornament or insignia of rank other than a single spotted eagle feather in his thick black braids. No second glance would be needed among my multitude of warriors, to place this one. His voice was deep and soft as a panther's grunting, and as arresting.

"Welcome to my tipi," said Crazy Horse.

"*Woyuonihan,*" I said, pointing to myself, then him, indicating I was full of respect for so great a chief.

He nodded and came silently to me, leaning over and touching me lightly on the chest with his right hand. Then, placing the same hand palm-flat on his own breasts, he uttered the single word, "*Tahunsa,*" which the black-blanketed squaw had used.

Crazy Horse and I were cousins.

In this simple way began my ten years as an Oglala Sioux; blood brother of the Bad Face Band, full chief in the Oyate Okiyu, the supreme council of the seven Sioux tribes; protégé and son by ceremony of the great Tashunka Witko.

I became other things, too: their constant companion of the war trail and buffalo pasture, of the summer grazing grounds and the snow-locked winter camps; their continual advocate in the Army councils with "Red Nose" Gibbon, "Star" Terry, "Three Stars" Crook, and "Yellow Hair" Custer; their champion, their disciple, their son.

In the two weeks between my regaining consciousness and my complete recovery I had many talks with Crazy Horse, becoming subject, most willingly, to his force and personality. He could not have been more than two or three years my senior, yet he had wrapped about him the ageless blanket of spirituality which seems to enfold great men, defying time to handicap or defeat them.

The first of these talks made me understand that I had found a man who felt as I did about the war between red man and white. Yet here we were, in a sense both men at war, he the greatest military genius of his race, an individual warrior without equal; I, a professional soldier by record and a fighting man by circumstance. He had killed my brother and I, his. Still we talked of peace and persecution.

He came into the tipi the morning following his acceptance of me as cousin, bearing a beautiful ceremonial pipe. Squatting across the fire from me, he carefully filled the pipe, lighting it and smoking in silence for some minutes.

I knew enough to realize this pipe, with its exquisitely carved stone bowl, long polished stem, eagle feather and dyed-hair ornamentation, was not the ordinary pipe carried by every brave and kept in every tipi.

If the pipe itself would not have held me silent, then Crazy Horse's smoking of it would, for he drew upon it slowly, with his eyes closed, then expelled the smoke upward, opening his eyes to watch its spiraling progress toward the tipi's smokehole.

Shortly, he handed the pipe across the fire to me. I took it and smoked as he had, saying no word nor giving any glance to him, concentrating every attention on the pipe and its smoke. When I had drawn several puffs from it, I returned it to him, the whole process then being repeated until the pipe was empty. When he had replaced it in its ornate elkskin cover, I asked him in halting Sioux, "My brother, what is this pipe we smoke?"

"It is the Pipe of Peace," he replied simply.

"I would know more of it," I said slowly, "for surely it is no ordinary pipe."

I had no idea of the literal truth of my statement, feeling only that I was taking part in a ceremony which was sacred to him and not wanting, in my ignorance, to transgress any propriety.

In response to my words, he retrieved the pipe from its cover, held it, bowl toward me, so that I might see upon it an inscription carved deeply in its stone surface.

"It is the honor-word of my people." Crazy Horse nodded seriously. "The motto of their lives."

"And it says?"

"Peace without Slavery." He lingered over each word, lovingly.

We talked then and he told me many things. This pipe was the sacred symbol of an entire people. No treaty made under its smoke was ever broken. Its delivery into any battle line, no matter how fierce the fighting, would bring immediate cessation of hostilities, and no truce held over its glowing embers could ever be violated. I learned this pipe was unique in the Sioux hierarchy. There was none other like it. Tashunka Witko was its present custodian. It was countless hundreds of years old, its physical origin lost in the legends of the past, but its spiritual force as strong as though ordained but yesterday.

In smoking it with me, Crazy Horse had extended an honor beyond calculation. At the conclusion of the first smoke I had no real idea of this but failing knowledge I maintained silence, always a safe course with an Indian.

I didn't see the pipe again for many years, never smoking it beyond that first time. But in the subsequent days of my recovery, we had many quiet councils over ordinary pipes. Thus, by the time I was fit to travel we had come a long way in understanding.

I'll never know why he treated me as he did. I can only explain it through his very real possession of spiritual power. In some way he knew of the reasonless fascination his race held for me, responding to it.

I came to know before we parted, that it was indeed he who had ridden up at the moment his braves were swarming me under. He had called them off, ordered me to be carried to the war camp on the Tongue. Here, for a week I was treated by Black Blanket, his wife, then, my condition showing no improvement, the whole band had traveled north and east to make a winter camp in the southeast lee of the He Sapa, the Black Hills.

This move had been made to bring me under the care of a great healing power. When I queried him about this power Crazy Horse shrugged, saying *"Wiyan Wakan,"* which in the simple Sioux tongue meant holy woman and might refer to anything from a wrinkled old hag of a medicine woman to a mountain or a pine tree; the Indians found magic and medicine in everything. My efforts to arrive at any identity for the power in the Black Hills to which I had been brought for cure were all balked by indirectness or even blank refusal to answer.

Still there was, in the replies I did get, a certain quality of uneasiness, hard to associate with a tree or a mountain. I felt a driving certainty that the Wiyan Wakan was a real woman, in my heart not admitting it even to myself, insisting on associating the haunting star-face of my unconsciousness with this imaginary, "real" woman. It was a strange, compelling association which no amount of argument on my part or obscurity on the part of my hosts would dispel. I could not forget that star nor shake off the thought it must shine again.

Further discussion disclosed the fact Dull Knife had told Crazy Horse of the tall white chief who rode and looked like an Indian, talked only with his guns, had the eyes and the beak of the hawk. Crazy Horse had seen me at the Fort Laramie council and knew me at once.

The night of that council, while leading his people north, even while his pony stumbled through a raging cloudburst, Tashunka Witko had a dream. In it a great hawk came walking among the Indians. He had struck at them fiercely, with bolts of yellow lightning shooting from each taloned hand. When the thunder rolled away, thirteen braves lay dead. The great bird then spoke aloud in the Sioux tongue. "I have done this so that you may know my medicine is strong and that I am the Hawk-That-Walks-Among-You-Like-a-Man. I do not fear you and I am your friend but you will not believe this. Once again I will strike you, just half so hard. Then you will know. From the time of the second striking you will know I come among you with a good heart and a straight tongue. The brave speak to the brave with the tongue of death, for it is the only true tongue."

Crazy Horse had kept this dream to himself.

Followed then the first wood-train fight in which, by

ridiculous coincidence, thirteen braves had died in the thrust which saw them break into the wagon circle. When Crazy Horse, who was not at the fight, learned this, he had known his dream was good, for with total untruth the lone warrior who survived the rush had borne back the tale that I, alone, slew all thirteen with the little guns that were my tongue and spoke for me.

Thus, when I blundered into the band of Oglala while fleeing the scene of the Fetterman Massacre, killing five of them before the others struck me down, Crazy Horse had seen his entire vision come true and had halted my killing. Prophecy had been fulfilled and the Hawk-That-Walked-Like-a-Man had come among them to stay.

When he had done, I told him of myself, saying that Geary was a joker, that there was no truth in his statement that I had Indian blood in my veins. I was all white.

"Your soul is red. You will stay with us."

He seemed not to have cared for my explanation, one way or another. I found this quirk increasingly true of the Indian character. They would see a thing as they wanted to see it, or as they believed it should be. I could be as pale as alabaster with hair of purest gold, and if Crazy Horse wanted to see me as an Indian, he would. I would actually become an Indian to him. As a matter of fact this odd character-transference was apparently already completed, for from that day he never spoke to me save as one red man to another.

This habit of accepting something at a value they themselves put on it, regardless of reality, can be the only logical explanation of their receiving me into their councils as a chief of the race. It is truly a marvelous ability, this thing of seeing another man in our own image, discounting that his skin may be one color, ours another. Hearing it propounded, in two short sentences by Crazy Horse, was my first lesson in Indian wisdom.*

I then told him how his people found great sympathy in my heart.

"It is truthful." He nodded. "In my dream I was told this, also."

Knowing their great reverence for the dream and any revelations which may come by way of it, I determined to approach him from this blind side on the subject of the

---

*The Indian color tolerance was complete. Several escaped Negro slaves were honored members of the various tribes, and in at least two instances rose to become chiefs of some standing.

mysterious healing power of the He Sapa, feeling at the same time great shame at thus taking advantage of his savage fantasy.

"By the dream is all truth known. Is it not so, my brother?" My question was sober.

"It is true."

"While I was walking in the evening I passed within the shadows of Wanagi Yata, the Place Where the Souls Gather. Do you believe this?"

"Even so, my brother. I believe it."

"Well then, as the shadows grew darkest over me, I knew a great dream."

"The place is holy."

"Even so," I replied. "And in this dream which was dreamed in this holy place, there came to me a face. It was more beautiful than any face." I waited, but he said nothing, only stirring uneasily. "The face did not speak but it smiled to me and it guided me out of the shadows, showing my way by its light." Again, I paused, and again he remained silent.

"This was the face of a woman," I announced, gambling on his Indian respect for the sanctity of another's vision. "And the face called to me, not with words but with a smile, saying I must follow it. Saying that as soon as Wakan Tanka returned my strength, I must follow it. Even with her smile she said this. My tongue is straight, my brother." It was the first time, but not the last, I lied to Crazy Horse.

I watched him closely, seeing he was deeply moved. For a long time he sat motionless, staring fixedly into the tipi fire.

"It is true," he said, at last. "My heart is not good within me but you have dreamed it and so I must tell you."

I felt deep shame for having imposed on his pagan credulity, but I was driven by an urgency greater than anything under the Indian sun or moon. I was in love with a dream face. I had to know if its counterpart existed in other realms than the disorder of a fevered mind.

"The face was a pale red star in the evening." My words tumbled now. "A mouth like crushed crimson berries, hiding teeth of snow. And the eyes were as green as mountain ice where the eagle flies. Tell me, brother, lives there such a woman?"

"She lives." His tones were heavy. "It is she. It is the Star of the North. Your dream was a true dream, my brother."

"And she is Wiyan Wakan, a holy woman?"

"Of them all, the most holy."

"She is as beautiful as my dream?"

57

"More beautiful than any dream."

"Her age then? She must not be old."

"Very young. Little more than a child."

"And will you show me where this star shines, my brother?" I tried, vainly, to keep the anxiety from my voice.

"It must be done," he said, gravely. "For you have dreamed it."

My heart leaped insanely within me. Gone now were all thoughts of Custer and Slatemeyer. That haunting dream face was real. It lived. And I was going to it. The whole time I had not dared believe this and yet I had been unable not to. Something of my agitation revealed itself.

"She cannot be yours, Cetan Mani." For the first time he used my name in Sioux, Walking Hawk. "Nor can she be any man's. She has so willed it."

"She will be mine," I challenged, recklessly. "Or I will be hers. For I cannot live without her."

"Then you will die, my brother," announced Crazy Horse, coming to his feet with easy grace. "For you cannot have her and live."

With that he left me, nor did I call out after him, but for an hour sat staring, motionless, into the fire.

Chapter 8

SINCE I had had a vision, Crazy Horse was bound by belief to accept it. He told me what he knew of Star of the North.

She had been captured, as a girl of five or six, by the Oglala, in a raid on a Crow Village far to the west and north. She was not a Crow, that tribe in turn having captured her, but where she was taken or what her origins had been, Crazy Horse's people had never been able to determine. There had been a sort of half-story related by an old Crow medicine woman, which said the child had been brought up from Mexico by the Apaches and sold into slavery among the Comanches, from whom the Crows stole her. But Tashunka Witko did not vouch for this.

She was, even then, a child of startling beauty, her peculiar green eyes at once commanding the imaginations of the Oglala, for in their legends the Sioux had all sprung from a common origin, the Earth Mother. The stories handed down by uncounted generations of old village tellers of tales, had dimmed somewhat the details of the Earth Mother's appearance, but on one particular all descriptions agreed: her eyes had been green as lake-ice.

The Crows, hereditary blood enemies of the Sioux, had no such legend of origin and treated the girl as they would any other captive child, which is to say with gentleness and kindness, as is the way of all Indians with all children.

The Sioux, however, at once venerated her, and in time she became in fact what they supposed her to be in fancy, a living legend, a Wiyan Wakan, a holy woman.

They built her a great lodge in the heart of their magnificent homeland, the mysterious He Sapa, the Black Hills. Throughout the year she divided her time, visiting various of the Seven Sioux Council Fires, living now with this tribe, now with that, carrying always and everywhere her magic power to heal.

This was in the hunting and traveling moons of spring, summer, and fall. When the first snows flew and hoar frost rimed the tipi's flanks, she returned to the Black Hills and her secret lodge. Crazy Horse knew the way and would ride with me. The trail was guarded; riding alone I would never get there.

Our course led through Pte Ta Tiyopa, the historic "Gateway of the Buffalo" into the Black Hills. We would ride at daybreak, as soon as Wi, the sun, pushed his burning scalplock above the world's edge. Crazy Horse would come for me, bringing me a mount fit for a chief. This set me to wondering what fate had overtaken old Hussein, but Crazy Horse interrupted that thought by arising, saying it was late and bidding me safe conduct "among the spirits of my enemies."

The Sioux believe nightfall releases the spirits of their slain enemies. The night is therefore ridden by the restless ponies of the ghost warriors, searching on silent hooves and with invisible lances for the living foe who slew them. It is no time for a flesh-and-blood warrior to be abroad. This, I thought, must account for the general Indian reluctance to fight or attack at night.

When Crazy Horse had gone, I sat alone in the tipi trying to make some sense of my predicament.

Here was I, J. B. Clayton, ex-colonel of Confederate cavalry, a white gentleman, proud by training as well as birth, squatting by an Indian tipi fire in the hostile heart of the

Dakotas, clad in doeskin leggings, shirt and moccasins, smoking a stone pipe loaded with reeking kinnikinnick leaves, rocking on my leather-covered heels, staring into a Sioux fire, talking in the Oglala tongue, thinking with an Indian mind, hopelessly in love with an Indian girl I had never seen and could never possess.

I lay back on a buffalo robe and gazed up at the cold stars blinking through the tipi's smoke-hole. Finally I closed my eyes and beheld again that glorious image: the haunting, half-curve of the berry-red mouth, snow-gleam of the perfect teeth, the beckoning fire-depths of the ice-green eyes. . . .

When I awakened I was stiff with cold. Above the smoke-hole gray dawn paled. Over me stood Crazy Horse, dressed in black wolfskin winter clothes, arms folded, a rare smile on his grim lips.

"It was a good dream, my brother?"

"Truly it was," I answered. "I have seen the Star again. And she has told me to hurry to her."

A shadow passed over his dark face. "The ponies are ready," he grunted. "Even now they are ready, standing outside."

"We shall depart, my brother," I muttered quickly and lost no time donning the gray wolfskin coat he had brought me.

As we passed through the tipi flap, a fierce neigh shattered the morning quiet. I was nearly beaten down by the rearing and hoof-lashings of a gaunted-up bay gelding.

Hussein!

Somehow the indestructible monster had survived another contest with whatever grim one it is who reaps among the equine sheaves.

Now, I think, the old devil was genuinely glad to see me, for he raced and ran about like a yearling stud, scattering the crowd of curious squaws and children gathered to watch us off. I thought he would kill a dozen of them before I could whistle him to me but miraculously no one was hurt. This was due, no doubt, far more to uncanny Indian agility than to any lack of evil intent on his part.

I girthed him with a strap and the crude Indian saddle handed me by Crazy Horse, swung to his back and joined the war chief. Together, we rode out of the village toward the north. As we went, I queried my companion about Hussein's history since last I'd seen him. His answer did nothing to dim my respect for the wicked Barb.

"We found him where you had tethered him. Since none could approach him, I shot his tether through. He ran with us, ever following the travois upon which we bore you. In each camp he stood by your tipi. Nor would he eat of dried grasses which I ordered brought to him. Surely he would have died but for North Star, who approached him without fear and with her magic made him eat of the grasses."

I tried to reduce this to logic, getting no better surmise than that the horse had scented my odor upon her hands, thus allowing Star to touch and feed him.

Regardless, horse and man both owed their lives to her, and it was a debt I meant to see repaid, and with interest.

Chapter 9

No BREATH of air stirred in all the Black Hills. Rank on dark serried rank, they stood as silent as though Yunke-lo, Death himself, held his tainted breathing against some foreseen movement.

A thousand feet above the highest granite scarpment, Wanbli the eagle hung motionless, a black speck in the winter-blue Dakota skies. Perhaps only he was aware of the flaw in the unearthly stillness below. For while the mind of man will conceive of postures to deceive the eyes of other men, these postures will not cheat the yellow orbs of old Wanbli. Half a hundred vermilion-smeared Sioux might lie among the boulder-dotted rubble in such a manner as to play false the searching human eye, but Wanbli could see every dyed quill, copper-wired earring and roach-crested scalplock among them.

He could see where belly-lay the old Lakota chief, Many Kills, with fifty picked Fox Lodge braves. And down-valley he could see something else. Far down there, where the North Fork of the Cheyenne snaked its flat, shining way athwart the slanting rays of the late afternoon sun, he could see the two dots crawling. . . .

As we left the North Fork of the Cheyenne, which we had followed since noon-halt of the second day, and began to climb the slope of its valley floor toward the towering cleft now looming in the seemingly endless fortress of hills on our left, it was late afternoon.

A heavy bank of purple cloud hung on the rim of the prairie to the west and as the sun settled into this cover every visible object became coruscated with deep crimson jeweling. The endless prairie snows, gleaming white a moment before, now were stained with scarlet from horizon to horizon. The shouldering hulks of the hills, black and bulky under the dense pine growth, softened into diffused walls of maroon and magenta, flashing here and there a hard battlement of crimson where the naked granite, armored in snow and ice, speared up out of the darker buttresses of forest.

It was a sight to draw the chest muscles of a less imaginative man than I. I simply stopped Hussein and stared.

Beside me, Crazy Horse sat his mount in silence, his narrowed gaze fixed upon the distant sun, his chiseled features ethereally handsome in its dying light. I knew he was praying in the way Indians pray; head unbowed, knees unbent, looking his God in the face, unafraid.

"The place is holy," he murmured at last, his deep, purring voice sounding soft in the unnatural stillness.

"It is true. It is the house of God," I said.

We rode on then in the gray winter twilight, the spell broken. "Ahead lies the Gateway of the Buffalo." My companion's words brought me back. "Within his mouth awaits my brother, Many Kills, with many warriors of the Fox Lodge."

I knew he had made smoke at the noon-halt and I had seen answering smoke from the Black Hills, still I was curious.

"How do you know they are there?"

"Before Wi put snow upon his fire, I saw Wanbli, the eagle. In the way that he flew he told me there were men beneath him."

"How is this?"

"When Wanbli sees nothing beneath him, he flies with eyes that do not see. He flies long and straight. When he is hunting, he flies as the dog runs the lost trail, back and forth. When he is seeing his prey, he flies down, coming in a smaller circle all the time, lower and lower. But when he is watching men, he flies very high and does not move.

"I saw him thus as we left the river."

Again I could not but wonder at the vast Indian wisdom of the wild. It goes beyond being born into a world of nature and being reared among its animal children. The Indian is created with an animal set of instincts which have been bred out of the white man. I saw numberless demonstrations of these infallible instincts in my years among them, but never an individual who equaled Crazy Horse in this gift. As hunter, scout and warrior, he was without compare among a people which has furnished the earth's best in all three categories.

As I thought this, the night came in around us. And with it came Many Kills, a crowding of murky-figured warriors at his back.

"Hun-hun-he!" he called out in the darkness, using the Sioux phrase reserved for sacred friendships.

"Hun-hun-he," responded the war chief.

"Hun-hun-he!" swelled in a chorus from the invisible ranks of the Indian horsemen. The sound was thrilling. I remembered at once this was the deep greeting-noise with which Tashunka Witko had been announced when he rode into the council at Fort Laramie. There could be no doubt of this man's position among his people. He was their chief of chiefs.

After a short discussion, during which I assumed I was being explained, we rode on, following a broad trail, hoof-ground to highway smoothness by untold centuries of passing buffalo. There was no moon, only the cold light of the giant stars serving to limn the course of the granite scarpments above our heads. From the constantly narrowing character of this overhead star-strip, I knew our passageway was continually closing in, growing all the while deeper. Finally the very trees atop the canyon walls seemed to meet, blotting out the stars.

How long we rode thus, wordless, through blackness colder than the dead belly of a crater on the far side of the moon, it would be impossible to estimate. But the way was often slow, the going tortuous.

Eventually, a faint grayness crept upon our progress, making it apparent we were no longer in the gorge. Shortly even better light sprang up, revealing before us a sight to be remembered.

We were high on a narrow scarpment which sloped steeply down into a broad valley. The valley itself was saucer-shaped, walled in by vertical cliffs a thousand feet high. A stream of good size traversed the level floor, entering the north of the valley by way of a spectacular waterfall, exiting to the south through a gaping cavern in the granite wall. I could see no means, other than the trail we rode, of human access to the valley or departure from it.

In the center of the saucer stood a monolithic granite mesa, which I judged to be about three hundred feet high, about half a mile in circumference. There was no trail either up or down that I could see. That there must be was plain, for the heavily timbered top of the mesa was dotted with Sioux lodges, all centered about a large, permanent, central lodge of white buffalo hides.

The whole atmosphere of the place was as wild and lonely as the cry of a curlew riding a high storm.

"We must go with caution," Crazy Horse said. "The way is treacherous."

He spoke with a straight tongue. That trail down into the valley was a nightmare. Even the sure-footed, unshod Indian ponies had to be hand-led the greater part of the way. We were an hour getting down what could not have been more than two miles of trail. I saw a dozen places where ten men could stand off a regiment. Noticing my appraising glances, the war chief nodded.

"*Wickmunke*," he said, gravely.

I looked at him quickly, not knowing quite his meaning. *Wickmunke* means "the rainbow," and also "the end of the rainbow." It also means "the trap." Did he imply simply that here was the end of my rainbow? This I doubted, for the end of the rainbow has, to an Indian, no significance comparable to the white fable. Did he mean to warn me, then, of a trap?

Only another Indian could know, for it is impossible for a white man to learn all the meanings a single word can have in their simple tongue when given various inflections.

Chapter 10

It was yet early when we rode into the lodges atop the mesa, the rear of which proved to hide a narrow, smooth trail, leading upward in a slope so gentle a heavily travoised pony could climb it with ease.

In the tipi of Many Kills, we were made welcome, his women hurrying to prepare us food. We ate a roasted tenderloin of elk together with the chopped parts of its heart, cooked in water, with the roots of the pangi, in a buffalo paunch into which the squaws kept dropping *tunkes*, red-hot stones, to maintain a boiling temperature. For dessert there was *wasna*, a sort of pemmican with sweet berries pounded into it. This was the only foodstuff which might be considered a confection I ever knew the Indians to prepare, their diet being almost entirely meat the year round.

After the meal, Many Kills brought out his pipe, lighting it with a coal from the fire, passing it around the circle until it had been smoked out.

Then I was made welcome with flowery speeches from all the several chiefs present. Once more I was amused at the peculiar humors of these people. I had just ridden with fifty of them for twelve hours, not one of them having uttered a syllable to me or to each other the entire time. Now they babbled away like happy children, laughing, joking, telling tales, asking for news, giving the same, in general carrying on like spirited youngsters on a holiday.

After a suitable interval of compliment exchanging, during which I flatteringly learned my undeserved reputation as a warrior had preceded me, I asked Many Kills if I were free to come and go as I wished. He was local head of the Fox Lodge, the law-and-order society of the Sioux Nation, the police force, if you will, of the Indian social system. This lodge was composed of picked braves, many of them chiefs, all men of respect and warriors of reputation. This small village was clearly detailed to guard North Star. Something more than courtesy required that permission to wander around be asked of its chief; this was touchy ground.

"Cetan Mani may go." The chief's words were easy, without hint of restraint.

"I would see the realm of Star of the North," was all I said rising to go and departing, without a backward glance. I was learning to talk Indian fashion; short and to the point.

Outside, I found Crazy Horse had followed me. He gestured toward the climbing sun, then the ground upon which we stood. I understood I was to return to this spot, "When the sun was in the middle." I nodded, swung up on Hussein and started off. He called after me. "You will not see the Wiyan Wakan yet. She is now in prayer to the morning, and will see no one while Wi is above."

"This must be true," I called back. "For surely such a star is best seen in darkness." He looked after me, not answering, leaving me with the uncomfortable feeling I had not said the right thing.

Taking the backtrail down off the mesa, I put Hussein in

an easy lope up the course of the stream toward the waterfall in the north. I had no idea where I was going. Later I thought, with such a broad valley to explore, there must have been some of my old hunch-power at work in the selection of trails I made.

A few minutes out, I picked up a line of moccasin tracks following the stream in the same direction I was taking. They were scarcely longer than my hand, their line of track being as true as a surveyor's string, with none of the turning-in of the toes typical of the Indian. Dismounting, I examined one of them. There was no blown snow in the tiny depression. Even as I watched, a small part of the sharp edge of it crumbled inward. They had been made that morning, possibly within minutes.

Unaccountably, my heart began to gallop. Urging Hussein into an alder clump I dropped his lead thong and left him, pursuing the trail on foot.

I had covered three-fourths of the distance to the falls before discovering the tracks. Hence, a few minutes' trailing brought me close in under the dizzy granite walls from which the water took its rioting plunge into the valley. Here were dense woods of pine, the ground rising sharply under me as I went forward. The sound of the falls was becoming deafening, indicating any moment must bring me to their base.

I have described this valley, with its waterfall, breathless cliffs, disappearing subterranean river, and thronelike mesa, as unbelievably beautiful. Nonetheless, I was not prepared for the sight which burst upon me.

Towering twelve hundred feet in the air rose the north wall of the valley. From a deep crevice, about halfway down its surface, leapt the headlong volume of the falls, thundering downward for perhaps three hundred feet to hurtle into a red granite basin two hundred feet in breadth. The water, a vivid copper-sulphate color, apparently from some deposit of the mineral in its upper courses, foamed and boiled in its basin confines in a cauldron of myriad blues and greens. From the basin, the water fell another three hundred feet to the valley floor in a series of spectacular cascades.

On the side of the main pool, nearest me, a great flat boulder jutted out. In the surface of this a depression about ten feet deep and thirty across had been formed by centuries of splashing backspray. This depression was kept full by the constant replenishing spray, forming a natural bathing pool complete with ever-showering overhead mists of green water.

To the rear of the pool a shelf of granite stood out from the encroaching cover of timber, providing a diving platform for entry into the water. I had scarcely time to note these things when any thought of natural beauty was devastated by the startling appearance of a girl on the diving-rock below.

She stepped quickly out of the darkness of the pines, walked to the edge of the diving-rock, stood a moment gazing eastward to the morning sun. Chin high, arms outstretched to the golden flood of light, she stood motionless for the time a man might slowly count ten.

She was absolutely, stark, skin-naked.

For an instant she poised on the rock's edge, balancing as lightly as a butterfly on a flower petal, then she was gone in an arching, clean dive and a rainbow spray of green water, her slim body cleaving the sun-dappled surface of the pool, a slender arrow of red lancing into a bright shield of blue-green.

As she swam, darting, diving, twisting, rolling in the icy waters below, I stood stunned.

This was she. This was my dream. I had found the North Star.

The blood came thick in my temples. I couldn't breathe. I couldn't swallow. I couldn't move.

But I could see! And what I had seen was: a body as perfect as the face it complemented. A wild, tigerish body, supple and lithe as a cat's, and yet a body no man would have to touch to know its powder softness.

Her neck was clean in line, elegantly poised, showing a provocative curve of nape where the tumbling hair had been piled high preparatory to entering the pool. Her shoulders were wide, straight as a boy's, the waist lean and slender as a child's. Her breasts, high, curving upward and slightly outward in their sculpture, were the full breasts of a complete woman, yet firm in their carriage as a girl's of sixteen.

Her hips were narrowed with the grace of years on saddle-less horseback. Her legs were faultless, the thighs full, as a woman's should be, tapering to slenderness at the knee, swelling again to the sleek curve of the calf, trimming cleanly into ankles as delicately chiseled and boned as a deer's. Her feet and hands were small, fine-boned, artfully graceful yet strong as indeed is true of her race generally.

Her face, slanting green eyes, luringly curved mouth and all, was exactly as pictured in the half-waking dreams of my delirium.

Her skin color had the gleaming coppery, peach-blow

bloom I had known it must. Her hair, not straight and blue-black like an Indian's, plunged around her head in an un-tamed mane of natural, soft curls, all gleaming with bur-nished auburn highlights over the dark inner masses.

My awe at this goddesslike apparition and the pure shock of having seen a beautiful woman absolutely nude after months of campaigning, during which even the thought of such charms had little time to haunt me, were now wearing off.

Below me the sounds of girlish gasps at the coldness of the water came interlarded with bursts of high musical laughter and just plain, lusty, boyish shouts of shock and pleasure.

In all she could not have swum more than three minutes before she was back on the rock, her gorgeous body dia-mond-dewed by a million-sun-glancing droplets of green water. She stood for a moment now, again with her arms to Wi, virgin breasts pointing with iciness of their recent im-mersion, slender legs tensed on tip-toe, straight back arching in a curve to bring the pulse thick in a man's throat and the iron of desire to the muscles of his hands and arms.

She was gone, then, and my long, held breath expelled itself with an explosive burst.

I do not know what madness then impelled me, for I leapt downward upon the diving-rock, lunging on unthinkingly to-ward the black pines which had closed behind her. Lust, con-scious lust that is, does not match my memories of that in-stant. Yet surely the thing which drove me had a depth as primordial as any which ever impelled man to seize his woman.

The blind spell passed and my mind cleared, but not be-fore I had burst through the inner cover and stood, dumb-struck, before her.

She froze as she had been at the instant of my entrance, leaning slightly forward to retrieve her garments of white doeskin and wolf fur from the ground where they lay. Her great green eyes widened imperceptibly, the ripe-berry lips falling apart in wonder. Yet no alarm nor least embarrass-ment marked her movements.

She came slowly erect, the long-lashed pools of her eyes holding mine unwaveringly. No gesture was made to cover her body and she stood motionless, holding her garments simply in one hand, slack at her side.

The haunting half-curve smile of my dreams was on her lips as she spoke the words which gained her a slave for eternity and lost me a heart forever.

"You have come to me, then, Cetan Mani." Her voice was soft and cool and musical as spring water among moss and smooth stones. "You have come to me and my heart is like a wild bird within me."

I could say nothing, think nothing, only stand there, dumb-struck by her words. I don't know what I expected, if I expected her to speak at all: possibly an angry tirade, a cry of alarm, a haughty rebuff. But this; this wide-eyed, simple, thrilling statement. I continued to stand, open-mouthed, my eyes looking but not seeing.

How long we paused thus, I cannot say. Surely it was no more than seconds, still, in that perverse way a man's mind will take when it is completely nonplussed, my memory of that moment concerns itself not with her beauty, her strange poise, nor yet her pagan nakedness, but with an odd detail; a minute, unimportant thing which had escaped my original notice.

She was not, in truth, entirely unadorned. It was this detail of ornamentation which now held my attention.

Around her neck ran a thin strong chain of silver, fitting snugly and high, like the choker ribbons affected by fashionable women in the States. Pendant from this chain, in the manner of a locket, was a silver amulet no more than two inches in diameter, heavily worked, and grasping securely in the exact center of its carvings a perfect cobalt-blue star sapphire of tremendous size and brilliance.

The opalescent fire in the heart of this great gem flashed and burned against the copper-red of the girl's skin.

The design which held the jewel was in the motif of two entwined reptiles supported on the spread wings of a bird. The former appeared to be renderings of the Montezuman feathered-serpent God, while the latter was most certainly a quetzal, sacred bird symbol of the Nahuatlan Indians at the time of Cortes. There could be no question, even in such a cursory examination, that the odd talisman was Aztec in origin.

What such an exotic bauble was doing around the slim throat of a North American Indian girl, three thousand miles and four hundred years from the land of its makers, was a question which probed my mind at the instant, but any further thoughts of the anachronistic charm were dispelled by its wearer's next words.

"I am cold, Cetan Mani. I would cover myself."

Immediately my mind returned to actuality, a region for which disposition and training had far better fitted it. Blushing in a style to shame any peeping schoolboy. I turned my back to North Star, standing patiently until she spoke again.

From behind me, presently, came a typically Indian instruction. *"Hopo,* let's go," said North Star, her low, husky voice setting me to quaking all over again.

I turned to see a vision no less lovely than the virgin nude of moments before. Clad from head to foot in cotton-white furs and snowy doeskins, replete with colored moccasin and legging beadwork of the rarest Sioux workmanship, caped and hooded by a parkalike garment of prime arctic fox pelts, Star's appearance made a memory with which any man might live forever, knowing he had held true beauty in his eyes for one precious parcel of time.

"Owanyeke waste, everything is good for the eyes," I managed, worshipfully, my gaze sweeping in the whole wonderful picture of her.

. *"Hookahey!"* she answered, laughingly, suiting motion to phrase by setting off down-trail, walking lithe-hipped and pantherish. I fell in by her side and we traveled silently, our tongues as hushed as the fall of our moccasins in the fresh snow.

We had not far to go to where Hussein awaited us, small ears up-pricked in curiosity, wicked eyes glaring as he saw I came in company with another. All this time my mind raced with my pulse at a hammering gait, but with a million questions thronging my thoughts, I could not voice so much as a word of one of them.

This was the time and instant every man lives for. Yet what could I say? Where could I begin?

I longed to pour forth poetic phrases, sounding her perfections to the uttermost lodge-pole of Wakan Tanka's tipi, yet as we came to Hussein's tethering place and she paused an expectant moment, turning to me with that little half-smile which seemed always to light up her entire face with its sudden, startling appearance, I could think of not one syllable.

We stood a moment thus, facing each other, her upturned child's face coming barely to my breast, my head bent forward and down so that her glorious hair lay just beneath my lips. A vagrant breeze lifted one of the soft curls to brush my cheek with the lightness of black eider-down.

Sioux is a language of reality. The Indian mind and tongue do not concern themselves with refined emotion.

"I love you," I said, hoarsely, in English. And seized her to smash my mouth against hers. It was a long kiss, harsh and cruel.

She staggered back from it as though from a blow in the face, her slim hand held with its back to her bruised lips, nostrils wide, emerald eyes on fire. I was aware then that her features mirrored a look which superseded any possible anger, hurt, incredulity. It was a look of fear, the fear of the unknown.

My voice was soft then, as quiet and sure as a mother.

"Wonunicun," I murmured, employing the sole word in the Sioux vocabulary which may be spoken in apology. Literally it means, "A mistake has been made."

"No!" she whispered, her voice thick with emotion, "no, not *wonunicun.* This thing was not a mistake. But I know not what it was and I am afraid. I am afraid, for I have never felt this thing before."

"It is a kiss," I said, slowly. "It is a sign among my people, sacred to lovers. Its meaning is that I would have you dwell in my tipi forever."

She felt her lips wonderingly with arched fingertips as I talked, meanwhile shaking her head in disbelieving negation. Only then did it occur to me, oaf that I was, that the kiss is unknown among her people. While I had been speaking to her, telling her of its nature, I had not consciously realized her complete innocence of the act and its implications.

When a custom is so deeply seated within a race as to be almost an instinct, it is hard to imagine another race being in ignorance of its use and import. So now, as I watched the color of her beauty following my kissing of her, I could not fail to think that any woman in any age or time, experience to the contrary, must by virtue of simply being a female understand and thrill to the implied end-promise of a passionate kiss.

Nor was I far wrong, for her next words revealed just such a physical picture, though to be sure her unsophisticated mind did not grasp the facts nor state them in clear phrases.

"When you have touched me now, with your mouth," pausing here to lay a tapering forefinger upon my lips, "I know that no other man may stand before you outside my tipi door. But neither may you stand there. For I am Wiyan Wakan and no man may wait outside my lodge."

I knew we had come upon dangerous ground so, like the good military man I assumed myself to be, my next move was to evacuate the position with the least possible delay and loss.

"This I have known and have wrestled with it in my heart, bringing therefrom a vision, a dream, which bade me come to you." I shot her a quick glance, wondering how I was getting across. No whit reassured, I stumbled on. "This I have told Crazy Horse, and he has brought me here to council with you. His heart is bad within him also, but he knows not what to do."

"Nor do I," she announced simply. "Though my heart is good and speaks to me with a straight tongue."

By this I took she meant she gave full cognizance to the feeling between us, but dared not question her further on it.

"We shall council then," I suggested, trying to sound casual, "with Crazy Horse, upon our return?"

"So be it. But my spirit lies quietly, breathing not of hope."

Thinking to retrieve our former, lighter mood, before her spirit began to lie any more quietly or breathe any less vigorously, I suggested a race to the foot of the mesa incline. This seemed to strike the proper note, for she was at once all smiles. I was later to find the pagan priestess and the delighted child never far separated in this strange girl.

At the moment my proposal was a lucky shot, serving to stave off a retreatless impasse.

As we spoke, we stood about ten feet from Hussein, who all the time had been conducting himself peculiarly; poking his head out in our direction, snuffling and flaring his nostrils to sample our scent, flicking his ears to catalogue our voices, in general acting more like an inquisitive weanling than the yellow-toothed old killer he was.

"And what will the wager be?" Star laughed, excitedly. Then, before I could answer, "I know. You shall bring me the heart of a great enemy of our people. And you shall lay it before my tipi, that I may know you are truly the warrior they say you are."

I wondered a bit at this bloodthirsty suggestion, not yet having it clear in my head that this lovely vision was in actuality a high priestess of the most warlike tribe of hostiles on the continent. It was hard, later, for me to remember this, for her goodness and gentleness were obvious. Yet in her veins ran the blood of countless centuries of warring ancestors and the savage in her was never so well-covered but what the first war whoop wouldn't bring it bounding into the open, naked, primordial, unveneered.

"The wager is fair," I laughed, in turn. "But what if you lose?" I had in mind, of course, a footrace, having no intention of allowing a slip of an Indian girl to outrun me. If there was one thing I could do well, it was run. From boyhood I had delighted in the joy to be found in effortless stretching of strong limbs. Later, in the bizarre climax of my life among the Sioux, I was to find a terrible use for this proud fleetness, but at the moment I merely wanted to impress my Indian love with my power and speed afoot.

"I shall not lose!" she shouted, wheeling suddenly. "For even the Hawk is not so swift as the Horse!" With that she leaped for Hussein with the speed of a darting hare. I had no chance to stop her, only being able to cry out in terror. "No, Star! Keep away from him! He'll kill—"

Alas, what fools we males are. And that goes for you, too, Hussein, you traitorous dog! Never again shall a word be said for your warrior's head nor hero's heart. Never again the buffalo trail nor warpath for such as you. You have become an old woman and from now on you shall pull a travois loaded down with squealing puppies and squalling papooses. You shall travel with the squaws and the dogs and the old men, that the sight of your craven carcass may not pollute the courage of true war ponies as they carry the braves. And in the end you shall be cut up for wolf bait, for even a village cur would not eat of your treacherous innards for fear of becoming in turn a gutless jackal.

Yes, I was left standing there, all fat and stupid, my terrified warning still resting peacefully in my strictured larynx, while Star, swinging gracefully to the willing back of my erstwhile warhorse, galloped off with all the ease and confidence of seat she might employ on any spotted butterball of a village pony.

Hussein, no doubt in ignorance of the fact I intended putting a rifle bullet through his black heart the minute I got my hands on a gun, had the temerity to look back and fling me a whinnying horselaugh before settling into his stride and skimming off over the valley floor, sailing over frozen creek and bush alike, as smooth and easy as any bird, quite obviously as happy.

Accompanying his laugh came one from Star, along with a shouted phrase in Sioux, which I could not translate at the time but which Crazy Horse later broke down for me into some such sense as, "Never trust a woman with your war pony!" To the Indian this means you can't mix love and business. A very good idea, Tashunka Witko, but one to which military history fails to pay a great deal of respect.

Chapter 11

THE COUNCIL with Star and Crazy Horse never came about.

Upon my tail-dragging return to the camp I sought out the great Sioux, laying my heart bare to him, telling him Star wanted me as I did her and that we had agreed to council with him on the matter. Protecting Star, I assured him she felt her position as a holy woman made any living love between us impossible.

Much has been written of the impassiveness of the Indian character, the dark nature of the red man's mind and heart, particularly those of the unconquerable prairie Sioux, most particularly those of the war chief's own band, the Oglala Bad Faces. Pure ignorance dictates in these cases.

A more gentle reception of an emotional outburst was never given a love story than was given mine by Crazy Horse, that very Indian who shall probably go down through white legend as the bloodiest red wretch of them all.

"My brother," he answered, soberly, when my tale of the morning's events had spilled out, "no man may truly say his words are those of Wakan Tanka." I thought of the host of his white counterparts who chose to announce themselves appointed to speak for God, making accordingly a deep mental bow to the Indian grasp of reality and lucidity of spirit. "Still," he continued, "I am my people's leader. What I say now is thus spoken. You cannot have this woman so long as she will not have you. But in our eyes, holiness is a personal thing. That of Star's being hers to keep or abandon as she sees fit. So long as she wills to remain pure, so long will the price of her holiness be held at the last drop of Sioux blood on these prairies."

He looked at me steadily, his slitted eyes unfathomable, his handsome face immobile as though hand-cut from living red granite. I returned his gaze, then dropped mine to the tipi floor, answering him with equal impassivity. "You speak with a straight tongue. My heart hears you."

"It is well, my brother, for tonight, when the moon is in the middle, we leave."

74

"So soon?"

"You have been brought to the Star of the North, as your dream was told you. I have done this, for the dream is sacred. But it is as your brother told you. You cannot have her."

"It is well," I echoed him, knowing that for now my quest was hopeless. I would be leaving at midnight whether I would or no. And fifty Fox Lodge braves would be along to see my respect for the physical sanctity of their priestess didn't waver somewhere along the out-trail. The Indian is a stern realist, an iron moralist, but he knows the hot hammerings of mating blood as well as the next man.

It is fair to set down here the fact I respected the Sioux beliefs and taboos so long as I was among them without, at the same time, sharing them. At no time was Star anything to me but a woman, the most desirable in the world, true, but always and simply a woman. Could I take her in compliance with Dacotah custom, I would. If not, I meant to have her anyway.

For the moment, though, I held a busted flush in a game where red-held fulls, fours, and straights crowded every corner of the blanket.

Crazy Horse signified the council was over. Casting about for some means of strengthening my contact with him, hence increasing my chance I might come upon to win Star honorably, I resolved to tell him of the plan which caused me to quit the Army at Fort Phil Kearney; the plan on which Carrington had turned thumbs down. Briefly, I did so.

He listened, gravely. When I had done, his answer was clear and succinct. "The Little White Chief was right. Whiskey has done the Indian harm, as have all white customs, but it is in my heart to know when he comes the white man brings death for the Indians, whether he comes with whiskey or with hands empty. It is in the hearts of the white soldiers to destroy us and take from us our lands. They will have the land. We will not let them have it. They make treaties, giving us broad lands, then they send spies and whiskey runners and many diseases among us to weaken us. Then they take the lands, killing the Indians. Those which are not killed are sent to the hot southlands to wither and die of the white sickness (tuberculosis), or to starve for want of meat. In my heart I know the white men mean to kill us, one way or another.

"There can be no peace until the last buffalo is dead and the last Indian held upon the reservation.

"Already the Ute, Cheyenne, Kiowa, Comanche, Pawnee,

Crow, and Arapahoe live upon the White Father's spotted buffalo (cattle). Only the Sioux remains free, and only upon the broad lands of the river you call the Powder does old Pte still roam to serve his red brothers. When Pte is done, the Indian is gone, the whiskey will not speed the day beyond a few moons."

What Carrington had said in ignorance and his brother officers in arrogance, Crazy Horse was now saying in thoughtfulness and in language I could appreciate. He painted a military picture.

Slatemeyer, to Tashunka Witko, constituted, with all his kind, but a delaying action in the white man's determination to extirpate the red. The main action would be the destruction of the Indian's commissary, the buffalo. Without this free-roving food supply the Indian was done. The war chief could see it. He knew it. His people were doomed.

For it was the buffalo which furnished all his life's necessities to the Sioux. He was not just commissary but whole economy.

Fresh meat came from Pte for daily cooking; dried meat and fat for pemmican, the "staple-storable" of all the plains Indians. From the hide of an old bull would come the bull-boats for overwater carriage of all gear and personnel. From the finer hide of the cow, all tipi coverings, clothes, leggings, moccasins, shirts, sleeping skins. The toughened neck-hide of a bull made the small round war shields that would turn a lance in full charge. Winter hunting capes, tipi rugs and sleeping spreads, were furnished by buffalo robes, the whole body-skin of the animal tanned with the thick curly hair left on.

Rawhide was used for trunks, boxes, ropes, and other camp gear. Sledge runners from rib bones, axes from the scapulars, hide-dressing tools from cannon bones. The horns, boiled and softened, were shaped into wondrous spoons and ladles. The paunch, removed whole, made a "kettle" for boiling meat.

Out of Pte's great body came bone and sinew to form sewing needle and thread; glue from the boiled hoofs for fletching arrows, cementing lance and ax heads, mending camp gear. His tail made a broom or fly-brush. The skin of the hock made an iron-tough winter boot. Saddle leathers, girths, bow cases, quivers, gun and knife sheaths, travois straps, garment lacings, duffel bags; all the thousand-and-one articles of the nomad tribesman's society came from the bountiful Pte.

No great mystery then, that the Sioux revered the buffalo

above all animals. And small wonder Crazy Horse measured the future of his race by the years of Pte's survival.

Still, I was a military man myself. I argued craftily with the war chief. A delaying action had been known to turn a major campaign. Better not pass any chance to twist the white tail.

As applied to the present case, the argument was specious. I knew I lied. Crazy Horse knew it. The only thing he didn't know was why I lied. I had not told him of the jesting wager Star had made me, but now in desperation I saw in it my best chance to come again to this valley. I meant to destroy Slatemeyer and his destructive trade, if it were the last act of my life. I hasten to say the original honesty of this intention, in which I saw myself a hero in the cause of an exploited savage people for whom I had an unaccountable sympathy, was now compromised by my love for Star.

While I did not agree with Crazy Horse entirely, I could see, with him, the end-hopelessness of his race. It wasn't that the whiskey trade was not a powerful weapon of harm, but that its breaking would not alter the outcome of the final battle. I still felt the hamstringing of the liquor runners would, by eliminating one big cause of the red man's bad conduct on the frontier, strengthen his position with the whites, possibly to the extent of gaining a keepable peace.

Nevertheless, I abandoned the thought of going to Custer. If I couldn't interest the field marshal of the Sioux, how could I expect Yellow Hair's ear to be any more sympathetic?

Still, I meant to have Star one way or another. Slatemeyer remained in my mind. I'd underestimated Crazy Horse. His next words made this excitingly apparent.

"I know the sun of my people grows short." As he spoke his gaze fell through the open tipi flap upon the distant walls of the Black Hills. In the harsh blue of the winter sky, a black dot wheeled in lazy circle above the highest escarpment. "But yonder flies Wanbli K'leska. This is his land. This is my land. The Land of the Spotted Eagle. So long as he flies above it, so long shall I ride and fight for it here below. You may have this thing you ask. But first you must be given rank. Tonight, on the hour of departure, you shall receive Canounye Kicicupi."

My heart rabbited up within me at these words. Since my capture I had been given no weapons, in consequence having no real tribal status. Now I was to receive Canounye Kicicupi, the Giving-of-War-Weapons, one of the highest of

Sioux ceremonies and the one which forever dedicates the warrior to the service of his tribe and race.

To accept this ritual meant my embracement of the Seven Tribes as the government of my allegiance, the acknowledgment that the blood in my veins was red blood, Sioux blood. In a word, literally, I would become an Indian.

I knew enough of their ways to realize this step, once taken, was unretractable. In any act I might perpetrate after the Taking of Weapons I would be judged, punished or rewarded, as the case might be, as an Indian. To them it meant the birth of a new warrior, Walking Hawk, into the band. To me it meant the death of John Clayton, Confederate States Army officer, southern gentleman, white man.

And to all other white men, wheresoever I should meet them, it would mean one case-hard word—renegade.

In retrospect, knowing as I do the crushing fortunes I endured thereafter, and the nameless, faceless end of those fortunes, I wonder at my decision of the time. Had I to make it again, would I have the courage, the will, the blindness of duty to race and nation, to do so?

Even now the vision which gave me my answer then arises before me and I know for all time what my answer would be: it would be two green eyes, long and slanting under raven lashes; the sound of a cool laugh, the flash of snow-clean teeth; the fragrance of pine and prairie air mixed with the smell of her in the perfume of her curls; the living feel of the slim red body lying warm and sweet and close, in hours any man will treasure above all his others on this earth.

Breaking the long silence which endured while Crazy Horse's statement turned in my mind, I said the words which took me into ten years of high joy and opposite sorrow. It was the beginning of the Sioux prayer which says in effect: "Father, receive my offering . . ."

From my use of it, the war chief would understand I accepted the honor, considering it sacred.

The trail was chosen, my moccasins already set upon it. In the distance the red light of war-fires burned on the bleak skyline. In twelve hours I would be an Oglala Bad Face member of the Dacotah Sioux Nation. A "red" Indian in fact and being.

THE OLD chief, Many Kills, came to me about sunset as I sat broiling a slab of buffalo hump for my supper.

"Woyuonihan," I said, touching my forehead with my left fingertips as I nodded to him. This is the little gesture of respect employed by the tyro warrior toward one of reputation. I could see the old fellow was mightily pleased.

Courtesy is very precious to the Indian, particularly when he has aged. Nor is the oldster frequently disappointed, for Indians believe that the old shall be deeply respected; another example of the innate graciousness of the race. It is hard to fault a social philosophy which venerates age and childhood, leaving the middle years of strength to defend themselves.

"It is time," he announced, squatting by the fire, regarding the sizzling humpmeat with what I thought more than passing interest.

"Have you fed?" I asked.

"Only a little. The rib of an old bull, boiled."

"This is from a young cow, fat and full with red blood."

"I will join you," he grunted. And together we tore at the succulent meat, taking the whole chunk in turn, seizing it in the teeth, severing what we wanted each time with our knives, passing the remainder back and forth until the last morsel was gone. The meat was done to the Indian-turn; fire seared only, the inside as red as the day before it came off the cow. The hot blood dripped and ran through our fingers, it and the delicious fat hissing as a droplet of one or the other found its way into the fire. The hump of a young cow, prepared and eaten thus, is the finest meat of all.

When we had finished, the old man got up and walked off without a word. I followed him, smiling inwardly at the verbal penury of his kind.

Many Kills led me to an especially miserable tipi before which squatted an old devil of a Sioux, ancient enough to be my wrinkled guide's great-grandfather. By the hair and feather charms, eagle-bone whistles, carved stones, buckskin bags and reed flageolets with which he surrounded himself, I knew we were in the presence of the village medicine man.

He spoke in Sioux to Many Kills, eyeing my face and fingering a villainous pair of large surgical tweezers the while. I wondered what smoking settlement ruin, or brush with the pony soldiers, had yielded this instrument, but was more interested by the gist of the old man's words to Many Kills.

"It will be a great thing," he crowed, gleefully, at the same time taking up a glowing hard wood faggot. "Like skinning the face of Father Pte, himself!"

I caught on quickly. The buffalo's distinguishing characteristic was his healthful growth of chin foliage. This wizened old goat was about to de-beard me.

"Touch one hair of my face and I'll smash you into so many pieces your ancestors will spend the next ten thousand moons just finding your fingers and toes," I demurred.

Many Kills reassured me. "No harm is intended, Cetan Mani. The tweezers are for the upper lip only. Here the hairs may be easily drawn out, one by one. For the chin hairs it is simple to use the hot stick, for here you are as thickly grown as Pte's tassel."

I had no intention of letting these two old murderers pelt me alive, yet here was the old business of protocol again. One had to walk softly. An inspiration came.

"Send me to the tipi of Tashunka Witko for the little bag which travels with me," I demanded, haughtily. "Therein I have magic to remove any part of the body; face, beard, nose, ears, anything. Even the entire head!" I added, impressively, looking meaningfully at the medicine man's wrinkled skull. The implication was a success. A passing boy was sent for the bag.

When I had it in my hand, I instructed both old men to go into the tipi, standing with their faces wallward while they might breathe two hundred times. This they did, I making the best of their absence with the magic available—a pair of barber's shears and a hand mirror, standard equipment for any frontiersman affecting the fierce beard and mustache I did.

Having gotten as close to the skin as I might with the scissors, I covered the remaining stubble and the white skin under it with a hasty ingraining of red dust and ashes. When my would-be depilators turned, they saw what they wanted —a face without hair.

They then cut and groomed my hair, Sioux style, in two

long braids with a roach-crested scalplock piled above my forehead. Following this I was stripped naked and made to bathe in the icewater of a nearby spring. I was furnished a simple loincloth of soft-tanned elk, with moccasins of the same material, before being smeared from toes to tonsils with vermilion, ochre and cobalt, not to mention some tremendously effective blazings of pure white zinc.

When they had done, they had created something to upset the digestion of any white settler.

Having a fine Indian face to begin with; high cheekboned, wide-jawed, hawk-nosed, hard-mouthed and ugly, topped with hair blacker and straighter than any Dacotah's, mounted on a six-foot-three frame of lean body, whose wide shoulders, long arms, spare pelvis and saddle-bowed legs couldn't have been by nature more nearly cast in the Siouxan mold; the removal of beard, application of war paint, and cutting of scalplock were the only touches to complete my outward transference to the red race.

The actual ceremony of the Weapon-Giving which followed took two hours in preparatory dancing before the moment came for me to receive my arms.

While Indian ceremonies of this nature are serious and binding no matter by whom performed, they cannot help but take on added prestige if administered by an individual of high reputation. To be confirmed as a warrior by any chief was honor enough, to be sponsored into the select Society of Warriors by the greatest fighter of them all, was more than I had dreamed of.

The chief who performs the actual handing-of-weapons to the candidate acknowledges by the act that he takes upon himself the responsibility for the initiate's skill, courage, hardihood. In effect he accepts, as his protégé, the new warrior. Imagine the thrill for me when I saw making his way through the waiting ranks of braves, not the local chief, Many Kills, but the great Crazy Horse. The stoic red men greeted his approach with an "A-ah!" of surprise. Subsequently, I learned he had never before sponsored a candidate.

He stopped in front of me, standing statuelike in the red light of the fires. He was naked to the waist, otherwise clad in leggings and moccasins of fringed white elk. Slanting through his black hair was the single spotted eagle feather of the Dacotah Sioux. His deep voice fell over the breath-held silence.

"*Ótotanla*." With the word, he placed the fingers of his right hand on my mouth. My tongue would be straight.

"Zunta." His left hand went to my right shoulder. I would be honest.

"Nakaciyin." The right hand on my left shoulder. I would be loyal.

"Wolakota wa yaka cola." Both hands on my heart. "Peace without Slavery." The honor-word of the people, the scripture on the Pipe of Peace. I would fight forever for freedom.

He stepped back, the oath given, the whole thing having taken no more than twenty seconds; a man's complete allegiance dedicated in a third of a minute.

Crazy Horse motioned to two tall braves behind him. These came forward, each bearing a bundle wrapped in skins, undoubtedly the weapons I was to receive. I pondered their nature, for some of the war instruments they make show superb craftsmanship.

At a word from the war chief, the first brave held forth his burden. His leader removed the skin wrappings, turning to me to reveal the two new Colts I had thought long-lost in the snows of Fetterman's massacre-ground. Quickly the chief buckled them around my waist, announcing as he did, loudly and clearly,

"Ohan! Wear them!"

The other brave, to my added surprise, bore my Winchester repeater. This in turn was given me by Crazy Horse. He then stepped back, removed the eagle feather he wore and, placing it deftly in my hair, called out the words of finality,

"Hohahe, Cetan Mani. Welcome is Walking Hawk to the tipis of the tribe."

"Ha-a-u!" echoed the watching warriors.

"Hohahe," muttered the women and old men.

"It is the decision of the Nation, done by the people," Crazy Horse's deep voice concluded.

I was Walking Hawk, full-blood Oglala Sioux. The crowd was still as I stepped back. Its silence was unearthly quiet.

Seized by impulse, I leaped toward Crazy Horse, Winchester high above my head, calling out the warning-word, "A-ah!"

The women and warriors watched intently. Crazy Horse looked at me sharply, his obsidian-black eyes glittering in the shifting firelight. The tension of the thing lay about me like a cobweb. I could feel the strands drawing. The Indian sense of ceremony does not include provision for unrehearsed demonstrations by the initiate. I was making an incursion on touchy terrain. My next move had best be just the right one.

But impulse has always maintained a full head of steam in the boiler of my being. Thrusting the Winchester into the war chief's hands, I called aloud, my voice ringing in the flamelit silence, "Wear it, that its charm may always protect your life!"

For ten seconds he stood, holding the gleaming new rifle before him, his gaze never leaving it. Not a moccasin-shuffle was heard. Then he looked up at me, his sculptured face unsoftened.

"*Ha-a-u,*" he said, touching first the gun, then his heart.

In a moment he was gone, the warriors' ranks dividing soundlessly for his exit. Crazy Horse had taken my war-gift into his heart.

Around me now the other savages thronged, congratulating me, patting me, holding my hands, grasping my arms. All were smiles and there was much talk. That I had given my rifle to Tashunka Witko had made a tremendous impression.

I had to smile at their simplicity. The real generosity had been theirs, of course, in their original returning of the gun to me. My gesture was nothing but a thin aping of theirs. It would never occur to an Oglala in such light. The Sioux vocabulary has no word for generosity.

Chapter 13

I DID NOT see Star again. We left at midnight, the night being moon-dark, traveling the out-trail as we had the in, in stygian gloom. But this time Crazy Horse talked, pointing out various trail marks, giving certain place names. My mind was still back in the village with Star but my military self automatically catalogued his remarks. In the game I meant to play knowing this trail might mean my life.

The journey out was uneventful. We parted from Many Kills and his braves in the opening of the Gate of the Buffalo, riding all the following day and night, north and west, to reach the war chief's lodges on noon of the second day.

Crazy Horse at once sent out runners summoning the Fox Lodge to council.

During the next days scattered groups of Indians drifted in until there were nearly two hundred lodges pitched along the Upper Cheyenne. There were Brule, Minniconjou, and a few Sans Arc; no Blackfoot or Hunkpapa, these tribes being winter-camped too far north, along the headwaters of the Missouri.

The council, held a week after our return, was crowded with names and faces of Sioux repute. Present were American Horse, Standing Bear, the elder, Bull Bear, High-Hump-Back, Buffalo Bear, Gall, Wolf-That-Limps, Paints-Brown and Spotted Tail.

Crazy Horse propounded my plan, neither advocating nor depreciating it.

Some of the older heads could see nothing in it, some of them being surprisingly hostile to the idea. I wondered if these might not be worrying about disrupting their source of supply, the Indian appetite for the white man's god-awful trade whiskey being what it was.

Here again I was brought up against the fact of the red man's terrible thirst, having cause to question anew whether or not my first impression of the great force of evil liquor wrought among the Indians was not the correct one; Colonel Carrington and Crazy Horse to the contrary notwithstanding.

As I write these words the signal blanket of the years will not cover the smoke of the idea that it was not the carbine of the cavalry, nor yet the musket of the infantry, that defeated the red militarists, but the bearded, hard-eyed men of whom Slatemeyer was the archetype, coming among them with no ass's jawbone but a brown clay jug loaded with white civilization's most potent ammunition, rot-gut whiskey.

The plains Indian had not known an intoxicant prior to the coming of the white fur trader. He had no racial immunity built up through an ancestry of guzzlers as did the European. The effects of drunkenness among his kind were plainly terrible. All the white scouts I ever knew have been agreed on this point: there's nothing an Indian won't do to get whiskey and nothing he won't do after he's gotten it.

I cannot believe the Army was innocent of the part whiskey played in softening up the red military. The Indians themselves, witness the burning patriot, Crazy Horse, did not understand this fact. But I am convinced the Army, if not its individual commanders such as Carrington, was beautifully aware if officially "blind" to the "terrible swift sword" they had in the lethal trade whiskey of the frontier.

The common recipe for this Sioux hemlock will speak more for its devastating potential than volumes of description. Here it is—

TRADE WHISKEY

1 quart raw alcohol

1 pound rank, black chewing tobacco

1 handful red peppers

1 bottle Jamaica ginger

1 quart black molasses

water from the Missouri River ad libitum

While the Army was suffering the existence of this trade, the traders themselves operated on another theory: the conclusion that the coming of the white settlers meant the ruination of the fur country and the end of their fat traffic with liquor-stupid natives. Although the fur supply was already far down from its earlier abundance, it was still well worth conniving to protect. An idea of the remaining heft of that supply and of the traffic which drained it, may be had from this trader's list taken by myself from the scalped body of a whiskey runner.

His bookkeeping began with the following entry:

> 16, 9 *gal. kegs liquor*
> (2 *gal. alcohol to* 7 *gal. water*)

And closed with this summation of what the Indians had traded for their throbbing heads and rotted-out stomachs:

> 628 *beaver skins*
> 78 *black bear*
> 53 *cinnamon*
> 8 *grizzly*
> 137 *wolf*
> 86 *red fox*
> 17 *kit*
> 101 *otter*
> 47 *martin*
> 117 *fisher*
> 36 *mink*

This was still big business. To protect it, the whiskey trader not only supplied the Indian with liquor but in case after documented case, incited him to attack white settlements and wagon trains. To keep the country free of whites and full of Indians added up to profits for the whiskey runner. Men like Slatemeyer never neglected looking to their profits.

But where the reactions of certain of the Sioux to my plan brought all these old suspicions to mind, the enthusiasm of the others confused me. The young braves and sub-chiefs were full of interest.

Upshot of the session was that I should have my way, with the added recommendation that I start "when the short grass was up and the first fat showing on the ponies." This suited my impatience well enough. Winter was already far gone; spring not more than three moons away.

Those three moons were spent on my education. Crazy Horse was away much of the time traveling the winter circle of war camps, laying out the spring campaign for the coming wagon-train season along the Bozeman Trail. When he traveled I went with him, meeting most of the famous Sioux chiefs and warriors.

While on these trips I had the advantage of studying under the top Sioux masters in each branch of the war arts. I hunted with the best hunters, rode with the finest riders, was instructed in the highest secrets of trailing, stalking, bird- and animal-call imitation, in short, learned under famous teachers, all the ins and outs of the Sioux's prairie-crafted war methods.

Because of these wide rangings up and down and across the Sioux homeland, my name and new tribal status became familiar throughout the Indian Nation.

Also, disastrously, my plans.

For somewhere in the red hierarchy was a warrior who loved his whiskey better than his native land. The whiskey runners had a full report of my intentions before I moved a moccasin in their direction. So efficient was Slatemeyer's intelligence he not only had my plans but my complete history since joining the Sioux, my capture, convalescence, subsequent journey to Star, the whole thing.

It is a wonder this wasn't foreseen, every army having its Arnolds, the Indian being no exception. Despite the concentrated nature of my experience I was new to the frontier, still enamored of the Sioux race and character. It simply didn't occur to me that one of them would turn against his own blood for a few demijohns of raw spirits.

But one of them did, may his soul wander the nightlands forever, and while I was still learning to become a Sioux warrior, Slatemeyer struck, revealing in the manner of his striking how criminally I had underestimated his brutality, imagination and cunning. Also, how I had overestimated my own position, or rather mis-evaluated it.

My attitude in going after him at all smacked more of bravado and derring-do than of real purpose. Thinking now, with the brains the horny hand of time manages to beat into the thickest skull, I know my motive was an immature male urge to show off in front of the girls. I saw in the whiskey runner a great chance to impress Star. Nothing else. Once before I had started after him with no girl involved and had quit the trail cold at the first cross-track. Now I was hotter than a two-dollar pistol. Star was the answer.

My scouts had located the barges of the whiskey runner frozen in on the Missouri, just south of Fort Kiowa. Slatemeyer, it appeared, had tried to squeeze in a last trip the season before, being caught by early ice. I had no idea he would be so close, assuming that this time of year would see him in Kansas City outfitting for the spring trip up the Big Muddy. I made another wrong assumption; that he had been caught by the ice on his way out, with empty barges.

So I started south for Fort Kiowa six weeks ahead of the expected spring break-up on the Missouri, having changed my mind about waiting for spring, figuring now to find his barges still frozen-in, sitting ducks for the shooting. With me went my first Indian Command, ten Oglala, all young men handpicked by Crazy Horse.

My plan was simple; find the barges and fire them.

My scouts had told me there were three of these, all small ones without living quarters aboard. This meant the crews would be winter-camped ashore, possibly at Fort Kiowa but more likely in the vicinity of the precious boats. Even with the Army's sub rosa compliance the runners usually observed surface precautions, hardly daring in this case, I thought, to winter in an Army post where their presence would need some explanation at least.

This assumption proved right. I found the barges lying in a blind slough a quarter of a mile off the main stream. The camp was ashore in a dense copse of poplar and willow. A fresh fall of snow showed no tracks between barges and shore. So far, so good.

Scouting the camp, we discovered it consisted of about fifteen white men plus an old Pawnee camp cook and two Arikaree, apparently either meat-hunters for the camp or guides for the coming trading season. I saw nothing of Slatemeyer but discounted the fact.

With nightfall I went aboard the barges, having instructed my companions to wait, giving me a hundred breaths before following me in.

A fine surprise awaited me. The barges were crammed with squat, nine-gallon kegs, certainly well over a hundred of them to the barge, each painstakingly stenciled with the innocuous legend, "*Caution*: *Kerosene*: *Keep Away From Fires.*" This honest claim was compromised by a certain haunting effluvium familiar enough to a thousand frontiersmen who probably couldn't even spell coal oil, let alone "kerosene."

From stem to stern and beam to beam the three barges reeked and stank of alcohol. I had caught my friend Slatemeyer with nearly three thousand gallons of trade whiskey.

Now I searched for what I had hoped to find aboard—and found it: three fifty-gallon hogsheads of *real* kerosene, one to each barge.

I had thought Slatemeyer smart enough for this. It was simple enough, if any *honest* Army inspector insisted on boarding the barges, to throw a few buckets of coal oil hurriedly around the cargo holds, cutting the whiskey fumes and lending olfactory support to the innocent illusion of the kerosene labels. Kerosene lamp oil was a very legitimate trade article sorely needed in the Montana mining settlements served by the Upper Missouri. Officious indeed would be the inspector who proceeded beyond his eyes and nose in such a patent picture of honest commerce.

Well, if Slatemeyer were courteous enough to provide such facilities, it would be rude not to use them.

Thus, a few moments later, when my fur-clad crew came slithering up through the snowfall then beginning, I gave them their orders promptly.

Any child loves a fire, and the Indian intellect is nothing if not youthful. My cohorts went about the business of smashing the big oil barrels and dousing kerosene all over the barge holds, each grinning as happily as any schoolboy pulling wing off a horsefly.

In minutes the night air was redolent with coal-oil fumes and Yellow Bird, my lieutenant, brought me the smoldering buckskin bag of live coals lovingly prepared ashore in a smokeless, hardwood fire no bigger than a man's two hands.

"Go now and wait where the trail leads from the camp," I told him, accepting the fire, "When you see the fire burst forth, all shall follow as we have planned it. Am I understood?"

He nodded assent, a sibilant chorus of grunts from the others backing him up.

"It is understood," he growled. "When the great flames leap toward Wakan Tanka, the white men will come running to see what has been. They will run on the trail where you have told us to wait. As they come, we shall meet them, knife and war ax—"

"And—?" I questioned, anxious to know he had the full text of his orders.

"And when we have struck once," he continued, "we shall flee—"

"Bringing with you, above all things—?" I quizzed, sharply.

"Bringing with us, above all things, one white man." He hesitated a moment, then added, reluctantly, "Alive."

"It is well then." My words were hurried. We had so far played in luck. I had no wish to stretch it. "I shall give you fifty breaths to make the ambush. We dare not use calls with those two Rees in camp."

"It is understood. The trap will be laid as you have said. In fifty breaths."

One moment there were ten Sioux within five feet of me, the next, nothing but invisible yards of swirling snow.

The following three minutes seemed ageless. I counted my breathing for what seemed an eternity. At last the fiftieth breath was expelled. Swiftly I dumped the living coals among the pile of oil-soaked shavings we had prepared; watched, fascinated, as they bit into the curls of oily wood, knew a heart-stopping moment as they sputtered and almost went out, then quick elation as they leaped to bright, clear life.

Slipping over the side of the barge I gave my anxious legs permission to get me the hell out of there.

They did, and none too soon. I had scarcely hit the wooded shore before the barges went up with a boom that lit the snow-smothered night for hundreds of feet. Kerosene may not be very volatile but that many gallons of it liberally laced over three winter-dry, wooden barges, lying beam to beam and loaded to the sideboards with raw alcohol, and you've got several shades better than a campfire.

As anticipated, Slatemeyer's men came bucketing out of their huts and off down the trail to the burning barges.

Yellow Bird played them perfectly, letting the first pack go by, falling on the smaller following group with the customary enthusiasm of his kind when the prospect is fair for a wedding of Sioux steel and Caucasian cranium.

Half an hour later when we rendezvoused he brought with him eight Sioux, the required "live" white man, five warm scalps, and an innocent-looking burden carelessly tied up in a hunting shirt.

"Good. Yellow Bird leads well. Who is with his ancestor?" My question referred to the missing Sioux.

"The-One-That-Limps," he answered.

"It is too bad. He was a fighter."

"He won't be lonely. He took his enemy with him. We could not see him smiling for the gun went off in his face and he had no face. But he *was* smiling. He had his knife well into the paunch and was cutting upward when the gun borrowed his face."

"It is well," I said, grimacing as I counted the grisly trophies dangling from the braves' scalpbelts. "I see where wailing will be held in the tipis of our enemies to the number of five."

"Six," he corrected me, unfurling the knotted hunting shirt to roll therefrom, a heavy, round object which thumped to a stop against my right moccasin, remaining there to look up at me with wide-open blue eyes. I caught myself in time to stifle the gasp that would have cost me face.

"Pesla," announced Yellow Bird regretfully, meanwhile giving the trophy a disgusted turn with the toe of his moccasin that I might see his statement was true. His tongue was straight. The human head at my feet was bald as a buzzard.

Yellow Bird felt called upon to apologize for the situation.

"It was a mistake," he stated, simply. "But our time was short and we wanted Cetan Mani to know the true count. Ordinarily," he added, humbly, "I would not take a pelt in such poor condition."

I nodded rapidly, half in understanding, half to keep my gorge from chucking the evening's pemmican all over the object of Yellow Bird's concern. After all, it might well be a puzzling thing to try to scalp a bald-headed man in the dark and in a hurry.

"It is understood," I gulped out. "Let us lay a line of

tracks away from here. You know the chief of these enemies. He has no fear. Even now his Arikaree hounds are
probably baying on our trail."

"With this snow they had best bay fast," said Yellow Bird,
laconically, "but nonetheless, let us go." Fingering his scalp-
ing-knife suggestively, he added, "What shall we do with
this one who still wears his hair?"

I had forgotten the prisoner! All this time the poor brute
had not said a word, standing gray-sick with terror. I thought
it queer he had made no plea to me, his fellow white man.

"Bring him," I told Yellow Bird, turning with the words.
"He shall tell me what I would know."

The thickening snow closed blankly over our tracks as we
headed north where our ponies were tethered. Behind us
three thousand gallons of "purified" trade whiskey crawled
skyward in a stinking cloud of oily smoke. The goods were
gone, now for the merchant. Slatemeyer was next.

"Score one for Walking Hawk," was my high-flown
thought, as I allowed myself a humorless smile.

Back at the pony-camp, knowing the storm would hide us,
we felt safe in enjoying a big fire.

The men needed warmth and food and sleep. We had a
fresh side of venison left among our supplies. This we
slashed into thick chunks, each man stick-roasting his own
dripping portion. The Sioux would thrust theirs into the heart
of the blaze for ten seconds, removing it and wolfing it
down while it was yet so hot you could hear it searing their
lips. For many minutes only the sounds of the fire, the tearing, chewing, and lip-smacking over the bloody meat broke
the wilderness quiet. Then when the last leg-bone had been
polished, cracked and marrow-sucked, the lordly Indian
belching began.

I stood this round of artful rumbling for a time then, de-
siring as always to be a man among men, sucked in a deep
breath of air, the while calling upon my own innards for a
comparable effort. Nothing I did subsequently, no act of
valor or feat of arms, advanced my standing as did that note-
worthy salute.

My braves squatted, staring open-mouthed. Then, to the
man, in awed unison, touching fingertips to foreheads, they
muttered *"Woyuonihan!"* Nine steel-eyed, hostile Sioux who,
within the hour had lifted the hair of five whiskey runners
and the head of a sixth, sat in touching reverence for my
gargantuan belch.

It is pertinent to their philosophy to know that this whole

exploit went down in tribal history not as, "The time we took five scalps and a head," or, "The night three thousand gallons of fire-water burned," but logically and simply as, "The time when Cetan Mani belched."

Yellow Bird, not a particularly religious fellow, complimented admiringly. "Wakan Tanka himself couldn't have done better! Even old Uncle Pte must bow his beard in shame before you."

This was rare praise. To be able to belch as loud as God and better than a bull buffalo, was as high as anyone might hope to soar in Sioux regard.

But my mood for levity passed. For the first time in months I felt the stab of my "Indian hunch" at work. "Bring me the prisoner," I barked at Yellow Bird.

When the man was brought before me I asked him bluntly, using English for the first time, "Why haven't you spoken to me? Why don't you ask for mercy? Aren't you interested in breathing?" He looked at me a second oddly, I thought, then dropped his eyes.

"What kinda mercy is a pack of Sioux hostiles gonna give a white man?"

"A good question," I agreed. "But how about me? I'm a white man."

He stared at me the way a man stares at an idiot. His short laugh had the rasp of desperation in it. "Sure, and I'm Sittin' Bull, er mebbeso Red Cloud."

I studied him, the full import of his statement beginning to settle in. This man was not joking. He thought he was going to be tortured, then killed. And he didn't see nine Sioux and a white man before him. He saw ten Sioux.

The jolt of this held me quiet a moment. Three months of snow-burning, winter sun and acrid lodge-smoke had apparently brought me to the point where a fellow white man could not discern my true color. I started to tell the hunched figure before me who I was, deferring the tale on second thought, till I had heard his.

"Where's Slatemeyer?"

"I dunno."

"Was he in the camp?"

"I dunno."

"Yellow Bird!"

"Aye, Cetan Mani?"

"Is my tongue straight?" This in English, of which Yellow Bird understood considerable and spoke a little.

"Aye," nodding soberly.

"If I tell this dog I shall spare his life, will it be so?"

"Aye."

"If I tell you to put his head in the shirt with that of the bald one, will you do it?"

"Aye!" Lips lifted swiftly over gleaming teeth.

"Now then my friend," I snapped, "you heard, didn't you? You can talk or have your hair lifted off at the neck. I don't much give a damn which, but it's going to be one way or the other, quick!" Yellow Bird eased forward, slipping a foot-long skinning knife out of its sheath as he came.

The man talked.

"Slatemeyer's gone north." The words tumbled all over each other now. "Left four days ago."

"Alone?"

"No."

"Who was with him?"

"Passel of Injuns."

"Indians?"

"Yup."

"What kind?"

"Crow."

At this, my braves came alert, their jet eyes glinting in the firelight. "Crow!" snarled Yellow Bird contemptuously. The Crow were the most precious of the Sioux blood enemies.

"How many?" I went on, ignoring the stirring among my men.

" 'Bout thirty."

This was a startler. What the devil was the whiskey runner figuring that needed thirty Indians of a tribe that, not even excepting the Sioux, was as tough as any that roamed the prairies?

"That all? Nobody else?" I said, not knowing why I asked.

"Nope. Nobody else."

There it was again, like a knife blade twisting in my thoughts; the "Indian hunch."

"You lie!" I burst out. "Yellow Bird, the knife." He almost had our guest decapitated before the words were well out of my mouth. I was barely in time to knock his arm up.

"Now talk fast," I snarled, raising the runner clear of the ground, my fists knotted in his greasy buckskin shirt, the muscles of my arms cording with lust to strangle him outright. "Who else was with him?"

"Another Injun, that's all. A little skinny Sioux."

A Sioux! The chill of the words ran into me like the bite

of a saber-blade. "Hurry up, damn you! What was he called? His name! What was his name?"

My eyes must have been blazing like an animal's, for the fellow recoiled, gasping, "Mouse, Mouse—my God, I dunno—I think I heard Slate call him 'Mouse.' "

Tonkalla. Tonkalla, the Mouse. So this was our traitor. Tonkalla, the sniveling, runted, unpopular Sans Arc chief.

"Tonkalla was present in the council of the Fox Lodge at the camp of Tashunka Witko?" I shot at Yellow Bird, thinking I remembered him there.

"He was," the Sioux answered, calmly, "and he will remember it as his last."

Facing the prisoner again, I put the pivot question. "And just what is Slatemeyer up to?"

I waited, my heart hesitating, having no right I knew, to hope this man might know this. Fortunately for him, he did. I think I would have killed him with my bare hands had he claimed ignorance.

"This here Mouse he come down the river last week and told Slate a white man is with the Sioux drummin' them up about whiskey runnin' in gen'ril, and him, that's Slate, in partic'lar. He told Slate this here feller was aimin' to come down here with his gang and smash up the whiskey boats. Slate gits out the jug and laces this redskin up with whiskey, proper. After he's got him his snootful, the Injun unpins his chin and really lets it wobble.

"He starts tellin' Slate all about this here squaw-man, and seems like 'bout halfway through his spiel Slate suddenly recollects who this white feller is. 'I know him!' he yells, jumpin' up excited like. 'So help me, God, I think I know who it is.' You know Slate, he don't git the wind up much. We all figured he was some upset.

"Well, the Injun goes on. Slate keeps lacin' him with the jug, and he keeps talkin'. But now Slate don't seem to give a damn 'bout anythin' but this white feller. Don't say nothin' 'bout the whiskey.

"Finally he gits it outa this chief that there's a gal in the deal. Some sort of a squaw medicine woman er somethin'."

"Star of the North," I interjected, tonelessly.

"Yup. Thet's the one. Well, anyway, Slate acts like he already knows all 'bout this here female but when he hears the white man has been sparkin' her he jumps up again. I never seen Slate excited before. He grabs this here puny little Sioux and yells at him somethin' thet sounds like, 'Hopo!' and him and the Injun departs instanter."

"Where did they go? Which direction?" My words sang like a strung bow.

"They went east. Then they come back a day later with this here bunch of Crow. This time they hit out north, the whole kaboodle of 'em. Thet was 'bout five, six days ago. Slate said he'd be back in a week and when we asked him what if this here guy comes after the whiskey while he's gone, he says, 'Jest don't worry none 'bout thet. I'll be back in plenty time fer him.' 'Pears like this little Sioux done told him the feller wasn't aimin' to come down until the grass was up short."

Well, there was one piece of good luck anyway. The Mouse had left before I changed my plan.

"Anything else?" My question was more automatic than anything. I already knew enough to sweat me for the rest of my natural days.

"Well, no, 'ceptin' I never seen Slate so kicked-up 'bout anythin'. He ain't persactly what you'd call a happy-jack, ordinarily, but when him and his Injun pals set out to leave, he's grinnin' like a crockydile. He yells back to us, 'Take care of the liquor, boys. I'm bringin' me back a squaw and we'll need ev'ry drop fer the weddin' party.' Never seen him act up thetaway. Reckon I'd nigh as soon be where I am as in thet white feller's moccasins."

I felt like vomiting. Every inch of my body was cold as the snow under my feet. My voice sounded flat, unreal. "The Mouse is a member of the Fox Lodge Council?"

"He is," answered Yellow Bird, knowing my unspoken fears.

"He will know the way into Mesa Valley, then? Through the Gate of the Buffalo?"

Nodding, my lieutenant answered quietly, "Let us put snow on the fire, Cetan Mani."

Chapter 14

ALL THAT night we drove through a high plains blizzard. By dawn the ponies and their riders were caked inches deep with frozen snow. Gulping pemmican as we rode, we pushed on crossing the Missouri above Fort Sully, following the Teton

River across the Bad Lands, reaching its headwaters two night later. Striking the Cheyenne the next day we got clearing weather, sundown raising the jutting headlands of the Gate of the Buffalo far ahead.

Here we parted company, Yellow Bird and the eight braves riding west for the Lodges of Crazy Horse.

On the trail we had talked plans of action. Since the season was late, this probably being its last storm, it was likely with its clearing Star would come out to the plains on her annual swing through the Nation.

The Mouse would know this. We had to gamble he would persuade Slatemeyer to hang outside Pte's entrance awaiting the Wiyan Wakan's expected exit. Actually this wasn't too much of a gamble. Even Slatemeyer would be given pause by the prospect of forcing Pte's passage.

Yellow Bird felt sure of this but I wondered. It seemed impossible anyone, thirty Crows or no, could gain that valley against Many Kills and his Fox Soldiers. But I'd seen the impossible done too many times by pitifully outnumbered bands of Confederates.

I would not yield to Yellow Bird's suggestion we travel to the lodges, pick up Crazy Horse's reinforcements, and move in on Slatemeyer in force. I said I would head on, my only thought being to find and kill Slatemeyer before he could approach Star. He being four days ahead of us, the thought he might by lucky chance run into Star's group coming out made me nearly crazy.

When I announced my intention upon reaching the point where the trail forked, the south branch following the Cheyenne to the lodges, the north skirting the Black Hills, not a brave moved.

"We follow you," scowled Yellow Bird, speaking for them all. "The white man may be yours, but the Mouse is ours."

The Indian military organization is peculiar. Nominally I was their leader. Actually I had no authority at all. This is true of their own war campaigns, the mightiest chief having no power to order the least warrior. If a man wanted to quit and go home, he quit and went. If he wished to ride away from the marching force on a little private buffalo hunt, away he went. If it suited his ego to sneak off ahead of the main body to strike the enemy a lone blow, off he sneaked and struck it. This hard-headed independence, after whiskey and the disappearance of the buffalo, was the third of the great weaknesses which made the Indians' conquest by the Army a matter of ten short years rather than the long fifty it should have taken. In no other society, pagan or polished, has the individual known the utter degree of personal freedom enjoyed by the plains Indian.

His democracy was impossibly pure, but it was beautiful.

Where they cannot be pushed, however, the Indians may be freely led. By cajolery and flattery I induced Yellow Bird to take the men and go. The ten of us could do nothing anyway if Slatemeyer had not gotten to Star, I told him, while if he had, a lone warrior could put a rifle bullet through Slatemeyer's brain as easily as could ten. "And," I wanted to know, fixing the lot of them with a hard stare, "who among you can put a bullet through a head better than Cetan Mani?"

That was the kind of straight talk they cottoned to. Among their number were several whose lodges were still mourning the loss of some relation in the first wagon-train fight or my subsequent capture at Lodge Trail Ridge.

After securing my promise that no matter what, not a fuzz-hair of the Mouse's scalp would be harmed, Yellow Bird quickly announced, "We go," as firmly convinced now I was right as he'd been positive I was wrong.

And off they went, whooping and ki-yi-ing their ponies up the Cheyenne. They had a forced twenty-four-hour run ahead of them. Then another twenty-four back. I could expect Crazy Horse and plenty of warriors along about sunset two days hence. And I had a hard twelve-hour ride to Star's valley facing me.

Chewing the last of the pemmican, I pointed the bone-weary Hussein for the Black Hills, giving him his head. Neither of us had rested for ninety hours, I having had no sleep for sixty, he no food for forty-eight. Stumbling continually, the ugly brown gelding ploughed unsteadily through the night.

As the moon rose the air turned off warm, a balmy wind blowing east from the Black Hills. In no other place can the weather be as crazy as in the Dakotas. Now, apparently, we were to get one of those weird warm spells which occur in late winter. I could literally hear the snow thawing. Soon Hussein was clay-slushed to his stifles, the going becoming more treacherous with each moment of the booming thaw. It was a time for careful work by man and mount and my eyes would not stay open. I rubbed spit in them, then tobacco, finally salt from my buckskin salt-pouch. They burned, weeping and searing with pain—but they closed.

The last I remember was putting Hussein down a steep

claybank into a small tributary of the Cheyenne, already swollen from its customary trickle to a forty-foot river. I recall the current hitting us broadside like a great smacking-wet sledge, and Hussein, all eleven hundred pounds of him, going hock over forelock, carrying me under with him.

The foul yellow water was paralyzingly cold, filled with plunging, swirling debris of every variety. Great blocks and chunks of honey-combed, rotten thaw-ice churned and crashed in a constant crush of roaring noise.

The shock brought me to the surface, wild-eyed and fighting.

Hussein was gone from under me and my eyes, blinded by mud and sand, could see nothing. I remember striking out blindly, swimming by instinct downstream, hoping, I suppose, to hit a sandbar or wedged log to get me out of the convulsive cascade. Before a dozen strokes my vision cleared to show an enormous jag of rotten ice booming down on me from upstream. I dove to escape it, recalling only a bright flash of light which seemed to originate inside my skull and to light up, for one glorious second, the whole broken river bottom.

Then there was blackness and a long quiet.

Chapter 15

I AWOKE to a late afternoon sun. It was warm where I was and very peaceful. Somewhere below I could hear the rushing of swift water. Song-bird calls, the saucy whistling of a marmot, a beaver gnawing placidly, the sleepy "pee-weet" of the prairie plover, the rusty cry of a blue heron, the bickering of a crow; these sounds with a myriad others of the lazy trivia of a late Dakota day, filtered restfully through the film of my half awakeness.

I gazed speculatively up into the darkening blue above. The feeling of well-being with which I had awakened began to settle upon me more deeply. My eyes closed, my body, stretching itself reflexively, sought a yet more comfortable pose for the return of blessed slumber.

Suddenly I was wide, staring-eyed awake.

My limbs, seeking to move, had remained motionless. I tried to sit up, found I couldn't. I was wedged in a tight mass of flood-drift, ten feet above the receding stage of the water pouring by beneath me.

The process of extricating myself brought me up to date. I was unharmed. Also unarmed. The latter perhaps not literally but practically. The rifle Crazy Horse had insisted I take from him in place of mine was gone. My Colts, soaked and full of sand, were still in place, thanks to my cavalry habit of strapping them down when traveling. But my ammunition had been thoroughly soaked, rendering it worse than useless. For while some of the shells were undoubtedly good, the question of which these were was not precisely the query for which one would care to seek the answer while triggering against a man like Slatemeyer. Playing the game to his rules there would be just one shot to a customer. It had best not be a wet one.

I wondered briefly if I might have lain for two suns around but a hasty check of my "Confederate calendar," * convinced me I had not. But I was afoot and one precious day lost.

Night came on abruptly as I set out for the still distant Black Hills. Twenty-four hours later, at nightfall, I arrived under the brooding hulk of the Gate of the Buffalo.

I was in a real tight. Somewhere in the blackness around me, by supposition at least, lay Slatemeyer and his thirty Crow warriors—if they had not already made their ambush and escaped.

Under no circumstance would they make a fire. If they were here they were just here, lying possibly within yards or feet of me, possibly a mile away. Adding to my joys a freak storm, building through the late daylight hours of my journey, now began furnishing fitful lightning flashes to make the situation even worse.

I hesitated, knowing my next step might land squarely in the squirming belly of a sleeping Crow, and bring a lance or knife blade into my vitals before I could so much as murmur an apology. Nevertheless my training had not been in a "wait and see" school. I headed straight into the yawning maw ahead of me, naked knife in hand, nerves drawn tight.

Twenty feet inside the entrance my moccasined foot

---

*Back in the war when some particularly hot, prolonged action made a meaningless jumble of days and nights, my men used to swear they could keep track of the time by the growth of my whiskers, the accepted rate being an inch a day. An exaggeration not without basis.

touched human flesh. I went up in the air like a cat, came down soundlessly, right side up. Apparently my man slumbered on. Two thoughts took the hurdle of my mind simultaneously. Was I in the middle of their camp? Or was this a solitary sentinel?

Due to the position well within the canyon opening, I judged the latter to be the case.

Figuring the angle and distance of my leap away from him I could theoretically place him in the blackness. I was satisfied he had not moved since I touched him. My body shot forward knife-arm driving downward through the dark. There was the sudden plunge of steel into flesh—any combat soldier knows the feel and sound of it. My foe didn't even convulse. It was as though he had been dead before I struck him.

He had.

I bent my knife hand to remove the blade. The butt of the turning hand touched naked flesh. It was fish-belly cold. My touch running over his body told me he lay stripped of clothing. Searching for his head, hoping to know by the hair-fashioning whether I had Sioux or Crow beneath me, my hand came away thickly wet. He had been scalped.

Before I could begin to figure my next play a looping chain of lightning limned every inch of the canyon sharply for five seconds.

Scattered within eight feet of me were the bodies of several Indians, all stripped and scalped. The body at my feet had run a bull elk with me the month previous. It had had a name then; Heyoka, The Clown. These were Sioux.

Nor was that all. Heyoka had been a Fox Lodge brave, one of the police detail for Mesa Valley.

So Slatemeyer had Star. I knew this as surely as I breathed. It was impossible at the time to imagine how he had made the capture. Later, when I knew, it appeared entirely simple. Yet pure simplicity is frequently the hallmark of genius and in his violent way Slatemeyer was undoubtedly a genius.

Arriving three days ahead of me he had placed his Crow in ambush, sent Mouse into the valley with a message. As a Fox Lodge member the entrance and authority of the Sans Arc chief went unchallenged. The message he bore was clear. . . .

A mighty chief lay very ill, almost within the portals of Wanagi Yata, the Gathering Place of the Souls . . . Would the Wiyan Wakan come at once? . . . Ay-ee, the Wiyan would know the name of the chief? May Wakan Tanka forgive her the hesitation. . . . It was the great Crazy Horse himself!

Of course North Star would come. There need be only an hour's delay while the guard party was organized, a number of them being absent at the moment hunting the upper valley.

No need of that. At the mouth of the canyon waited thirty of the finest warriors to escort the Wiyan.

Star had gone then, taking with her only such braves as were present. The ambush and massacre within the canyon mouth had followed. As simple as that. The whole thing took scarcely a day's time.

Slatemeyer had thus been gone at least a full day when I arrived. At the time, knowing only what I could see, ten dead Sioux, I was forced to await daylight where I was.

If Star's guard had repulsed the attack and withdrawn to the valley, which was not impossible, she was of course safe. If Slatemeyer had her I must find the trail. That took light.

I crouched there among the dead, miserable with cold and hunger, keyed up to the point of craziness by the forced wait. Then, an hour before dawn, it rained as though heaven's belly had been knifed from breech-clout to breastbone. When daylight came sick and pale through greasy gray clouds, a Pawnee couldn't have trailed a picketed pony ten feet.

For the first few minutes I ran around the throat of the canyon whimpering like some fool hound which has lost his line on the fox and thinks to find it by sheer obstinacy. Then I began to think.

Slatemeyer's course was not hopelessly unpredictable. To his north lay the yawning canyons and impassable crevasses of the Black Hills. To his west the land of the Oglala and the lodges of Crazy Horse. He could go either south or east with his prize—if indeed he had it. Perforce, I had to assume he did.

I had just come over the most logical route east, having seen no fires or camp-sign, no pony dust. It was possible I had missed him, also that he had skirted the hills, turning north. But the best bet was he had gone due south to strike the headwaters of the White, this stream running east to empty into the Missouri at Fort Kiowa only ten miles above his camp. In reducing his course to this choice, I took into consideration his precious whiskey. Slatemeyer wouldn't want to be absent from his stock-in-trade any longer than necessary.

As I started south across the prairie grasslands sloping down and away from the Black Hills, I wondered at the delay of Crazy Horse. By schedule he should have been at the valley last night.

Perhaps he had. That idea was yet another angle. He could have come in daylight, read the gruesome sign, taken off on Slatemeyer's trail. There was no way for sure of knowing, except for one thing which argued against the possibility: an Indian will bear his dead away in all but the most extreme cases. Whether Crazy Horse would estimate the abduction of Star to be such a case was pure hazard. But if he had, it meant Slatemeyer had only a twelve hour start on tired ponies. It meant this same day might bring the Sioux up with him. My hopes began shooting skyward like Wanbli, the eagle, riding an air current up out of a dark canyon into sunlight.

About noon I reached the Cheyenne. The weather holding warm, and with fatigue and hunger riding me double, I decided to shed my clothes and plunge into the turbid stream. Refreshed, I emerged to hear a moving noise in the poplar scrub to my right. Flattening, I waited.

Presently more noise and movement. Then the sight of a rusty brown rump through a hole in the foliage. Moose! Possibly elk. And I starved!

Emptying my cartridge belt I selected the twelve least-mildewed-looking shells, reloaded the Colts, bellied forward. The big brown body moved again and I could hear the sounds of the heavy ruminant grazing. Waiting for one more movement I triggered the right-hand Colt into what I could see of the beast.

Results: four straight misfires which so unnerved me the fifth shot which was good as gold went banging wildly away over the poplar-tops and a fizzling blopper of a sixth shell exploded with just enough interest to shove its lead out of the barrel. It wouldn't have penetrated the skin of a baby's butt at diaper distance.

Naturally this comic opera cannonading brought my quarry out in the open. Poking through the scrub eyeing me with patent disgust hung the only head in the world uglier than a moose's. Flicking his good ear, flopping his bad one, Hussein ambled out of his cover.

Any horseman—cowboy, buffalo hunter or scout—will appreciate my delight, especially since my mount was in good condition. I climbed aboard and we made tracks away from there. After clicking around to a good shell while holding on a running antelope, I felt my own spirits begin to lift. I made a mounted scoop-up of the little animal, threw it across Hussein's withers and, slicing out the heart and tenderloin, butchered and ate as I rode.

An hour's journey brought us to the end of the territory pelted by last night's storm. On a hunch I ran out a quartering movement, striking a broad trail within fifteen minutes. I counted no more than twenty-five ponies and knew I had Slatemeyer in front of me.

Another fifteen minutes and a still broader trail of at least fifty ponies struck in from the west. Crazy Horse, too, was ahead of me.

A new thought arose to frost the warmth of this discovery. Trusting the generalship of the great Oglala I could not help but remember he had the sanguine Yellow Bird along, together with fifty other Fox Lodgers, all doubtless loyal to Star but possibly even more intrigued with the prospect of arranging for brother lodge member, Mouse, to lose his dues-paying status instanter.

I could guess the temper of the trailing Sioux, imagine quite easily the mad spate of *"Hookaheys!"* which would announce their sighting of Slatemeyer's band—and the ensuing rush which would just as surely mean death for Star as for the whiskey runner and his crew.

The first thing an Indian will do when hard pushed is abandon all equipment save horse and gun. The second, kill any captives he has along. Even if Slatemeyer willed otherwise, the first cornering of his crew by Crazy Horse would wing a Crow lance into the body of the Indian girl.

I put Hussein's heart and lungs once more on the auction block of necessity. Had my own life been at stake I might have held some reserve in him. As it was I drove him to the limit, rating him slow all the same. According to my figures, if we were to beat the Sioux to the death, Hussein had to last through the night without more than blowing rests. I meant to see that he did, getting me to Star before he dropped dead, if I had to hand-carry him the last mile.

As the cast-iron gelding drummed steadily down the broad valley, I made my plan.

Slatemeyer, having no reason to expect such immediate pursuit as was already upon him, would travel at an accented trail-gait, only a moderate speed-up of the ground-covering, shuffle-trot of the Indian pony.

Crazy Horse would travel faster, probably at a canter, but knowing his prey was within reach would rate his pace to overtake Slatemeyer at dawn, always the Indians' favored attack hour.

I, holding a rolling gallop through the night, would outdistance the Sioux, coming up to Slatemeyer an hour ahead of both dawn and the Oglala.

These were assumptions, the kind any fighting man makes daily. If he's right, he wins. If he's wrong, he doesn't care. The dead never do. What I meant to do when I came up with my enemy I didn't know. The hour itself would have to decide that.

I tightened my grip on the braided leathers of Hussein's hackamore, slacking his gait. Under my clamping thighs the flow and rhythm of his gallop felt perfect in reach and timing. Not tiring yet. The miles rolled endlessly back into the night.

Slatemeyer's way led down a long shallow valley, a well-traveled Indian track familiar to me, reaching from the Cheyenne to the White River. When I had gone as far down this as I felt I could without running over Crazy Horse's camp in the dark, I slowed Hussein, swinging him wide of the valley trail, heading for the foothills to the left. He was trembling under me, very tired now.

I hoped he would get a fair blow while we walked our way around where I supposed the Sioux camp to be, this respite being out of no consideration for him but due to my respect of the fact an Indian can ground-hear a running horse for a good two miles.

As we padded through the thick dust of the hillsides I got the first satisfaction in days. Off to my right and directly below us the querulous whickering of ponies carried up on the night air. My in-the-dark computations hadn't missed by four hundred yards.

Once around the Sioux camp I put Hussein back on his gait. He was running unevenly with probably not more than an hour's effort left in him. His breath came scraping into his lungs metallically. Under my knees the exhausted hammering of his heart was ragged and heavy.

Pity came thick in my throat. I loved this vicious horse not knowing, until this night, how well. But now as he ran dying under me, his whole body faltering with every stride, I knew. Leaning far over his outstretched neck I buried my head in the ragged backstream of his forelock. My mouth close to his flop-ear I spoke to him, my words as soft as a mother's whisper.

"*Hopo. Hookahey*, Hussein."

His evil eye rolled back at me, his good ear flattening to catch my voice. I felt him steady up under me.

"*Hopo, hopo,* you ugly ass-eared crowbait. Do you know I love you? Do you know I am killing you? Hi-yee. Easy. Easy."

Staggering brokenly, then finding his stride, he managed a racking whicker. His neck then, at the spot my face lay against it, was wet not from lather alone.

Three miles more and I eased him down and left him. He stood spraddle-legged, head to the ground, gaunt flanks whipping in behind slatted ribs with every gulping breath. His eyes protruded fixed and glazed, his tongue hung swollen and lifeless between the long yellow teeth. Thin blood ran in twin streams from the bell-flare of his nostrils. As I turned to leave him he raised his head, looking for me, then staggered a step or two as though to follow. He moved directly away from me. He was stone-blind. . . .

Chapter 16

FINDING thirty Crow Indians and a renegade white gunman in three miles of pitch-black prairie was no easy chore but I did what I could. I began quartering the wind from a spot I considered to be well to the nearside of their camp. Luck was with me, the fresh morning air shortly bringing what I sought—the high clean pungency of their pony herd.

I worked upwind to a point I thought would be about a hundred yards from the horses. Here I holed up, for an Indian will always sleep between his horses and his enemies and I had no irresistible desire to find myself wading knee-deep in Crows with nothing to paddle my way out with but an eight-inch knife.

In an hour a ghost-glow of light appeared. Fifteen minutes more and the true dawn would start fading the night. In twenty the camp would come alive.

In the uncertain gloom, not two shades off real darkness, I could make out the black lumps of sleeping men all about me. These lay singly, Indian fashion, with the humping shadows of the pony herd just beyond them.

The wind and the luck held in my direction. Not ten paces

away, sheltered from the main group by a low clump of
elder bush, lay a double shadow. Star and Slatemeyer! From
the larger shadow came the stertorous breathing of a fatigued
man in deep sleep, from the other no sound at all. The smaller shadow, then, was awake.

It seems unreal to me now as it did then. I went over that
intervening ten yards as noiselessly as a hawk's shade over
hard rock. The whites of Star's eyes rolled up at my looming figure. She had no way of knowing who or what this was
crawling in at her out of the black prairie, but Indian-wise
made no outcry or motion. She was between Slatemeyer
and me, leaving no way to get at him save over her. The
heavy figure by her side stirred uneasily, grunted sleepily.

The next instant my knife was buried hilt-deep, this time
in living flesh. I struck once only, for I felt the powerful
body stiffen and convulse with that all-over contracting spasm
peculiar to the paralyzing shock of a lethal heart wound.

I cut Star free of her bonds and we fled. It was still dark as
we stole away but morning was bare minutes behind us. Out
of earshot of the camp we began to run for the hills, and as
we ran I panted out hoarsely, "You are all right, Star?
Not injured?"

"Not with wounds, Cetan." The sound of her low voice
thrilled me but her words struck my heart.

"He harmed you then? Oh, my God!"

She didn't answer but the glance with which I accompanied
my agonized query showed me great hot tears coursing down
her cheeks as she ran.

"Thank God I killed him. Oh, thank God!"

"What did you say, Cetan?" In my passion I had cried
out in English. I repeated in her own tongue.

Her next words belted me behind the knees like a giant-
swung wagon tongue.

"The one you slew was Fox Runner, the Crow chief. The
white *sunke manitu* left camp an hour before you came. He
went scouting the back-trail, on foot."

Would I never learn to respect this man? Could I still be
stupid enough to think to catch him sleeping like a log with
a captive Sioux medicine woman in the heart of Oglala country? How love and anger can blind a good soldier! If I
didn't smarten up fast there was apt to be mourning in my
lodge, not Slatemeyer's.

To Star I snarled out between gulps for breath, "You have
said I shall bring you the heart of a great enemy."

No answer save a silent upturn of tear-stained face.

"Will you say this enemy is great enough?"

Still no word, this time not even a glance. But I felt the tear as it splashed hot on my naked arm.

"His heart is yours. I shall bring it to you when I bring my own."

We reached the shelter of the hillside rocks in safety, the last few hundred yards being made in full daylight. There we lay quietly for several seconds, Star, tight-held in my arms, not moving nor speaking, our hearts pounding in rapid unison. After an ageless minute thus, my face buried in the dark masses of her hair, her cheek pressing fiercely into the bare hollow of my neck, we drew apart for our first real look at one another.

I can imagine what my face looked like with its week-old accumulation of beard, mud-cake and multiple abrasions. Star's was in little better repair, dirt- and tear-streaked, gray-drawn, hollow-eyed. Still all the wild passion and beauty of her smoldered in the green eyes, lingered on the irresistible slight petulance of the full lower lip.

"Star, Star—" I murmured, my voice breaking.

She came into my arms. It was a long kiss and our breaths came hot and hard with it.

But her next words, when her mouth at last parted clingingly from mine, were those of an Indian. "Is there any pursuit, Cetan?"

My mind and body came back to the present. Rolling over, I peered between the rocks. Far below and cross-valley there was consternation in the Crow camp. As was only natural, conditions down there being what they were.

"None!" I answered, jubilantly. "Nor shall there be. Come and see for yourself."

She joined me at the rock, her eyes widening at the sight below. And I should say, speaking cautiously, that as sights go it was an eye-widener.

In a huddled knot the Crow horsemen milled their ponies over the ground of their last night's camp. They seemed confused, starting now one way, now another, then halting and going neither, as though with all this prairie to ride in they didn't quite know in which direction to go.

At first glance I was as muddled as they, but Star's slim arm pointing northward gave me the first clue. Following the direction of her gesture, I saw thirty horses, standing in a wide-spread line atop a small rise four hundred yards upvalley of the Crows.

Ordinarily thirty horses wouldn't cause an Indian maiden's

eyes to burn with the fire now glowing in Star's. But these were special horses. Atop each one sat an impassive, war-feathered Oglala Sioux.

Star's slender arm was now pointing southward.

Fifty more horses were strung out across the south flank of the Crow camp. Here again no sound or movement came from the waiting Sioux. No wonder the Crows were showing a bit of indecision.

"Where did they all come from?" I wondered aloud, thinking of the fifty-odd Sioux I had counted in the track of Crazy Horse's band.

"Many Kills," she answered, indicating the south line of Sioux.

Peering intently I made out a lone horseman sitting slightly in advance of his fellows. It was the old chief from the valley. Apparently his forces had joined those of Crazy Horse sometime during the night. Here was another example of the marvelous Indian system of communication.*

Scanning the battle lines again I thought I made out Yellow Bird commanding the north group but peer as I might I could not see Crazy Horse in either band. There was no time to wonder at this. Below us the Crows had made their decision. I watched, fascinated, for the plains Indian is the world's finest natural cavalryman and I, something of an expert in that line, was professionally intrigued by their tactical position. I had been in equally tight spots and gotten out. It interested me to observe how closely the methods of wild experience might follow those of the written textbook.

I believe the Crow indecision resulted from the finding of their chief, Fox Runner, dead. For when they did move there was no hint of confusion. Their maneuver was a classic of its kind. They began by forming a closed phalanx of three columns of ten, riding slowly down upon the southern Sioux, the three-width presented forward. Behind them the northern Sioux closed in at a following pace, keeping their spread line. Here was none of the whooping and yelling popularly associated with Indian battles. Here were thirty men trying to outsmart eighty and not aiming to bring it off by out-whooping them.

The whole myth of the Indians' "blood-curdling" vocal ef-

---

*A system which even after ten years among them I was not able to understand completely. Smoke, drum, mirror, and ground-vibration signals were in common use with them but at other times they were able to convey messages where the use of these methods was definitely ruled out. I was never able to identify this "fifth sense signal," and in the end was left to conclude it was just that—a mental telegraph of some sort.

forts in attack comes from his use of this psychological weapon upon the whites. Here it works. But where a high-screaming war whoop may serve to unnerve a white settler, a Crow knows a Sioux and a Sioux knows a Crow, and both know nobody ever got killed by a war whoop.

Below, old Many Kills showed hesitation, then shouted for his line to pull in and bunch to receive the Crow assault. Exactly, I imagined from my field-view, what the Crow leader wanted. For the minute the Sioux bunched, the Crow horsemen split, and not in two or three sections but in thirty. Every man for himself. The old-scatter-and-ride-through which until that moment I had believed we Confederates practised better than any cavalry. But the way the Crows pulled it off put us to shame. They bombarded out of that tight phalanx like quail from a stepped-on berry bush.

It worked, too. The following Sioux broke out their best yells and charged wholesale. The fronting Sioux tried to scatter to contain the Crow maneuver. But too late. In seconds the whole well-ordered trap became a military mess. Arrows, lances and war axes hissed, stabbed and swung. In twenty seconds fifteen or twenty of the Crow had broken free, regrouped, and headed south for freedom, the shadows of their flying ponies skimming the short prairie grass like swallows. The other ten or fifteen of their number were already riding far out ahead of them. But these were casting no shadows. The dead seldom do.

In the rear of the fleeing Crows went the howling Sioux, the whole pack of them being lost in a down-valley dust-cloud in less than two minutes. Turning to Star I laughed aloud, the first genuine release from tension in days.

"Our troubles are over. We're in the clear."

"Everything is good for the eye!" she cried delightedly.

And surely it was. Star was alive. The night was gone. The sun climbing. The world, at least from the Platte to the Powder and the Missouri to the Musselshell, was ours.

"In all the world," I announced joyously, seizing her out-stretched hands, feeling now the full post-danger letdown, "we haven't a thing to worry about but Slatemeyer!"

"Isn't that enough?" The question fell with singular flatness in the morning stillness of the hillside.

The words weren't loud. They weren't triumphant. But they came in that purring monotone which once heard was never forgotten.

Beside me I felt, rather than heard, Star's stiffening gasp. Slatemeyer stood on the hillside behind us, his back to the morning sun, as quietly at ease as though in Market Square at Kansas City.

It was my first real look at the man and, as I took it, all the old fear of him came over me.

Standing there black against the sun he looked enormous. In the card game at Kansas City I had been able to study him only as he squatted on his haunches. I had been impressed then, but not as I was now.

His hair had grown long, its ashen mane falling nearly to his shoulders. His mustache was still close-cropped and he was cleanshaven. His dark face and pale eyes were as I remembered them. His dress was a black leather shirt, buckskin trousers and moccasins, all in the heavily fringed, simply beadworked Arapahoe design.

Two silver-mounted Colts hung low and forward on his thighs, the holsters and crossed cartridge belts in black leather and silver. In the cradle of his right arm rested a new Winchester. A flat-crowned black stetson and black neckcloth with heavy silver slip ring completed his outfit.

"Turn around slowly and drop your holsters."

I looked at him, hesitating.

"And the knife," he added, his throaty tones level.

My guns were useless anyway, but a knife is a knife and man's best friend when in doubt or the dark. I had no intention of parting with mine.

Turning slowly, I unbuckled the Colts, letting them slide to the ground. Reaching inside my shirt for the knife thong I tensed my body for what would likely to be my last lunge. If I could strike fast enough to get the blade into him before the lead that would be in me weighted me down, Star might—

"If that knife touches your hand the squaw gets gut-shot." Behind me the dry click of a cocking rifle put the period on his warning. "Pull the thong over your head. Let the knife dangle where I can see it all the time. Then drop it."

I must have hesitated even then for he added, spacing his words deliberately like a man to whom talk is distasteful, "I don't want to fire a shot. Indians get curious about shots. Drop the knife."

The threat was no less effective for its being implied. If I didn't drop the knife he would lever that Winchester into Star's belly if it brought the whole Bad Face band down on him. Thank God I knew him by this time. He was literal. What he said you'd better believe. He meant his words to the letter. I dropped the knife.

"Now turn back around."

I obeyed.

"Pick that stuff up, girl."

Star glanced at the guns and knife disdainfully, making no move. He stepped in close to her, repeating, "Pick it up."

She spat in his face. He stood expressionless, letting the spittle course his cheek untouched.

"Pick it up, Star." This, tersely, from me. "Pick it up or we're both dead."

"I would rather be," she snarled, her lips drawn back savagely over the white teeth.

"One—" said Slatemeyer.

"Two—"

"Star. Pick it up. I order you to do it." I used the Sioux phrase with which the brave terminates all tipi arguments when he has heard enough. She looked at me, surprised, hesitated, smiled quizzically and dropped to one knee, picking up the knife and guns.

"Yes?" she queried, turning obediently to me.

"Do as he tells you."

"Throw them over the rocks behind you—down the hill," Slatemeyer ordered.

As she turned to do so he stepped quickly in behind her. When she threw the weapons he struck her across the head with the barrel of the Winchester. She dropped soundlessly. "She'll keep," he said, not even glancing down to see if she would or not.

Facing me, he added, "Back up, in between those rocks. Those two high ones that wedge together."

I stepped back until my shoulders touched the boulders. They were twelve feet high with smooth vertical sides. A puma couldn't have gotten out of that spot. The only way was *through* the figure fronting the opening.

Unbuckling his own Colts, Slatemeyer threw them contemptuously up onto the hillside behind him, following suit with his Winchester.

"They're yours," he grunted. "All you have to do is go get them." As he spoke he drew his knife, starting in toward me. "No noise," he explained, tonelessly, making a slight twisting gesture with the blade.

I suppose no man is totally without some shred of the actor in him, some raveling of humor in the cloth of his makeup. Deep inside Slatemeyer lurked a maverick strain of mirth. His weakening to it in this moment was one of those weird split-hair things; the sort of featherweight foolishness that has cost many a man many a battle. Pausing five feet from me, his eyes never leaving mine, he made his memorable sally into sarcasm.

Between the pause and the speech I gathered myself to counter his attack.

"In all the world," he began, his mimicry of my stupid announcement to Star being painfully good, "I have nothing to worry about but Slatemeyer—"

"—and Crazy Horse." The deep Sioux guttural dropping onto the end of Slatemeyer's sentence left no room for argument.

The whiskey runner froze and I swept my gaze upward past him. Fifteen yards up the hill stood the war chief and ten Oglala braves.

"Hohahe. Welcome to my tipi," I called to him weakly.

"I can believe you mean it," he answered, flashing the rare Sioux smile. "What do you want done with this sunke?" he asked, referring to Slatemeyer as a "dog."

"I want him taken alive."

As he heard me speak, the whiskey runner pivoted slowly on his heel until he faced the Indians. I watched the muscles of his back and knife-arm, seeing them tense. Being a white man I could read that sign where the Sioux might not. If they saw it at all they would see it wrong; figuring he meant to make a fight.

"A-ah!" I called the Oglala warning word to Crazy Horse as I launched myself at Slatemeyer's back.

I caught his arm in the downstroke deflecting it so that the knife ripped harmlessly through his leather shirt instead of into the lower gut where he had aimed it.

In a second the braves swarmed over us.

But the giant white man reared up like a cornered grizzly, throwing warriors off like a huge dog shaking himself free of water. Crazy Horse stepped in close, faster than I have seen any man move, and brought the haft of his war ax ringing across Slatemeyer's skull.

I stood up facing the Oglala chief across the body of the whiskey runner. "Two times now you have saved my life," I acknowledged gratefully, extending my hand.

He took it in both his but looked past me out over the valley as he answered, somberly, "It is nothing. In the end you will save my life. Then there will be another battle and you will lose your own. I am seeing this now. This is a great battle. A great victory for the Sioux. But you are lying among the enemy dead. A chief dressed in black riding a black horse is bearing you away. It is I. It is Tashunka Witko. I am alive. I am carrying you away. You are dead." No one spoke then, the Indians stirring uneasily in the silence following Crazy Horse's vision. . . .

Neither Star nor Slatemeyer were any the worse for their "walks in the evening," Star recovering as we lashed the still unconscious form of her abductor to a pack pony.

On the journey back to the lodges she told me of her experience with the whiskey runner. She spoke in short, hard sentences, sparing no detail, embellishing none, finishing with a plain statement which summed up the sordid adventure from her viewpoint.

"As you see me now," she said, her voice low, head bowed, "I am no longer holy."

I could not tell whether her words carried relief or remorse but as our eyes met I felt the sudden pressure of her hand in mine and my heart leaped uncertainly.

So we rode the home trail, silent in thought.

Ahead of us lay we knew not what, behind us our captive enemy and ninety Sioux warriors. Not exactly ninety, either. In the rear of the savage caravan, the ninety-first Sioux bumped and jolted along enjoying the double comforts of rawhide lashings and the bony back of a baggage pony. Tonkalla, the Mouse, was headed for his last lodge meeting.

I knew our arrival at the lodges would be celebrated with a victory dance. Thirteen Crow scalps, a traitor and a big white enemy captured, Star of the North rescued; these were feats demanding commemoration.

Riding back to Crazy Horse I told him of my plans for a part in the ceremony. He listened seriously, calling up Yellow Bird and Many Kills that they might hear also.

"Cetan Mani will honor the victory dance," he told them. "He has requested a trial-by-knife for the white *sunke*."

Many Kills nodded vigorously. "Good, good."

Yellow Bird, that unreconstructible blood-lover, burst forth enthusiastically, "By Pte's beard! This should be a fight to paint on a shield. Now, Cetan, let me tell you. I have a knife given me by Black Moccasin, the Cheyenne, he in turn receiving it of a Comanche who took it home in his ribs from an Apache raid. It is said the blade was once owned by Mangus Colorado, old Red Sleeves himself. This is a rare knife. No Indian knife. And it carries great *hmunha*. Now with this knife a man . . ."

113

WE CAME into the lodges late in the afternoon of the second day. Our reception was an epic of its kind.

The Indian appetite for celebration, ceremony, and conflict is endless. Hence when the word bombarded around camp that tonight's affair was to start with a Scalp Dance, intermission with a Fox Lodge Traitor Trial, and terminate in a knife fight between Cetan Mani and the big white man, the pandemonium of preparation became deafening.

Out came every cooking pot in the village and into each went the presently handiest ingredient of the Indian larder. Since the spring buffalo hadn't drifted north yet, this meant a heavy drain on the current canine crop. The early night echoed with the anticipatory scramblings and yelps of the poor animals scurrying desperately away from the swinging club of one squaw only to skid around a tipi corner into the brain-crunching ax of another.

I never got use to what followed and the sight tilted my white belly as always.

A squaw would whistle up a fat young dog, grab the bewildered beast by a hind leg, swing it free of the ground, knock-in its skull with a club, drop the animal whole, hair and all, usually still kicking, into the nearest boiling pot.

Other preparations went forward. Blazing dance fires were set and the scalplock pole was reared in place and festooned with its clotted trophies. The Fox Lodge was closed while the medicine man went within and purified it for the coming trial of the Mouse.

Throughout the village streets ran the News Walkers, shouting out the story of our journey, its untold dangers, its vast triumphs. Each one in his own tipi, the warriors dressed and painted themselves for the ceremony. Children scurried like rabbits everywhere, their black eyes shining with excitement.

I sat alone watching all this activity of which I was to be the main feature. The giddy hours of dancing and feasting sped by, and my guts began to draw within me as though they had been salted and dried. I could neither eat nor rest but only sit and think of Slatemeyer and the knives.

The Sioux trial-by-knife is a legal simplicity. When two litigants have reached the impasse where one or both of them is unwilling to settle for less than the life of the other, they are stripped naked, handed knives and told to fight as loud as they have talked.

Knife duels were by no means uncommon to the frontier, the white traders, trappers, and rivermen using them just as freely as the Indians in settlement of impacted personal opinions or desires. But the Bad Face Band of Oglala had certain refinements of the contest. For purposes of better and more dramatic entertainment of the spectators, always a prime consideration with Indians, the duel was held at night.

A circle of fifteen long paces' diameter was drawn on bare ground. Around this, boundary fires were built, these providing light for audience and principals alike. Between the boundary fires and around the perimeter of the circle squatted the more efficient of the tribes' lancemen, each armed with a short, razor-headed buffalo javelin. If either fighter got beyond the circle for any reason, tricked, forced or frightened there, the nearest Indian was delighted to lance him back into the contest.

There are just two ways these duels can end. First: one of the fighters kills the other. Second: by virtue of mutual conviction that both have had enough, neither fighter will kill the other. In this case the waiting lancers happily move in and satisfy them both.

The Sioux have no word for "tie" or "draw."

As to the survivor, no matter what his status prior to the contest, he is entitled to the full rights of the tribe. In Slatemeyer's case this meant one thing: if he killed me he went free. And he would go with honor, riding my best horse, wearing my weapons, being escorted in full honor to the boundaries of the tribal lands.

So much for the legal aspects of the trial-by-knife. Both contestants knew the rules, the forfeits, the prizes.

About midnight Yellow Bird came to me and said, "It is time. I am to be *kola* (friend or second) for you. Crazy Horse will announce the rules."

"What has happened to the Mouse?" I asked, not wanting to appear concerned about my own case.

"He is with his ancestors."

"Did he die like a man?"

The tall Sioux spat viciously as though to rid his mouth of a bite of rotten meat. "He died like a mouse," he said.

Together we strode toward the distant clamor by the fires. Still trying to fit the pose of the calm and collected, I questioned, "And Star? Where is she?"

"You will see her."

He would not talk further and then as we reached the dark outskirts of the crowd, stopped short. "Here," he announced stiffly. "Here is the knife of Mangus Colorado. Wear it."

I took the long thin blade, feeling its beautiful heft and balance at once. I had never felt such a knife. It seemed alive in the hand. *"Ha-a-u,"* I said. "I take it."

"I give it. It is yours." Turning, he was gone in the dark.

Alone I went forward, the cold rising from the ground, creeping through my legs, settling in my belly.

A deep *"Hun-hun-he!"* ran around the packed circle of savages. Every eye swung in my direction as those nearest me parted to let me through. I walked looking neither right nor left, head high, warrior fashion; or as nearly as I could simulate warrior fashion, feeling the crawling fear I did.

Then that eerie heavy silence which infests Indian crowds descended.

I could hear my own halting moccasin-falls in the powdery dust of the dance-ground. Before me the ring loomed and I entered it, standing irresolute for several seconds, my eyes temporarily blinded by the leaping flares of the boundary fires.

Slatemeyer wasn't in the ring yet. I took the moment to examine the knife Yellow Bird had given me. It was a Spanish blade of the rarest Toledo, its mirror surfaces as polished and gleaming as four centuries of bathing in soft flesh and warm blood could keep them. The haft was of leather rings pounded close down over the tang, Apache fashion, and I assumed it had been re-hafted several times in its long life. The blade itself was just over an inch in width, about eight in length, very thin and straight after the way of Iberian blades, with a shallow drain-channel grooved in either side from guard to point.

Peering closely at the shoulder of the blade I made out the flowing Spanish inscription, *M. Villalobos, Toledo, MCDLIV.* Mangus Colorado indeed! Cortes himself may have sheathed this slender cuchillo.

My fingers tightened on the aged haft. A strong warmth flooded up my knife-arm, seeming to come in pulsing waves from the strange foreign blade lying so lightly in my right hand.

"Cetan Mani!"

Hearing my name called, I glanced up. Star was seated upon a raised dais across the ring, behind the row of lancers. Around her squatted and stood the medicine men, vision dreamers and *wawahokuns* of the tribe. As my eyes found her she raised a slender arm toward me calling out softly, "Courage!"

Smiling in return, I noticed she was carrying something in her other arm. I perceived it was the sacred buffalo-hide doll owned by every holy woman. I had not seen her carrying one before, wondered idly why she did so now.

But now I had a figure more compelling than a rawhide doll to examine. Slatemeyer was entering the ring.

All the man promised by the way his buckskins drew over the curve of thigh and biceps now stood revealed, for he was dressed as I, save for a loose doeskin breech-clout and bare-bladed knife, as naked as the day of his delivery.

There is no use describing that physique. It was faultless. A big, powerful, highly-trained fighting man with shoulder, arm, belly, back and leg muscling to shame the best imagination. Looking across at his easy slouching stance I met his pale gaze and knew he in his turn was "looking across the ring."

For some reason this gave me comfort. What did he see? Did it look dangerous to him? Was he knowing fear, too?

Somehow I didn't think he was. Yet it is dangerous to underestimate one's self.

I had been with the Sioux seven months, the last two spent in "summer dress," loincloth, moccasins, gun, even though light snow still lay on the ground. The spring sun, glaring off the late snows had burned me a dirty mahogany. I was no pygmy in structure. There were 215 pounds of me carefully distributed over six-foot-three of big-boned skeleton. Where muscle and sinew are expected to be, there they were. I was big. I was tough. I was fast. Since boyhood I had done little but practice the protection of my own life, at the usual price of such a profession—someone else's.

Slatemeyer may well have been totting up some of these points as he watched me, but if he was, his expression gave no indication he found the sum total impressive. He stood, slowly flexing his arms and hands, watching me with that curiously indifferent glance I had noted in the Kansas City card game.

Without knowing it I found myself imitating his gestures, flexing my arms and hands spasmodically. The palms of my hands poured perspiration. My breathing was as though I had just run a hard-pressed mile. With time running out, there remained no doubt of my true feeling toward my opponent.

I was mortally afraid of him.

Crazy Horse entered the ring and with no delay issued his brief statement. Any fighter stepping out of the ring would be lanced. The fight could end only with the death of one or both fighters. The survivor held full right to all the status of the vanquished. If Cetan Mani won he had his life. If the white *sunke* won he had his life *and* his freedom. It would indeed be a fight for the hide-painters to record.

He looked at both of us carefully, stepped quickly to the edge of the circle, called out sharply.

"*A-ah!*" the Sioux warning word. "Look out!"

Slatemeyer crouched, his amber eyes pinning me where I stood. I felt my whole body draw inward.

"*Hopo!* Let's go!" The feral voice of the Sioux leader released Slatemeyer almost before I heard it. He struck across the ring at me with a speed I couldn't follow. To this day I don't know how he got to me so fast, only remembering he was in front of me with the echo of Crazy Horse's order.

I could see the sweeping arc of the broad bowie knife coming from the ground up, coursing like a firestreak directly for my crotch. There was no time to go forward or to either side. I leaped and fell backward, expecting to feel the bite of the steel in my vitals as I went over. Instead I felt a searing bolt strike through my right buttock. Instinctively, I rolled over and forward. My backward fall had taken me out of the ring and into the ready lance of one of the slit-eyed ring stewards.

Slatemeyer had recovered from his charge with a twisting pivot and, even as I rolled back into the ring, launched himself upon me again. This time I drew my knees upward to protect myself, turning hunched side and buttock to him as I twisted to roll free.

I felt his blade enter my side but the momentum of my roll ripped it free as it entered. His own diving drive carried him past me and into the ground. We came to our feet simultaneously, about ten feet apart.

I believe had he leaped a third time without hesitating he would have had me. My eyes were full of dirt and ashes from my fall out of the ring. The lance wound in my haunch had temporarily spasmed the muscle there, rendering the right leg almost useless, while the coursing blood from the ragged rip in my side contributed its share to my general shock.

But he did not charge a third time. He had not seen me get lanced, didn't know of my impaired vision. All he could see was the side wound and he knew that wasn't serious.

He stood a moment, then began moving to his left, coming around my right. I turned with him in the ages-old "circling for an opening" tactic.

I had a few seconds' respite to realize why I had been so badly used thus far. I had made the gross error of applying my own thinking to the enemy. I had envisioned the fight beginning with the wary circle we were now in. Slatemeyer by his unorthodox opening lunge had very nearly eviscerated me. Blind luck and a superior set of reflexes had saved me. Now, twice wounded, half blinded and humiliated, I was beginning to think.

With the pain and the blood, came anger.

A soldier can go into any action knowing beforehand he may get killed, even that he probably shall. Yet not until the enemy wounds him personally does he seem actually to get the idea that death is involved.

Well, Slatemeyer had blooded me and I was beginning to fight.

It may seem peculiar that one who claims the combat record I do could be so unstrung as was I in the opening of the duel. Part of this awkwardness can be attributed to my nearly hysterical fear of the whiskey runner, yet I had faced him down over a six-gun without exhibiting the ineptness I now showed.

The full answer lay in the knives. A knife is not the white man's weapon. He fears it, hating those who use it. The white gun-fighter who will brace any man with a Colt grows weak at the sight of bare steel.

I was surely suffering this knife-fear as the fight began. Now it was turning to rage and hate. And with the turning all the coldness and awkwardness went out of me. I circled inside Slatemeyer, each slow, cat-footed move matching his.

Then I remembered a cute little thing Yellow Bird had taught me. Dropping both hands to my sides I moved straight in. My opponent stopped, crouching. As I came up to him he struck at me, his right arm throwing the knife at my left side. I moved to my right, shifting the Spanish blade to my left hand in the movement, whipping it at him in a backstroke as his body rushed by me.

Classically, this maneuver is designed to make your enemy

miss, his miss carrying him past you, his left side grazing your right. Without the shift of knife hands you would also be out of position, but with it you are ready as his body passes yours to strike to the rear into the kidneys. The danger lies in making the shift of hands too soon, allowing him to twist away from it.

I made the shift beautifully but was so jarred by the impact of his body brushing past mine that the backstroke was deflected. The blade found not the soft kidney fat but the hard fiber of the great back muscle.

Slatemeyer turned in mid air as the steel entered his back, freeing himself of the blade. But I felt it go deep.

Spinning on my left heel I was in time to slide in under his sweeping return stroke and lock his knife-arm, at the same time feeling his left hand lock my knife-wrist with bone-powdering force.

Arm-locked, we struggled, his weight and strength driving me backward.

The pressure of his left hand was paralyzing my knife grip. Another moment and the blade must drop. At the same time my own left arm was yielding to his right, the point of his bowie knife was coming with quivering, agonizing slowness down toward the shoulder juncture of my neck. A second more would have brought it thrusting home but even as its point pricked my skin I felt the sudden weakening of his left hand.

The severed back muscle was giving way.

Exerting my whole force I threw my knife-arm up and forward. The thin blade found his left side, low down, just above the hip-point, and again I knew it had gone deep.

In staggering back and away he nearly tore the knife from my numbed grasp.

I could not follow him, for neither of my hands had survived the pressures of his strength with enough force left in it to grip the blade properly. I could not risk losing the knife by striking at him.

Luckily, he too hesitated. I saw why. His left arm dangled useless, the slashing kidney wound and its twin I had just delivered having made control of the member impossible.

He began sidling toward me, crabwise, his wounded left side forward. Apparently he meant to let me take my best shot at that already-crippled target, using the time I thus employed to twist his own blade into me. He was going to let me get my blade into him so that he might get his into me in return, trusting he would get his in deeper. I backed steadily away as he crabbed around the ring after me. Once or twice I leaped in, feinting a lunge, to see if he would come out of his pose. He wouldn't, simply turning to present that huge hunching shoulder and dangling arm.

The Indians began a dull chanting in the background, at first begun by the warriors then taken up by the higher voices of the women, finally by the piping shrills of the children.

"It is fear, fear, coward, coward!"

I did not know if they jeered Slatemeyer or me and it made little difference. If action were not forthcoming they would take some of their own.

I stopped, spread my feet, swung my knife-arm free, determined to stand and let him come in at me. There was no other course.

Then as I watched him approaching I saw something. A little thing. The kind upon which battles turn. Just before he began to move in, the fingers of his left hand, the "useless" one, flexed, unflexed, then flexed again.

My mind jumped. Either that dangling arm had been a ruse all along or he had just gotten back use of it. At any rate he was playing it as a ruse now, not knowing I was on to the game.

Now was the time for some inspired guesswork on my part. What did he intend to do with that arm? How would he use it when I struck or when he struck? Watching him come in, I thought I knew, and acted on the thought. If I were right the fight might end instantly or it might continue. If I were wrong it would just end instantly. It was now my turn to take a gamble. I took it and fast, moving cautiously in to meet his advance.

When we were six feet apart Slatemeyer erupted into motion. I saw his jaw muscles twitch a hair of an instant before he leaped and I released my whole power toward my one objective, his "useless" left arm.

The knife came sliding from his good right into his bad left hand a light-flash before my teeth buried themselves in the bones of his left wrist. The heavy bowie knife thudded into the dust beneath us. The guess had paid off. He had tried the Sioux handshift. Had I not seen the fingers of that left hand flex themselves before his leap, the broad blade would have been resting in my vitals, not dust.

We went rolling over and over, he snarling and grunting as he sought crazily for my knife-arm. I felt his thick left arm around my body, then his right seize my knife-arm below the elbow. He had me under him, crushing me inward, toward him, with all his bear's strength. His right hand began inching down my arm to the knife-hand.

Surging upward I managed to bridge my body enough to free my left arm. Flinging this upward I seized the knife from my pinioned right, just before Slatemeyer's groping paw closed over it.

My head was buried on his right shoulder, so that I looked over it and down his back. Looping the left arm clear, around behind his head, I struck, burying the blade hilt-deep in the muscles of his right shoulder, ripping downward and deeply from shoulder-point to elbow.

The white bone showed sickeningly as I felt the arm go limp, allowing me to roll free.

I was on my feet in time to see him gain his and come for me, right arm a sodden motionless mass of blood and dirt, left hand flopping grotesquely as the fractured wrist strove vainly to control it.

I think he was in shock those last moments, for he was not a man but a white-faced, slavering, staring eyed brute. Giant that he was, he had taken three gaping wounds, of which either of the first two would have killed an ordinary man. He had been suffering intense pain and heavy blood loss for ten minutes.

His jaw sagged and wobbled crazily as he came forward. He gestured meaninglessly with the futile club of his left arm. His steps faltered, the thick muscles in his white thighs jumping and jerking in failing spasm. And all the while those great pale eyes kept looking at me and past me and through me. But now in truth they didn't see and were in fact fastened on some distant view.

I stepped inside his blind groping then, whipping the lean length of the Toledo blade into him as I came in. A shudder ran over the big body and, as I stepped quickly back away from it, it slid slowly to its knees in the dust.

The fingers of the right hand felt aimlessly across the chest, found the knife haft, plucked wonderingly at it, fell away. With the falling hand, the body went forward, twisting down into the trampled dirt on one shoulder before rolling over to lie in awkward silence.

Slatemeyer died as he had lived—with his eyes open.

I stood over him, motionless, while a thousand Oglala joined me in the payment of a respect of silence to this strange, fearless man. Not a Sioux there but knew he had seen a warrior die.

Then I did what I had to do, working quickly with Yellow Bird's thin knife.

Coming to my feet I faced the Sioux. A low swelling *"H'gun! H'gun!"* swept their ranks, dying away into the night as I stepped across the circle toward Star.

Halting before the fire in front of her dais, I raised the Spanish knife toward her. Her green eyes were wide in the yellow-red fire gleam. Her full lips parted and she leaned slightly forward, her high color seeming to flow and ebb with the leaping up and dying back of the flames.

"Receive my offering," I intoned harshly, and snapping the upraised knife blade downward and forward, I flung Slatemeyer's heart into the center of the fire before her.

Coming to her feet, Star held me with her eyes. In a voice hardly loud enough to carry above the crackling flames, she replied, "And receive you, *my* offering."

With the words she raised the sacred buffalo-hide doll high above her head and flung it after the heart of the whiskey runner into the fire. The little doll burned brightly for a moment and was gone. There was a long gasp from the watching Sioux, then silence.

Star stood defiantly, her eyes sweeping the ranks of her tribes-people. A shadow fell between her and me. Crazy Horse stood before us.

Here was another of those unpredictable Indian instants. I had brought the heart of her violator to their holy woman and this was right. But she in turn had cast from her the symbol of her holiness, renouncing, in the passion of the act, her holy status. This might prove very much wrong.

Judging from the shocked mutterings among the medicine men, this latter seemed very likely.

"I respect them," called out Crazy Horse, unexpectedly. "It is our way of doing things."

An angry, sullen growl sprang up among the medicine men.

The war chief continued, facing them challengingly, "That which was holy within her she has flung after the heart of him who destroyed it in her. She had already told me this on the sun of her capture. Now that which is woman, remaining in her, she would bestow upon him who avenged her. I say this is right. Let them walk in peace."

The scowls and bitter denunciations of the medicine men were lost in the thundering shout which went up from the warriors.

"Hun-hun-he! Let them walk in peace. *Hun-hun-he!"*

I leaped over the fire to Star's dais and she rose to meet me, casting from her shoulders as she did, the white elk robe of the Wiyan Wakan, to stand revealed in the red light, slimly naked but for copper breastplates and the briefest of beautifully beaded breechcloths.

I swept her into my arms and together we made our way to my tipi through the milling, howling mass of warriors already beginning the celebration dance of our nuptials.

Outside our tipi the throbbing drums and wild voices of our savage people welled up in a pagan wedding hymn.

But far to the south, and nearer still, to the north, other drums were beating and other wild voices calling out. And they were beating and calling out for me.

PART TWO

Interlude

. . . THE NINE years I spent with the Oglala Sioux erased the last question of my white allegiance.

I rode and hunted with the Indians, sharing with them their feasts and famines, their customs, manners, fortunes and misfortunes. I learned to ride a charging buffalo off and drive a thick hunting arrow feather-deep into him from a squat war bow of Osage Orangewood. I learned lance-work, ax and war-club handling, all their marvelous tricks of horsemanship. Their language became mine, my thoughts theirs. I stood high in their councils, their hunting, their wars.

And always I practiced and worked with the Colts and a succession of new rifles, beginning with the beautiful Winchester won from Slatemeyer. My skill with firearms became legend through the prairie country, allowing me to enjoy a repute far above fact.

Through this skill I was made chief hunter for the annual buffalo kills. My time among the Sioux was painted onto the tribal record skins as "the sunny days of plenty."

Star and I lived with Crazy Horse and his wife, Black Blanket. Our tipis were pitched side by side in every camp. By association my power in the Sioux hierarchy rose rapidly. By '74, when the Indian War began its final abortive eruption, I stood second to Crazy Horse in the Bad Face Band. He stood second to no one in any band.

Red Cloud rose and fell in final disgrace through his bumbling in Washington. Spotted Tail, Lone Horn, Whistling Elk, Pipe and others knew their day before deserting to the security of the reservations. Of them all, Tatanka Yotanka, Sitting Bull, remained aloof, climbing steadily in power among the warlike Hunkpapa.

But always Crazy Horse was there, behind and above all,

the supreme war leader of the Sioux Nation, worshipped and held in awe by his own people, hated and feared by the whites.

During this time I made war when the Indians made war, made peace when they did. I sat in on the Peace Council of '68, that farcical treaty which led to the dismemberment of the Sioux race, that spurious pledge of white honor which was in fact the white race's conscienceless gut-slashing of the red.

I sat in subsequent councils with the Army and with Indian Bureau agents and Washington statesmen; with Generals Sanborn, Harney, Terry, Augur, Hancock, Crook, Gibbon, and "Red Beard" Sherman, with Indian Commissioner N. G. Taylor (who had known me as a white scout at the Laramie Council in '68), Senator Henderson of Missouri and many others.

I argued the Indian cause before these white chiefs interminably. Not once did one of them treat or address me in any way but as white to Sioux. In the Army records of the time you will find the name of Walking Hawk along with such Sioux unforgettables as Pawnee Killer, Man-That-Walks-Under-the-Ground, Standing Elk, Swift Bear, Turkey Leg, Cold Face and Crazy Lodge. I even sat in one memorable, two-hour session with Custer, without the least sign of recognition from him.

In these years the tide of fortune rolled steadily against the red man. He had only two friends on the frontier, Harney and Custer: the one "promoted" out of the way, the other broken and sent east by his rashly honorable exposé of President Grant's corrupt relative and henchman, Belknap.

The southern plains Indians, Comanche, Pawnee and Kiowa, were rounded up and reservationed forever by '75. In this campaign Custer was the leading figure. There remained then only the indomitable hostiles of the Sioux Nation, with a thin scattering of Cheyenne, under Red Cloud, Sitting Bull and Crazy Horse.

Red Cloud went over to the whites, taking thousands of Sioux onto the reservations with him. When Gibbon and Terry came up into the Powder River country for the climactic campaign which ended with the massacre on the Little Big Horn, only Crazy Horse and Sitting Bull remained hostile.

Those were memorable, exciting days, the chronicle of

them making another entire story.* Here they can be only indicated, my history being important only as it touches on that great, unknown moment of Custer's death on the banks of the Greasy Grass. Knowing this, the reader will appreciate the roughness of this treatment, skipping with me over these years of "restless truce on the frontier," to the winter of 1875-76, when the ill-famed unconditional surrender order was issued by the U. S. Secretary of the Interior.

Crazy Horse got a copy of this order which I saw. It read, addressed to the Indian Bureau:

> Referring to our communication of the 27th ultimo, relative to the status of certain Sioux Indians residing without the bounds of their reservation and their continued hostile attitude toward the whites, I have to request that you direct the Indian Agents at all Sioux Agencies in Dakota and at Fort Peck, Montana, to notify said Indians that unless they shall remove within the bounds of their reservation (and remain there), before the 31st of January next, they shall be deemed hostile and treated accordingly by the military.

This was dated December 3rd, 1875.

It was a terrible winter, even for that land of bitter snows. The camps of Sitting Bull and Crazy Horse, the "certain Sioux" and "said Indians" referred to in the order, were three hundred miles north and west of Standing Rock, the nearest agency.

The runners sent out from there had not even reached the

---

*A story of many "little things" which have no bearing on the present tale. Little things such as the way, three months after he had "died" of exhaustion, the super-tough Hussein calmly grazed his way into camp, hog-fat with spring grass and sassy as a stud colt in saptime.

Or the way Little Wolf and I, together with ten picked young Cheyenne bloods of his tribe, went moseying down to Fort Phil Kearney when we heard the Army was abandoning it and, lying in wait along the out-trail one fine dark night, stampeded their whole horse herd into the Powder. And how, when Sergeat Kelly counted up the losses next morning he was delighted to report just three head short. But how Colonel Carrington was very unhappy, for they were three fine brood mares heavy in foal, left at the fort by a white scout named Clayton who was killed in the Fetterman Massacre.

Or how my friend with the bloody sense of humor, the irrepressible Yellow Bird, invited me along to a lecture he proposed delivering on honest trade methods to a certain Indian agent down at the Pine Ridge Agency, a chap who insisted on weighing his heavy right hand on the scale with every supply issue he made to the "ignorant" Sioux. And how, after Yellow Bird had rebuked him in his own dignified way, said agent never weighed his right hand again. For the simple reason the hand accompanied a couple pounds of pemmican back to the Oglala camp in the *parfleche* of the noble Yellow Bird.

Sioux by January 31st, the date set for their surrender at
Standing Rock. Not a single runner even got back to the
agency before the expiration date. There is no doubt this
impossibility was deliberately set up. The Army wanted the
Sioux to stay out. In planning a murder it's best to catch the
victim out in the open, away from any witnesses.

The Army got its wish. If it wanted a war it was going to
get it.

I was in the council where this decision was taken by the
Sioux. Crazy Horse was determined he would not force his
families through three hundred miles of snowdrifts and hammering blizzards to reach an agency where no food awaited.
Even then, as I recall positively, our lodges were filled with
agency Sioux who had drifted "home" to the hostiles simply
to get something in their bellies beside wind and promises.

Crazy Horse's life-long ally and my good friend, the bat-
tle-scarred and influential old He-Dog, led his followers out
of our camp and into the lodges of Two Moons, the Cheyenne leader, who had already announced his intention to go
in. Crazy Horse and Sitting Bull sat alone amid the swirling
snows of the Big Horns and the Powder River. War would
come with the short grass. They would be ready. . . .

Chapter 1

OUR LODGES, over a hundred in number, were nestled along
the Tongue in the same stretches where I had scouted the
Oglala Scalp Dance which preceded the long-gone Fetterman
Massacre. The weather had turned blue-cold, the snows piling
deeper by the minute, the temperatures scudding far below
zero.

Yellow Bird and I, dispatched by Crazy Horse to scout the
agency at Standing Rock following his refusal to "come in,"
had just returned. We brought big news; big enough to call
up a Fox Lodge council at once. I made the report, backed
by Yellow Bird.

"It is as you knew," I began, addressing Crazy Horse where
he sat on a pile of buffalo robes, wearing his war garb of
black wolfskins. "There will be war."

He nodded, all the other chiefs grunting assent.

"Already the Grandfather has ordered it," I hurried on. "Many troops began a march from the Big Muddy all the way to our lodges here on the Tongue and the Powder. It was so ordered. This is the way we were told the order read. We had these words from Spotted Tail." I looked to Yellow Bird for agreement.

"Aye," growled the lean fighter, "but the snows came too many. Ponies and men all froze."

"They lost heavily from the bitter weather," I corrected him, "and the attack has been turned back to the Big Muddy. But as we came away from Standing Rock our trail crossed that of Little Wolf. He had seen the troops and scouted their retreat. He had with him a Crow Army scout, one who had been with the troops which turned back. This Crow told them heavy news."

"Heavy indeed," grunted Yellow Bird. "Three Stars."

At the mention of General Crook's name the council came alert, for he was respected among the Sioux.

Crazy Horse challenged at once. "Three Stars is coming? You are positive?"

"From the south and soon," I answered. "He has made vast preparation to march when the moon is new. He is at Fort Fetterman."

Crazy Horse arose. "Three Stars will come if he has said he will. We are to be ready.

"Walking Hawk and Yellow Bird will travel south when the night is in the middle. They will scout the way that Three Stars comes, telling me of his strength. White Bull and One Bull (nephews of Sitting Bull, in our camp as liaison with the Hunkpapa) will travel to warn our Uncle of the danger."

Turning back to me, he concluded, "Moving south you will pass the lodges of He-Dog and Two Moons. Warn them. Their tipis are in the path of Three Stars. I think the heart of Three Stars is good but I do not trust his grandfather (President Grant) and I think He-Dog and Two Moons will have their lodges burned and their ponies stolen if they wait. They are fools if they wait. I will make all things ready here."

I went to bid Star farewell, my heart slow within me. After eight barren years she was now six moons heavy with our child. My "Indian hunch," that odd prescience which had never failed me, rode the withers of my spirit as heavily as a travois heaped with stones. I knew I should never know this first-born of ours.

Star was cheerful as always, helping me dress for the journey, packing my *parfleches* with pemmican, hard-fat, and marrow butter, setting out my weapons.

"You shall return soon, Cetan Mani. Then you shall see me as big as a buffalo cow. But never fear. I will need to be to deliver your son. He shall be as great as his sire!"

Whether her spirit was genuine or she thought to raise mine I could not know. In any event I failed to respond, my presentiment of evil sinking its spurs deeper into the flanks of my feelings with each passing hour. We left the lodges an hour before midnight, heading south in a stinging cold sleet storm.

Four days we traveled; then, on the morning of the fifth, far up the Tongue, we sighted the fires of many men. This proved to be Crook with a very strong outfit, nearly a thousand army men, the whole column supplied by trains of tough army mules. Here were no clumsy field wagons, baggage coaches or ambulances to impede action. This was a fighting outfit pure and simple. Our report to Crazy Horse would indicate these were very seasoned troops indeed. No green boys with muskets here.

Crook was headed down the Tongue, his Crow and Pawnee scouts out in front, searching for the camp of Crazy Horse's Oglala.

We had passed the lodges of He-Dog and Two Moons the day previous, delivering Crazy Horse's warning. They had refused to believe Crook was coming and that if he were he meant them any harm. After all, their hearts were good. Covering their ears, they sat still.

In his camp Crook was halted to re-shoe his mules, their worn irons being too smooth for the icy work ahead in the rough hills of the Tongue. Yellow Bird was for rushing back at once to bring the news to He-Dog and Two Moons, but I bade him wait, for I needed something in that camp.

Crook pulled out about noon. An hour later we went down into the deserted camp, Yellow Bird muttering darkly about Crazy Horse's stupidity in entrusting such a mission to a hawk that walked like a man but thought like a sparrow.

Once in camp, I sought out the farrier's fire, bidding Yellow Bird to alight and help me load an old supply bag with the wornout mule shoes. He shook his head, calling upon Wakan Tanka to witness the grade of goose feathers which stuffed this hawk's empty head, but nonetheless joined me with good humor.

Shortly, he threw the big bag of shoes over his pony's

withers, mounted with a grunted, *"Hopo,* let's go!" and away we went, making long tracks out of there. By circling wide, riding all night, we reached Two Moons' camp at daybreak, some hours ahead of the Army column.

We slid our lathered ponies to a halt, showering ice and snow all over the door-flap of old Two Moons' tipi. I shouted at the top of a voice never noted for haunting delicacy, "Let Two Moons come out and see what a fool he is."

"Aye!" barked Yellow Bird, to a group of gathering curious. "And let all the warriors come to see what fools they are. Ho! He-Dog! Where are you? For you are the biggest fool of them all!" He had never forgiven the Oglala sub-chief for his disaffection from the beloved Crazy Horse.

In minutes there was a big crowd of warriors around and for a change they were making plenty of noise, a sure sign of apprehension. They seemed to sense the trouble and in a moment, when He-Dog came riding up and Two Moons stumbled sleepily out of his tipi, we gave it to them.

"By the time Wi is overhead," I bellowed dramatically, "there will be pony-soldiers and walk-a-heaps among you to the number of a thousand!"

"You talk with a big mouth," growled He-Dog. "We know there are soldiers. And if they come they'll find peace here."

"Aye," I sneered. "He-Dog speaks straight. Too bad he cannot think that way. He knows there are soldiers. He is bright. Does he also know these soldiers are riding mules?"

At once a murmur of concern swept the listeners. The Sioux knew the average Army expedition, with its awkward baggage vehicles and preponderance of green infantry, was intended to impress them, not actually make war on them. They also knew a column of mule-mounted veterans, supplied exclusively by pack animals, meant something else again.

"Mule-riders?" queried He-Dog, uncertainly. "How can this be? Have the eyes of the Hawk begun to see like those of an old squaw?" The doubt in his questions was more than polite.

Two Moons seconded his implication but with a more admirable directness. "You lie!" he shouted, angrily.

"Yellow Bird."

"Aye, Cetan?"

"Two Moons says we are liars. He-Dog says, squaws."

Grinning broadly, the tall Sioux heaved the clanking bag off his pony's withers, crying aloud that all might hear, "When one is dealing with iron heads, one must produce iron proof." Before even I could guess his intent, he drove his pony up to Two Moons and emptied the contents of the bag over the old chief's head. When the clatter of mule shoes had cascaded off the Cheyenne's scalplock to lie in a bright pile around him, Yellow Bird turned to He-Dog, sneering, "None for you, Dog Mouse. Even a mule shoe wouldn't dent that iron head of yours."

Within half an hour there wasn't an old moccasin left in that camp. Bag, baggage, tipi and travois, the Oglala and Cheyenne dusted out, heading east and north for the Powder. Yellow Bird and I remained behind to cover Crook's approach.

It was well we did, for less than two hours later Crook's scouts rode into the deserted campground.

Beside me, I heard Yellow Bird curse. "By Pte's navel! There rides Sitting-with-Upraised-Hands."

"The Grabber?" I whispered, excitedly.

"Aye, the Grabber. May his food turn to calf-dung in his mouth."

"The Grabber" was a nickname for Frank Grouard, one of the ablest scouts the Army had. And a traitor of the yellowest belly-color by Sioux standards. Some years earlier, young Grouard had been captured by Sitting Bull. He was a bright youngster who, due to the rough time he gave the Sioux in their capture of him, gained the ready Indian admiration for courage and daring. Sitting Bull adopted him exactly as Crazy Horse had done me.

Before long he became one of the best scouts and hunters among the Sioux. I had not met him but had heard Sitting Bull's nephews speak of him with respect.

Such an Indian-trained man made a dangerous element to have in the camp of the enemy. When Grouard went over to the Army, the Sioux apprehension mounted understandably. But the campaigns in which he figured had been largely in the south with the result the Sioux had forgotten him with that childlike "out of sight, out of mind" ease, which so pervades the Indian philosophy.

Now that Yellow Bird saw him back in the homeland, all was changed.

The click of a cocking rifle in my ear warned me in time to roll over and thrust my hand over the breech of Yellow Bird's gun. "Heyoka!" I snarled. "Would you bring every trooper in Wyoming down on our shoulders? Is your scalp getting too loose for your skull?"

He glared at me, his black eyes snapping. It's never safe

to run rough on an Indian. For an instant I thought he was going to drill me. Then he lowered the gun. "A mistake," he said, no anger in his words. "But he must die, Cetan. He will lead Three Stars into our people without fail if we do not kill him."

"Look at that trail," I urged, pointing the broad track our allies had left in their hasty removal. "A blind quill-pig could follow it. They don't need the Grabber for that trail. Let him be now. We'll get him later." He said no more, settling his gaze on the scene below.

We were in the branches of a gnarled old cedar which formed a part of a small grove which stood overhanging the sight of the cooling embers of the Sioux cooking fires, our ponies well-hidden and nose-wrapped half a mile away. We had chosen the site hoping to overhear something when Crook should come up. It was risky as all hell but we weren't disappointed.

Grouard had no Indian scouts with him. I remembered Spotted Tail telling me the Indian Bureau had succeeded in getting their use ruled out in this campaign. Thinking back to the Crow and Pawnee outriders we had seen the previous day only confused the picture. The good old Army. Still never letting its right hand know whose throat its left was cutting.

Grouard halted under our tree after scouring the campsite for sign. Shortly, Crook rode in with Colonel J. J. Reynolds and Captain Anson Mills.

"Well, Frank, where do we go from here?"

"They've ducked out for the Powder. I count over a hundred lodges of them. Some Cheyenne. Mostly Sioux.'

"Crazy Horse's outfit?" This from Mills.

"Dunno. Mebbeso, mebbe no. Reckon it is, though."

Crook sat a moment fingering his famous braided beard. "The weather's bad—" he began.

"And gettin' worse," interrupted Grouard.

"Yes. I don't see the sense of taking the whole outfit into that rough country with a storm blowing up. Fact is, I won't do it. Reynolds!"

"Yes, General?"

"Take the troops of Mills, Egan, Moore. Go on in there and find that village. Grouard will go in ahead of you to make sure it's Crazy Horse's village. If it is, Reynolds, I want it wiped out. If it isn't, leave it alone and report back. Get that straight. We're after Crazy Horse. We get him and the rest will come running in. I can't stress the fact too much that I want the identity of that village made certain. It's Crazy Horse we want. Nobody else."

Here Captain Anson Mills, an Indian fighter of reputation, broke in. "General, there's some feeling in the command that Grouard is still sympathetic to the Sioux. I don't believe he is, but—"

"I don't know about that." This interruption from Reynolds who seemed obviously unhappy with his "big chance." "Perhaps for this action the Pawnee or Crow might—"

"Colonel, you know those orders as well as I do. The Crow and Pawnee are along as hunters, not to be used in scouting." I exchanged glances with Yellow Bird over this tightrope-walking tidbit, as Crook concluded. "Frank will take you in and you are to act on his information. Further, I suggest you let him lay out the best plan of going in with the troops. All clear?"

No one answered at first, then Reynolds and Mills replied together. "Right."

"All clear."

In the entire discussion of his loyalty Grouard hadn't said a word, devoting his talents to the careful mouthing of a monstrous cud of cutplug. The thin black streams which he spat out as Reynolds talked were his total contribution to the discussion of his possible villainy. I never saw a cooler man.

The column left an hour after dark, Grouard going on foot ahead of it, the snow by now coming hard, piling deeply. It was growing intensely cold, probably fifty below, as Yellow Bird and I crept out of our tree, bellying our way through the dark to our tethered mounts. We freed the ponies and I gave Yellow Bird his orders.

"Ride like Yunke-lo had his teeth in your flanks. Tell Crazy Horse what we have seen and heard."

"And you—" he wanted to know arrogantly.

"I trail the Grabber, trying to come before him to the lodges of He-Dog and Two Moons that they may be warned."

"I could do this better than you," he growled.

"I am seeing inside your black skull," I answered him boldly.

"What do you see there?" He was scowling, his mouth corners coming down hard.

Breaking out my most infectious grin, I chided him quickly. "I see you sticking a knife in the Grabber while all the rest of our plans go flying away to a hell."

He gave me his slit-eye stare, then grinned like a wolf with his mouth full of hot buffalo veal. "Cetan, may your son feed always on humpmeat." With that, he pivoted his snow-caked pony, whirled off northward at a high lope. Crazy Horse would get my message.

Chapter 2

THERE WERE perhaps three white men on the frontier who could run a trail better than I. Frank Grouard was one of them.

When I found the Sioux-Cheyenne camp, troopers were already falling into attack positions around it.

The camp was in a low, level bottom in a tight bend of the Powder, its hundred tipis dotting the willow brush and cottonwood timber of the stream-side. My cover was in very close to the camp, the whole terrain being heavily fogged over. This enabled me to hear the village better than I could see it. A rusty voice crying out the early morning news carried clearly to me.

"Walking Hawk has spoken with a straight tongue. Soldiers are following. Mule soldiers. But scouts sent back by He-Dog to locate the troops found nothing. All is well for now . . ."

This at a moment when the hills on three sides of them were filling with heavily armed soldiers. I cursed. Apparently the scouts had gone but a short distance down their backtrail. Finding no pursuit sign they had returned with the good news. I had seen where the wily Grouard had pulled Reynolds' troops off the village trail five miles back. The scouts had quit too soon.

Suddenly a file of men loomed out of the fog, pausing within five feet of my hiding place. I recognized Captain Anson Mills, Reynolds, another captain, a lieutenant and Grouard. Their subdued voices carried clearly to my cover.

"I know it's Crazy Horse," Grouard was saying, apparently in reply to a query from Mills. "I been in his camp plenty times when I was with them. This is his outfit. I heard pony bells, then got in close enough under this sopping slop to spit on their damn rumps. I know this village by those horses. This is Crazy Horse's village."

"How shall we place ourselves, Grouard?" Reynolds' voice had lost none of its petulant anxiety.

"Well," the scout replied, unhesitatingly, "we split in fours. One bunch to rush the lodges. Second bunch to foller up behind the first. Third bunch to hit the horse herd and run it off. Last bunch to stay up here on the mesa so's to be between the Sioux and the hills back there. No horse is gonna git into those hills but we gotta keep the Injuns from gittin' into them on foot. If we kin keep them down there on the flat none of them'll git away."

Again I cursed. Very clearly the object of this tactic was to trap and kill, not maneuver for a surrender. There was to be no quarter if they could spring their surprise without warning.

Reynolds accepted the plan. Captain Egan would charge the village. Captain Mills follow in reserve. Lieutenant Moore's detachment would defile on the mesa and cut off any retreat to the hills behind him. Reynolds would run off the horse herd. My opinion of this officer rose none as I heard him ration out this plum for his own group. Looking the bunch of them over, thinking of the orders, I selected Moore as the soft spot in the picture, silently thanking Reynolds for handing the youngster the hot corner.

Before I could hear more, the speakers drifted away through the fog to put the attack in operation. But I had heard more than enough. It was no time for caution.

As soon as Grouard and the officers had departed I busted out of my cover like a bunny coming out of a brushpile with a beagle at his rump. I got over the fogged-in quarter of a mile to the village without interception. As I shot down the deserted street, my hoarse voice lifted above the quiet tipis, bringing braves and squaws rolling and tumbling out of their buffalo robes like sowbugs out from under kicked-over buffalo chips.

"A-ah! A-ah! Look out! Armed soldiers! A trap!"

Even as I ran, yelling, and the warriors sprang to their weapons, the fog lifted off the hillside revealing Grouard standing within twenty yards of the camp. Cupping his hands he shouted aloud, "Crazy Horse! It's me, the Grabber. You told me you'd rather fight than make a treaty. Come out then. You'll git all the fight you want. Soldiers are all around you."

He dived for cover as a dozen rifle shots dug into the hillside around him. There were a couple of Colt slugs mixed in with the Sioux lead but I didn't think they hit the ground. I found later I was right, Grouard carrying the scars for life to prove it, one under the right arm, one in the left shoulder. Bad shooting, and no second chances. You never get them with Grouard's kind.

No sooner had he made his challenge than Egan came galloping into the south end of the village. I took over the fight for the Indians, ordering He-Dog and Two Moons to hold Egan while I rallied the rest of the village. They took the orders. With the handful of warriors ready to fight, the two chiefs held Egan's troopers for thirty minutes, even starting to drive them out of the village before Mills came roaring up with the reserves.

But by now I was ready. *"Hookahey!"* I yelled to He-Dog. "We are all ready here. All are to break for the hills. It is our only chance. *Hopo,* let's go!"

"What of the ponies?" howled old Two Moons, his nomad's mind thinking always of his horseflesh. I shouted, "The hell with the horses! Run for the hills on foot. Now. *Hopo!"*

"Hookahey!" screamed He-Dog. "Follow the Hawk." With a rush the village went up the hill at my heels. On the way out I counted ten troopers on the ground, at least four of them there for keeps. We lost exactly one toothless old buck and a blind squaw.

Lieutenant Moore who could have and was supposed to cut us down if we tried the very thing we were trying, lost his nerve, pulling his men back onto a hill to one side, contenting himself with directing his fire into the empty lodges below.

From their places in the rocky hills my Sioux poured what fire they could into Reynolds as he moved into the village. But we had few guns, fewer good shots. I ordered the shooting slowed to conserve ammunition. Still no pursuit developed. It became clear Reynolds had had all he wanted of fighting Sioux and was clearing out. He then demonstrated his complete stupidity.

Did he put his exhausted command to rest in the snug warmth of the tipis? Did he issue a big feed from the captured tons of dried buffalo meat? Did he slaughter the pony herd? Did he send back for Crook as instructed? Did he load a batch of captured ponies with meat and furs to feed and warm his frozen, frazzled-out command? Not Reynolds. He piled everything up and burned it. Then he got out, leaving one tipi standing to shelter the blind squaw. Otherwise not a stick or a skin was left of the camp or its supplies.

That night I followed them up and with a hundred braves ran off the captured horse herd—over seven hundred fractious Indian ponies left in the guard of five soldiers. What a commander! That man couldn't have been a corporal in the Confederate Army.

Once mounted, we swept back in on them at three A.M., out of the belly of a howling norther, and stole their beef herd. They were left without a mouthful of food other than the mules they rode.

Reynolds' men were starving, yet he had destroyed enough prime meat to feed a regiment two months. His command was loaded down and riddled through with men crippled by frozen limbs, yet he burned a mountain of furs and robes. No wonder Crook arrested him on sight and put him on file. A little late, obviously, to help Army-Indian history avoid another abortive miscarriage.

Many of the Cheyenne and Sioux in the camp were agency Indians. The presence of big stores of agency issue goods in the lodges must have proved this to Reynolds' command. All the Indians in the camp were avowed "comerinners," runners establishing this status having been sent to Standing Rock weeks before. The troops knew the minute they occupied the village that this was true and that it was not the village of Crazy Horse.

General Sherman whitewashed this blunder with the following masterly statement: "The result of Reynolds' fight was only the destruction of the tipis of the Indians, with their contents."

Sherman was wrong. The result was Custer's massacre.

Chapter 3

WITH THE recapture of our pony herd I soon had the Sioux and Cheyenne moving, the whole tribe beginning the long freezing journey down the Powder an hour before daylight. The bitter weather held, making our progress one of pure misery. Several old ones made their last ride that night and four of the very young.

As soon as we had put ten miles behind us with no sign of pursuit, I sent for He-Dog. We rode knee-and-knee that we might hear one another above the hammering of the storm.

"I understand the village of Sitting Bull lies ahead," I shouted above the rising wind.

"A long day's journey," he replied. "He is camped on the Creek of the Beavers, under the Blue Mountains."

I knew a swift wish before continuing: what a different reception Reynolds would have gotten had he blundered into the camp of the Hostile Hunkpapa instead of that of old Two Moons.

"I ride ahead to council with Sitting Bull. You will see that our people are kept moving. No one is to stop. If the dead cannot be carried, let them lie in the snow. It is peaceful there."

"I will see to it. I have been a fool."

"Do not think about it. You fought like a real he-dog in the village."

Changing to a fresh horse I set off alone through the blizzard. It was long after dark when the snarling and yelping of Indian curs told me a village lay ahead. Sitting Bull saw me at once, for while we had not talked before I had seen him many times and he knew me as the son of his war chief, Crazy Horse.

Here let it be said that all talk of jealousy or rivalry between these two was thin rot. To Crazy Horse, Sitting Bull was his "Uncle," revered and respected as the civil head of the Sioux. By the same token Sitting Bull regarded Crazy Horse as "Nephew," holding him without reserve to be the war head of the wild tribes. Tatanka Yotanka was lawmaker; Tashunka Witko, warmaker. It was an arrangement understood, honored, never violated.

Sitting Bull was a short squat man with an enormous head, passive countenance, wide between the eyes, broad of forehead. His eyes were rather an odd grayish color, very level-set for an Indian. His hair was feeling the iron of many winters and showing gray as the badger's. I judged him to be nearing sixty.

When I ducked under his tipi flaps he was seated by a small fire smoking a long, eagle-feathered pipe. He looked at me, nodded, grunted shortly. *"Hohahe,* welcome to my tipi."

"Woyuonihan," I answered, quickly. "I am Cetan Mani, son of Crazy Horse."

"Even so, I remember you. Are you hungry?" He gestured to some dried buffalo beef hanging from the lodgepoles.

"I cannot eat with my heart so bad within me."

"When a man's heart is bad his tongue is no good. Tell me."

"The last sun, a day's journey south, Three Stars fell upon the village of He-Dog and Two Moons. Without warning. Every lodge and all the food was burned."

I went on, giving him details in answer to his brief questions. When I had finished he made a memorable speech for an "ignorant savage." He was remarkably well-spoken at that; an Indian intellectual, philosopher, prophet.

"Ever since the Black Robe * came to smoke with me eight snows gone, I have kept the peace. They have lied to me and they have cheated and stolen from my people. But I have kept the peace. I am a man of much suffering. I am patient. I am gentle. I have been a great fighter, too.

"Many insults I have taken for myself and this is right. For a chief must be able to suffer, holding back his thunder. For myself I want nothing. But now they have attacked my people when there is no war. They are trying to kill us. That is all they want, to kill the Indian. They do not want peace. All they want is war.

"I have no more patience. I am not gentle. I am angry now. And when I am angry, things are different."

He stopped and we sat for some minutes, passing the pipe, staring into the fire. At last I spoke. "May I go to see that meat and tipis are made ready for our poor cousins?"

"Go!" He nodded, his old eyes brightening visibly. "Go in peace and say a prayer to Wakan Tanka. For soon there will be war." As I parted the tipi flap he added, his voice warm, "Crazy Horse has a good son. He is blessed who has a good son. I no longer have a son."

I knew he was thinking of Grouard. Glancing back I saw him gazing through the smoke of the fire, his eyes seeing far away days and places. A lump came in my throat, for I could think of no way to answer him. "My heart is full of pity for all," I murmured, and went out into the night.

As the survivors of Reynolds' raid drifted in during the black hours of that morning, they were fed, clothed and

---

*N. G. Taylor, the Indian High Commissioner who made the Laramie Treaty of '68 here referred to by Sitting Bull, and who, prior to his Indian Bureau duty, had been a Methodist minister.

made warm. All the following day preparations were made for removal of Sitting Bull's camp. Minutes after my arrival, runners had gone out to summon the chiefs of all the local hostile bands to a big council on the Tongue. I was sent to carry the call to Crazy Horse.

Thus it was I came again to that great war camp on the Tongue, where so much of my history had already been plotted; and came again, too, to the beloved arms of my Indian wife.

Star was well and we had much to talk of as we lay there in the warm dark of the tipi, the blizzard yelping and bellowing outside like a pack of dogs tearing an old bull to bits. But we, snug and warm in our shaggy robes, for the moment were far beyond the cares of Crook or Crazy Horse.

Present at the council which met in three days, beside the two head chiefs, were the Sioux—White Crow, Gall, Two-Bull-Bear, White Bull, Gray Eagle, Old Bull, Elk Nation, American Horse, Black Moccasin and Paints Brown; the Cheyenne—Hump, Bob-Tail-Horse, Comes-in-Sight, young Two Moons and Half-a-Horse.

By contrast to his usual style Sitting Bull's statement to the council was abrupt.

"The whites are a great lake around us, and the Indians are an island in the lake's middle. We must stand together or they will wash us all way. These soldiers have come shooting. They want war. All right. We will give it to them."

Crazy Horse now arose, being greeted by an acknowledgment not afforded even Sitting Bull—the guttural *"hun-hun-he!"* always a thrilling sound, now made more so by the gravity of the hour. For never out of Sioux minds was the fact the Oglala chief was the mightiest warrior in their history—and none of Sitting Bull's powers of civil government shaded that situation. He was, by common consent of the Army commanders who opposed him in the field, the greatest natural cavalry commander of modern times.

This was to prove the first of the last three general war councils of the Sioux. None of us could know that, at the time, but there was none there who didn't feel it might indeed be the very last rather than the first of three.

Crazy Horse stood there in the leaping firelight of the council tipi, a figure to be etched on the mind whether of wild-born Sioux or adopted white son. Seated cross-legged on the ground beside him, Sitting Bull invited comparison: the Hunkpapa, short, squat, dour, ugly; the Oglala, lean, pantherine, elegantly handsome. When he spoke it was with his customary succinctness.

"Our Uncle has put a tongue to the hearts of all of us. *Hopo. Hookahey!*"

The council broke up on a final word from Sitting Bull; the word which cost many a white his hair and horses in the following weeks; the word which smashed Crook's vaunted fighting force clear back to its base on Goose Creek; the word which ran the Greasy Grass red with the blood of Custer's men.

"Runners will go at once to every hunting band on the prairie. To every agency of the Sioux, Arapahoe and Cheyenne, to the sunward of the Big Muddy. All the agencies. The riders will ride hard. When their ponies stumble at last into the villages they will tear aside the flaps of the chief's tipi, speaking the word of Sitting Bull. 'It is war. Come to my camp at the Big Bend of the Rosebud. Let us all get together and have one big fight with the soldiers!' "

"*Hopo! Hopo!*" echoed the chiefs, their deep voices bounding off the drum-tight skins of the council lodge.

"*Hookahey!*" boomed Crazy Horse, throwing his rifle above his head. "It is the way of our people!"

Then the tipi was empty save for three figures. Sitting Bull and Crazy Horse remained by the fire, the one standing, the other still seated, cross-legged.

"Our sun grows short." The voice of the Hunkpapa was far away.

"May it set in splendor," his companion answered, grimly.

"I will never surrender." The old man's mouth was hard, but his words were tired.

"Nor I, Uncle," said the war chief, his voice oddly gentle. "We shall ride together, you and I, faces to the enemy."

"Aye," breathed the other. "As it is written on The Pipe. 'Peace without Slavery.' "

I stood, unmoving, just inside the tipi door, knowing I had heard the valedictory of a brave race.

Chapter 4

THE DAYS following Sitting Bull's declaration were without sun or moon. Around the clock the war camp on the Tongue seethed. Arrivals and departures were endless: warriors leaving for the trading posts and agencies to barter for guns and powder and ball; heading for "tame" tribes to the west and south to trade for fresh war ponies. Riders traveling all points of the compass carrying the words of Sitting Bull. "It is war. Come to the Rosebud." Warriors going out with empty pack trains, returned with ponies staggering under loads of dried buffalo beef, robes and hides for outfittings of new moccasin, harness and shield leathers. Squaws and old men trailing away with empty travois, appearing again with tired ponies grunting under mountainous stores of agency-issue goods; flour, salt, sugar, blankets, cooking pots, knives, axes.

And always, once the grass appeared, the uninterrupted stream of faithful striking their lodges, moving; warrior, woman and child; tent, tipi and travois; north and west across the Powder and the Tongue; moving slow, moving fast, coming with doubt, with fear, with desperation; but all coming, all moving to one destination—the Big Bend of the Rosebud River.

The arrival of one group in particular is fresh in my mind, serving as a pattern for the hopes and hearts of all the red pilgrims.

This was a small band of Oglala, all the way from the Spotted Tail Agency. There were no women or children, just warriors, all youthful, all heavily armed. In their lead rode a young giant of a Sioux, revealing in his carriage at once the bearing of a hereditary chief and something vaguely familiar in a personal way. As he brought his band in, riding alone ahead of them toward the tipi of Crazy Horse before which Yellow Bird and I were hunkered down over a blanket measuring powder, my companion looked up, muttering a name which took me back through the years to the hillside beyond Fort Laramie and the splendid figure of a tall chief in a blazing scarlet blanket and white-feather warbonnet.

"Jack Red Cloud," commented Yellow Bird. "Our Uncle will open his eyes at this. Ho!" He called toward the tipi behind us. "Come out, Uncle, and see who approaches."

Sitting Bull, who was within counciling with Crazy Horse, came to the tipi flap, peering intently. Behind him, closer than his shadow, moved Crazy Horse. Neither showed emotion as the young Sioux rode up, touching left hand to forehead and calling out the courtesy word. *Woyuonihan,* Uncle."

"*Hohahe,*" answered the imperturbable Hunkpapa. "Where is your father?"

"The old man has been to Washington and measured the big guns there with his fan. His heart is weak within him, like a sick squaw's. He says there will be only despair, no victory. He advises his people to cover their ears and sit still. But I am his own son and I would not listen to him. I would not listen to the old man. This day is a day for a young man. Sitting Bull's medicine is good. We rode away."

So came the son of the great Red Cloud to fight with the people his father had forgotten.

The Army made the mistake of delaying its "winter campaign," until May. The grass was not only up by then but tall. Ponies were fat. Pte, the buffalo, had come north. The Sioux were full of fresh meat and fight.

Many accounts have spoken of the ways in which the Army caught the Indians napping, outsmarting them time and again. To my knowledge the only times the Army surprised a red camp were the occasions of such shallow treacheries as Reynolds' unprovoked attack on Two Moons, where the Indians regarded themselves as known friendlies, never dreaming of being set upon by forces to which they had already surrendered.

At other times, such as that of the Yellowstone Expedition to the Rosebud, the Sioux knew every plan and disposition of the white soldiers.

We knew Terry had two columns in the field, one coming from Dakota, one from Montana. (I was strangely excited to learn from our scouts that Yellow Hair Custer and his pony-soldiers were with this command.) And that Crook was coming north from Wyoming with the third column. Our scouts estimated fifteen hundred men with Terry, a thousand with Crook, missing the actual count less than fifty men in each case. All three columns were converging on the Big Bend of the Rosebud.

We knew their basic orders as well as they.

"Find Sitting Bull and Crazy Horse, destroy the camps and horses of their hostiles, so bring the Sioux to surrender."

Two months earlier there would have been little question of such a campaign's success. Now there was no doubt of its failure. But the Army had taken off its kid gloves.

Gone were such bureau-born idiocies as the non-employment of red man against red man. Chief Gall, third in power to Sitting Bull and Crazy Horse, and entrusted with covering the approach of Crook from the south, reported Three Stars had 250 Crow and Shoshone scouts under the great Shoshone chief, Washakie. Over Washakie, as chief of all scouts, red and white, was Sitting-with-Upraised-Hands, Grouard the Grabber.

This report upset the red command more than Crook and Terry put together. All white boasting to the contrary, the Indians never feared the Army troops. They rode circles around them, shot hell out of them, rode off home when they were tired. Their casualties never amounted to more than one or two men out of a hundred. But their fellow red men, armed with Army carbines loaded with new copper cartridges, were something else again.

Those Shoshone, under Washakie, narrowed the slant gaze of Crazy Horse more than any other report we got in. "You will see," he told me, simply, "they will be very bad for us."

"Very bad," proved mild description indeed for what they were for us when the time came.

Gall also reported Crook had parked his wagons far up the Tongue, mounting his whole outfit on mules again. "Even the walk-a-heaps are thus riding," the famed chief informed us, "and they look as stupid as the flop-eared ones they ride." Crazy Horse at once ordered me to take over the scouting detail from Gall.

It was mid-May when Crook reached the headwaters of the Rosebud. From his movements followed by Little Wolf and me, together with ten Cheyenne trackers, it was clear he did not regard himself as being under surveillance.

Now, in the gray dawn of May 16th, we judged from the bustle of activity in his camp that he was readying his attack. Apparently he planned following on down the Rosebud to take our village by surprise. And so he might have done, too. Except that our ponies were very fast and we were awake earlier than he. We rode the twenty miles to camp at a yellow-lather gallop.

Five miles from the lodges the whole pack of Cheyenne riding with me set up a wild clamoring of wolf howls, the ages-old alarm signal of their tribe. As we came down on the camp I could hear answering wolf howling within it. I made my report to Crazy Horse, that, "The whole valley of the Rosebud is swarming as black with soldiers as a buffalo wallow with flies in the dog-sun."

In the following council I was to know the Indian military mind opened wide and laid bare to the incredibly hard red skull. It was a frustrating experience. No two chiefs saw the problem alike and none of them, not excepting Crazy Horse and Sitting Bull, had any conception of a true military viewpoint.

We knew where Crook was, his strength, where he had to go. We had as many men as he, better fighters, and over half of them armed with modern breechloading carbines. We had superior mobility, knowledge of the terrain, and the most valuable of all advantages, choice of time and place of attack.

Result: the decision to move en masse up the valley, meeting Crook head-on, when, as, and where, we might contact him—or he, us.

It would have been the simplest thing in the world to outflank him, take him in three-pronged ambush, with the main force coming down on his rear in two groups. I argued this course, saying it could be done yet today, while there was still time to catch Crook where we wanted him—in the open, on the move, tired from the day's march. Failing this, we could hit his camp half an hour before sun-up the following day, with his mules on picket, his carbines stacked, his men fogged with sleep.

But no. First there must be the big ceremony of painting and arming. Then the great parade around the camp so that all the squaws might gawk and faint over the splendors of their men. When all this falderol had been gloriously brought off, time enough to ride out hell-for-halter-rope and smite Three Stars for once and all.

This nonsensical view was traceable to the ineradicable Indian weakness for "counting coups." In their early days, the Sioux fought hand-to-hand, having nothing to outrange a lance or club in getting to any enemy. Hence all their warrior tradition came down in a vein of "body contact." The bravest warrior was the one who got in the closest, actually laying his hand-weapon on the greatest number of the foe. The advent of the bow and rifle, far from changing this concept, cemented it. The Sioux took no pride in killing an enemy with arrow or ball. Too easy. But the added danger created by these weapons in the hands of the enemy immeasurably enhanced the risk, hence the fun, hence the honor, of counting coups.

Then again the Indian had no idea of defeating an enemy in pitched battle the way a white man does. The Sioux in this case had no thought of wiping out Crook's command, which they certainly could have done, but figured only in terms of how many coups might be counted before the battle was over; which meant before the Indians got tired, or figured they had gotten enough scalps, and rode away to get on with the really important business of the victory dance.

The true picture of their concept of war can be most simply gained from the fact their casualties seldom ran over one or two per cent. What might be a big fight and a notable victory to a bunch of Sioux would be a routine patrol skirmish to any effective white cavalry outfit.

The Army surely acted at all times as though it were playing at "bluecoats-and-redskins," while with the Indians such an attitude was no act. They really were playing. War was a game. A hell of a lot of fun, sure. But as soon as the other side began to get too rough, you picked up your marbles and went home.

This childish outlook was hammered down my gullet by chief after chief the day of that council. Nothing would have it but that the whole swarming horde would ride up the valley next morning and lift the hair off a couple of hundred of Crook's boys, before knocking off for lunch.

Disgusted, I stomped out of their midst, realizing what was going to happen when they tried their wild and woolly tactics on Crook's tough regulars.

Well, I've been more wrong—many times. But for the life of me I can't recall one of them. My Sioux damn near murdered Crook and his entire command. Only the thing Crazy Horse had worried about to me prevented a wholesale slaughter; Washakie and his Shoshone scouts.

I FINALLY prevailed on Crazy Horse, who was in full command (Sitting Bull, as usual, sitting safe in his tipi), to take our forces down through the Wolf Mountains under cover of dark that night, rather than wait for daylight to prance up the valley on dress parade.

I got another point across. Fox soldiers were thrown out in front of the main body to see that no coup-crazy brave or bunch of them sneaked off ahead of us to spoil the surprise.

When we were about a mile from where I figured Crook to be, I went ahead accompanied by Little Wolf, Elk Nation and Yellow Bird. Ahead of us on the west side of the river rose a commanding hill, the highest for miles. I calculated there was a good chance Crook might be on the other side of it.

I calculated right.

When the four of us wormed our way over that hilltop we looked down on a sight to uncover the canines of any Sioux or Cheyenne. There was Crook and his command all right—every horse and mule in the outfit, unbridled and grazing, spread on both sides of the rosebud. The men were lying around on the ground resting.

"Look, by the spring down there," gloated Yellow Bird. "Old Three Stars still braiding his beard."

Sure enough, there was Crook taking his ease alongside a beautiful little spring, carefully plaiting his long beard into twin queues while an orderly held up a polished frying pan the better for the general to admire the effect.

"He wears his tent as usual," commented Little Wolf, referring to Crook's canvas fatigue suit, a sort of cover-all garment looking as much like Little Wolf's simple description as anything else.

"The troops have eaten," observed Elk Nation, pointing out the cooks at work washing utensils in the stream. "This is well, for it is said a man dies happiest over a full paunch."

"If we can get our people up here without discovery," I

interrupted, bringing the discussion back onto hard ground, "there won't be a pony-soldier left alive by sunset."

"*Hopo,* let's go," growled Little Wolf.

Slipping down behind the ridge we ran for our horses. As we came up to them, Elk Nation's pony threw up his head, flicked his ears upward and behind us, whickered challengingly. At the same time a shot cracked out and Elk Nation pitched over a steep ledge, his body tumbling and sliding down the hill like a wet sack of feed.

I dropped, throwing myself sideways and slapping the Colts out as I went. Coming up out of the dirt, I saw silhouetted above us atop the ridge we had just quitted, the figures of four Indians. Three of them flashed down out of sight but I fired five shots from my right-hand gun before the other could get out from against the sky.

His horse came cascading down our side of the ridge, hit through the body, bearing his wounded rider with him. The dying animal plunged into a mass of rocks ten feet from where I stood. When the Indian staggered up and away, I shot him twice through. He slid down the remainder of the slope, the body coming to rest at my feet. It was that of a Shoshone Army scout.

As this action went on, Little Wolf and Yellow Bird had fanned their ponies up and around the hill and down the other side, hot on the haunches of the other scouts. I could hear their wild firing now. And more. Down behind me a great roar went up. Across the Rosebud, shattering the line of Fox Soldiers, screaming up the hill toward me, came our thousand Sioux, only a hundred or so Cheyenne among them.

Washakie's damn scouts had ruined our surprise party right. They were to shorten our lances in a worse way yet, though, before the day was out.

The Sioux had three or four miles to cover to Crook's camp, giving him time to "Boots-and-Saddles" his command into something like readiness. I threw my pony in alongside Crazy Horse's black stallion as the Oglala chief swept by me at the head of his howling Bad Faces. "*H'g-un! H'g-un!*" he shouted, his handsome face contorted like that of a snarling animal.

"*Hookahey!*" I screamed back, as our ponies went over the rise and down the long two-mile roll to Crook's position below.

Around me rose and fell the most ungodly bedlam imaginable. In my immediate field were three hundred Oglala,

149

superbly mounted and armed. Their ponies were going two jumps above top speed down a grade that ordinarily would have been slid down at a careful walk. Man and beast were feathered and painted up hideously and while the horses neighed and whinnied crazily their riders bombarded the open sky above with a nerve-rupturing cacophony of whoops and screams. On every side and behind us came more and more warriors, till the immense flat of the hillside seemed covered with twisting red bodies.

As we rushed down I got the picture of Crook's defenses. On our side of the river were two cavalry battalions and the mule-mounted infantry group, beyond the stream another two battalions of cavalry. Commanding one of the cross-stream groups, I could see the tall figure of Captain Anson Mills, but the other officers were strangers to me.

Crook managed to get a number of his troops into the bluffs north of the river before we could get down to prevent it. Mills spearheaded this move. From their position these troops had a field of fire which enfiladed our advance, breaking it up and forcing our momentary retreat. Crazy Horse then took command of the sector, trying with repeated suicide charges to knock Mills lose. He wouldn't knock. He had a sound position and held it. We took heavy casualties there.

I yelled to Crazy Horse that we should leave these troops there, concentrating on preventing the others from joining them. He shouted back agreement, sweeping downstream to take the battalions of Van Vliet and Henry on the flank. Fronted as they were by Gall, Hump and Little Wolf, held on the opposite flank by Yellow Bird, Jack Red Cloud and American Horse, these commands began to break up. In a matter of minutes their demoralization became complete.

The Indians were spreading through them like prairie fire, riding and fighting in their beloved every-man-for-himself-and-an-arrow-in-the-butt-for-the-hindmost style. In this tactic they were incomparable, the troops stampeding badly, standing for a few minutes in danger of a wipe-out.

Indians were everywhere, riding down the cavalrymen by sheer force, deliberately colliding horse with horse, lancing, stabbing, clubbing. Wherever a trooper was knocked off his horse, three Sioux were on him before he hit the ground, their knives and war axes flashing.

Time and again I saw an unhorsed white rider seized and held while his arm was severed at the elbow before he was shot through the gut and left to "die slow." This was the Cheyenne trademark, this arm amputation, their Indian sign language name being literally, "Cut Arms." The Sioux had their own butcher's stamp, its character again best described by their eloquent tribal symbol, "Cut Throats."

It is only logical to wonder with what conscience I rode into this battle. The answer is, "To begin with, none."

My four years in the War between the States had seen plenty of white brothers killed. And in all ways: in groups by shell-burst, in windrows by sweeping rifle fire, and in single combat, hand-to-hand knife, bayonet and clubbed-rifle fighting. Coming into this battle was, at first, no different to me than riding up Cemetery Ridge or Massanutten Mountain into the throats of the Union artillery or caving in the Yankee flank at Chickamauga.

But when the mutilation began my Indian blood thinned rapidly. For the first time in fifteen years of fighting I had no answer to the questions which must pound at every man's mind when the battle grows desperate: "Why am I here? Who am I serving? For what am I about to die?"

God knows I could not plead innocence at this late hour. I had been with the Sioux nine years. I had seen and helped them in fights which resulted in the deaths of white men during that time. I was with High-Back-Bone, Big Crow and American Horse when the Army's Captain Powell handed us one of our few lickings, in the Wagon Box Fight.

White men had died that day and I had pulled down on my share of them. I had been visiting south with the Cheyenne when they trapped the buffalo hunters at Adobe Walls, and again when they themselves were trapped and routed in Palo Duro Canyon. True, I had killed no whites there, but I had been ready to.

No, I could not plead innocence. I had been an Indian for nine years. What matter that those nine years had been years of "official peace" on the frontier? That in my whole time with the Sioux no formal war had been going on with the whites?

I might claim that shaky peace as an excuse but I will not. During that time isolated settlers, freighters and emigrants had been burnt-out, shot, scalped. Irregular brushes with the cavalry had occurred. Troopers had died. If I hadn't killed them I had been with those who did.

About all I could say up to the moment I found myself in the Battle of the Rosebud, was that I had never shot a mother or child or scalped a husband and father. Still I ran with the red men and some of the color had rubbed off on me. I was an Indian. An Oglala Bad Face Sioux. Signed and sealed

"Cetan Mani" on more than one Government treaty to prove it.

But here and now, with these terrified, sweating, chalk-faced men of my own repudiated race being gutted and dismembered alive, began the retching wave of shame and remorse which seven suns later rose up in nausea to vomit me out forever from my adopted people.

At the same time I was in the vortex of two thousand battling humans.

Remorse was no weapon with which to cut my way out. As well as I could, I refrained from killing as I tried to force my way out of the rolling dust and constant charging and counter-charging of the mêlée. But again and again a trooper would loom before me, his carbine or saber aiming for my Sioux scalplock. Again and again the Colts in my hands would jump.

When I could I shot the horse. When I couldn't I tried to ride-off the trooper without shooting. Yet there were times when my lead went home, sending some brave boy or hard-case sergeant sliding groundward to lie luckily among the dead—for when I had to shoot, I shot to kill. I wanted no injured on my conscience, no thought I had sent a brother white to die under the scalping knives of the Sioux and Cheyenne.

Yet there can be no washing of that day's blood from my hands. You cannot handle guns the years I have and not know when your shots hit home.

When I was almost out of the fighting a sudden hostile charge carried me back in. Crook's whole line faltered and broke. Only Vroom's command held the center. It was soon cut off completely. Captain Henry led a counter-charge which succeeded in reaching and relieving Vroom. Henry fell back, covering Vroom's retreat, riding at the rear of his troops, facing the eagerly following Sioux. His courage in this was so rash, his luck in escaping injury so miraculous, his command began to rally strongly and would in another minute have gone over to the attack.

At my elbow I heard a familiar bass voice. "A-ah! Cetan. That one must go down. *Hookahey,* come on!"

Turning, I beheld Crazy Horse, face and body streaming dirt, sweat, blood. He gestured wildly toward Captain Henry. I kicked my pony behind his into the charge.

The Sioux chief drove his black stud squarely into Henry's backing, whirling mount. Henry fired his carbine twice, then clubbed it to swing on the Indian. The Oglala came in under the upraised weapon, literally throwing his six-gun up into the white man's face. At the report of the revolver the whole lower half of Captain Henry's face, below the eyes, seemed to melt away. One moment there was a face, the next a bloody, nameless maw.

I had no time to see if Henry rode on or fell, for his clubbed rifle had completed its swing at the moment the Colt blast took him in the face, knocking Crazy Horse as cleanly from the back of his rearing horse as you might knock a possum out of a 'simmon tree with a spade-handle. He hit the ground like a rock and I went diving after him. Running to him, I stood astraddle his body to face the three troopers who were riding up fast, apparently with the idea of finishing off the fallen chief.

I levered the Winchester from the hip, managing to get all three horses down without hitting the riders. The three soldiers, young and white-scared but full of fight, came rolling up out of the dust of their collapsed mounts, unharmed.

Behind me I heard a burst of wolf howls topped by the unmistakable baritone voice of Yellow Bird. *"H'g-un, Cetan! We are coming!"*

I leaped toward the three white boys, waving my Colts, screaming hoarsely and crazily. "Get the hell out of here, you damn fools. Don't just stand there with your Yankee tongues hanging out. Run!"

Their looks of amazement at these English words bursting out of a naked Sioux were ludicrous. But ludicrous looks or no, they beat Yellow Bird's scalp-collectors back to their lines.

I got a leg-up behind Yellow Bird who ran me alongside Crazy Horse's big black stud which was still galloping loose. Swinging aboard the black I wheeled him in time to see the stricken Captain Henry succumb to shock. The following Sioux, seeing him hit the ground and sensing the fall of a leader who had been keying the resistance, swept in to finish him.

The troops scattered and broke before their insane charge. Henry's still form lay unprotected.

At this moment, with Crook's line shredded on both flanks, his center chewed to pieces and being held waveringly by Henry's staggering command alone, the Sioux had a tremendous victory in sight. When Henry went down the whole hostile front rolled irresistibly forward. A general massacre of Crook's outfit loomed.

Into this juicy prospect lanced a brave bolt of friendly red lightning. Washakie, the Shoshone chief, stood on a hill blanking the surge of the Sioux advance. Behind him ranged his Crow and Shoshone scouts. They had been driven to this retreat by the Sioux under Gall only minutes before. They had fought hard and taken many casualties. Now they were safely, honorably out of the fight.

But Washakie saw Henry go down, saw the Sioux surge forward to get at his body.

Alligator-Stands-Up yelled happily across his Crows to their chief, Plenty Coups. "Come on. Let's go. Everybody wants to go!"

But Plenty Coups was already gone, the Shoshone and Crow yelping after him. They struck the seesawing struggle as the Sioux reached Henry.

The hostile ranks, surprised and hard hit on an unprotected flank, broke. Washakie went in at the head of his braves, Plenty Coups and the Crow right behind. They made a hollow square around Henry, the hot fire from their new Army carbines driving the Sioux backward. This was Indian fighting. In no way does the warrior so love to show his bravery as in the rescue of a wounded, fallen comrade. Henry's situation was the kind of thing they understood. To save him from the Sioux was far more important than winning or losing the battle.

In the lull their attack created in the Sioux advance, the troops of Captain Vroom and Royall were able to organize a counter-advance. They drove the foremost Sioux, my own Oglala, back across the spot where Henry fell, retrieved the unconscious form of the captain, even held his hard-won position for a time.

But Crazy Horse was back in the fight now, recovered from his knockdown, refreshed and remounted. He was intensely humiliated at being bested by Henry in personal combat, furious at his warriors' failure to kill the fallen captain, raving mad over Washakie's successful diversion. He was the Sioux' best soldier. He had seen an epic victory snatched from his grasp by 250 enemy scouts. He knew he had lost a great moment while he lay unconscious.

Now he came back with murder in his heart.

The troops could not withstand his assault. Once more they broke and this time they stayed broken. Back across the Rosebud fled the pony-soldiers, our hostiles shooting, stabbing, clubbing among them at hand's length. We held the west bank of the river clean and free.

Crazy Horse called up the head chiefs.

The Oglala, still mad, still burning from humiliation, still sensing a possible victory, wanted to cross the stream at once, tackling Crook in the north bluffs. The others, having been over there earlier in the morning getting a memorable taste of the general's lead in their bellies, were not so eager. They had already achieved a fine victory over the bluecoats. The light was failing. Perhaps it was time to hit the home trail. To light up the victory fires, start the drums for the celebration.

While Crazy Horse harangued them I held my silence. I too had my belly full and wanted to go home, but the lead which lay in my gut was of a different kind than that which weighted the paunches of the chiefs. In my belly was the lead of remorse, the sickness of self-hate. I knew I would never again ride and fight with the red hostiles.

Over the Valley of the Rosebud settled a quiet broken only by the shouting and arguing of the chiefs.

Without warning, a heavy rifle fire broke on our north flank—behind us—from the hills out of which we had just pushed "all" of Crook's men. We were amazed to see a big column—I counted eight troops of cavalry—pouring down upon us from a direction where "there couldn't be any white troops." Nevertheless, there they were, with the ubiquitous Anson Mills riding in command.[*]

I looked at Crazy Horse, seeing doubt in his dark eyes for the first time. *"Hopo,"* I said. "Come on. Let's get out of here."

"Hopo! Hopo! Hookahey!" chorused the others, nervous ponies edging away as they spoke. Still the war chief hesitated.

"We have won. We are tired. Let's go along," stated Hump.

"It is late. It grows dark," seconded Bob-Tail-Horse.

"We can come back and get these others in the morning," suggested Gall.

"It is time for the dance."

"My ammunition is gone."

"My pony is lame."

"Our medicine grows weak."

---

[*]We found later that Crook had sent Mills to destroy our village, which he supposed to lie only a few miles down the canyon, hoping by this maneuver to draw most of the warriors off his own neck. Mills found no village, naturally, since it was fifteen miles away, and in returning he had cut across country to hit us in the rear. This was his own hard-hitting idea—not in his orders from Crook.

"See! Yonder comes Washakie and his Shoshone dogs again."

"Ay-eee!" I caught Yellow Bird's bull-bellow above the excited exclamations of his fellows. "Let's stay and kill the stinking curs!"

"No, no, let's go."

"Aye."

"Aye."

"Let's all go!"

Listening to this babble of disorganized shouting, I knew Crazy Horse had lost. Today was done. There would be no tomorrow. The fight had gone out of his braves.

Some of the same thoughts were passing in the war chief's mind, for with a quick pivot of his pony he threw his rifle up, firing a string of four shots, the Sioux and Cheyenne "good medicine" number. There had been enough. The battle was over. Their medicine had been good. Time to go home.

"Hookahey!" shouted Crazy Horse.

"Hookahey!" echoed the crowding chiefs, no single shout carrying more conviction than that of Crazy Horse's only son, Hawk-That-Walks-Like-a-Man.

Southward up the Valley of the Rosebud streamed the Sioux. Swinging in a wide circle behind Crook's position we headed northward for home, the Sioux looping long rifle shots and screaming insults at the whites as they rode by. Mills showed no disposition to follow up his flanking move, I suspect under hurried orders from Crook, for I knew Mills and he would certainly have come after us.

But Crook had had enough. Throughout the long hours of darkness, huge watchfires burned along the Rosebud and no white man slept on its banks that night—save those who would sleep there forever.

With dawn, Crook returned out of the Rosebud all the way back to Goose Creek, where he holed up and stayed. Captain Mills reckoned their forces had been "humiliatingly defeated and were lucky not to have been entirely vanquished."

I share his views but where twenty-four hours previous I had been bitter and angry because the Sioux would not listen to my tactical suggestions, I now thanked God they had not. Following even the simplest order of organized battle plan such as mine, the Sioux would have wiped Crook's outfit clean off the face of the prairie. As it was, their own harum-scarum assault, plus Washakie's Shoshone, plus leather-tough

Anson Mills, robbed them of any such blood bath and kept me from twisting forever on the spit of responsibility.

The news of Crook's retreat came days later, by scout, for the same night which saw his command sitting up wide-eyed by the watchfires, saw all the Sioux he was worrying about, drumming and dancing fifteen miles to the north.

The only Indians to prevent his command from walking peacefully away down the Rosebud were four second-rate young apprentice warriors detailed by Crazy Horse to keep an eye on Three Stars. Even these four upstarts grumbled that such was "squaw's work" and that, if Crazy Horse would leave them one good man—Yellow Bird volunteered at once—they would go down and run the Beard-Braider back to Fort Fetterman.

The Oglala chief had no mood or time for such histrionics. Already his warrior's mind was out-traveling his tired, stumbling pony. Custer and Terry and Red Nose Gibbon still hung in the east. Three Stars had been defeated but the vision of Sitting Bull had promised "hundreds of American soldiers all dropping suddenly dead around his feet." Crook's casualties had been considerable but by no means had hundreds dropped dead. The Rosebud was not the Hunkpapa's dream. There would be another great fight.

Little Wolf rode back to me, bringing a summons from my "father." When I came up to him, Crazy Horse spoke of Sitting Bull's vision, stressing the fact that today's battle did not fit it. His final words, coming on top of the deepening foreboding in my own heart that my days among his people were numbered, found me too dispirited to do other than nod dull assent.

"Tonight, with fresh ponies from the village, we shall ride north, you and I. Uncle must know of this fight from my own mouth. Something is wrong here. My heart is bad."

Chapter 6

WHEN we reached our village on the headwaters of Beaver Creek, Crazy Horse altered his plan. Unknown to me, Sitting Bull had pulled out for the rendezvous on the banks of the Greasy Grass at the time we were riding to meet Crook. The war chief had known this but had thought it better to say nothing about it before the battle. Now he gave me his new orders.

He would ride on alone to council with Tatanka Yotanka, the tribes would strike their lodges, moving at once to follow him. As his second-in-command I would head them. It was a great honor but I suspected it fell to me because he could not trust any of his warriors to carry out his orders without substantial embellishments of their own.

However, nothing could have pleased me more. I had the old "Indian hunch" working full tilt by the time we approached the tipis, the burden of its message being that the Sioux and Cheyenne were heading for disaster.

I knew nothing of Terry and Gibbon, though both were Indian fighters of reputation. But I knew Custer personally, was thoroughly familiar with his record in the War between the States, and I had followed his Indian campaigns with close interest. I had sat in council with him, talked with many Indians who had been in the field against him, had been in at least two Indian camps as a "visitor" while Yellow Hair was on their trail. I knew the inside facts of his fall from President Grant's grace, a fall, incidentally, more honorable than most promotions.

Much has been written of him, much more will be. But few men knew him as I did, from both sides of the fence. My opinion is that he was intellectually brilliant, personally warm, friendly, string-straight and professionally tough.

Thinking now as a professional soldier myself, no officer the Army had could run a dead-heat with his frontier record let alone finish in front of it. He was certainly the Crazy Horse of the U. S. Cavalry. And very, very dangerous.

The thought of him hovering now to our east in part command of two thousand men and full command of his own hard-boiled Seventh Cavalry kept my hunch working overtime. This prescience warned only of disaster, a simple premonition without details. In mentally balancing "the Sioux against the Seventh," the scales came down heavily on Custer's side. It never occurred to me that disaster is a double-headed dragon.

I thought to speak of my fears to Crazy Horse, then thought again. Profound changes had taken place in him following the Rosebud clash. He showed none of the high elation so common to the red warrior after any humbling of the hated white troops. Clearly he was in one of his "black vision moods," the mystic in him holding quirt-hand over the fighter.

At the same time my own mood plunged lower with every homeward step of the ponies. I could not know whether he had noted my behavior in the fight or his odd clairvoyance was warning him against me, but his parting words as we stood outside of the Village prior to his departure for Sitting Bull's camp, showed one or the other factor at work within him.

"Cetan, I think we have fought our last fight together. My heart lies in my belly like a cannonball. Let us say goodbye and then no more of it."

Not knowing what he meant, not daring to probe, I answered him in like generality. "I have seen what my father has seen. My heart is heavier than his." We shook hands white-man fashion, parting without another word.

I went back to our tipi but for once Star could not soothe me. We lay quietly close in the dark of the lodge, I feeling the young life in her jump and struggle as I held her, she saying no word, her slender arms around me, her slim hands caressing me with cool slowness.

I turned restlessly. What good the coming of this only child of mine, now? What joy this beautiful creature, his mother, who lay beside me carrying within her the final proof of my allegiance to her kind? Where all the blessings of our promised free life on the plains? What had become of my dreams for these red people? How had I ever seen any future for them but the calamitous one that loomed now? Had I ever thought really to be an Oglala brave? A Sioux war chief? A son to Crazy Horse? What sense was there to the death of Slatemeyer? To my wild love for an incredibly beautiful Indian medicine woman? To my part in the endless councils and clashes with the Army?

It seemed after nine years visiting among a strange alien race, my mind had gone home to my own people. I saw again the broad savannahs of my native state, heard again the roar of Union artillery, the angry crack of Rebel rifles, the ringing clash of saber steel. The dark air of the tipi was suddenly warm, redolent of magnolia and night-blooming jasmine. Lovely women in white floating gowns and wide Dixie bonnets drifted in with the fragrance. The sound of southern voices, ice in tall glasses, polished compliments softly drawled, whispered at me tauntingly.

Then there was Lee, his beloved face ruddy in the sad light of that last fire in Appomattox Wood. There was gentle

John B. Gordon, fiery Fitzhugh Lee—and Yellow Hair riding up from the Union lines. . . . The vision of Custer must have brought me back, for I awoke.

Through the open tipi flap the morning star rested low over a shoulder of the Wolf Mountains. Dawn was not an hour away.

"Peace, Cetan." The voice beside me was softer than any southern belle's. "You have slept with much muttering and turning. Strange words have sprung from you and you have been restless in my arms these many hours."

"You haven't slept?"

"How may I when my warrior wanders the nightlands? And beside, your son is restless, too. He butts like a two-headed buffalo calf sucking at a dry cow."

I took her in my arms then and for a brief cool dawn-hour all the old peace and beauty of her stole into me. Come Custer, come calamity, come anything in God's power, I knew for all time my heart and soul belonged to this Indian girl.

Chapter 7

THE PROBLEM of being grand marshal for a dress parade of two thousand Sioux, five miles long, is one well calculated to take any man's mind off his troubles. The next three days of our travel to the Greasy Grass were among the most exciting, perhaps almost the happiest, I had known.

Yellow Bird burst into our tipi with the sun, indignant as a male dog with a strange nose under his tail. "By Pte's tassel, they'll not have it so!" he shouted. "I'll not eat the dust of any Cheyenne."

Questioning revealed the chiefs of the allied tribes were up early, wrangling over the order of the march. Dull Knife, the top Cheyenne, was adamant. His people would march first. It was courtesy rules. Gall and High-Hump-Back would not see it. Who had twisted Three Star's braids? Who had carried home the most scalps? Whose dead were in the greatest number? Aha! Of course, the Sioux. That was settled. That was easy. But getting into the finer points of protocol, who among the Sioux had precedence? The Hunkpapa, naturally. Had not Sitting Bull ordered this fight?

Ha! The Hunkpapa? Never! Who had struck down Henry? Who had run the pony-soldiers across the Rosebud? Not Sitting Bull, for sure. He had been moving safely to the Greasy Grass even as the fight ran hottest. He had not even waited in camp to hear the news. The Hunkpapa! Very funny. Crazy Horse had won that fight. His Oglala would make the dust for the others to hide in—this, that their shortcomings as men and warriors might not be so apparent.

By strict convention, Dull Knife was right. By the courtesy code his people should lead. But I had eight times as many Sioux as Cheyenne on my hands. It was a time for dainty treading.

"Yellow Bird, is there any question who are the greatest?"

"None, the Sioux of course."

"Very well then. Who does the work of the march?"

"Squaws, naturally."

"Fine. Will the Sioux then argue like squaws as to who shall ride first in a thing which is squaw's work in the first place?"

"Never."

"Who shall ride first, then?"

"The Sioux, of course."

I could see we had missed connections somewhere. Another tack was in order.

"Very well. And suppose Three Stars tricks us, coming up behind while we travel? Will the Sioux then be able to explain to Dull Knife why they ride where the safety is? Do you want Hump and Little Wolf to fight your battles?"

"Not while I breathe."

"Who rides first, then?"

"The Cut Arms. It could never be any other way. Surely you can see that, Cetan? How could it be otherwise?"

"You are right, Yellow Bird. Your mind is clear as a trout's eye. It is a wonder I had not seen you were right all along."

"You are sometimes very ignorant, Cetan."

"It is the price of my inferior blood. We are agreed then?"

"Aye."

"You will so give the order, then? Cheyenne in front, Oglala and Hunkpapa in the rear, where the danger is."

"Good. I'll go and tell the dogs right now. We ride in their rear to protect them from Three Stars."

It was time to pull still a little more sail. I laughed. "Yellow Bird is the best joker of them all. He would never tell the Cheyenne what he has just said, for he is too clever. But it makes a good laugh, eh? But if they thought danger threatened they would run away, making even more dust for the rest of us."

"Of course." He grinned, after searching my eyes a dubious moment. "You know, Cetan, not everyone appreciates my qualities as you do."

"You are a born chief. We are agreed, then?"

"Naturally. *Hopo,* let's go."

That trip to the Little Big Horn was the sort of thing I had read of as a boy in the fascinating journal of Father De Smet, even then, though bug-eyed with interest, clucking in disbelief. It made great reading but anyone could see it was spiked and re-spiked with the uncut pepper of the author's imagination.

It was June 19th. Early summer hung like a blue benediction over the lazy sweep of the plains. Our course lay through the finest of all the prairie uplands, leading in a graceful westward semicircle through the northern foothills of the Wolves. The grass was thick and fat everywhere, standing up to a tall pony's belly in its waving endlessness. Groves of towering cottonwood and clustering willow, burgeoning with the first thick summer green, flanked the splashing waterways as far as the eye could follow. The surrounding hills and mesas were covered with fragrant growths of conifers, intermingled with alder, birch, aspen, oak and sycamore. And always, behind and above everything, there were the mountains—the distant "Shining Mountains," of De Smet's pioneers—the lofty, snow-shrouded Big Horns.

Through this paradise my Sioux moved with all the dignity and sureness of hereditary owners. What a pageant of color they presented!

From Dull Knife, fronting his Cheyenne in the lead, to Yellow Bird in charge of the Fox Lodge police flanking and tailing the line of march, the body of the caravan stretched a long five miles.

First came the warriors mounted on the best ponies, flaunting aloft their gayest lance-pennons, arrogantly proud in their heron and eagle feathers. Next, the vast concourse of pack animals and travois ponies, heaped and loaded with the camp paraphernalia, tipi skins, lodgepoles, robes, blankets, dried buffalo beef, cooking utensils, spare weapons, hides, furs, and all the endless personal trivia of a nomad people.

Among and on these animals, walked and rode the squaws, old people and children.

Last came the immense pony herd, nearly three thousand wall-eyed, dish-faced, pot-bellied, squealing, kicking Indian ponies: bays, blacks, grays, chestnuts, piebalds, roans, whites, buckskins, apoloosies, line-back duns; a shifting, wheeling, crazy palette of every color in horsedom.

Shot through and through the length of the column, skirting it, leading it, following it, flanking it, trotted the yapping, bickering hords of Indian curs. It was a sight dustier, dirtier, noisier and wilder than anything I'd read in the journals of De Smet or Marcus Whitman. My humble apologies to those old plainsmen. Their prose, far from being overpainted, lagged short of the colors of reality presented by these naked, feathered savages.

The second day out, Little Wolf, whom I had ordered ahead to scout our foretrail, rode in with news. He had spotted an immense buffalo herd four hours ahead. If it were remotely possible that Cetan Mani might consider a hunt the column must be halted at once. For Pte, slow and stupid as he was, could hardly be expected to stand still for the clamorous approach of several thousand dogs, horses, and Indians.

I had no interest in this hunt but even less in the rendezvous which lay ahead on the Greasy Grass. Accordingly, much to the delighted surprise of my warriors, I ordered the march to bring up.

The men were immediately wild with excitement. They had thought to get a refusal, my ready acceptance taking them happily off guard. An Indian will interrupt anything to go off on a buffalo hunt. As to Crazy Horse's orders or Sitting Bull's vision—well, they would wait. Pte wouldn't.

The hunt was a good one. By late afternoon we had made our kill, the vast herd moving about six miles during the shoot. Now the tens of thousands which composed the herd were far to the south, the dust of their going hanging thick and high on the rim of the prairie.* The grasslands back over

---

*This was one of the last great herds I saw. I estimated it to number close to 200,000 animals, for it took the group which rode around to get on its far side three hours to get there, their ponies going at a lope. I remained with the group on the near side of the herd, passing the waiting time in fascinated observation of the brutes.

It was the opening of their mating season, the whole herd being in a turmoil from the bellowings and clashings of the enraged bulls fighting off the fury of the rut.

Everywhere across the unbroken miles of their black bodies, the huge-maned

the course of our run were liberally sprinkled with the lumpy black splotches of buffalo carcasses. The Colts in their holsters at my thighs, the Winchester in its scabbard under my knee, were still hot with their half-hour's hard handling.

I don't rightly know how many animals I downed on that last buffalo hunt with the Sioux, but I used up three ponies and four belts of ammunition. And on certain record skins of Crazy Horse's Oglala will be found pictographs of a very tall, bowlegged hawk, armed with two short guns, surrounded by heaps of Pte's defunct relatives. Occasional oldsters, yarning of better days, will probably pop the shoe-button eyes of their grandchildren with lying tales of how, in the days of Tatanka Yotanka, a lone Oglala brave slew buffalo to the amount of *opawinge nunpa* in the space of a hundred breaths.

His name? Oh, Walking-Eagle, or Stalking-Hawk, something like that. No matter. He was a great warrior.

Well, even though I hadn't slain two hundred buffalo in five minutes, it had been a fine hunt. Now for the butchering and feasting.

The tribe, following along slowly after its halt to let the hunters find the herd, came up to us in time to join the cutting-of-meat. The Sioux skill in this was considerable. Four or five braves would seize on a carcass, rolling it up on its belly, the four legs spread out like braces beneath it to hold it upright. Then all the Indians around that particular animal would attack it like wolves.

First the huge skull would be caved in with an ax and the raw brains scooped out and passed around. With these devoured the formal butchering went forward. A knife was run down the line of the spine from neck to croup, the skin being flayed down to the belly on both sides and left to lie outspread on the ground as a receptacle for the meat cuts to come. The tongue and tenderloin came out first, frequently being eaten on the spot, raw. The squaws slit the beast's throat, draining the copious blood into prepared paunches brought along for the purpose. Other squaws cracked the bones and extracted the marrow—the Indian butter—placing this too in a paunch.

The two long strips of fat lying along either side of the

bulls were either struggling in skull-crashing battle or rearing up in the work of their gigantic couplings with the bawling cows.

The rank, wild-ox stench of their close-packed bodies carried powerfully to our hiding place, five miles off, cross wind. And constantly there were the hollow roarings and coughings of the bulls in action, the middle bawls of the old cows satisfiedly submitting to, or petulantly demanding, service, and the panicky tenor lowings of the heifers, vainly seeking to elude their manifest genital destiny.

spine were stripped out, smoked, dipped in tallow, hung up to cure. This delicacy formed "Indian bread." The hump and ribs were the favored red-meat cuts, these being taken to camp for boiling. The blood and marrow were mixed to create a thick soup of surpassing taste.

When the carcass had been butchered down, the squaws lit a small fire and collected "boudin sticks." The animal's viscera was opened, the "boudins," or small intestine, carefully extracted. These, full of blood and the pre-digested remains of the buffalo's last meal, were wound in long loops around the sticks and roasted instanter. With that done, the ponies were brought up, loaded with hides and meat, and headed back where the oldsters had meanwhile set up the lodges.

That night I attended my final Sioux buffalo barbecue. The gorging which took place was fantastic, the Indian belly-capacity being about four pounds more than that of a bull buffalo. The Sioux ate for hours, cramming themselves with baked tongue, boiled ribs, hump and sidemeat, broiled steaks, huge lengths of boudins, roasted, great greasy chunks of Indian bread, slabs of Sioux butter, raw strips of heart, liver, and kidney, and hors d'oeuvres of the uncooked, tender young testes of a bull calf or the sweetbreads of a yearling heifer, the whole menu being washed down with repeated gulping drafts of hot blood-soup.

I sat with Star on the sidelines, for neither of us was hungry. I, the excitement of the hunt having passed, our journey's end in sight for the next day, relapsed into the fitful depression which had hung upon me since the Rosebud; she, the young life surging painfully in her now, sank into that despair which seems to afflict first mothers. Her time was very near and the birth-fear was upon her.

With us sat Black Blanket, the faithful, silent wife of Crazy Horse, her mind, like mine, I knew, wandering ahead across the darkened plains where her husband sat in final council with Sitting Bull.

MY SIOUX horde straggled into the war camp on the Little Big Horn in the late afternoon of June 20th. We came up the west bank of the winding, shallow stream, the air being so still the towering clouds of our yellow dust rose straight up to hang over us in a choking, ochre pall. So long was the strung-out order of the march, the Cheyenne who led had their lodges pitched and the buffalo ribs simmering in the pots before the Hunkpapa and Oglala came into the campground. It was after dusk before I had all my tipis up, yet as the moon rose it looked over a city of skin houses as ordered and integrated as though it had sat there a thousand years.

The arrangement of the camp saw the Cheyenne camped farthest north, downstream, then the Sans Arc, Minniconjou and Oglala Sioux. At the south end of the camp, where a large slough had been formed in an old channel, clustered the tipis of the Hunkpapa, the Blackfoot Sioux, the Two Kettles and Santee. The camp was four miles long, containing something over two thousand tipis.

By the Indian rule-of-thumb of two warriors to a lodge this meant between four and five thousand men of battle age, at least three thousand of them mature, seasoned fighters. By the same rule of five inhabitants of all ages to a lodge there were no less than ten thousand Sioux and Cheyenne in that camp, by far the largest concourse of Indians I had ever seen.

While the lodges were going up I had my young men take our pony herds to water in the river, then drive them up to the heavy grass benches behind and west of the camp. The river flats north and south were already covered with the grazing thousands of the other pony herds.

As soon as all was in order I reported to Crazy Horse. I found Sitting Bull and him, together with Black Shield, Paints Brown, White Wolf, Mad Wolf and Lone Bull, hunkered down in front of Tatanka Yotanka's big red and black lodge. The Oglala bade me speak and I gave my accounting right there.

When they heard I had brought in two hundred ponies loaded with fresh buffalo meat their enthusiasm nearly skinned the hides off the lodge poles. The encampment by its size had scared all game away from the river so that fresh meat was an invaluable item.

For the next three days scouts came in with corrected information, almost hourly.

Terry's column, moving from Fort Abraham Lincoln, was very close, only a few suns away . . . Crook was still on Goose Creek, out of the fight . . . Gibbon's troops, coming from Fort Ellis, were closest of all . . . The other two commanders apparently didn't know that Three Stars was cut off and would not meet them. His messengers would not ride across the country where our warriors swarmed . . . Terry and Gibbon had made contact at the confluence of the Yellowstone and the Rosebud . . . Terry and Gibbon were waiting for Crook . . . Now Terry was coming, and great news, Yellow Hair Custer was with him . . . Major Reno had found the trail of Sitting Bull . . . Yes, it was the true trail of our village. They would find us now . . . General Custer, Terry and Red Nose Gibbon, were going aboard the fireboat-that-walks-on-water (the Army supply steamer, *Far West*) . . . They were in a big conference . . . Now big things were beginning to be . . . This very afternoon (June 22nd), Yellow Hair and his pony-soldiers set out on the trail of our village . . . Many of the troops looked very young. (This was a surprise. Later we knew forty per cent of his troopers had never shot at an Indian before.) . . . Yellow Hair had soldiers to the number of six hundred . . . Major Reno, who had found our trail, was with him . . . Yellow Hair was traveling very fast, he was getting close, he was heading for the Little Big Horn thirty miles upstream of our camp . . . Red Nose was at the mouth of the Little Big Horn, downstream of the camp. Both were four suns away. It was clear what Star Terry had ordered . . . Red Nose to come upstream, Yellow Hair, down . . . Between them lay our war camp.

During these high-tension days my mental state may easily be imagined. It was clear in my mind, had been since the Rosebud battle, that I could not go into another fight on the Sioux side. Yet look at my situation:

Nine years with the Indians. A full chief in the highest war councils. A ranking brave in the Fox Lodge police society. A son and constant associate of the number one Sioux bad man, Crazy Horse. A known hostile to the U. S. Government, my name on three treaties, my face familiar to every commander on the frontier. Married to a famous Sioux medicine woman. And carrying, among white settlers, Army personnel and reservation redmen alike, the reputation of a bad Indian.

Up until the Rosebud the "bad" part of that rating had been unwarranted, was in fact, due to my heated arguments on the Sioux side in the various councils with the Army. Being white I cut through many of the thin dodges they sought to perpetrate on the Sioux, becoming thereby a constant thorn in their flesh.

But in the Rosebud action I had blown my last chance of redemption. I'd played a conspicuous role in that engagement, my part in the rescue of Crazy Horse having singled me out beautifully. Even had I not labeled myself by this personal act I could not have escaped association, for in any roster of that day's top hostile command the name Walking Hawk must have been included.

With the approach of the troops my moral position became intolerable. The most obvious thought was to desert, fleeing to a pre-arranged rendezvous with Star. Next thought was to throw myself on Crazy Horse's military mercy, explaining I would not lead my red people into certain defeat by overwhelming Army forces. This wouldn't wash, I knew. A third course would be to "have a vision," always a good bet with an Indian. Text of this dream would be that I had seen my warriors dying like deer-flies around me until suddenly I died. Then they all sprang back to life, etc. This would mean it was bad medicine for them to have me fighting with them. But Sitting Bull was too smart. Deliberately and with cold knowledge of their falsity, he used such dreams for his own purposes and would never tolerate my usurpation of the device.

In the midst of my indecision Little Wolf came in with a report which changed everything. He and his patrol had captured one of Reno's Pawnee scouts. This scout had been astounded at the size of the camp.

"Why?" Little Wolf had wanted to know.

"We thought to find no more than a thousand warriors," the scout admitted.

The implications of this intelligence were deadly. To the Sioux it meant only they were not getting the right kind of publicity, were being rated a second-class outfit. They were quick to be insulted, slow to realize the enormous advantage such a wrong impression of their strength gave them.

You may be sure that for once Cetan Mani held his

council. But the moment I heard this I knew Gibbon and Custer were on thin ice, knew the odds had dropped from ten to one in the Army's favor to even money all around. Perhaps if they persisted in their pincers, keeping their respective forces intact, they could effect the subjugation of the Sioux. But now it would be no easy slaughter. Now they had a fight on their hands. It requires no stretch of the military mind to visualize the difference in campaign preparation to take the field against one thousand rather than four or five. I felt sure now that the Army groups under Custer and Gibbon, which heretofore I had assumed were only spearheads being backed by close-following reserves, were in reality the whole attack.

My moral position had shifted once more. With the odds as I saw them hopelessly against the Sioux, my disaffection would have made little difference except to brand me in my own mind a coward. With the better than even chance to whip the whites which now emerged, my desertion would assume some strategic importance, both from the fact of their need for me as a war chief and my potential danger, if I left, as information bearer to the enemy.

Hard on the heels of Little Wolf's startler, Yellow Bird came lathering into camp with news which lifted every hair off the nape of my neck.

"Yellow Hair is coming!" he shouted as he fanned his pony up the village street. I was with Crazy Horse as the excited scout slid his pony to its haunches in front of the war chief's tipi. Present were Gall, American Horse, Sitting Bull. It was late afternoon, the 23rd of June.

"Yellow Hair is coming!" repeated the scout breathlessly, throwing himself off his mount, striking a suitably dramatic pose.

Crazy Horse looked at him coldly. "Next you will tell us Red Nose is on his way, too. Or that the Sioux beat Three Stars five suns ago on the Rosebud. Or that the fireboat-that-walks-on-water is waiting on the Yellowstone. You fool. We know Custer is coming."

Yellow Bird would have his little joke. Turning away as though utterly crestfallen, he muttered, voice low, but not so low that Crazy Horse wouldn't hear, "True, true. I must be failing in my advancing winters. But I thought the war chief would be interested to know that he is coming straight across the hills, for this very tipi—"

Crazy Horse leaped at him like a tiger. Seizing the tall Sioux by the arm he spun him around. The Oglala's eyes were blazing, his lips drawn white over his teeth. "Did you say he was coming straight? Over the hills? Not going up the river to come down on us from above?"

"Aye." Yellow Bird's voice was weary with simulated self-pity. "But then you knew it all the time. I will go help the squaws wipe the babies' bottoms. I am of no further use as a war—"

"Enough!" Sitting Bull's thin voice knifed into the conversation. "If you want to chatter like a magpie we'll slit your tongue for you. But if you don't talk like a Sioux, and suddenly, we'll cut it out of your empty head, entirely."

Yellow Bird, favorably impressed with Sitting Bull's frank approach, talked suddenly enough. He told us he had been with Hump and White Bull, tailing Custer. It was true many of the troops were young. It was true Custer was headed south, by-passing their camp as it had been thought he would. But then this morning the pony-soldiers trotted due west. Right through the hills, this way. They were trotting fast. Hump would follow them, reporting in the morning. White Bull would follow them, reporting tomorrow night.

It was a shame, Yellow Bird couldn't resist adding, the Sioux didn't have more foolish magpies like himself.

My mind, for days trapped in a trunk of confusion, jumped out of its prison like a jack-in-the-box.

Custer was cutting the line of march we understood Terry had given him—to the headwaters of the Little Big Horn—by fifty miles. Apparently some of what I'd heard of the boy general's irrepressible love of the limelight was true.

If he marched as Yellow Bird said, he would hit the Sioux war camp thirty-six hours ahead of Gibbon's thousand men. There would be no contact with Red Nose and Custer would jump four thousand fighting Sioux with six hundred regulars, half of them never having fired a shot in anger in their lives. Custer was thirty-six hours away from being a hero. And unless some way could be found to stop him, a very dead one.

Was there any way to stop him? There was. Just one way.

The moment the war chief got this new report he exploded into action. All scouts were immediately put into the field covering Custer's line of approach. Gibbon could be forgotten now. The scouts would ride back on the hour from Custer's sector. There would be great activity as soon as his attack plan became clear. The vision of Sitting Bull was a true one. Before the sun darkened the second time from now, the soldier dead would be piled high around the Uncle's moccasins.

A war council would be held now, tonight, as soon as all had fed. All the chiefs would attend. Crazy Horse would lead in the field. Two Moons, Hump, Little Wolf and Dull Knife would head the Cheyenne; Gall, Bob-Tail-Bull, High-Hump-Back, American Horse and Walking Hawk, the Sioux. Sitting Bull was supreme leader. Sitting Bull had the medicine. All would be as he had dreamed it. Crazy Horse had spoken.

As the dusk deepened, the chiefs began to gather. All dancing and drumming, both of which had been going on interminably since my arrival, were ordered stopped. Throughout the darkened village only the barking of the curs and the occasional high voice of a child broke the ordered stillness.

The side-skins of Sitting Bull's big lodge were rolled up. Under its shelter, facing the council fire burning in front of it, sat the top ten chiefs of the allied tribes, myself among them. Beyond the fire, facing the tipi, squatted row on row of minor chiefs, as nearly as I could estimate, some three hundred of them. Behind them, packed on every side, the braves and warriors of every rank, their number disappearing and continuing into the outer darkness beyond the fire's reaching light.

I had spent the hour before the council reaching my decision. The fact I was present indicated its nature.

The easiest thing in the world would have been for me to ride out of the camp without a word, my rank carrying me above question past the warrior-society guards and Fox Lodge police posted throughout the valley.

In the final analysis I couldn't do it. I was a fool not to and make no attempt here to justify my conduct. The decision I did reach was a vainglorious one on its face. But it was the only course I was able to see which satisfied at once my obligation to the Sioux and my own birthright.

When it came my turn to speak after most of the other chiefs had made their orations, I arose, stepping forward clear of the tipi, out into the open in the full light of the fire.

I felt no particular fear, no elation. I thought of myself as a man condemned to be executed and having been asked if he had any last word to say. In such state of mind a man sometimes finds a curious detachment of feeling frequently passing for cool courage. In my case I was just numb with the struggle of making an impossible, hopeless choice. All I wanted now was to get the public admission of that choice off my chest, satisfying my own conscience if nothing else.

I had purposely come to the council unarmed; I wore only breech-clout and moccasins. The silence deepened around the ring of intent listeners as I began.

"I am Cetan Mani, son of Tashunka Witko. When I have spoken the lodge of my father will be dark with shame."

A murmur of interest spread through the crowd. I could just see Crazy Horse out of the tail of my eye where he sat on my left. His lean frame stiffened at my words but his face remained immobile.

"Nine snows ago I came among the Oglala, a captive, my life spared by the war chief. He sponsored me, gave me back my weapons. He was my father even as Tatanka Yotanka was father of the Grabber." At this mention of Grouard, another ripple of sound coursed around the gathering. I watched Sitting Bull but he would not look at me.

"As is known to all, I am a white man." Actually some of them did not know this. Others had seemingly forgotten it, for as I said it another sound sprang up among them. It was not a good sound. They sensed now what was coming. "The Grabber was a white man, too, and he is known among us all as a traitor. Even now he rides up the Greasy Grass with the scouts of Red Nose.

"Five suns ago when we counted the big coup on Three Stars, I rode by my father's side. The magic of the little guns spoke many times, leaving the pale blood of my white brothers red upon these hands." Hence I presented my hands in a dramatic upflung gesture. Not a sound greeted the pose.

"Suddenly there came to me a dream. Even there among our enemies the dream came. It was big medicine, for as I dreamed there the little guns were silent. Many enemies shot at me. Many long knives sought my throat. But my medicine was strong. Nothing could harm me."

This was "vision talk" and it impressed them. I could feel the lessening of the hard tension, a return of a gentler spell of pure interest. I took a little heart, but catching the eye of Sitting Bull upon me, I lost it. His stare was as flinty as an arrowhead. Visions were his business. I was encroaching on a closed field.

"In my dream appeared the face of Yellow Hair—"

"A-ah!" There was no doubt of their interest now. Custer's was a name they knew. I used it deliberately, for as I talked a last-minute plan began to form. If I could bluff them into thinking I was bad medicine for them, that my presence among them was dangerous to their cause—

"Yellow Hair spoke and his voice was deep as summer thunder. These were his words. Uncover your ears. Hear them well.

" 'Cetan Mani, you are not a Sioux. Cetan Mani, you are a white man. Once you saved my life—' " Here I paused, interpolating. "This is true, my brothers. In the Great War, Yellow Hair and I were enemies. I spared his life when I could have taken it.

" '—and now I would save yours. If you fight with the Sioux against me, you will die and the Sioux will die with you. You are bad for them. I should leave you with them for you will help me defeat them if I do. But I shall destroy them anyway and to you I owe a life.

" 'What I owe, I pay.' "

Again I broke in on Yellow Hair, prompting my silent listeners. "This is true, my brothers, as you know. Yellow Hair's tongue is always straight."

"Aye, aye," rumbled several of the lesser chiefs. Crazy Horse and Sitting Bull made no sound. I quickly went on with Custer's peroration.

" 'Leave this fight. Fire no more shots against your own people. Go to the Sioux and tell them Yellow Hair warned them against you. Say I will kill them all and I do not want them saying it was because of you. Tell them to cast you out. I want their medicine to be strong, for I can kill them anyway. I seek no advantage. Tell them that.'

"Then Yellow Hair was gone. I have seen him no more. But I have told you what he said to tell you.

"Now I shall tell you what I say. My heart is bad for my red brothers. It is good for my white brothers. I cannot fight with you. My tongue is here but my heart is with Yellow Hair. My words are as straight as a lance haft. Hear them.

"If I go from this camp alive, I go to join the long knives. I shall tell Yellow Hair how many you are and that he rides upon you with Death riding behind him on his black horse. I shall tell him to go back. I shall tell him to run away. For the Sioux must not kill him.

"If the Sioux kill Yellow Hair the troops will come from the east as many as the stars which sprinkle the sky. It will be the end of the Cut Throat People." A pause here to let this sink in.

"If I ride away from here I will make Yellow Hair go back. If I do not ride away he will come on. If you kill me I cannot go to him and he will come on. Let the responsibility for that fall upon him among you who dares receive it." Here I stared hard at Sitting Bull. This was his war pure and simple and I wanted every brave out there to realize it.

His return gaze was furious; I had made a jabbing point.

"I am worse than the Grabber. For I leave you in your hour of need, while he came away in your greatest strength. But I go. I go to take the curse of my presence from the withers of your war ponies. I go to warn the long knives. I go to stop Yellow Hair.

"If I go, I go as a white man. If they will not stop I will come back with them. I shall be at Yellow Hair's side. But if I can stop him, all will be saved for the Sioux. Peace will be in this land of the Spotted Eagle.

"I am a traitor, yet who among you will say I have lied? Who among you will stop me and so lead all his people to their deaths? I have spoken. I go."

I did just that, turning slowly to walk, head-high, among them, my course laid straight through the thronging crowd of warrior onlookers. For perhaps ten paces no voice spoke, no watcher moved. Then the high, angry words of Sitting Bull lashed out.

"Stop, *sunke-mani!*"

My steps continued, their rhythm unbroken. But another voice now fell across the circle of firelight, a guttural, vibrant voice. "Cetan, my son."

I stopped, turning with my answer to face him. "Aye, my father."

"You are not going. I think we will kill you."

"If this is the voice of my father, I hear it. But the tongue is strange. Crazy Horse knows I speak the truth. His own visions have told him the same story." This was a shot in the dark worth taking. He had been very moody since the Rosebud. I felt sure he had been "seeing things." I didn't know yet whether I was right for all he did was announce, flatly, "Tie him up. We shall council at once on Cetan Mani, the traitor."

A dozen braves seized me, threw me roughly against a convenient ceremonial pole, lashed me there with rawhide. From my position I could see the fire in the council lodge. It burned very late.

About three that morning, the 24th, Yellow Bird came for me, a detachment of ten heavily armed Sioux with him. They untied the bonds which held me to the post, leaving my hands bound. Yellow Bird led me away like a captive animal, a heavy leather lead-thong around my neck, five ugly-eyed Sioux on either side.

"Is your heart bad against me, my brother?" I had a real affection for this tall, clown-minded killer. If any among the Sioux would remain constant, it would be he. But his answer let me know where the wind lay before ever I heard my sentence.

"As bad as the green gall of a gut-sick buffalo." There wasn't so much as a hint of regret in his tones. "If Crazy Horse tries any of his big talk to prevent the peeling-off of your skin there'll be trouble."

"Do you expect him to?"

"I do not know. He is your father."

"But you are no longer my brother?"

"Do not talk to me. I am full of baked tongue and boudins. I do not want to vomit."

We entered Sitting Bull's lodge, which now had the side-skins down tight. Only Sitting Bull, Crazy Horse, Gall and White Bull were present. "You may go," Sitting Bull directed Yellow Bird. The latter gave me a hard shove forward into the tipi, so that I would have fallen face into the fire, bound as I was, had not Crazy Horse sprung up. In one smooth move the war chief checked my fall and severed my bonds.

"It is not good for a chief to stand among his equals bound like an animal."

"A dog that will bite shall be muzzled," snapped Sitting Bull. The others nodded grunting assent.

"Cetan," Crazy Horse began, "here are no more pretty speeches. Every vote here but mine would have you given the Fox Lodge traitor trial, even as the Mouse had it. But I have argued for you, not because I love you and you are my son, though both of these are true things, but because you are a great warrior. You have lived among us with bravery always. You have risked you life for the honor of our people before this.

"Some among us"—here his gaze lingered speculatively on Sitting Bull—"do not have so long a memory as Crazy Horse. When you could have escaped on the Rosebud, you did not. You could have gone from this camp, and did not.

"Though you are ready to betray us, you stand forth like a man, saying, 'This I am going to do, and I am not afraid of any Sioux.' And in my visions, even as you have said, I have seen you are sick of heart and will be bad medicine for us.

"Because he honors my vision of this, Tatanka Yotanka

who has the final word in all points of our law, has consented to place your fate on the knee of Wakan Tanka. You shall be given a fair chance."

"In what way?" I demanded suspiciously.

By now, stung by Yellow Bird's treatment, beginning to fear Sitting Bull strongly, puzzled by Crazy Horse's position, I was beginning to get my Rebel blood up. For the first time I began to feel like a fool. Why hadn't I sneaked out of the camp with three good horses last night, making a run for it? Why hadn't I simply gotten the hell out of there any one of the six nights since the Rosebud?

But I knew why I hadn't. Of course it was Star. And maybe I wasn't a fool. When a man loves a woman as I did the exotic Indian girl, has loved her for ten years without issue, then finds, on the eve of his first child's birth, his white man's conscience crying out for him to go back to his kind, to forsake his Indian love and life, and the little Indian life-to-be, he is quite apt to deny his moral urge, yielding to his heart, telling his better-self to go to hell, and doing what his body passions tell him—staying by his wife and child—color be damned.

Drifting in this course as I was, had it not been for that final report on Custer's deviation from his orders, I would surely have gone into the battle of the Little Big Horn, a red Sioux, moral convictions disregarded.

As it was, when I heard of Custer's move, knowing at once it was theoretically in my power to prevent his ambush, I gave in. I could not stand by watching six hundred white men march into a death trap while I played the anxious father outside Star's tipi.

As these thoughts crossed and re-crossed my mind, Crazy Horse answered my dour question.

The answer curled my hair.

"When the sun tops the hills of the Greasy Grass, you will be made ready. You will be stripped naked, with no weapons. Behind you in a long line will stand fifty braves, also naked, but each armed with a buffalo lance. At the signal you will take ten paces forward and halt. Then will come another signal and you will begin to run. You will begin to run because behind you the fifty braves will begin to run. And they will have lances. If your medicine is good you will reach Yellow Hair. If it is bad your blood will be on your own hands."

"A little on the prairie, too, maybe?" I interrupted, sarcastically. I was mad now, as I always got mad when it penetrated my rawhide skull that people were shooting at me.

"It is fair," concluded Crazy Horse. "You saved my life on the Rosebud. I give it back to you."

I looked at him hard. His face was graven as granite. But in his eyes was something I had never seen there before.

"It is fair," I answered, adding softly, "my father."

We stood a moment, glances locked. Then I touched my left hand to my forehead.

His right hand swung up to rest over his heart.

Chapter 9

CRAZY HORSE accepted my parole, allowing me to go unbound to my tipi to spend the remaining hours with Star. What matter that snake-eyed old Tatanka Yotanka had a cordon of his hardcase Hunkpapa squatting around the scene of my farewell. It has always been the business of the medicine man to hedge the bets of the warlord.

Star was calm enough, largely I think, because of her monumental faith in me.

"Remember," she chided, "how you boasted of your speed the day you would race me back to the mesa in my valley? Surely no bull-footed Sioux may hope to head you."

I could see she either actually believed there was nothing to it or else was putting on for my benefit. She would not talk of any possible danger, assuming, for fact or fiction, I would easily outdistance my pursuers, reach Custer, stop the battle, make a great peace, be crowned King of the Sioux, and have myself skin-painted into tribal immortality.

Such things might take a bit of doing by your ordinary hero but for Cetan Mani, hah! Nothing to it but a bit of limb-stretching.

I found her aboriginal simplicity anything but refreshing. She must have felt my restlessness for she grew quiet.

"Cetan, within me your son struggles to be free. You will not see him born. This is not our last good-bye, however. You shall reach Yellow Hair, and live to see your son.

"You think I am light of head and heart in this sad time but I am not. Yunke-lo stands by our tipi flap but you will live. You will live and our son will live. I know these things."

I had not missed the omission of herself in the prophesy. "What of you, Star? You have not spoken of yourself?"

"Oh, there is nothing about me. Do not think of it."

"But you said Death stood by the tipi flap?"

"He stands there," she answered, gravely, "but I am not afraid. Yunke-lo always stands by the tipi flap when the young are born. Didn't you know this, Cetan? Sometimes he enters. Mostly he stays outside. But I am not afraid."

I was. And deeply so. For my life among the Sioux had taught me one thing: it was foolish to disregard their visions, particularly those of a known "dreamer" such as Star.

Living with nature as they have for uncounted generations, their animal instincts have remained uncloyed. Their strange sixth-sense warning powers were as delicate as those of a dog. And who has not known in his own life, or heard first-hand, where the unaccountable, sudden howling of some dog preceded the unexpected death of a friend or loved one?

You may put it down to anything you will; nerves, ignorance, fear, hysteria; but when Star saw Yunke-lo standing outside our tipi, I knew he was standing there. I knew why he was standing there. And I knew for whom he stood.

He stood for Star.

But now her wonderful hands were upon me, her soft lips at my ear, her breath sweet and clean on my cheek. "Perhaps, Cetan," she murmured, "you may strike down even Yunke-lo. Who knows? I am not afraid if you are not."

"I am not afraid," I whispered. "I am not afraid and I shall strike him down." We knew peace then for a last, quiet hour. But my words became stark lies, three suns later.

With dawn I left her, before the guards might come for me, striding off up the village street, alone and free.

Behind me, materializing out of the ground mists, trotted Sitting Bull's watchdogs, thirty silent Hunkpapa, grinning like a pack of waiting wolves trailing a wounded buffalo bull.

I halted before the somber lodge of the medicine man, calling out in a voice which carried the length of the sleeping camp, "Come out, Tatanka Yotanka! I am ready for your yellow dogs! It is the son of Tashunka Witko who waits here."

Within seconds the camp was alive, warriors tumbling half-dressed from their tipis, squaws hurrying up the street tugging on deerskin dresses, children running naked. Soon the crowd was hundreds deep and old Sitting Bull, probably all the while peering narrowly through his tipi flap judging the proper dramatic time, made his entrance.

He was dressed in an ornate "hair shirt" fashioned from the sewn-together scalplocks of various enemies. His leggings and moccasins were of black elk. A single white eagle feather adorned his iron-gray hair. His entire face was painted black, broad bands of vermilion and ochre slashing the cheeks. It was plain Tatanka Yotanka was bent on giving the faithful their money's worth this time out.

Nowhere among the watchers could I see Crazy Horse. Subsequently I learned he spent the night and morning retired in prayer on a hilltop west of camp.

No time was frittered away. Sitting Bull led the crowding pack out of the village up onto the flats east of the river. I could see the course had been carefully selected. As far as I could see over the area into which I must flee, the ground was covered with the small, flat, needle-spined cacti the Indians call "little green quill-pigs." I found my dislike of Sitting Bull enjoying a healthy enlargement.

Tatanka Yotanka was not the foe to overlook the least refinement of the odds in his favor.

The fifty braves who were to pursue me were selected on a volunteer basis. It is enough to say the number of those willing to have a try at heaving a lance into my buttside were legion.

I was pleased to note the first to leap to the call was my erstwhile chum, Yellow Bird.

It is an odd quirk in the human make-up, but a true one, that when a best friend turns against you, you hate him for it with a genuineness reserved above all other hates. On his part Yellow Bird may have felt the same way, though I could see nothing personal for him in my declaration-of-intention to go to Custer. For me, though, his arrogant disavowal of our long friendship was horse-dirt in the teeth. It constituted, in all fairness to him, a typically Indian attitude, one of the few I never liked in them: a bitter quickness to twist like the wild winds of their Dakota homeland, from due north on the compass of personal faith, to due south, without reason or warning. In this case, watching him jump so happily to be in on the white-pig sticking, my last feeling for him drained away.

"Take off your moccasins," the reedy voice of Sitting Bull ordered. I did his bidding, disdainfully kicking the skins free, being careful to shy them at him. My medicine was good. The second of the flying footgear took him full in the face, causing him to flinch and step back. Sitting Bull turned as livid as a red Sioux can.

"*Ohan!* Wear them," I laughed. "My feet are big enough to fit even your bull-head."

Again someone guffawed, for the Indian democracy is a real one, the followers having no fear of the leaders.

"Take you ten steps." His voice was level, controlled. My nerves tightened in response to it.

I began to step and the Indian crowd to chant the count aloud: "*Wance, nunpa, yamini, dopa—*" I was thinking clean, my mind uncluttered by any notion but that of survival. I suspected trickery from Sitting Bull. It would be his way. I thought I knew how it would come, my memory flashing to the way Slatemeyer had anticipated Crazy Horse's signal in the knife fight. Behind me I could "feel" the fifty braves straining on their marks. I gathered every power in my body, trying to hide the tensing as well as possible under an appearance of ease.

It would be natural for a man to unconsciously relax on the count of ten, expecting a pause, no matter how slight, to precede the following go-signal. It would also be natural for Sitting Bull to know this and to shout accordingly his go-signal right on top of his ten-count, the braves having been briefed beforehand on the treachery.

This time, I thought, easing into the tenth stride, if anyone jumped the gun it was going to be—

"*—wicksemma!*" yelled the crowd, as my reaching foot touched the ground. And "A-ah!" came Sitting Bull's signal-shout, so close on top of it as to seem unseparated.

But neither the yelled ten-count nor Sitting Bull's shout came soon enough. Before either reached my ears I was running, that tenth step, far from anticipating the expected pause, being in effect my starting jump.

It gained me five yards over the pack at my heels, each yard at the moment measuring not space but life-span. I was lifted on my way by a howl of rage from Tatanka Yotanka and a chorus of irritated yelps from his fifty red foxhounds.

But another sound came too, this from the crowd. It lent me real speed. Up out of hundreds of throats sprang a spontaneous, "*Hun-hun-he! H'g-un! H'g-un!*" The red heart dearly loves trickery. It has no whim as to what's "fair in love," but worships delightedly the premise that "all's fair in war." That shout of, "Courage, friend!" was for *me*.

For the first half-mile I ran straight away, intent only on bursting speed. There was no time or reason to look back.

The first driving strides of my bare feet among the carpeting cacti brought stabbing, searing pains. But I had more than pains stabbing me soon enough. At least a score of lances whistled by me to ricochet crazily off the stony ground or stick quivering in the sun-baked earth. Two of them grazed me, one my thigh, one my side, bringing blood but no retarding injury. Instead they brought hope, for I knew their owners, overanxious for the kill had literally thrown away their chances with their lances, any weapon-retrieving stop at the present pace being enough to force them out of the contest. The odds were down to thirty to one.

After the first flurry, no more lances were hurled. Either the other braves were saving their weapons or I had opened up sufficient ground to put me out of range. An overshoulder glance as I topped the first rise of the foothills, confirmed the latter hope. The main pack was a hundred yards behind, a few stragglers even farther. Fifty yards back ran a clump of five Cheyenne headed by Black Wolf, a famous runner among them. These braves were all running well but using so much wind in uttering their tribe's frantic wolf howls, I felt they would tire.

A scant twenty-five yards behind me loped a lean Sioux, running easily yet with speed to match my own, stride for desperate stride. As this one saw me throw my look, he yelled, "Fly, fast, Hawk. Yellow Bird flies faster!"

Five miles were covered, then ten.

I ran in a dry gully which led where I wanted to go, toward Custer, and which I knew lay straight enough to prevent any short-cutting to an ambush by the pursuing Indians.

My feet were sodden pulps, stone-bruised, cactus-shredded. But I no longer felt them. My breath came in painful spasms, my second wind having come and gone long ago.

I figured if Custer had made an early start I had forty miles to go. I had no illusion about running that far, and knew no Indian to be capable of it, either. My first objective had been accomplished: the outdistancing of the main pack. The six Cheyenne were still in the race as was Yellow Bird, but the latter had fallen a hundred yards behind while the former were a good mile back. In fact I hadn't seen them for several minutes.

The country ahead began to flatten out. Five miles of open prairie lay between me and the next range of hills. At the base of this range a dark ribbon of foliage announced a stream. I knew this to be the Sweetwater, a swift sparkling river of some volume. To reach it became my next goal.

Once out in the flat, I began to falter. At the same time Yellow Bird came on stronger. At three miles he had closed to fifty yards. At four, to twenty-five. With the river a short mile ahead, ten yards separated us. Nothing I had been able to do, no effort of mind or muscle, had staved off his closing rush. Behind him, also coming stronger, Black Wolf and his Cheyenne had closed to a half a mile.

My bones, muscles, every fiber and tendon strained. But Yellow Bird had me. Ten yards fell to five. To four. To three.

"You are going to die now, Cetan!" His voice screeched with exhaustion. "My lance is at your back. Father receive my offering—!"

The urge to look was too much. I couldn't run on waiting for that feathered shaft to lance through my kidneys. At his words I turned instinctively to look—and struck my toe on a rock. Lead-footed with fatigue, the slight stumble sent me sprawling face-down into the grass.

As I had turned it was to see Yellow Bird's lance-arm drawn far back, the razor-bladed weapon speeding toward my back even as I stumbled and fell. The lance whistled through the space where I had been a moment before, hurtled over my head, shattered itself on an outcropping of granite not three feet from my face. Yellow Bird's momentum of both running and throwing carried him into my falling body, his knees striking my back and side to send him flying over me to smash into the dirt practically on top of me. Had the maneuver been rehearsed I couldn't have sent him sprawling more beautifully.

These thoughts of course were not crowding my mind at the time. The only thing I knew then was that I had stumbled. My pursuer had thrown and missed, collided with me and gone down in turn, and the lance had been broken in two, leaving three feet of the haft on the blade-end.

Perhaps Yellow Bird struck his head on the ground in falling. Perhaps the fall knocked the wind out of him. At any rate, I clawed my way over his impeding form, seizing the spearhead of the lance before he could recover. As he got his hands under him to come up, I raised the lance blade high over my head, grasping the shortened haft in both hands.

His head came up, following his body. For one startled

second his gaze mirrored the picture he was to take with him to another land.

I drove the honed steel of the lancehead deep through his back, missing the spine and heart, penetrating the right lung, sinking a foot of the head and haft into the hard ground under him. His body hung, a shaving of a second, a foot off the ground, transfixed there by the lance. Then it slid slowly down the shaft of the weapon to rest finally on the clay from whence it had first sprung.

The tremendous animal vitality of the Sioux rallied. His head came up off the ground, the face contorted with pain.

"*Woyuonihan,*" groaned Yellow Bird.

"*H'g-un,*" I answered. "You ran better than I."

"No one ever appreciated me the way you do!" He grinned, before the bright lung-froth vomited out of him and he died.

This action took perhaps three minutes. I looked up at the sound of slogging moccasins. Black Wolf was upon me, his five companions not two hundred yards behind him. The Cheyenne was weary. He made a bad lunge. As I rolled over the body of Yellow Bird to escape Black Wolf's lance, I ripped the dead brave's knife from his belt—the same lean Spanish blade I'd used against Slatemeyer.

Black Wolf saw it coming, saw the blue arc of the knife sweeping up at him. But he was off balance following the missed plunge of his lance-stroke. The Cheyenne lacked the iron of a true warrior. He screamed like a woman in labor as the steel got into him.

I guess Black Wolf had a scream coming. As he fell, flopping grotesquely in mid air like a beheaded fowl, to land heavily on his back, I could see he was belly-slit from navel to breastbone.

I stood over the dying Cheyenne, my belly, legs and knife-arm splattered as a hog-butcher's in October, the sweet, hot stink of his blood everywhere. Froth and slime from my running labors flecked and roped my chin. On my heaving chest were the caked, sour stains of the bile puked-up as exhaustion had sickened me ahead of my second wind. Perspiration laced spidery channels through the crusting dust which covered my body. I shook and slavered like a trapped wolf as I crouched there with Yellow Bird's knife, awaiting the uprush of the last Cheyenne.

They were almost on me before the blood mist cleared away.

Then I ran with my last burst of speed, headed for the

river. For a weird minute I had thought to take on five Cheyenne lancers with an eight-inch knife. Now my mind was clearing, wondering what the hell I was going to do with the Sweetwater when I reached it.

The question was still unanswered when I hit the bank of the stream, turned right, scurrying down its edge for a clump of willow and cottonwood ahead. Then, as I staggered up a rise just before the trees, I saw that beyond the grove the stream was backed up by a beaver dam. Perhaps fifty of the animals' big stick-and-mud lodges dotted the pond's expanse. Here was my last slim chance. I could not run on. I was done.

Pausing atop the rise, I screamed back at my enemies. "Cetan Mani is going to fly to Wanagi Yata from this very spot! You will never see him again. His spirit will haunt you. You have killed him."

Topping this melodramatic pronouncement with a silent prayer that there were no Indian atheists among my devoted followers, I took a short run across the top of the rise, leaped as far as I could and landed twenty feet away and below in a patch of matted wire-grass. From here I made my way through the wooded tangle employing every trick of trail-hiding I knew, making them wonder if I really hadn't flown into thin space off the top of that rise.

The dry tangle persisted right up to the stream's edge, allowing me to dive into the water without leaving a toe-track to point my passing. I swam under water as far as I could, surfacing well out in the pond behind one of the beaver lodges. A glance showed me the figures of the five Cheyenne milling excitedly atop the rise. Apparently my leap had broken the trail. Taking a breath I dived again, surfacing under the lodge's interior.

Fortunately there was no one home. The last thing I wanted was to have a couple of evicted beaver indignantly making big, broad water-tracks away from that particular lodge. The water was a bit cold but otherwise I was very snug, these lodges being from six to eight feet across with an air space on the inside of about a foot and a half's height. My retreat was as black as the unopened gut of a grizzly and fully as fragrant. But to me no more elegant castle could be imagined.

Ashore I could hear the Cheyenne crashing about in the thicket, calling back and forth in challenge and puzzlement.

"Ay-eee, Elk Man. Any trail yet?"

"None here."

"Have you searched the water's edge, Short Bear?"

"Aye. To the bend and back. No tracks."

"I saw him leap in the air. I, Young Crow, saw him do that."

"Aye. Even as he said he would, he did it."

"You saw the leap, too, Cow Runner. Don't say you didn't."

"I saw it, but that is foolishness. He's around here somewhere."

I shrank down in my mud palace. Here was my unbeliever, this damn Cow Runner. Let it be hoped Wakan Tanka would rip his profane tongue from his heretic head when he got him up in Wanagi Yata. I began to wish fervently he had been as swift as Black Wolf. But then a moment later I was flattered, most pleasantly, to hear I also had true believers out there among the cottonwoods.

"By Wanbli's wishbone! I believe he's gone."

"I, too."

"Short Bear agrees."

"And Elk Man."

Cow Runner was obdurate. For three hours he kept the others beating and re-beating the brush. But any chance they had of finding my trail was gone after the first hour of their passing back and forth.

Finally Short Bear had had enough. "The sun's going," he announced, flatly, "and so is Short Bear."

"Young Crow is ready."

"And Little-Pony-Stealer."

Elk Man concurred with feeling. "Cow Runner may stay and have talk with Cetan Mani's shadow. I am laying a long trail away from here."

With darkness crowding him, Cow Runner's enthusiasm faded. "I hate to do it," he blustered. "No one can jump all the way to Wanagi Yata. But the coyotes will be after Yellow Bird and Black Wolf. We must bear them home."

"Aye. Let's travel."

A realist showed up in the crowd. "What do we tell Tatanka Yotanka?" someone wanted to know.

"Tell him Yellow Bird slew Cetan. No, better make it Black Wolf. It might as well be Black Wolf."

"Sure. A Cheyenne, by all means."

Cow Runner had a question of his own. "What do we show for a scalp? Tatanka Yotanka will want a scalp."

"We'll bring him Yellow Bird's. He won't need it where he's going."

"Yellow Bird is going somewhere?"

"He is going in the river with a big rock tied to his middle."

"*Hopo,* let's go. We'll just have time."

So it came about that Yellow Bird lost his hair as well as his life; scalped and thrown in the Sweetwater by his stout comrades; not, I might add, an altogether un-Indian procedure from start to finish.

Chapter 10

IT IS not easy to tell time while waiting in black dark. I counted a thousand slow breaths before swimming out from under the beaver lodge. I judged it to be about seven o'clock, still quite light, true dark coming about ten-thirty in that northern country.

Hearing no Indian sound and reassured by the fact that beavers were active in the pond, almost certain sign no humans were about, I swam for the far shore, clambered out and made off easterly at a swinging dogtrot. I was much refreshed by my hours in the cool water as well as by the pleasant feel of the hair still on my head. Once I had the stiffness out of my cramped limbs I made excellent time.

I found Custer's camp about ten o'clock, only some ten miles from the Sweetwater, not over twenty-five in all from Sitting Bull's war camp. It was a "dark" camp, fires out, men sleeping. Still, in circling it twice, coming in closer as I went, no guards were encountered.

In one tent a lone candle gleamed, showing me the occasional shadow of its occupant moving about. Watching, I caught a brief-held pose of the figure, limned sharp against the backing light of the tiny flame. It loomed misshapenly tall and twisting on the pitched angles of the canvas. As it moved to lean over the candle for some purpose, the head inclined, showing a definite length of hair shadowed for a fleeting instant on the tent's wall. Journey's end! The question now was should I work on in, locating a picket and calling out "Friend!" or should I go in unannounced?

The latter course won after very little consideration. Cavalry pickets are as triggery a group as I'd care to harangue with under any circumstances, while these, in the heart of hostile Indian country and maybe green at that, would likely be as edgy as a sow grizzly.

I was particularly proud of my approach to Custer's tent when, a few moments later, I learned no less than four hounds were sharing it with him. A notorious dog-lover, he always had a pack of hunting dogs with him on his campaigns. Not one of the brutes so much as woofed as I bellied up through the shadows.

A sentry nodding over his rifle was posted outside the general's tent, posing my first real problem. I didn't care to test his reflexes so I oozed up out of the ground behind him, my fist closed lovingly over an apple-sized rock. Tapping him behind the ear with it was no trick but catching him and his rifle, both falling simultaneously in different directions, was harder. Laying man and rifle comfortably out in the warm dust, I stepped over them to the flap of the general's tent.

"Colonel Clayton calling on General Custer."

"What the devil!" Custer's words were a combination of surprise and interest. He was, withal, about as cool a cucumber as you will find in many a patch of pickle plants. But soldier-like he backed his interest with a long cavalry Colt, scooped smoothly off a map table as he turned to face me.

I dare say we made a picture, he in his long underwear and a pair of Lakota moccasins, I, stark naked; for when I say the Sioux stripped me for that race, I mean they stripped me. Remember, too, my skin was burned copper-bronze by nine years of Oglala life, my hair shoulder-long in two thick Sioux braids with the scalplock of a Fox Lodge soldier roaching up in front.

Custer may have absorbed my introductory line but for all practical purposes, six-foot-three of slit-eyed hostile Sioux, complete with eight-inch scalping knife, had just walked through six hundred cavalrymen, appearing, without so much as a polite cough, in his tent.

I suppose such a moment should call for deathless words, something to enclose in proud quotes in the general's memoirs. They weren't forthcoming.

"Now, wait a minute, don't move," Custer commanded. "If this is a joke you'll find my sense of humor very rough."

"If it's a joke, it's a bad one," I answered. Catching his eye flicking to the knife in my hand, I tossed it into a corner. "I'm John Clayton, a white man, living nine years with the Sioux. I come from Sitting Bull's camp on the Little Big Horn."

"Guard!"

"He won't hear you. He's unconscious right now."

"Ho, guard!"

"I knocked him out with a rock just now. But I come in peace, to save your life."

"Well, talk fast. And move away from that flap. Over in the corner, there." He gestured with the Colt and I moved. Sliding past me, he pulled the flap, bellowing out to the sleeping camp. "Guard! Get a guard detail up here. On the double!" Within seconds a sleepy sergeant and four privates stumbled up.

"Bates," Custer ordered the sergeant, "send a man to round up the officers. I want every officer outside this tent in five minutes. And I want the camp ready to move in ten."

"Yes, sir!" stammered Bates, bug-eyed. "Do you want any more guard here, sir?"

"No. Get that man on his way. Come on, jump to it. The rest of you men stand guard on this tent. I've a hostile Sioux runner inside. He's going to talk. If I call out, come in fast. Otherwise, stay out. Is that clear?"

"Yes, sir. All right, men. Spread out. If the general calls, get the hell in that tent. Flannagan, go get the officers. Wake up Stover and have him blow a call."

Custer's head shot back out of the tent. "If I hear one note of a call I'll bust you clear back to a buck, Bates. Do you hear me? Where do you think we are? On parade at Lincoln?"

"Yes, sir. I mean, no sir. Flannagan! No call! Wake up Sergeant Butler. Tell him 'Boots and Saddles' with no bugle."

"All right, now," said Custer, dropping the flap and turning to me. "Let's have your story before the others get here."

"All right, General. First I'll tell you what you're heading into, then who I am.

"Twenty-five miles west you've got ten thousand Sioux and Cheyenne in camp on the Little Big Horn. Between three and four thousand warriors. Lots of modern rifles. Lots of powder. They're ready and they'll fight. They'll not only fight but they know you're split off on your own. They mean to wipe you out.

"They know Gibbon and Terry are down below and that you apparently intend to swing in and hit them before your support can come up. That's what you're doing, isn't it, General?" Without giving him time to answer, I went on. "Well, if you do you're finished.

"Now listen, for God's sake. They know you think they have only a thousand warriors. They know all about you. Have had scouts on you since you came into the country. They've got a contact somewhere among your Indian scouts. You know Indians, General. A sister in this tribe, a son-in-law in that one. You can't keep anything from an Indian. They've done everything but read your orders.

"Sitting Bull has got them ready to fight. Gall, Hump, Crazy Horse, all of them. And they'll fight. Don't ever think otherwise. These Indians won't run when you blow the bugles and flutter the pennons."

I could see his color mounting. His interruption was in tones of anger. "Who did you say you were?"

"Colonel John B. Clayton, Fourth Cavalry, Second Division, Confederate Army. I did you a favor at Appomattox."

"The devil you say!" His gaze narrowed. "A favor? Not that I believe your crazy tale but just what kind of a favor was it, now?"

"A private of mine tried to shoot you. I knocked his rifle aside. You were coming over to our lines with our truce officer. You were Third Cavalry, then, with Sheridan. Remember? You said, 'Colonel, my compliments. You have doubtless saved my life. Should our paths cross again, I shall remember you.' Well, General they've crossed again and I'm asking you to remember me."

"I remember all right. Every detail. Except one. You. What I want to know right now is who you really are and where you got all this information. You're no more Colonel Clayton than you're General Lee. Clayton was a high-born gentleman, a white man. You, my friend, are as red as a Sioux can get. Don't forget I know your people. You speak well but you speak like an educated Indian. There's no hiding that guttural."

It was true. Ten years of living, eating and breathing Sioux were coming up in my face like a red finger of accusation. I knew he was right. I did grunt and bark my words like any blood Oglala.

"You're clever," Custer went on, "but not clever enough. When you talk you make signs constantly with your hands, Indian style. Your tongue is crooked but your hands are straight. You're an Oglala by your hair. Bad Face, isn't it? Come on, now, what's your Indian name?"

"If I give it to you, you'll only be that much more unwilling to believe me."

"You'll give it to me or the talk's over."

"Cetan Mani. Walking Hawk."

"Aha! I knew it. Knew I'd seen you. Never forget a face or a voice. You're the smart Indian. The one with the big tongue. Always there with the right answer. Yes, I know you now. A real big hostile, aren't you? Colonel Clayton, indeed." His voice was brittle as first-frost ice. "All right. What's become of Colonel Clayton? How did the Sioux pick him up? How did they get all this detail you've been giving me, out of him? Be careful. I know some things myself."

"General, I don't see how any man would give up the detail I've given you. I mean, exact words you spoke eleven years ago, precise details of your bearing. Now I'll give you more. If you persist in refusing to let your intelligence stand over your apparent eagerness to lick the whole Sioux Nation with six hundred men, the blood of this command will be on your uniform so long as military history is taught."

"That's enough," he broke in, blue eyes snapping-mad. "I don't know what the Indian game is, sending you here but—"

"The name of the truce officer was Peyton, Colonel Green Peyton. You took the surrender from General J. B. Gordon. Fitzhugh Lee, Pendleton and Longstreet were active on your front."

"I said that would be all." I don't think he even heard the names. The man appeared obsessed. I knew he was brilliant but, as the Sioux say, "A bat's squeak is as loud as an eagle's scream to a deaf man." If he wouldn't listen he couldn't hear. Still, I tried. I did all I could to convince him. We talked for ten minutes while the camp came alive and the officers waited nervously outside the tent.

He wouldn't convince.

I was a red spy sent to stall them where they were, for an ambush, or turn them back for the same purpose. In any event, a spy, amazingly well-briefed on Clayton's life, peculiarly well-spoken in English, but nonetheless a perfidious decoy, to use his actual expression, and a red Indian by birth and blood.

Even, conceding an impossible point, if I were a renegade white, I was not Clayton. The general would prove this to my satisfaction within the next five minutes. I wondered how he meant to do this but was given no time to indulge the thought.

"Sergeant Bates."

"Yes, sir." The sergeant's face thrust in at the flap.

"Have the officers come in."

"Yes, sir."

Bates withdrew and Custer's command filed in, a good-looking group of officers for the most part though several appeared to be well within the grip of "Indian nerves." All looked at me with undisguised alarm. I'll qualify that statement. Reno's appraisal showed nothing but curiosity. His words, however, reflected the thought and feeling of all.

"What's all the fuss about, General? And who the hell is this hostile?"

"This, gentlemen, is Cetan Mani, Walking Hawk, a Sioux war chief. Very distinguished guest, gentlemen. The adopted son of Tasunka Witko, no less."

"Crazy Horse's son? Walking Hawk?" Reno was incredulous.

"The one and only." Custer's tones were mocking. "He tells me he is really a white man. Been living with the Sioux nine or ten years. Now he's turned soft. Come to warn us that four thousand warriors wait on the Little Big Horn."

"Four thousand! I thought your scouts told you one thousand, Reno?" Captain Benteen's challenge jumped with nerves.

"Wait a minute, Captain," Custer interrupted. "Here's the rest of it. This man claims the Sioux are only twenty-five miles from here, know all about us, are expecting to wipe us out. He says turn back or we're all dead. Does that sound like an Indian, gentlemen, or doesn't it?

"Go ahead," he ordered me. "Tell them your story. It's really quite interesting, gentlemen, from a professional standpoint. I would never have imagined an Indian capable of concocting such a yarn much less having the gall to come here with it. My hat's off to old Sitting Bull. You'd almost think this savage he sent us *was* a white man."

I repeated my story, but these men listened. Several nodded as I went along. At the finish there were some of the same questions and challenges the general had made but the average feeling was by no means what Custer's was. These men were thinking and they were worried. Some of them quite clearly, believing my story or not, were ready to accept its burden: that they were vastly outnumbered, in great danger.

Reno phrased it well. "General, it seems to me this man's identity, the detail of his story, are unimportant. We can check them later. What he says about the Sioux strength is what counts. I can see no logical reason why they would want us to know that. We've been satisfied they want a fight. Why should they try to scare us off at the last moment? I don't like it."

Custer broke in impatiently. "I've told you what I think. They're trying to stampede us into an ambush or keep us squatting here for one."

"Well, sir," Reno plodded on, his obvious concern overcoming any hesitation to cross his commander, "my scouts could have been wrong. If so we're in bad trouble. Can I go ahead with two troops to scout that camp?"

"Sounds logical," agreed Benteen. "If the situation's what this man says it is, we'll have to wait for Gibbon."

"What do you say, sir?" Captain Keogh pointed the big question.

"I say we're marching in twenty minutes," Custer's face was suffused with excitement. "Double-time. Right for the Little Big Horn!"

One officer spoke up brightly. "Good, good! Catch 'em sitting, eh General?" This was a captain, unknown to me.* Otherwise not an officer uttered a syllable. Even Custer's brother-in-law, Lieutenant Calhoun, looked down at the dirt of the floor, silent.

If ever a man took a command into battle against the will, wish and better judgment of every officer under him, it was Custer. Professionally, I was stumped by his attitude. In the five minutes of discussion which followed with his officers anent the plan of march and during which I was ignored, it developed he had not had scouts out, other than immediately in the path of march, for the past forty-eight hours. He knew approximately where the Sioux were but had sent no one ahead to check the exact location or number of them.

To me, knowing his Civil War record and the subsequent thoroughness of his Indian campaigns in the Southwest and the Black Hills, such oversight was beyond credence.

I had not seen his orders, of course. But our scouts had learned their gist as heretofore given and unless the Sioux intelligence was wrongly informed, which I could not believe because the very nature of the country and the known situa-

*Captain Tom Custer, Yellow Hair's younger brother.

tion of the Sioux camp made a juncture with Gibbon elementary, Custer was jumping those orders.*

If so, he must be held personally responsible before the bar of history for what followed. In the light of what did follow, the charges could be no less than criminal negligence, dereliction of duty, professional incompetence, and moral guilt of murder—all in search of personal glorification and aggrandizement.**

Custer heatedly talked down all objections of his officers. With his famous personality and magnetism going full blast, he soon had them giving at least lip service to his views. He was in very high feeling, flushed and garrulous. For the moment he had forgotten me. His résumé of the situation and his subsequent orders were rapped out with all the assurance of a commander taking a brigade of regulars against ten lodges of sick squaws.

"The idea, gentlemen, is this: the Sioux have sent their de-

---

* Author's note: The completeness with which Custer's actual orders bore out Colonel Clayton's reasoning makes their inclusion here of interest.

Camp at the Mouth of the Rosebud,
Montan Terr., June 22nd, 1876.

Lieut. Col. Custer, 7th Cavalry.

Colonel: The Brigadier-General commanding directs that, as soon as your regiment can be made ready for the march, you will proceed up the Rosebud in pursuit of the Indians whose trail was discovered by Major Reno a few days since. It is, of course, impossible to give you any definite instructions in regard to this movement, and were it not impossible to do so the department commander places too much confidence in your zeal, energy and ability to wish to impose upon you precise orders which might hamper your action when nearly in contact with the enemy. He will, however, indicate to you his own views of what your action should be, and he desires that you should conform to them unless you shall see sufficient reason for departing from them. He thinks that you should proceed up the Rosebud until you ascertain definitely the direction in which the trail above spoken leads. Should it be found (as it appears almost certain that it will be found), to turn towards the Little Big Horn, he thinks you should still proceed southward, perhaps as far as the headwaters of the Tongue, and then turn towards the Little Big Horn, feeling constantly, however, to your left so as to preclude the possibility of escape of the Indians to the south or southeast by passing around your left flank. The column of Colonel Gibbon is now in motion for the mouth of the Big Horn . . . Of course its future movements must be controlled by circumstances as they arise, but it is hoped that the Indians, if upon the Little Big Horn, may be so nearly inclosed by the two columns that their escape will be impossible . . .

Very respectfully
Your obedient servant,
E. W. Smith,
Captain, 18th Infantry,
Acting Assistant Adjutant-General.

** In his original journal, Colonel Clayton reports a rumor brought into the Sioux camp before he left it, to the effect that Yellow Hair had made a speech to his Crow and Pawnee scouts before setting off up the Rosebud, promising them great rewards, saying that a smashing victory would result in his becoming the Grandfather (president), and that then his faithful Indian friends would be remembered. Colonel Clayton generously discounted this report at the time but it is to be wondered what he thought of it as he viewed Custer's actions the night of the 24th.

coy in here to get us to do one of two things; either huddle down where we are, or back up. What we shall do, of course, is exactly what they wouldn't dream we'd do. The last thing they'd want us to do. Go forward. Tonight. We'll be on that camp in the morning and brevets will be flying around in this command thicker than crows in a cornfield."

As a soldier, looking around that circle of worried faces, I could not help thinking this was not the first time, nor would it be the last, that a general officer has sent brave men to useless deaths under the black banner of personal glory.*

"We'll divide up the regiment in two squadrons. Reno will take Companies A, G, and M, Captain Moyland, Lieutenant McIntosh, Captain French, respectively.

"Benteen will take the second squadron, with Lieutenant Godfrey and Captain Weir. I'll take the other five companies, with Keogh, Calhoun, Smith, Yates, and Custer. B company, under Captain McDougall, will convoy the pack train and ammunition. All clear? If so, let's go."

"How about the prisoner, General?" Sergeant Bates wanted to know.

---

*Colonel Clayton could not know the exact temper of Custer in this hour. The following letter provides the explanation if not the excuse for what Clayton had to see as pure glory-hunting: (and shows Grant striking back at Custer for the latter's perpetration of the Belknap scandel):

HEADQUARTERS DEPARTMENT OF DAKOTA,
SAINT PAUL, MINN., MAY 6TH, 1876.
ADJUTANT GENERAL,
DIVISION OF MISSOURI, CHICAGO.
I forward the following:
   To his excellency the President
   (through Military Channels):
I have seen your order, transmitted through the General of the Army, directing that I be not permitted to accompany the expedition about to move against hostile Indians. As my entire regiment forms a part of the proposed expedition, and as I am the senior officer of the regiment on duty in this department, I respectfully but most earnestly request that while not permitted to go in command of the expedition, I may be allowed to serve with my regiment in the field.
   I appeal to you as a soldier to spare me the humiliation of seeing my regiment march to meet the enemy, and I not to share its dangers.
                                        (signed)
                                        G. A. Custer,
                                        BVT. MAJ. GENL. U. S. ARMY.

General Terry added to
this appeal:
   In forwarding the above, I wish to say expressly that I have no desire whatever to question the orders of the President or of my military superiors. Whether Lieut. Col. Custer shall be permitted to accompany my column or not, I shall go in command of it. I do not know the reasons upon which the orders already given rest; but if those reasons do not forbid it, Lieut. Col. Custer's services would be very valuable with his command.
                                        (signed)
                                        Terry,
                                        COMMAND DEPARTMENT.

"Put him in irons and let McDougall have him. I want to talk to him when this is over."

"Why not take him along?" suggested Reno, who I was beginning to suspect had the best head in camp. "He might be of some use if his story's straight. If it isn't we might still use him to some advantage up there. Maybe to show the Sioux what we think of their espionage system."

Custer, whose enthusiasm was so high by this time as to strike me as purely boyish, thought this would be fine. "Why not?" He laughed. "We might have some fun with him, at that. Bates! Get him a mount. Tie his feet under its belly. He can ride with you, Reno, but don't lose him. I want him back. He's a *rara avis.*"

As the officers went out into the camp and Bates started to lead me away, Custer, already pulling on his boots, called out, "Wait a minute, Bates."

Sauntering over to me with that famous grin working for all it was worth, he drawled, "You see, chief, one of those officers just in here was with Carrington, at Kearney. He knew Clayton when he was scouting there. I meant to have him tell you. The real Clayton was killed by Crazy Horse's Oglala, at Lodge Trail Ridge, in the Fetterman Massacre. That's ten years ago, chief. Unless I miss my guess you know the details better than I. And also unless I miss my guess, you'll spend the rest of your suns in the Dry Tortugas. You won't lack for high company, though. I'm going to put Sitting Bull and Crazy Horse down there with you. Now get out!"

As he turned on his heel, he added, sharply, "If you're lucky, you'll stop a bullet tomorrow."

Chapter 11

WE BROKE camp at midnight, going forward for the remainder of the night in one column, our progress necessarily slower than the mercurial Custer would have wished. The country was rough, unfamiliar to his scouts, and he had only a general idea of the Indian camp's location. I could have gotten him there hours earlier and, knowing well the advantage of an early dawn attack on Indians, repeatedly urged my services on Major Reno. He was receptive, even sending to Custer to inquire about using my services. With his off-hand refusal, the latter threw away his last chance.

Could he have hit the Sioux at dawn with an undivided command he still might have had his glory and wallowed in it, too.

"Tell Major Reno," he relayed back, "that we'll have breakfast in Tatanka Yotanka's tipi. Crazy Horse will serve." It was clear "The Boy General" wasn't losing any of his high spirits along the way.

Where Custer was unwilling to listen, Reno was not. Through the night we talked, he getting into his head the exact lie of the camp, the disposition of the tribes, the nature of the terrain. Post-battle accounts may give his subsequent "retreat to the bluffs" as a disorganized or cowardly withdrawal.

It was neither, being a sane choice by a competent officer who, through the information he got from me, plus his belief in its authenticity, was the only man in the command who had a sound picture of the tactical situation as it developed later. And it was the only course which saved his command from the fate suffered by Custer's.*

Major Marcus Reno was a brave man, a competent officer. In this case he was the only commissioned man, outside of Benteen possibly, who seemed to have any comprehension of the military gravity of the hour. The others thought like dime-novel heroes and acted like state militiamen on a high bender.

At daybreak we were still some miles from the village but the bluffs of the Little Big Horn were clearly in view. We were following a tributary stream which came in below the camp. I judged we had ten miles to go. It was 9:45 A.M.

The Sioux gave no sign they'd sighted us, a fact which puzzled me and put my claim they had Custer under hourly surveillance in a bad light. The truth of the matter was Custer's

*Colonel Clayton was right again: At the court-martial which Reno himself requested following the slanders on his courage after the battle, every officer and man declared that Reno's retreat to the bluffs was the only factor which prevented their annihilation. Immediately after the abortive action, the surviving enlisted personnel of the Seventh petitioned the War Department to advance Reno to regimental command, replacing Custer. Scarcely the honor veteran troops would afford a cowardly commander.

The decision of the court itself: "The conduct of the officers throughout was excellent . . . there was nothing in Major Reno's conduct that requires animadversion from this court."

Nevertheless, pitiful footnote to the career of a gallant soldier, the slanders persisted, and Reno, unable to face them, drank himself out of the service and into disgrace.

bold move had caught them asleep. With that luck which seemed to ride so consistently with the brave, he had gotten up this far without discovery. But his luck was running out. Halting the column, he ordered Benteen to cut across country to the left, scouting the bluffs mentioned above. He and Reno went on down the stream, one taking each bank.

About 2:00 P.M., on our side, we jumped two Sioux braves watering their ponies. Carbines cracked and one of the braves went down. The other made it away, clean. Sitting Bull's warning was on its way, riding low over the neck of a spotted warhorse.

Custer dashed across the shallow tributary wanting to know what the shots were about. When he learned he ordered us across to march with him, the two columns continuing up the right bank at a stiff trot.

At 2:15 a lone Sioux tipi was sighted. Around it were signs of a large number of lodges recently moved. Cooking-fire ashes were still warm. The single tipi contained a dead warrior. When the soldiers ripped the skins from the tipi to reveal this warrior I knew him at once. I dug my hobbled heels into my pony's flanks, forcing him toward Custer. As I came up, he was leaning over his horse's neck, examining the body, saying to Reno, "What the devil do you make of this, Marc?"

I had told them of my race with the Indians and of the way Yellow Bird and Black Wolf had died. Custer had laughed then. I wondered if he still would.

"That's Black Wolf, General, the Cheyenne I told you I killed on my run to you. They've given him the honor of facing you first. That's his reward for 'killing' me. If you'll pull off that hair shirt you'll find him slit open from belly-button to breastbone."

"Pull off that shirt," barked Custer. Two privates jumped to do so. The garment came off, sodden and crusted. A cloud of blow-flies swarmed lazily away from beneath it. I hadn't liked the look of that wound when I'd given it to Black Wolf and it hadn't improved any sitting in the steaming air of that sun-drenched tipi.

"All right, men. Cover him up." Wheeling his horse to face me, Custer continued, the sober tone of his words the only indication he gave of any change in attitude. "Now then, 'Clayton,' give us that camp lay-out again. Quick. Who's on this end?"

"Hunkpapa."

"Then?"

"Oglala, Minniconjou, Sans Arc, Cheyenne."

"Tough ones all on this end, eh?"

"We're on Beaver Creek,* three miles south by a shade east of the Hunkpapa. They and the Minniconjou are on the Little Big Horn, side by each. Crazy Horse's Oglala are right back of them, on Medicine Creek."

"Do we dare believe him, Marc?"

"I do!" Reno exploded almost fervently.

"Cooke?" His adjutant shrugged, passing the question in a manner which said "no."

"Moylan? Keogh?"

"Sounds straight to me."

"Yes."

"Tom?"

"Whatever you say, General," his brother agreed.

Custer wasn't sold yet. "Seems to me that Cheyenne warrior being here might indicate we had the Cheyenne in front of us." No one answered him, so he concluded, "Well, all right. Let's go on. We're getting hot now, anyway. Bring your protégé along, Marc."

The column clattered into movement, Custer and Reno heading it, I riding with them.

"If I know my Sioux," I advised Reno, "we'll see a hell of a dust-cloud any minute now."

"It's a wise spy who knows his own side," laughed Custer, overhearing the remark.

Within five minutes a towering cloud of dust became visible on our direct front, right where I had placed the hostile camp for them. "There it is," I called to Custer. "They're milling the pony herds to throw up a dust cloud around the lodges. There's your village."

"Let's take a look," cried Custer, spurring his horse up a hill in front. We followed him, accompanied by Fred Girard, his civilian scout and Sioux interpreter. It was a bad look for me. A much worse one for them.

Crazy Horse had forty decoys waiting behind that hill and by damnable luck alone, they were all Cheyennes. It was a bad break for my Hunkpapa story. The Indians simulated alarm, fanning their ponies off upstream, yelping and calling out as though in fear and warning.

"There's your Indians!" yelled Girard. "Running like devils."

*Now Reno Creek.

"What are they? What band are they?" demanded Custer, eagerly.

"Cheyenne," echoed the interpreter.

Custer whirled on me. "You hear that, chief? Marc, did you hear that? Cheyenne! Just what his nibs here said was on the other end of the camp." Before Reno had time to say yes, no or go to hell, Custer rattled on. "You see what that means? The heavy strength is up at the other end. It's soft down here. This rascal wanted us to keep our power down here and send a weak column up ahead to be wiped out.

"All right, Hawk Walker, we'll take care of you in time. Marc, get on back on your command. I'll be down in a minute. Take your hangdog hostage with you. And watch him. Girard, send the scouts on after those Cheyenne."

Girard bawled down to the Indian scouts to go ahead, pursue their fleeing brothers. The scouts bawled right back at him. They wouldn't go. Those Cheyenne were decoys. Plenty Hunkpapa waiting right behind.

Furious, Custer ordered his adjutant to take the scouts' ponies and rifles. Then he sent the order down to Reno which precipitated the action I had done everything in my power to prevent.

From where I waited with Reno, below, I could see the general's motions but not hear his voice. Hence, while I could read what was happening to the scouts, it was not until his adjutant, Cooke, rode up, that I realized we were at last committed.

Sliding his horse into us, Cooke shouted at Reno, "General Custer directs that you take as fast a gait as you deem prudent and charge afterward, and you will be supported by the whole outfit."

Reno blanched and I laughed in Cooke's face. "What whole outfit?" I demanded, as if I had business to. "Benteen is ten miles away, lost in those bluffs." I might have added my doubts that Custer, the glorious, had any intention of "following" Reno, or anybody, where there was a hero to be made. I didn't have time.

"You goddam Sioux!" shouted Cooke, whipping out his service revolver. "I'll—"

Reno struck his arm up. "Not an unarmed prisoner, Cooke, for God's sake!"

The adjutant wheeled away, red-faced. "You've got your orders, Major. You're to attack at once." Up on the hill, Custer was now marshaling his five companies. Reno waved up at him; Custer waved back.

"French, take the right flank; Moylan, the left. Lieutenant McIntosh, center, with me." Major Reno gave his orders quietly, almost resignedly. "Let's go."

And they went; 112 officers and men, riding blind into the swarming thousands which awaited them under the boiling dust over the Little Big Horn.

In ten minutes we were at the edge of the dust. As it lifted, Reno saw in front of him more mounted Sioux than his scouts had placed in the whole camp. One look and he shouted to a nearby sergeant, "Cut that prisoner free and give him a gun. He's the only damn man in this valley who knows where he is and what he's doing!"

I was hustled to the rear, given a carbine with four belts, a service Colt with two. "Got another of these beauties?" I asked the supply sergeant as he handed me the revolver.

"Hell, chief, we ain't got nothin'. If McDougall don't git up here with ammunition we ain't gonna be in this fight long enough to warm up our barrels. I got fifty rounds a man over what they're carryin'. After that we're gonna use rocks. And I'll tell ya somethin' else. Them there new carbines ain't worth a hoot in hell. Fire 'em ten times and they jam. Pin swells up. Won't extract. Fire 'em five and blow 'em out. That's the only way to keep 'em pumpin'."

"Thanks," I yelled back, kicking my horse around, heading for the front. Heavy fire was beginning up there and the fever that always gets in a fighting man at the sound, accordingly began to run up in me.

To get the picture of what followed it is best to study my map of the Little Big Horn Valley. It's drawn from memory but is as accurate as one you'd do of your own backyard. Reno was boxed in by the river on his right flank, Medicine Creek and the bluffs on his left. The hostiles had him almost circled, only the route directly to the rear, by which I now returned, being open.

As I galloped up Reno saw me and shouted, "Over here, man. Over here!" I rode over.

Reno was not a cool man but he was nervy and smart. Still he was in a tight, cut to squeeze a bigger man than he. He had his command mounted and firing, that was about all. They were bunched and backing, crowded and jamming. Many couldn't get a clear field of fire because of their own fellows in the way. On every side I heard wild curses as the new carbines jammed. I rode through the men repeating the supply sergeant's wisdom.

"Hold your fire, men. Fire five and blow your guns out.

200

They'll work. You're jamming them by firing too fast. Shoot low to knock the horses down. Shoot slow. Shoot low. Fire five. Blow out." Some of them looked at me and threw their jammed arms away, pulling Colts and blasting away futilely. But others took heed, steadying down. We soon had a fair volume of fire going out into the Sioux.

But twelve hundred of them were riding our front and flanks, mostly Hunkpapas, the best the Sioux had. They didn't give a hoot in a hailstorm for our fire and their own was getting intolerably hot. We began to lose men. Fifteen casualties in ten minutes, eight dead.

*Colonel John Clayton's Map
of the Battle of the Little Big Horn*   June 25th, 1876

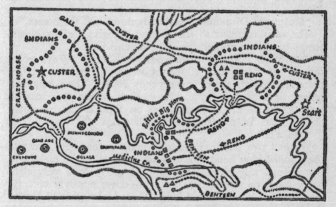

COLONEL CLAYTON'S map is historically accurate. The star at the right shows the spot from which Reno and Custer started, and from which Custer had promised to follow Reno in support. Actually he swung wide (dotted line), circled through the hills, was rat-trapped there (star at left), by Gall and Crazy Horse. Reno's route (dotted line), shows him stopped at the river, trapped in the bend, and retreating to the blufftops (indicated by squares). Here he holed up, waiting for Custer. Benteen's route came up to the east bluffs overlooking Reno's boxed-in position in the river bend, returned along the bluffs, down them and across the valley to Reno's position on the west bluffs.

From the map it would seem that had Custer kept to his word and followed Reno in support, paying credence to Colonel Clayton's intelligence on the layout of the hostile camp, there would have been no massacre; probably no worse than a stinging defeat and, again as Clayton observed, a very possible victory for Custer.

Reno rode up to join me. "Major"—I held my voice down so the men wouldn't hear—"we've got to get out of here. We can't take this. The Sioux are cooling down and getting their shots into us."

"Where can we go, man?" Reno's question was uttered in desperation. "I know they're killing us but we can't go ahead and I won't go back. Custer's coming up behind. I'll be damned if I'm going to fall back in his face."

"Listen, Major, something's gone wrong with the general. We've been in here fifteen minutes. He wasn't three behind when we moved in. We've got to get out. Now."

"Well, what do you say?"

"I say, dismount. Get the men off the horses while we've got some men left. Then into those woods over there, on foot."

"McIntosh! Dismount. Everybody down. Off the horses."

The men tumbled to the ground, hanging on the cheek-straps of their terrified, plunging mounts.

"McIntosh!" Reno's commands were terse. "We're going out of here. Into that clump of woods in that bend, right there off the right flank. Is everybody down?" The young lieutenant signaled they were. "Now. Four horses to a man to lead. Every other man out front on foot, firing. No cover on the rear. We're risking that. All clear?"

"Yes, sir!"

We had two hundred yards to make across open grass to the wooded river bend. We took six more casualties making it. Our refuge was a thick cottonwood grove in a very tight bend, water on three sides, the entire cover not over seventy-five yards wide, a hundred long. Reno, McIntosh and I were the last three men in. The following Sioux were forty yards off our tails. As we were almost to the trees a terrific shout went up from them.

Before starting from Custer's camp the night before, Reno had gotten me an old uniform from supply. A sergeant's faded chevrons adorned the sleeves of the jacket. It had been a dark, hurried issue, the supply sergeant not giving a ruptured damn whether he made me a corporal or a brigadier. This uniform had covered my identity at longer ranges but once the hawkeyed Sioux got in close they spotted me.

"Cetan!" . . . "Cetan Mani!" . . . "The Ghost!" . . . "The Traitor!" . . . "How's your hair, Cetan?" . . . "Ay-eee!"

The howls went up from them like a pack of blue-tick hounds belling a dog-coon in a swamp hollow at midnight. White Bull, one of Sitting Bull's nephews and apparently in command on our front, lashed his pony forward in a last frenzy. Four or five other Hunkpapa followed him jump for jump. We were so surprised by their suicidal rush they were into us before we got a shot off.

Then the Colt was bucking in my right hand. Three empty ponies blundered on into the wood. McIntosh knocked one off his pony with a clubbed carbine and I put my last two shots into him as he fell.

Reno, either dazed or just too slow a man with a gun, got belted out of his saddle by an ax-blow from White Bull. He hit the ground hard, lying quiet. By this time the troops were firing briskly, and the Sioux, having had theirs for the nonce, dashed off hanging on the far sides of their ponies.

We pulled Reno in and bandaged his head. It had been a glancing blow but had laid the scalp open to the skull; a great flap of grisly flesh and hair hung down over his left ear. From that moment he was a blown man, and though he fought his command through to the blufftops he was sick with pain the whole time.

"Clayton, listen," he rasped, as McIntosh left to fetch Moylan, the senior captain. "I can scarcely hear or see. That damn Sioux ax! Listen. Don't tell French or Moylan. You stay here with me, you hear?"

I nodded, smiling. Then my lips to his good ear, I shouted: "You've picked an aide. Got my degree under Jeb Stuart. Post-graduate with Fitzhugh Lee."

He bobbed his head, dark pain stabbing his eyes at the movement. "I believe you. You fight like a Rebel. You took us into this cover like a professional."

We waited for Moylan and McIntosh, the Sioux meanwhile slacking fire as they moved their forces into new positions around us. When the officers showed up Reno excused me by saying, "I'm satisfied this man is an ex-Confederate Cavalry officer. He's staying with me as aide. He's a fighter and we need him."

"He's all of that and I don't give a damn what else," agreed young McIntosh, feeling, I suppose, he owed at least the forelock of his fine red scalp to me.

"All right, Major." Moylan nodded. "Where do we go from here?"

"God knows. But I say up to those bluffs is our only chance. Get up there and stay there. What do you say, eh?"

"My God, we can't make it!"

"Well, we've got to, Captain." I talked fast, before he could worry too much about my qualifications. "If we stay here they'll get the horses. I know Indians and their thinking. Right now they'll be seeping in around French's flank over there on the right, trying to get in and stampede the horses. We can't handle the mounts if they get panicky. Not and have any men left to keep up a fire. If the Sioux get us afoot down here on the flat, we're dead."

"Oh, where the hell is Custer?" broke in Reno, querulously.

"And Benteen," added McIntosh.

"God knows about Benteen," I hurried on, "but I think Custer's tried to go around. He was convinced the Hunkpapa and Oglala were down south. He's gone around to hit them. We can't wait any longer, anyhow." I had to shout over the rising Sioux fire. "We've got to mount up and make a run for those west bluffs."

Reno acquiesced at once, backed by McIntosh. But Moylan hesitated, as well a man might in such a spot. His hesitation was short-lived. A runner from Captain French panted up with the news the Sioux were infiltrating his flank heavily. "Captain thinks they mean to run off the horses. Corporal Pickens savvies their lingo and he says he hears them keep hollerin', 'Sunke Wakan, Sunke Wakan.' Says that means 'horses' in Sioux."

"He's damn right it does," I exploded. "If you don't think so watch my dust. I'm going for those bluffs while I can get my hands on a horse."

"Give the command, Moylan." Reno's instruction was decisive.

"That's an order?"

"It is."

"Very well, then, here we go."

Reno then started yelling excitedly, "McIntosh! McIntosh! Where the hell are you?"

"Yes sir? Right here, Major." The youthful officer hadn't been ten feet away, in plain sight.

"Clear out. Every man mount up and make for those bluffs. Do you hear?"

"Right."

"Moylan!" the wounded major bawled out after the retreating figure of his senior captain. "Get out when you can. Everybody out. Hurry it up."

These shouted orders coming over the constantly building Sioux fire, upset the command. Whether by misunderstanding or simple panic will never be known but our charge out of that wood was almost a rout. Some of the men either never got the order to clear out or else ignored it. I think the latter. There was no actual unity of command left.

Moylan went out first, not waiting for anybody. With him went what was left of A Company. McIntosh and ourselves with G Company were next and French with M, last. It was part of this company that got left behind, about twenty men in all, whether by choice or accident is the guess of the devil, but the Sioux drowned those woods with an avalanche of warriors which lapped our heels as we fled, and those twenty were dead before we were out of hearing.

Once in the open riding hard, we were able to bunch somewhat, hitting the river in fair order, making the bluffs in a last rush. Casualties, as will happen in such crazy actions where they should be heavy, were light. Through a blizzard of lead which should have sent half of us to hell on a short-term ticket, we made it with only four wounded. Dug in on the blufftops a quick count showed fifty-eight men on their feet and fighting. Our surgeon was dead, his three corpsmen wounded. Reno was partly irrational from his head injury. Most of our other wounded were blanket cases.

It was 3:00 P.M.

Chapter 12

WE HAD been in the fight only forty-five minutes and taken more than two score casualties. It took no mathematician to figure our future at that rate. Almost a man a minute. We had less than an hour to go.

"Where in the name of God do you suppose Benteen is?" Moylan asked, joining me where I was directing the fire of G Company downhill on the advancing Sioux. I didn't get a chance to answer, for a trooper rushed up waving his carbine excitedly.

"Captain, there's a million of 'em comin' up that north ravine on our side. We can't stop 'em."

"You think *you've* got Indians? Look down there." I joshed him, gesturing to the slopes below, up where three or four hundred braves were belly-snaking and hip-firing their way. "What do you think those are?"

"Damn'f I know," answered the trooper, a wild grin lighting up his dirty face. "But I sure as hell know what *those* are!" His words and cross-valley-pointing arm were exclamation-marked by the sweetest sound this side of Gabriel's trumpet—a U. S. Army bugle blowing the charge.

Across the valley, down out of the bluffs overlooking the grove we had just evacuated, came Benteen's wanderers. They'd seen us trapped below and had started down at once but by the time their mounts drummed past that grove it was silent as a graveyard at midnight.

Reno, out of his head by now, jumped to his feet, started to run down the slope toward Benteen before we could stop him, yelling and waving his arms hysterically. "For God's sake, Benteen! Halt your command and help me. I've lost half my men!"

A minute later and Benteen's battalion had joined the remnant of Reno's on top the bluff.

A fine officer and a cool one, he at once took command. Far from questioning my new status he singled me out at once. "What do you suppose ails those Indians? They split off to let me through and now they're running off up the valley. I don't get it."

It was oddly true. The Sioux were streaming south up the Little Big Horn by the literal hundreds, obvious excitement stirring through them like a giant whirlygust in the powdered dirt of an old campground.

"Well, they've got us up a stump and we'll damn well keep. My idea is they've got their eye on bigger game."

Benteen looked at me sharply as I spoke. "The general?"

"Damn right. Our flush is busted right now. Custer's up there somewhere and he'll never in God's world make it down here."

"Hope you're right on the busted flush," Benteen replied. "Looks more like a dead man's hand to me."

"Yeah."

"Say, how long has Reno been out of his head?"

"Just the last few minutes, clear off like this," I responded, grinning and nodding to Moylan who had just crawled up. "He rode into a trap down there. Custer never showed and we had to fight it to here. Reno did a good job while he lasted. Saved what you see of the battalion, anyway."

"Reno's all right. Anybody'd go crazy in this. God, what a mess! Where in the devil do you suppose Custer is? Heard any firing?" Moylan and I shook our heads. It was then he fished in his pocket and tossed over a crumpled scrap of paper. "Read that."

I took it and read: "Benteen—come on—big village—be quick—bring packs." There was the signature of Custer's adjutant, Cooke, in the same scrawl as the brief note, and then hurried, "P.S. Bring pacs."

"When did this come?" I asked.

"About an hour ago."

"What happened?"

"We were on our way to him when we saw you down in that grove."

To my knowledge that was the last communication from Custer.

Reno, who'd been sitting by all the while holding his head, turned a white face up muttering incoherently, "Not a shot. Not a shot. And what I want to know is, where the hell is Custer? Damn it, he was supposed to support me. Where the hell is he?"

Where indeed? The question was on the lips and in the minds of every weary frightened man on that hill. And why didn't the Sioux come on up and finish us? We were beaten, broken, whipped. Just sitting up there dull-eyed, waiting to be wiped out. Why didn't the Sioux come on? Why were they stopping, fleeing up the valley? Was Custer coming up at last in support? Could Gibbon's column possibly be near? Where was Custer?

"Well?" Reno's face was gray, his eyes walled with desperation. "Answer me. Where the hell is he? Damn it, where's Custer?" He wasn't talking *to* anybody, just shouting aloud, under shock.

"God only knows, Marc," Benteen answered, soothingly.

"And he's not telling," Lieutenant McIntosh finished the phrase, hopelessly.

The lieutenant was wrong. God *was* telling.

To the south, upstream, out of the strange lull which had palled the whole valley for the past five minutes, a heavy, continuous rifle fire began. Through the barking, cracking rattle of the general wild Indian firing, rolled a cadence terrifyingly familiar to every soldier among us—the repeated, controlled volleys of men firing on command.

"God," breathed Benteen, his voice hushed with fear, "it's him . . ."

Captain Weir, commanding D company under Benteen, leaped to his feet. "That's Custer for sure."

His lieutenant, Edgerly, seconded him. "It's got to be him, and we've got to go down there."

"I'm going to ask him," exclaimed Weir, meaning Reno who, though laid out on a blanket by this time, was still nominally in command. "But if he won't take the command in himself, will you go with me and D Company, alone?"

"I'll get the company mounted up," Edgerly replied eagerly. "We'll be ready to move when you signal." With that he ran, low-bent, over to the lines across the blufftop where D Company was firing.

"Fred," Weir addressed Benteen, his senior, "have I your permission if I get his?"

"Captain, if you've got the guts to go down there, I haven't the guts to stop you."

Weir ran for Reno, but not alone. "Need an orderly, Captain?" I grinned, falling into stride beside him. He looked at me irritatedly, then panted, "No. Hell no. Go on back."

Since I outranked him, in my own army at least, I chose to ignore the order and was at his side when he drew up to Reno. Two more heavy volleys rolled down the valley as we stopped.

"Major, that's Custer firing down there. I want permission to take D Company and go down there to join him."

Reno had recovered somewhat, his answer indicating near rationality. "We're here and we stay here. With luck we might last till Gibbon gets up. It's a chance. Down there—no chance. Not for anybody. If that's Custer, he's already beyond help. I won't sacrifice these men. Nobody leaves this hill with my orders."

Weir knew he had no time to argue. "Then somebody is leaving without your orders. And it's I." Turning, he started angrily for his horse, in doing so nearly running me down. "Still feel like playing orderly?" he challenged, his tone implying his certainty I would not.

"What's the first order, sir?" I threw him a Johnny salute and a grin.

"Get a horse and come on. Reno refused. I can't take the company but I can take myself. And you. If you want to go."

We mounted, putting our horses over the edge, down the precipitous south decline. We weren't a hundred yards down when Edgerly and D Company came sliding over the rim to join us. When the lieutenant came up it proved he had seen us ride off, assumed permission had been granted, followed along.

We went in silence a few minutes, riding hard. But forty

men and horses trying to keep company formation over terrain as rough as a porcupine's back don't make the kind of speed I knew was necessary. I drove my mount in alongside Weir's.

"Captain, I'm going ahead. I know a gully route that shortcuts up to where I think they've got him cornered. A man can get through but not a company. All right?"

"Go on, for God's sake. Tell him to hold on. We're coming."

As I topped the last rise before plunging into the gully which was to take me to Custer and the end of the trail for Cetan Mani, I had a last clear view of the blufftops we had just quitted.

Down the slopes we had come, now came others. Judging from my quick glance, the whole outfit. Checking my horse, I waved both arms above my head, shouting to Weir and Edgerly two hundred yards below. "Reno and Benteen are coming up. Right behind you."

The two officers waved back signifying their understanding, Weir shouting something I didn't hear in return. It made little difference. I was not to see any of them again. I'd had my last look at Reno's and Benteen's ragged remnant of the gallant Seventh.*

---

*"Weir and his troop advanced to a hilltop overlooking the battle-scene. They could see the Indians, some of whom were gathered in groups, while others rode about, shooting at objects on the ground. But no engagement was in progress. Whatever of combat there had been was finished now; and if the sounds of battle they had heard, the volleys that had reached their ears, had indeed come from Custer it was evident that he was no longer fighting there.

"Weir's troopers searching out that field with straining eyes, wondered what had become of their commander. Little did they imagine the truth. Nor did any member of Reno's command, which soon followed Weir's advance, draw any other inference from what they dimly saw in the distance than that Custer had found the Sioux too strong and, repulsed, had gone to join forces with the advancing columns of Terry and Gibbon. They had but to hold their own yet a little while, they thought, and Custer would come charging back with reinforcements.

"Soon the Indians began to press upon Benteen, who had followed and reached Weir. They determined to retire to the hill they had just left and there to stand and fight. The attack lasted until a merciful darkness, settling down upon the hills, put an end to the conflict.

"That night, there in the Indian village across the Little Big Horn, there was revelry and celebration. That night, among the little band of soldiers on the hill, there was feverish preparation for defense against the attack that all knew would be renewed with the first blush of daylight; and many were the muttered curses, both of officer and man, that Custer and his five companies had deserted them.

"All night long the little band burrowed in the dusty, flinty ground, scooping out, with such implements as they had—three spades and two axes were the only tools they possessed—shallow holes which would afford some cover. Working, perforce, with knives and spoons, all except Benteen's company dug in as best they might. During the night, positions hastily taken the evening before were revised; gaps in the line were closed; the animals were picketed and protected as much as the terrain would permit.

I found Custer where I thought I would, caught in the flat of the broad trail leading from the east hills down to the ford across the Little Big Horn at Beaver Creek. This put him precisely between and in front of the Oglala and Minniconjou camps, these being the very boys who now had him fronted, flanked and hamstrung as I topped out on a ridge four hundred yards north of the battle.

It was 4:00 P.M. when I got my first sight of Custer.

The scene was one of the wildest pandemonium. Sioux swarmed everywhere. The shrill outcries of crazed and dying men and animals carried clearly to my position. The volume of fire from the hostiles was deafening, that of the Seventh, though still under command-volleys, already ragged and disintegrating. The sum total of the battle noise was frightening, now. Thirty minutes later not a single rifle shot echoed within ear's-reach of the Little Big Horn.

But those thirty minutes were the wildest of my life.

Here is what I saw before abandoning my refuge and going in: Custer, with his Gray Horse Troop, was in position on the hillside. What was left of the other companies was strung in a half-mile line along the top of the last ridge fronting the river, an advance force being on the slopes in front of the ridge itself. This placed the whole force of them in Custer's immediate front.

They had apparently just advanced to these positions, for the field between them and the Gray Horse Troop was littered with kicking, dying cavalry mounts, and the twisted, still forms of their riders.

A long deep gulch led from the river up into the heart of the defended ridge. Into the mouth of this I could see hundreds of mounted Sioux galloping. Its walls gave them per-

"At daybreak the attack began, the Indians firing from cover. From time to time on the 26th bugle calls were heard. The soldiers also saw among the Indians men in white men's clothes, even uniforms. This distracted the soldiers between alternate hope that relief was coming, and fear that deserters were fighting with the Sioux. Not until long afterward was the truth revealed; that the Sioux had stripped the clothing from Custer's dead, soldiers and civilians alike, and donned it in the hope of drawing Reno's men from their secure position; that the bugle which they had heard had been torn from the body of an ill-fated trumpeter of Custer's battalion, and had been sounded by an Indian warrior with the same crafty purpose.

"All that day they fought, now charging to disperse the Indians near their front, now retreating to shelter. When night came bringing temporary relief, they buried some of the dead and shifted positions to be nearer water and get away from the stench of the dead animals. But all the time and in each man's mind was the question, 'Where is Custer? Why doesn't he come?'" (R. G. Raymer: *History of Montana*.)

Note: It was 5:00 P.M. when Weir reached his vantage point overlooking the battleground. By that time Custer was thirty minutes gone, up along the dusty trail to nowhere.

fect protection from the fire of the troops, who could not even see them entering the gully, and allowed them passage into the very center of Custer's advance lines. At the same time, deep gullies flanked both ends of the position. While the troops could see the side gullies they were obviously unaware of the danger of the middle gulch.

To Custer's south the hills were covered with Indians, more of them pouring out of the gully which serviced that flank, by the minute. Even at my distance I recognized a lone figure momentarily outlined against the sky directing the assault. Who could miss that lean panther's body, the single spotted eagle feather, that careering black stud, the black wolfskin body trappings and ineffable grace of bearing: Tashunka Witko, Crazy Horse, was tearing at Yellow Hair Custer's bleeding right flank.

Below me spread the line of hostiles trapping him on the north, his left. With a good wind I could have spit on them. Riding their lines, firing, yelling orders, issuing warwhoops wholesale, raced another familiar red man: squat, ugly, capable Gall. Gall the good soldier, the fearless fighter, the white-hater.

Flanked by Gall and Crazy Horse, the best war chiefs in the business, fronted by two thousand other charging Sioux, three deep gullies giving covered approach to the very doorstep of his flat, wide-open, undefendable position, Custer was through, finished, done for.

Between me and the dying Seventh lay four hundred yards of open ground. I got a good grip on the reins with my hand, a better one of my lip with my teeth, slammed the spurs into the good horse under me, laid the barrel of my Colt flat aslant his haunch and fired one shot.

The lead ploughed a shallow furrow across the beast's rump and this, with the spurs and my warwhooping "*Heee-yaahhh!*" sent him bursting down into that ravine full of Gall's Sioux like a buck deer with a bobcat clawing his butt. We were up and out of that gully before the Minniconjou realized what'd hit them.

Then they came after me with a rush. But not quite rush enough. I cut down the slope for the troops on the ridge, hoping to reach them before the Sioux came up into their midst out of that center gully. I lay over my horse's off-side, Oglala-style, leveling on my pursuers to see if Cetan Mani still had his eye. With the five shots left in the Colt I knocked three of them flopping; accepting that as "fair," considering my Army-trained mount's aversion to having his rider operating under his belly.

The troops, seeing a lone sergeant on a cavalry horse tearing up, gave me covering fire as I came in. The Sioux sheered away cheated for the moment. But again they'd recognized me.

Bob-Tail-Horse, the noted Cheyenne warrior, shook his rifle angrily.* "We saw you, Hawk. You're dead!" I couldn't help but agree with the possible logic of his sentiment, but just for the hell of it, snapped a long shot at him with the carbine. I had the pleasure of seeing his pony buckle sideways and fall, neighing crazily, over the lip of the gully.

"Who's in command, here?" I yelled, sliding off my horse into the midst of a group of enlisted men. A pickerel-jawed non-com spoke up in a voice as calm as though he were directing the general's wife to the ladies' latrine.

"Nice ride, chief. Captain Keogh. Over there on that clay-bank sorrel." This sergeant proved the finest fighting soldier I ever knew. I won't forget his name and hope history doesn't either: Sergeant Butler.

As I ran hunched and dodging to Keogh's position, I constantly had to leap the prostrate, frequently still struggling bodies of downed horses and troopers. Nobody was attending the wounded. Nobody could. Every hand that could hold a gun was holding, and every finger that could press a trigger, was pressing—hard.

"Keogh! Get your command back at once. Pull them in. Get those men on the other side of the gully back over here at once. Pull them in. Pull them in!"

"Who in God's name are you?" gasped Keogh, getting shot out of his saddle the minute he spoke, a Sioux slug low through both lungs. I pulled him back of a dead horse and flopped on my belly beside him as I answered.

"Runner, from Reno. He and Benteen are coming. But so are a thousand Sioux. Right up that gully in your center. I could see them pouring into the lower end of it from up there where I just came from. If you don't get those men out of there right—" But Captain Myles Keogh wasn't listening to me. He wasn't listening to anybody. He was bleeding to death.

"Trumpeter! Hey, trumpeter! For God's sake, isn't there a bugler in this outfit?"

---

*This is the warrior who led the four Cheyennes who bluffed Custer into his fatal stop on the hillside.

"Here, sir." A boy, not over seventeen, his right ear shot away, answered. "What's the call?"

"Retreat. Blow your lungs out, boy!" I was on Keogh's horse now, riding the lines, bellowing heavily. "Back! Get back. Get away from that gully. It's full of Indians. Fall back. Run!"

The men needed no further invitation. Most of those who still had mounts under them streamed up the hill, making it to Custer, safely. The others began to run for it on foot. Captain Yates, Sergeant Butler, two corporals and myself, all mounted, stayed with the men on foot giving them what cover we could.

Even in the weird disorder of that broken rout I couldn't fail to note Butler. He was everywhere, riding and firing with amazing rapidity. He was the best shot with a carbine I ever saw.

Yates and the two corporals were loading and firing well, too, and I don't think it immodest to feel our gunwork alone allowed what of the command did get up the hill, to make it.

The last man away from the ridge wasn't fifty feet from the gullyhead when the Sioux began to vomit out of it by the score.

The fire from our five carbines was just enough to hold them up for a couple of minutes, then they came on, anyway.

As the final inundation of Sioux broke from the gully, Gall and Crazy Horse came in from both flanks. There was no stopping them. They knifed, lanced, shot and clubbed our fleeing troopers. Yates went down, knocked out of his saddle by a collision with Crazy Horse's black stallion. I saw the war chief fire down into his fallen foe's body, then an Indian voice was howling, "Get him. That's him. Get the Hawk!"

It was Gall, urging his warriors toward me through the litter of dead and dying.

At the call of my name, Crazy Horse whirled and came for me, too. *"H'g-un!"* I yelled at him, and shot his black stud out from under him.

That finished the carbine for shots, but I was just in time to turn and give it a fond farewell by wrapping it around Gall's ugly skull as he rode in to lance me.

Down on the ridge I had picked up another Colt from the dozens lying around on the ground, so had both hands full for his faithful followers. I shot my way through them, headed for the only white man standing short of Custer's hillside—Sergeant Butler. He was still horsed, still firing. He had two Colts, also, and the way he snapped and rolled them was sheer magic.

I got to him though it cost me two dear friends: Roan Calf, a Cheyenne, and Gray Bear, a Minniconjou.

We had a second of respite as we came together, for no Indian likes well-directed belly-fire on the intimate basis we'd been pouring it to them—say from about two pony-lengths. Butler gestured up toward Custer, said, laconically, "Let's go."

"Right now," I assented. "And here comes our escort."

We made it up to Custer who still had sufficient organization to give us enough of a covering volley to knock the redskins off our tails.

We had left the ridge with about seventy men, arrived on the hill with thirty-five. The retreat took five minutes. It was now 4:15. Custer had 115 actives left.

Now came a five-minute lull while the Sioux gathered for the kill. "Lull" is used advisedly. The tremendous Sioux fire continued and we took casualties every one of those five minutes. What I mean is there was no mass charge made in that time, no concerted rushing advance. During those minutes I learned all any man is ever going to know about Custer's movements up to the time I found him.

The general was a sight to stir the heart and pride of any soldier. His shoulder and chest were soaked with the blood which still ran from a deep head wound. His left arm was in a torn-scarf sling, shattered by a large-caliber ball. He sat on the hot, bare ground, his back to a small boulder. The Gray Horse colors and the red and silver regimentals of the Seventh, with his big, red "7" on the lower half of the pennon, flanked him. On the ground to his right hand lay a stack of loaded carbines. Two Colts were strapped around his waist. In all that welter of bare-headed, naked-waisted, shot-torn men, he alone held to dress; hat, gauntlet, blouse, sash. No history book could possibly gild the truth of his appearance there and then.

Wounded, down, defeated—he was still, unquestionably, The General.

His mind was clear as a piece of glass. He knew me at once and no words were wasted.

"Where are they?"

"Both coming. Benteen with Reno. They've caught hell, too. Reno lost fifty men. Benteen not so many. Reno's out of his head with a bad scalp wound. They ought to be getting close."

"How close?"

"Forty-five minutes, maybe thirty." I saw the shadow flick his eyes.

"Which way?"

"The way I came in. North by east."

"Who's between us?"

"Gall. With about six hundred Minniconjou and Hunkpapa."

"Over there?" he gestured south.

"Crazy Horse. A thousand Oglala."

"That's out. What's below?"

"Everything. Maybe two thousand. Mixed bands. That's out, too."

"How many men came up from the ridge with you just now?"

"Thirty-five or forty."

"That gives us about a hundred."

"Or a little over."

"Cooke!" Custer raised his voice, calling in his adjutant. "Take this down. I'm going to talk fast. It's a statement of responsibility." Cooke squatted by his side and the general began talking, his voice low, swift. Other than Cooke, I was the only immediate witness to the whole story.

"Get this straight. If any of us get out of here, I want it known I take full responsibility, not only for my own position but for that of Reno and Benteen. I pulled out from under Reno on a hunch. I've always played hunches, but this one played me."

"It happens to all of us, General," I tried reassuring him, pity for this great soldier rising up in my throat like a fist-sized rock despite my certain knowledge of the terrible blunder he had made. "We all play hunches. We've got to in this business." He passed my interruption, unnoticed.

"We came around behind the east bluffs, heading for this track down to the ford. When we got here I saw the big village below, unguarded. I sent my trumpeter, John Martin, to Benteen with a message to come quick."

"He got it," I interjected.

"Good." He paused to wipe the blood away from his mouth. "I started on down. As I did, four Indians rode across the ford and right up the grade at us.* I couldn't figure that. Thought it was a trap. Halted the command up there." He gestured back up the hill where I noted for

*The Cheyenne—Bob-Tail-Horse, Roan Bear, Big Face, Calf.

the first time a litter of troopers' bodies. "I gave the order to dismount.

"That was a terrible error. It gave Crazy Horse time to get around behind us. He struck us there while we were dismounted. Calhoun is up there with twenty of my troopers, little Autie Reed, and my other brother.*

"I mounted and started on down then. Too late. Every foot of ground on all sides of me was covered with hostiles. A charge would have been murder by then. My hesitation over those four incredibly brave Indians finished me. Had I charged at first sight of the village I could have cut it in two, relieved Reno, joined Benteen on the other side, swept back through and broken them up for good.**

"If any man here lives, let him remember what I've said. "All right, Cooke. I'll sign that now."

That speech wasn't made any the less remarkable for the conditions under which it was delivered. During it, the officers and enlisted personnel had been pressed back by the Sioux fire until we were the center of a tight, sweating, jam-packed huddle of desperate men.

It isn't to be thought Custer and I just sat there and watched his command being chewed up while Cooke was taking his statement. The whole time we were firing carbines from the loaded pile by his side. Officers were rushing up for orders, riderless horses raced and reared everywhere, men fell, noiselessly or shrieking with pain. We fought as he talked.

I can no more understand his use of me as a witness than you might. I feel that in his final hour he faced his guilt like the soldier he was. At the same time such a burden of conscience was more than any man might wish to take with him. Faced with death, most men will talk. Custer did, and I just happened to be there.

Just as suddenly as he had given his statement he forgot it.

"Tom!" His brother, Captain Tom Custer, ranking officer left alive, hurried up.

"Are you all right, General?"

"Certainly. Listen. Tell Lieutenant Smith we're going out of here on our feet."

---

* Boston Custer, the second of two brothers the general had with him. It was a hard day for the Custer family. Autie Reed was his nephew, Calhoun, his brother-in-law.

** Many military historians agree.

"George, we can't do it. The Sioux are coming at us again any second. Can't you see them massing?"

"Tom, we're going out. Right now. Tell Smith."

"All right. Which way do we go?"

"Benteen and Reno are coming in over there, from the north. Maybe thirty minutes out. We're going to meet them."

Captain Custer's face brightened. When he shouted the news to the men, a ragged cheer went up. I cinched up my holsters, belted on some more ammunition, slung two extra carbines across my back. All around me others were doing the same.

We had five horses left.

Chapter 13

CUSTER, Lieutenant Smith, Captain Tom Custer, Sergeant Butler and I took the horses. Custer had decided to try and get up to the top of the hill, regrouping there for a continued retreat toward Reno or, if the field of fire appeared good, to try to hold onto the hill until darkness or Reno relieved him. It was as sound a plan as any and the general's calm orders outlining it gave us all hope. He made it sound like once up there we had the Sioux at our mercy.

"We'll divide the command into four companies. [By now no formal companies existed.] I'll take Company One. Captain Custer, Two. Lieutenant Smith, Three." His next words affected me deeply. "Colonel Clayton, Company Four.

"We'll go up the hill this way: Company One will retreat ten yards, halt and fire back while Two proceeds ten yards beyond, halts and fires in turn, and so on. Each company thus covering for the other. This will give us seventy-five per cent continuous fire, also provide the enemy with a reduced aiming point. Is the action clear?"

"All clear." The three of us nodded our understanding.

"Do the men understand it?" Custer shouted to the ranks. The sum total of their answers added up to, "My God, yes. Let's go!"

"Sergeant Butler, I want you to stay with the last company, right on up the hill. I want to hear that carbine of yours firing all the way. All right?"

"You'll hear it, General." The sergeant's lean jaw worked in a wolf's grin, his carbine barking three times in period to his remark.

"Now boys"—the general's words were heard clearly in one of those strange lulls which bloom in heavy fire—"we all know what we're heading into. Let's head into it like men. There's one force to help us now. May God bless us one and all." A terrific burst of Sioux fire cannonaded into the delivery of his last words. With it the hostiles came screaming in at us from every eighth of the compass. Only the short route up the hill behind us lay open. Spurring his horse in that direction, Custer shouted, "All right, men. Let's go!"

We didn't go far. The Sioux had a good general, too.

At first we went up fast, Custer's chain retirement working well. It looked like we would make it. The Sioux below and flanking us didn't seem eager to come on in, contenting themselves with shadowing our retreat, firing from cover as they followed. Even so their fire was hitting in, troopers dropping by twos and threes every yard of the way. Hot as the fire was and busy as we all were aiming and firing back and running, I still wondered what the devil was holding the Sioux back.

I found out soon enough.

Fifty yards from the top of the hill Custer regrouped us. There were about sixty men remaining alive.

Tom Custer and Lieutenant Smith were on the slope below. Custer shot through the head, killed instantly, Smith, with his pelvis shattered, struggling to drag himself up the slope by his hands. We couldn't cover him. I saw Cow Runner snake in like a ferret under the drifting rifle smoke, seize Smith by the hair, whip his knife into and around the head. I got a bead on the Cheyenne but another burst of rifle fire rolled more smoke between us and when it cleared I could see Smith still moving, still groping blindly upward. But now he had no hair. Cow Runner had it.

Cow Runner didn't have it long. As he ran for the gully, he shook the grisly trophy aloft, howling the wolf howl of his people, and my first shot broke his back to send him jerking spasmodically around on the ground like a trout flopping on dry grass. I hope Cow Runner died slow. But I shot him again as he flopped, just to make sure it wouldn't be too slow. I owed him two. One for Lieutenant Smith. One for Colonel Clayton.

He was the son-of-a-bitch who very nearly talked me out from under that beaver lodge.

We now started on up the hill in two companies, Custer commanding the first, I the second, Butler fighting with both. Not once did I see any trooper between the sergeant and the enemy.

We covered half the distance to the hilltop before it happened. I had just moved my men back through Custer's when I had a sudden impulse to turn and look up. To the end my "Indian hunch" played faithful.

A lone Sioux horseman stood lean and black against the skyline. As I saw him, he threw up his arm in signal. A single, high call broke from his lips. It was a sound to curdle the courage in any white vein. Harsh, shrill, ululating. The scream of the panther hunting in the night. The tribal war cry of the Oglala Bad Face band.

No red throat could put the terror in it Tashunka Witko's could.

"Custer, look out!" I bawled down to the general. "We're flanked."

Crazy Horse followed my words down the hill, three hundred yelling Oglala at his back.

Custer had the time it takes a racing Indian pony to cover fifty yards, to prepare his last defense. All any man could do, he did—kept levering shells into his carbine and firing them. I can hear his last given orders as clearly as though he were calling them as I write. "Stay together, men. Don't break. Fire low. We'll make it." His unforgettable voice carried over the panic disorder which had seized our men at the appearance of Crazy Horse. They actually pulled together and stood to take the Oglala charge. This was bravery in its highest hour. But like so much of bravery, futile, senseless, pointless.

Crazy Horse rode into us on the gallop, the momentum of the impact carrying the fight down the hill. His warriors threw themselves from their ponies and the battle was instantly hand-to-hand. Knife flashed against knife, Colt against tomahawk, clubbed carbine against war ax and lance.

My memory of those two minutes is necessarily incomplete. You can't be fanning two Colts, dodging war clubs, ducking axes, grabbing up fallen rifles and firing them, all the while leading a frightened cavalry horse, and still be making comprehensive tactical observations.

These things I remember, though: a crazed corporal, snatching the reins of Sergeant Butler's horse, swinging aboard the brute and galloping out through the Sioux lines. The Indian horde opening like a gaping, red mouth to let him in. The poor devil throwing his Colt to his temple, blowing the side of his head out before the Indians could touch him. The ripe-pumpkin "pop" of skulls opening under rifle butt or war club. A tall, drawling southern private fighting shoulder to shoulder with me. The soft pelting across my cheek of what felt like half-a-dozen small, wet sponges—his brains dashed out by an Indian rifle slug, spattering into my face. The sudden, dull realization that no more than ten white men remained alive and standing. The picture of Custer among them, hatless now, uniform slashed to ribbons, yellow hair flying, fighting like a madman. The following flashes of shock-image recording on my mind that we were now eight. Now six. Suddenly, three. Butler and Custer and I.

The general died first.

How history or the legend-makers will draw that death, God alone knows. Probably with yellow curls streaming, a gun blazing in either hand, a defiant burst of laughter on the smiling, boyish lips, a last-second, heroic flinging of the empty guns in the snarling faces of the enemy.

Well, if so, they won't be too far amiss. General Custer was on his horse at the last. A smother of Sioux fire cut man and beast down together, the horse falling sideways to pin Custer's left leg beneath it. Butler and I started for him but a wedge of Sioux cut us off. Firing into their galloping ranks, we saw the end.

Custer, still alive, twisted up to rest his Colt across his dead mount's withers. Crazy Horse and a shrieking knot of Oglala rode over him. The general emptied his Colt up into their ponies' bellies. One—three—five shots, and they were on him, lances driving, axes swinging. Their charge carried them on beyond the sodden, motionless figure. As they wheeled their mounts, Custer stirred. His right arm reached out toward them, the Colt in its hand, half-raised.

Then they shot down into him, there on the ground. We were so close we could hear the soapy smack of lead hitting into flesh. The Colt barrel wavered, plunged earthward. The finger on its trigger stiffened. Custer's last shot. It went ploughing into the trampled dirt of the hillside.

He didn't hear its sound.

Two Sioux braves seized him by the arms, wrenching the lifeless body from under the horse. A third sprang in, knotting his left hand in the thick yellow curls. Up went the scalping knife.

A rifle shot cracked. The knife went spinning crazily out of the warrior's shattered hand. A guttural voice boomed angrily one vibrating word. *"Woyuonihan!"* I saw Crazy Horse standing beyond Custer's horse, the thin blue smoke still wisping from his rifle barrel.

"Woyuonihan," he repeated, ominously. *"Wakan pecokan sunpi."* Literally, "Respect him. This is a holy scalplock." The two warriors holding the general's arms released them, stepped quickly away.

Again it is not possible to know what history will ascribe as the reason for the Sioux not scalping Yellow Hair. I have given the real one: one great warrior's personal respect for another. For the fact that forty-eight hours later, Terry's column found Custer's body unmarked save for the wounds he took in battle, future generations of hero-makers may thank an "ignorant, vicious savage." Tashunka Witko, the war chief, Crazy Horse.

There had been a pause in the furious action such as must grace the actual moment of a great soldier's death. But now the Sioux turned on Butler and me like so many hunt-eager hounds. Yellow Hair was dead. The battle was over. They had won the greatest victory over white troops in their history. Now all that remained was to chase down the great soldier with the chevrons and Cetan Mani.

Best not to spoil such fun too quickly. Let them run. Let them have a start. Especially Cetan Mani. It never does to let a traitor die too fast. *Hopo! Hookahey!*

Swinging up on Keogh's horse, Comanche, I grabbed Butler by the arm, shouting, "Let's go, Sergeant. They'll want a run before elevating our wigs." His hard jaw broke in that fast grin as he swung up behind me.

"By all means. Let's not disappoint the little red sons-of-bitches."

I let Comanche go a dozen jumps across the hill. Suddenly Butler called out, "Hit for the top, Colonel." I swung the horse hard left, putting him up the last few yards of the incline. "We'll make that goddam hill even if Custer couldn't." The soldier's words were gritted between clamped teeth and I knew he'd been hit.

The Sioux came right on our haunches, yelping and warwhooping but holding their fire now.

As we hit the rise, Sergeant Butler yelled, "Give 'em hell, chief. Here goes the Seventh." He'd flung himself off the horse, hit the ground, rolled to his knees and had the Colts smoking, almost before his words were out.

The Sioux split around the hilltop and came for me. But now the lead was singing and the fun was over. They meant business. Behind me I could hear Butler's guns still going.

Two slugs whined by my ear and I had no more than time to think the Sioux were beginning to range me when the third whanged across the side of my head, knocking me out of the saddle as neatly as you'd swat a bull-bat off a fence post with a broom handle.

I hit very hard but managed to end up on my elbows with a gun going in either hand. I got two or three shots out of the left, one out of the right Colt, then just ringing, flat trigger clicks. The Sioux were haunch-sliding their ponies, piling off, running toward me on foot. I saw Crazy Horse, Hump, Gall, White Bull, in the van. Beyond them, on the hill, gunsmoke still drifted. Butler was still alive, surely the last man of Custer's 7th U. S. Cavalry, to die.*

I saw no more. A great flap of skin from my torn scalp sagged down over my vision. Blood filled my eyes.

I groped to my feet, blind, drew Yellow Bird's knife and started forward.

Hearing alone remained to me of my senses. I "heard" the blows striking into me. But they were without location, meaning or feeling. If I thought I heard a familiar, deep voice calling, *"Woyuonihan! Woyuonihan!"* it was probably only that I relived in that last flash of consciousness the memory of Tashunka Witko's gallant crying-out of "Quarter!" over Yellow Hair's fallen form. . . .

Chapter 14

THE FACT that I opened my eyes again at all will strain a generous credulity. That, once opened, they looked upon the scene they did, may prove too much even for the most willing believer. But however incredible, the fact still remains that I had the privilege of listening to my own funeral oration: the speaker, my Sioux "father," Tashunka Witko.

---

*He was. All hostile Indian accounts of the battle agree on this. And add, succinctly: "That soldier with the three chevrons on his sleeve, he was the bravest of them all."

The Oglala bury their honored warrior dead on a high scaffolding. On the bed of this, along with the hero's body, are placed his finest weapons and ample food for the long trail out to Wanagi Yata. Beneath the platform is tethered the favorite war pony of the departed. In exceptional cases where the silent one has died especially well, a fine funeral pyre of tinder-dry kindling is laid beneath his airy couch; to be lit when all the speeches are done and the ceremonies completed. In the case of a Fox Lodge soldier, the one who sponsored him in the "giving of weapons," delivers the eulogy which precedes the torch.

Apparently Cetan Mani had "died well," the above description picturing to the last detail the situation in which I regained consciousness. The only added touch worthy of mention might be the identity of the pony below.

Beneath my cottonwood bier, gray with the snows of fourteen winters, scarred and stiff from a hundred hunts and war raids, rolling his pendulous lower lip over the snaggled, yellow cusps of his remaining teeth, stood old Hussein. The Sioux might have picked fifty better mounts from any of the pony herds but they have a fine sensibility in such matters. This was undoubtedly the horse of Walking Hawk's heart.

One other thing: the weapons they'd provided gladdened the touch of my searching hands. A new Winchester, two holstered Colts, plenty of ammunition for both, Yellow Bird's knife.

My presence there, alive, and to superficial testing, without crippling injury, was seemingly the result of one of those rare cases wherein the cumulative, multiple shock of many injuries, no one of which is in itself disabling, produces a cataleptic condition so closely resembling true death as to deceive even a physician. Marveling at my own escape, I could recall Confederate Army medics discussing similar freak cases of catalepsis in battle shock.

The compounding stroke of luck in my case may have been the bad look of the scalp-wound which had unhorsed me. This had the appearance of being much worse than it was and might well have convinced the warriors the corpse needed no further attention.

So far I could reason, no further.

Why hadn't they shot into my body on the ground as was their custom? Why hadn't they fired arrows into it? Driven lances through it? Why wasn't I scalped?

Crazy Horse's voice was rolling now, supplying the answers. I listened while "scouting" my position.

My scaffold stood on a rise beyond the Oglala camp, this putting it very close to the east bluffs and Medicine Creek. It was distant perhaps two hundred feet from the edge of the restless throng listening to the war chief. Huge victory fires burned up and down the Little Big Horn, from the Hunkpapa on the north to the Sans Arc on the south. The shallow Greasy Grass seemed afire with their lights, its surface blazing orange-red for four miles.

A dozen victory dances were in progress in as many camps, the scalp-pole wheels spinning and jerking crazily with their ghastly ornaments. Drums, war cries, rattles, reed flageolets, eagle-bone whistles echoed everywhere. The buffalo-skulled, elk-antlered medicine men gyrated in their dances from one village to the next, intoning in endless shouts the burden of their master's oration.

"The vision of Tatanka Yotanka has been fulfilled. These soldiers, these white men who had no ears, who would not listen, have come to his camp and met the doom that he prophesied."

Even the great Oglala, who surely engineered the whole trap which destroyed Custer, began his speech with a verbal bow to Sitting Bull.

"Today we have had a great victory. The dream of Tatanka Yotanka was true. His medicine was good. The vision of Sitting Bull has been made to come about. Today we saw many brave enemies die, but three were braver than them all. Yellow Hair was braver. The soldier with the three chevrons was braver. Hawk-That-Walks, my own son, was braver. He was braver and so I would not let you touch his body.

"Yellow Hair and the chevron soldier lie in honored peace upon the hill, for they are white men and soldiers. Cetan Mani lies yonder on the burial sticks, for he is a Sioux and a warrior. He told us he was going to Yellow Hair and he did it. He outran fifty braves. He killed Black Wolf. Now we know that. He came back with Yellow Hair as he promised. He fought like a mad bear. . . ."

I didn't know how long Crazy Horse would talk but one thing I did know—when he finished, I got the torch.

Fortunately, he had his listeners' rapt attention. I was able to work atop the scaffold with comparative freedom. I slipped the Colt belts under me, buckling them on. I stuffed a *parfleche* with pemmican, smoked fat, raw buffalo steaks, and three dozen cartridges for the Winchester. My head hammered with blinding pain. Every move brought some new agony from the abrasions and contusions which covered me.

My throat was on fire, I was dying for water. Still I worked frenziedly, for down by the fires Tashunka Witko was reaching his conclusion.

"He shot my horse. He shot that of Bob-Tail-Horse. He counted coup on Gall. He killed many warriors. He killed three in the gully. He killed Roan Calf and Gray Bear. He led the soldiers up the hill. He killed Cow Runner. And plenty more. He killed Fox Man, and Red Dog. He killed . . ."

I was ready to go. What to do about Hussein? It would be easier to leave him, still if he winded me as I started away without him he might raise hell. It might be better to take him, anyway. If we both disappeared the Sioux might figure we'd made the ride to Yanagi Yata. Of course, in the morning they would see our tracks.

I slipped down off the far side of the scaffold. Hussein whickered and my heart spasmed. I went over to him, whispering quickly, soothingly, knotting the lead rope hard around his reaching nose.

". . . All the things he did, that he said he would do. His tongue was straight as the shot of a star across the sky . . ." Crazy Horse droned on.

I led Hussein over the rise on which the scaffold stood, down into the dark of the gully beyond. The gully was deep, paralleling Medicine Creek and the east bluffs. Now a refinement of my "disappearance act" occurred. Tying Hussein, I ran back up the ridge, flopped on my belly, snaked back down through the grass. After all, a booming fire never was bad theater.

". . . His heart was never bad, his medicine was always good. He was a true Oglala. He left himself among us, even now his mate laboring to deliver the son of Cetan Mani. . . ."

In the pocket of the sergeant's jacket was an Army tinder kit. I fished it out, wadded a pile of dry grass into the faggots crammed under my last resting place, began quickly striking the flint.

". . . He was no traitor. I deny this. He had had a vision. It told him to go to the people of his fathers. He went . . ."

The fat sparks flew into the stuffed grasses, my breath puffing steadily behind them. A cherry-glow began to spread and a wisp of white smoke wobbled upward. Another breath and bright, clean flame ate up the smoke, began to lick swiftly around the ball of dried grass, bit into the faggots above.

". . . *Woyuonihan*. I honor him. He was my son. He was a great warrior. I have spoken."

"*Hun-hun-he! Hun-hun-he!*" The vibrating growl of the packed audience accepting Crazy Horse's speech, rolled in my footsteps as I ran for the ridge-top. I no more than slid over into the dark of the gully than the whole skyline, campward, lit up in flush of red.

I could hear the sucking boom of the mushrooming flames leaping around the scaffolding; then the alarmed shouts and moccasin-falls of the running crowd. The hillside thronged with watchers seconds after I'd quitted it. My medicine was good. A milling, pushing mob of Indians trampled the slope over which Hussein and I had passed.

Our tracks wouldn't be found tomorrow or any morning.

I waited no longer than to know my trip to heaven had been an unqualified success.

I had my doubts what the crafty Uncle of the Hunkpapa would think of such a spontaneous combustion of a miracle, but I would bet anything that the lodges of the rank and file Sioux would grow hushed for generations to come as some wrinkled oldster sucked his stone pipe reverently and launched into the true account of the night Cetan Mani rode the flames to the Gathering Place of the Souls. I'll wager the skin-painters had their color pots out before I got Hussein over to Medicine Creek and tethered in a thick cottonwood clump.

If I never gave the Sioux another thing, I gave them the finest damn funeral-fire in their history.

Leaving Hussein, I went through the night back into the deserted Oglala camp. Sioux villages are always pitched according to rank. I knew exactly where Crazy Horse's tipi would be. And if I didn't know all the dogs in camp by their first names, they knew me. Not a cur whined as I threaded my way in and out among the homes of my lost people.

Before the flap of Crazy Horse's lodge hunched a familiar ugly figure, close-wrapped in a dingy black blanket. All was silent within.

Slipping to the rear, I slit the skins with my knife, slithering into the tipi a second later. Inside, a tiny fire smoldered, rose-red. Its feeble light danced and flickered on the sooted wallskins, chased waveringly over the floor hides and sleeping-robes, came to frightening rest on the figure lying so quietly across the tent from me.

I bent over Star, the great tears splashing my blood-caked cheeks.

Her breathing was stertorous, her color, pale as the dawn

sky in winter. As I watched, she stirred fitfully, mouth drawn back over her teeth, like a frightened animal.

"Star, oh Star!" My whisper couldn't have been heard across the tipi, yet she awoke. Her great green eyes were dark with pain, her faultless face hollow and drawn skintight over the slanting cheekbones. She said no word, reaching up like a sleeping child to take me in her arms. I could feel the hot fever in them as they circled my neck. Her skin burned my lips as I kissed her again and again.

"Star. Listen. Do you know me? Do you hear me?"

"Yes. Oh yes, Cetan. You have come for me, have you, Cetan? I shall not be long. I—"

"Star. Listen to me. Get rid of Tasina Sapewin. Hurry. Do you understand? Send her for water. Do it, Star. Send her away." She nodded, called out, "Mother, Mother, come in to me."

I flattened against the wall behind a pile of buffalo robes. The flat, dark face showed in the flap opening. "You called, child?"

"Mother, I must have water. Fresh. Medicine water. Bring it from the creek."

"Aye. You shall have it." Quickly, she was gone, padding through the dark toward Medicine Creek. I noticed for the first time the small, lumpy bundle slung in doeskin across her back. As she passed the knife-slit a tiny, querulous cry lifted every hair on my head.

My beautiful, poor, wasted Star was in my arms then, my tears splashing shamelessly into the dark glory of her hair.

"Star, you—you are all right?"

"I am going to die, Cetan." She was calm now, her eyes clear. "And in peace now that you are here. Oh, Cetan, I love you more than the breath which feeds my life. When I heard you had died with Yellow Hair, I—"

"Star. Hear me now. I am alive. Believe that. I have escaped, feigning death. It has happened before. But I cannot stay. They think they burned me on the burial scaffold. Listen, Star—"

"It is no use, Cetan. I am done." A hard chill racked her frame. "I lost much blood. The blood came out of me as from the throat of Pte when it is cut. I care not, even so, for he is alive. Your son is alive, Cetan, and so beautiful." I had forgotten the baby, forgetting him again, instantly.

"Tasina Sapewin will return quickly." My words sped with desperation. "I cannot be here."

"Cetan——" Another trembling shudder ran over her. "Will you leave me now? Will you go out, letting Yunke-lo come in? Cetan, you are my life. Cetan!"

She was going now. Her arms clamped in spasm around me then slacked away. I let her back on the robe, tucked it gently around her still figure.

She still breathed, very thinly. But when her eyes opened, they were full of all their old beauty. A flush of high color mounted her cheeks, bringing fleetingly with it the remembered berry-blush of other days. For a magic moment then, I saw the face which guided me safely past Death's gate those many moons ago; which gazed in startlement up at me that long gone morning in the forest above the bathing pool; which peered, wide-eyed, at me the moment before I hurled my knife into the sleeping Fox Runner in Slatemeyer's fugitive camp; which blazed at me that wild, fire-lit instant when I flung the heart of the renegade rapist into the flames at her feet; the face which had blessed my last sight on a thousand nights since, and graced my first as many mornings after.

The face whose memory I would take to hell with me as the most beautiful thing God ever made and man ever looked upon.

I scarcely heard her voice. "Cetan, take the charm." Her pale hand moved to the Aztec amulet around her neck. "It is for him. Name him 'Hawk' after his sire. Here, in this hand" —her other hand fell toward me, tightly clenched—"is his own charm, to be worn into every battle, carried always." She paused, a quiet peace lighting her features. The thin arms reached out.

"Cetan—my love."

That haunting half-smile was on her curving lips. I covered them with mine. And when I brought my lips away, hers still held their graceful, taunting arc. Would hold it forever.

Yunke-lo had entered behind me as I held her.

I eased her slight form onto the deep pile of the great robe, quickly removed the Aztec trinket from her throat, opened the clenched hand she had extended to me. In its small palm lay a wrinkled string of dark tissue, the war-charm every Sioux mother bequeaths her first-born son—it's bloody umbilical cord.

Outside, the shuffle of moccasin steps padded up through the dust. Quickly, I reached for a blanket, spread its gray warmth over my silent Star.

I went out through the knife-slit as Crazy Horse's wife entered the flap, carrying as my last memory the legend which leaped up at me from the blanket as my hands came away from it. "U. S. Army. Seventh Cavalry. Fort Abraham Lincoln. . . ."

I stripped my clothes off, bundled them along with my Colts and ammunition, carefully wrapped in oiled skins, into the war-bag across Hussein's withers. Carrying the Winchester, I grabbed the lead rope and guided Hussein into the middle of the stream. Down the black waters of Medicine Creek we went, man and horse, feeling our way like the veterans at such things we were.

Where the creek entered the Greasy Grass the water was wide and deep. We had to swim for it, heading south up the Little Big Horn, away from the camp.

For two hours we held that watery course, now wading, now slipping, plunging, swimming. With the moon beginning to sag down over the bluffs of the valley behind, I began looking for the right place to take Hussein out of the water. Shortly, I found it, a broad, rock-strewn slope running from the water's edge well back to the hills. I mounted up and we went away from there.

Once free of the valley I swung around to the west of the bluffs on which I was forced to assume Reno's men still remained, awaiting dawn and, as they must have felt, death. (I had no way of knowing how long I had lain unconscious, figuring, for lack of certain knowledge, that the night I awoke was that of Custer's disaster.) Daylight was graying the walls of the Big Horns to the west and my supposition was borne out. To my ears, faint and from far off to the east, carried the sounds of scattered rifle poppings. By the time I had passed out of earshot, the fire had grown heavy.

It was June 26th, about 5:00 A.M.

All that day I rode down the Valley of the Little Big Horn, late afternoon at last bringing to my straining eyes the sight they sought—the heavy dust cloud of marching column moving slowly up the Greasy Grass.

An hour later I rode into the point band of Terry's scouts.

Fortunately these were Pawnees and Rees, strangers to me. Speaking Crow, I demanded to be taken at once to Star Terry or Red Nose Gibbon. The scout captain, a heavy featured slob of a Pawnee, felt inclined to question the whereabouts of my credentials.

"Right here," I said, patting the two Colts, "and if you don't get me to Star or Red Nose at once, I will give them to you. Right between the eyes." He started to raise his carbine. The Colts were on him before the rifle barrel had climbed four inches. Holding his eyes, I added ominously.

"I come from Yellow Hair. He is dead."

Twenty minutes later I was talking with Generals Terry and Gibbon. I put the Crow act on very heavily, wanting no part at the moment of establishing my true identity.

"What do you want?" demanded Terry, suspiciously. "Who sent you? Who are you?"

"Crow. Scout with Oak Leaves Reno. Yellow Hair is dead. Hundreds pony-soldiers dead, too. All dead up there."

Terry and Gibbon were incredulous, not wanting to believe my story, not daring to doubt it. "They can't *all* be dead!" challenged Gibbon, irritatedly. "What the hell are you trying to tell us?"

"Heap Sioux. Hump, Gall, Crazy Horse. Three, mebbeso four thousand, warriors. They chase Oak Leaves up big hill. He is still there. Mebbeso dead now, too."

"My God!" ejaculated Gibbon. "It sounds like he's trying to tell us Custer's been wiped out and Reno's surrounded."

"Yes, and apparently being wiped out, too. Better start the column moving, on the double."

"I doubt his whole damn story," snorted Red Nose. "He could be leading us into a trap. There's no proof whatever he's a scout. Look at him. Naked as a jaybird. And if that's a cavalry horse he's riding, I'm a buck private."

"We don't believe you," Terry said to me. "You have no paper, not even a uniform—"

I smiled as vacuously as I knew how, laughed happily, pulled the rumpled sergeant's uniform out of the war-bag. "Nice suit. Swim river to get away. Keep suit dry, no spoil."

That did it. Gibbon started bawling for his adjutant. The column started forward at once.

"We'll go on up tonight," I heard Terry say. "God knows, it could be true."

With darkness, I deserted the marching troopers, continuing my own way not knowing if the column reached Reno in time or not.*

---

*It did: Accounts vary as to whether their arrival saved Reno, however:

(1) "During the 26th Terry's scouts came upon a Crow scout who informed them that Custer and hundreds had been killed by the Sioux and that the survivors were besieged and in dire distress. Although he could hardly believe this report Terry urged his column forward and this approach which called the Sioux from their concentration on the remnant of Reno's command was all that prevented its annihilation." (Raymer—*Hist. of Mont.*)

(2) "The soldiers were in a tight place. Everybody, both whites and Indians,

Chapter 15

FOR NINE months I lived on the prairies like a buffalo wolf; lean, starving, hunted and hated by all. My first move after leaving Terry had been to go to the Standing Rock Agency with my story as I have told it here. But unknown to me, the very night of his disastrous march on the Sioux, Custer had scribbled a last dispatch, including my capture and his suspicion I had murdered the real Clayton and that I was, in certainty, a full-blooded Sioux, a wanted hostile. I was arrested and sent under guard to the Spotted Tail Agency. On the route I escaped, making my way back to the high prairie homelands on the lonely headwaters of the Tongue and Yellowstone.

The surviving men of the Seventh, Reno, Benteen, Weir, et al., who might have supported my story, had all been shipped east on furlough. On top of that came a dispatch runner from Crook, listing twenty top hostile chiefs participating in the Rosebud clash. Walking Hawk's name was well up on the roll.

As though matters needed further complication the Agency Sioux got the tale of my death from their wild cousins. They spread this around the reservations, making me officially a ghost. This closed my last trail out, for while the tame Indians might have given a live Cetan Mani sanctuary, they would

---

agree that, if the Indians had charged all at once from all sides, a retreat must have followed, and a second retreat under Reno must have become a rout. There was no place to run to: every soldier would have been rubbed out . . . the books say the Indians stopped fighting because they feared the troops coming with 'Red Nose' and 'Star' Terry. But this is nonsense. The Indians could easily have killed all Reno's men before the infantry arrived, and then have run away on their fleet war ponies. Long before noon the women were already striking their tents. The truth has never been told about this: it was Sitting Bull who saved Reno.

"About noon he came to the Sioux line again. He told the young men to stop shooting. 'That's enough!' he yelled. 'Let them go. Let them live. They are trying to live. They came against us and we have killed a few. If we kill them all they will send a bigger army against us.'" (Bob-Tail-Horse: as told to Stanley Vestal.)

Author's note: This scarcely sounds like Colonel Clayton's "slit-eyed, Tatanka Yotanka." All respect to Mr. Vestal, but for me, it is difficult to place the credence in Bob-Tail-Horse's story, he apparently does. Colonel Clayton's has far more of a red "ring" to it.

have no part of any night wanderer from the Gathering Place of the Souls. At the same time I figured their wild brothers would have made short change of me in either event.

In all those months through the blue-cold of the northern winter I dared let no man, red or white, see me. I became in effect the ghost I was supposed to be. Still, I was seen.

The loneliness of that endless journeying through the snows, coupled with the necessity of stealing food and ammunition, forced me into periodic night visits to various hostile camps. I was stopped on several occasions and, Hussein being as readily known to them as I, the story of the spirit-shade of Cetan Mani roaming the snowlands became widespread among them.

In its way this was good, for while no Sioux would knowingly ride the trail of a dead warrior, neither would he dare ignore his existence. Small offerings of pemmican, buffalo jerky, smoked fat and ammunition began to appear outside villages where I'd been sighted.

In this way I lived through the winter, being forced by its success to cater somewhat to my occult status.

I shot a very pale yellow cinnamon bear, almost an albino, on the Upper Tongue. Tanning its thick pelt, I rode henceforth clad in its furry white shroud. Old Hussein seemed to grow grayer with each frosty moon and since his rough winter coat was generally coated with snow or ice, we no doubt made a compelling sight. Seen through a howling half-swirl of Montana blizzard, the effect heightened by the eerie, long-drawn wolf call I had perfected, the impression was notably productive. Rarely did we fail to find our offering awaiting.

These silent visitations upon my Indian hosts were productive not of sustenance alone. Lying in the banked snows outside the council lodges on selected moon-dark evenings, one could learn much of the news of the Nation.

American Horse had been killed, his forty-eight-lodge village, destroyed. Captain Anson Mills had led the raid . . . Three Stars was back in the country, campaigning . . . Colonel Nelson A. Miles, "Bear Coat" Miles, most respected of white soldier chiefs, was up in the Yellowstone country with a big force . . . Sitting Bull had counciled twice with Bear Coat, the second council ending in a battle . . . The white chiefs in Washington had passed a law that until the Sioux gave up all claims to the Powder River country and the Black Hills, no rations would be issued . . . Starving, the hostile chiefs were signing.

Red Cloud had been deposed as chief on the reservations and Spotted Tail was in full agency charge . . . General MacKenzie had captured and burned to the stick, the village of Dull Knife's Cheyenne. In the fight, Last Bull, chief of all the Cheyenne Dog Soldiers, was killed . . . The Cheyenne were done . . . Little Wolf had fled with the survivors, seeking aid from Crazy Horse. Crazy Horse would have none of Little Wolf's war on the whites, was thinking, in fact, of surrender . . . Little Wolf, angered, went to the Army and joined as a scout, requesting duty in the field against his old war chief, Tashunka Witko . . . Crazy Horse was now camped on Reno Creek . . . Sitting Bull had struck out for Canada with two hundred lodges . . . Spotted Tail, Crazy Horse's uncle, respected by all Sioux, was coming to council with the war chief. . . . Crazy Horse had agreed to surrender! He was going in without a fight! . . . There were rumors abroad that he had vowed to murder his old enemy, General Three Stars Crook . . . Crazy Horse was very angry, he denied this lie stoutly. He was going to meet Three Stars face-to-face, and tell him what a lie this was.* He was going in, very soon . . .

By the time I heard this last news winter had soaked away into the warm earth, spring was jumping the short grass up an inch a night.

Knowing the great Oglala, I believed neither that he would utter such vain boasting as the Crook murder rumor, or that he would contemplate surrender. His enemies among both Army officers and jealous agency chiefs, were too well known to him. He would realize surrender meant death or, worse yet, life imprisonment.

I returned to my wanderings half-satisfied these were but campfire gossipings. Still, somehow, I drifted north and west, toward Beaver Creek. I would hear for myself what was being talked in the village of the war chief.

And so once again I came to the Tongue Valley under the Wolf Mountains, where ten years before my Indian career had begun. And again, from my hiding place in the hills, I watched as I had that long-ago night when the scalps of the wood-train troopers had danced on the wheeling pole. And again I heard Tashunka Witko speak.

It was a moonlit May evening, as still and quite as a trout pool at dusk. The words of the war chief carried clear.

*Crook himself believed this story, refusing to council with Crazy Horse because of it. It would seem, with thousands of troops backing him up, a rather weak-livered belief.

"My uncle, Spotted Tail, has said there is no use fighting any more. You all heard him. He is right. I have fought long and I love this Land of the Spotted Eagle. But I am tired and they are too many. I am done now. I am going in. I have asked Tatanka Yotanka if he will surrender, too. Here is what he said. He said, 'I do not wish to die just yet.' That is what he said. He has struck his lodges for the Land of the Grandmother.* The trail is broad. Anyone can see it. Those who will, may follow it. But it is not my trail. My home is here on these lands that have been taken from us. I will not run away. I am going in. I am going to the Red Cloud Agency. I have told Spotted Tail I would do this. Tashunka Witko has spoken."

I shrank down in my cover, stunned. He was really going to do it. My ears had heard but my heart wouldn't listen.

Next morning the lodges came down, about half of them traveling east with Crazy Horse, the other half, a hundred or so, turning northward for Canada and Sitting Bull.

As the Oglala moved down on the Red Cloud Agency I hung on their trail like a shadow, not knowing why I followed or what I hoped to do. At the agency, Crazy Horse's wife fell ill with the white sickness. (I had long since determined she no longer had my son, but was not able to discover who did have him or even if he still lived.) Crazy Horse asked permission to take her down to his trusted friend, Dr. McGillycuddy, at Spotted Tail. Permission was refused.

The war chief wasn't used to asking permission, far less having it refused. Black Blanket was dying of tuberculosis. He went anyway.

I trailed the twenty Government scouts sent out from Red Cloud to arrest and bring him back. When they rode up to him the war chief whirled his pony on them, his handsome face distorted.

"I am Crazy Horse!" His words rapped out like shots. "Don't touch me; I'm not running away!"

This was too much medicine for the scouts. They hadn't enough war honors among them to entitle the laying of one finger on such as the war chief. They fell into the dust of Tasina Sapewin's travois, forming an honor escort for the mighty Oglala's approach to Spotted Tail.

Spotted Tail rode out to meet Crazy Horse. The two halted,

*Canada.

hands upraised. With no preliminaries, the old chief spoke.

"We never have trouble here; the sky is clear, the air is still and free from dust. You have come here and you must listen to me and my people. I am chief here. We keep the peace. We, the Brules, do this. They obey me. And every Indian who comes here must listen to me. You say you want to come to this agency and live peaceably. If you stay here you must listen to me. That's all."

This speech was punctuated with the flat clicks of loaded rifles cocking. A hundred Brule warriors backed Spotted Tail.

When the old Brule chief had finished speaking, Crazy Horse said not a word, simply kicking his pony in the ribs, riding straight for the Brule ranks. They drew back and made him a path through them. The war chief rode, hard-faced, looking at no one. Here was Crazy Horse. Do not touch him. But the agent at Spotted Tail, Major General Lee, had the Oglala's confidence. Crazy Horse agreed to return to Red Cloud on Lee's guarantee that no harm was intended him; and that not a hand would be laid on him. Also that they would ride alone, he and the war chief, unattended, both un-armed.

The two set out, Lee in an Army ambulance, Crazy Horse riding his pony.

I shadowed the return journey. All along the route, groups of agency Indians appeared out of the hills, falling word-lessly into place around and behind the war chief. By the time they neared Red Cloud no less than two hundred Brule friendlies were riding along.

Crazy Horse grew uneasy. This looked like treachery, a trap. What had Lee to say to that?

The agent quieted him by saying the Indians were riding an honor escort out of respect for his fame. But I knew the war chief's heart must be bad within him, for his ramrod figure slumped dejectedly, proud head bowed to the chest.

I had gotten in close enough to the agency lodges while Crazy Horse was at Spotted Tail, to hear some night-talk.

At Red Cloud, Lieutenant "White Hat" Clark hated Crazy Horse. He it was who had spread most of the evil stories about him: that the Oglala chief planned to murder Crook, skip the reservation, start another war . . . Where would he get the guns for this new war? The horses? No matter, the rumors flew anyway. And the white chiefs in Washington be-lieved them . . . Orders had come to arrest Crazy Horse . . . He was to be sent to the Dry Tortugas for life, and with-out trial.

These were rumors, true. But Tashunka Witko had ears. What I had heard, he had heard. And, no doubt, much more.

It was dark when the cavalcade reached the Red Cloud Agency. More rumors were crawling. Crazy Horse's friends began to show up. Soon they were as many as the friendlies. Ugly talk ran through them. Crazy Horse had been promised a council with the big soldier chief at Red Cloud, General Bradley. He was to be given the chance to state his own case about the lies his enemies were spreading . . . Crazy Horse was innocent. His enemies were killing him with crooked tongues . . . That promise had better be kept. If it wasn't—look out!

Just as ugly was the talk running through the agency Sioux. "Crazy Horse makes trouble. He stirs up the dust all the time. We are tired of him. If that damn Crazy Horse tries anything funny there will be big trouble!"

In the darkness and confusion it was easy for me to mingle with the Indians. I stood by Bradley's quarters as General Lee walked up with Crazy Horse. The adjutant stepped out of Bradley's office, saying, "General Bradley directs you to turn Crazy Horse over to the officer of the day, at once."

Lee stepped quickly out of earshot of the war chief, taking the adjutant with him roughly, by the arm. "My God, man! I can't do that. I've promised him he could talk to General Bradley. That's the only reason he came along. He wants to tell his story and by God I've given him my word on it!"

"I'm sorry, sir. The general was absolutely definite."

"Well, so am I!" Lee's voice whipped with indignation. "You just hold that order. And don't touch that Indian whatever you do. Not a hand on him, do you hear? I'm seeing Bradley right now." Going to Crazy Horse the agent asked him gently, "Will you go in the little office and wait there, Tashunka Witko? I must talk with the White Soldier Chief first."

Crazy Horse nodded seriously, shook hands with Lee, went quietly into the office. With him went his friends, High Bear, Touch-the-Clouds, Swift Bear, Black Crow, Good Voice. Outside the door, armed Indian police stepped quickly in to set up a guard. At this, an angry murmur lashed through the watching Oglala.

Lee came out of the general's office minutes later, his face as black as a buffalo's. Nearing the office where Crazy Horse waited, he set his face as pleasantly as he could.

"The night is going and the Soldier Chief says it is too late for a talk. He says to go with the officer of the day and not a hair of your head will be harmed." *

Crazy Horse's friends were happy. All had turned out well. In the morning there would be the council; things would be cleared up.

"See, Tashunka? No reason for worry, after all. Don't you feel foolish, now? And you thought they were trapping you! The Soldier Chief's heart was good all along. *Woyuonihan!*"

The war chief smiled that rare, quick smile. I knew a sudden fear. Was I now seeing its dark flash for the last time? Out went his hand, seizing that of Captain Kennington, the O.D. eagerly. But Kennington wasn't smiling. He and two armed guards led the great chief away, as peaceful and trusting as a child. My heart sank like a spent bullet in clear water. They were headed for the guardhouse.

The yard in front of that building was well lighted, filled with soldiers, and I dared not follow across it. But all of us there in the shadows saw clearly enough the tragedy which came now with such stupefying speed.

As I watched the white Judases leading the last of the Sioux fighting chiefs into that dingy frontier-post guardhouse, I knew why I had followed Tashunka Witko all these weary days from the Tongue. I would break him out of that stinking prison if it were the last act of my mortal life. Suddenly I heard my own voice, crying out, *"H'g-un! H'g-un!"*

I do not know that he recognized my voice but he stopped dead, half-turned in his tracks, peering intently back.

On the echoes of my cry had sprung another, deeper one. The whole crowd, hostile and friendly alike, burst forth in a spontaneous, *"Hun-hun-he!"* It was a last, grateful salute to a warrior whose kind would ride the northern plains no more. Crazy Horse quit peering then, waved to his friends, stepped toward the door.

The portals swung inward, the war chief following its invitation without hesitation.

We saw the stiffening which shot up through him like a lance. Even we across the courtyard could see the iron-bound cells within, the manacled and chained occupants, the patrolling guards with their bayoneted rifles.

Too late now the proud Oglala saw the treachery. His hand

---

*This was a black lie. Actually Bradley, a martinet, refused point-blank to hear one word from Crazy Horse. He had his orders. They read: "Arrest and imprison." That was that. Lee, I think, may be excused his part in the treachery. He was in an impossible position.

flashed to his buckskin shirt, came away with a short hunting knife. Where or how he had gotten it, was never found out. With a scream which I have heard reported as one of terror, he wrenched from his guards, sprang for the guardhouse door. That heart never knew terror. The cry which burst from his lips was that of the hunting panther. The war cry of the Oglala Bad Face People.

As a man, the watching Indians surged toward the guardhouse, carrying me with them.

We saw Crazy Horse crouching like a tiger just inside the door, Captain Kennington with drawn saber barring the way. The two bayonet-armed guards could not fire or lunge for fear of hitting the captain. The crazed Oglala, probably one of the greatest knife fighters of his race, came at Kennington straightaway. The officer demonstrated far more intelligence than he had so far shown, by getting the hell out of the way. Crazy Horse leaped out of the door, the two guards after him, yelling. "Kill him! Kill him! Don't let him get away!"

As the fleeing chief hit the courtyard, his own friends, not wanting to see him shot down in cold blood, grabbed him. Little Big Man, a very powerful brave, pinned both his arms behind him.

But Crazy Horse had seen the iron-house. He knew now the Dry Tortugas rumor was no rumor. He was insane. Little Big Man fell away with a slashed arm. Even in his desperation, the chief would not kill a friend. Swift Bear and other Brule friends seized him.

Kennington rushed up, slashing at the war chief, yelling hysterically. "Stab him, kill the son-of-a-bitch!"

The Indians whirled their captive out of reach of the maddened officer. All the while Crazy Horse wrenched and twisted to get free. He fought furiously, whining like a mad bear. "Let me go. Let me go. Can't you see they're killing me?"

The guards were on him now, with their bayonets. The first lunged at the struggling Indian, missing and jamming his bayonet into the guardhouse door. The second stabbed twice at the war chief—and both times the bayonet blade came away bright red.

A low roar leaped up from the Indians, Crazy Horse stopped fighting, drew himself erect. His voice was the old purring voice. When he spoke the silence was thicker than winter fog over a river swamp.

"Let me go, my friends. You have got me hurt enough."

These were soft words but all the Indians took their hands from him, shrinking back like coyotes from the presence of the king wolf. The war chief turned slowly and began to walk. One. Two. Three steps. Without a sound, he slid forward into the dirt of the courtyard, his shirt and leggings already black with running blood.

The camp broke into an uproar. Here was the white man at his old game. Arrange a peace talk and while the tongue of friendship was wagging, slip the steel into your back. Friendly Brule, reliable Minniconjou and hostile Oglala alike, hooted, yelled and war whooped. Crazy Horse's worst enemies' hearts were bad within them. Cold murder had not been in the bargain. Homicide is a crime almost unknown to the red man. Sudden death to be sure. But in battle, man against man. That an armed man would stab another while that one was being tight-held, helpless to fight back, passed belief.

But it had happened. There wasn't much to be done, either. Soldiers came running with fixed bayonets. Crazy Horse's friends, including Cetan Mani, made themselves very scarce. The day of the Sioux was gone. His power broken. His medicine spilled. He was a dog. A rabbit. Run, Sioux, run!

I dived around and hid in the last place a soldier might poke his bayonet-following nose; smack up behind the O.D.'s office.

Touch-the-Clouds ran up to his fallen leader's body. "Let me take him to the lodges of his people," he cried, brokenly. "You have killed him here. Let him die with the Indians."

"Carry him into the office." Captain Kennington's voice was shaking. "And get out. All of you. Guard! Clear out this yard."

"I will not go. Where my friend goes, I go. You may shoot me, but I am staying." Touch-the-Clouds was defiant. Kennington must have known he would indeed have to shoot the chief or let him stay.

"You may stay if you give up your gun," replied the captain, anxious to get Crazy Horse inside. Touch-the-Clouds' words held that dignity which somehow the white man's treachery and smallness have not tainted.

"You are many. I am only one. You may not trust me, but I will trust you. You can take my gun."

Stooping, the tall chief lifted the huddled form as tenderly as he would a stricken child. Two bent figures stumbled wordlessly in his wake as he bore the dying war chief into the office. None challenged them. Who would dare? And so they came along. The aged, bewildered parents of Crazy Horse.

Within minutes the camp was dark and silent. Armed guards and Indian police roamed the shadows. Only the dim light in the O.D.'s office gleamed in the black of the deserted yard. The door opened, outlining the departing figure of the post surgeon.

"He's dying." He spoke back into the room. "The bayonet passed through both kidneys. There's nothing I can do." His footsteps went across the yard and faded.

Crouching there against the rear wall, I knew only that I must see my "father" before he died. I slipped around the corner of the building, flattening to the ground as the door opened again. Touch-the-Clouds came out, spoke to the two guards. "He wants to see General Lee, the agent. He wants to tell him he does not blame him. I am going."

One of the guards nodded. "All right. Call out when you come back. Jack, here, is jumpy. Ain't you, Jack?" The other guard growled an answer and then, in the closing flash of the door, I saw him.

Jack had better reason than he could possibly know, to be jumpy. Jack was the guard who had bayoneted Crazy Horse.

The first guard was nearest me and, since shadows are hard to hear, didn't hear me. But the "tunk" of a rifle butt on a skull makes a noise no matter how deft the technique. The second guard, the one called Jack, whirled as his companion slumped groundward.

Jack managed to get his mouth open to yell. But no sound came out of it. None, that is, but the splintering crush of his teeth and face bones as the steel-plated butt of my Winchester drove into them.

"One for Crazy Horse!" I whispered, stepping back to let him fall forward.

Then, as his body came past me, I slashed the barrel of the rifle across the base of his skull.

"And one for his son!"

Inside, all was quiet. Well, almost. Crazy Horse's old parents were across the room, squatting with their faces to the wall, heads blanketed, moaning softly like hurt animals.

The chief lay on a pile of Army blankets on the bare floor. His color was gray, his eyes closed.

Bending over him, I placed the fingers of my left hand on his forehead. *"Woyuonihan,"* I whispered. His black eyes flicked open, looked at me dully, then widened.

"Cetan. Cetan Mani! *Hohahe,* my son."

"Hohahe, my father."

"We are not in Wanagi Yata. Where did you come from?"

I knew there was no time to tell him of myself. "From out of the night. And I must go back into it again. I had to bid my father farewell. Is your heart good, Tashunka Witko?"

"It is good. I am ready. I do not blame them." It was on my tongue to add a bitter curse to this but I thought better. If it gave him peace to be generous with his murderers, why, let him have it.

"Aye, father."

"Even so. Give me your hand, Cetan." I took his hand in mine. It was small and slender in my clumsy paw, like a woman's hand. The touch seemed to quiet him.

"Father."

"Aye?"

"Your daughter, my Star—you buried her well?"

"On the Creek of the Beavers, fifty paces sunward from the headwaters of the last branch."

I held the Aztec charm close to his face that he might see. "She gave me this as she died." He opened his eyes, nodding at the amulet. "She said I must bring it to the child. Does he live? Is he with our people?"

A spasm of pain flushed his face. When it passed, he muttered, "Aye. With Tatanka Yotanka. The Uncle took him at my charge." Here a shiver of a grin flicked the blue lips. "He calls him, 'Cetan Mani Sni, Hawk-That-Cannot-Walk.' "

"Thank you, father. I am saying good-bye now. We shall meet again." He looked at me, steadily.

"My son, I am bad hurt. Yunke-lo is holding my black warhorse outside. Tell the people—" His jaw clamped hard, but the thin trickle of bright blood would come anyway. "Tell the people it is no use to depend on me any more."

"I will pass the word. Sitting Bull himself shall have it. Rest now." He seemed satisfied, speaking once more, however.

"Cetan." His hand fumbled for my arm. "Will you pray with me?"

"Aye"—gathering both his hands—"I remember your favorite—

To ke ya inapa nun we
To ke ya inapa nun we

He wakan yan inapa nun we
He wakan yan inapa nun we

Kola he ya ce e-e-e yo. . . ."

I finished the prayer, backing for the door. Footsteps were approaching outside. Crazy Horse lay quietly, hearing nothing. Tashunka Witko, War Chief of all the Sioux, Fox Dreamer, Keeper of the Sacred Pipe, Spearhead of the Fox Lodge Soldiers, Blood-head of the Oglala Bad Face Band, First Warrior of the Seven Council Fires, was dead. The time: crowding midnight, September 5th, 1877; his age, only the moon before, thirty-three years!

I opened the door, brushing past the astounded Touch-the-Clouds. "Cetan Mani!" He gasped.

"Woyuonihan!" I answered, knuckling my brow. "Greetings from Wanagi Yata. Wakan Tanka gives you good hunting and sends you this message. He hopes all your squaws will have breasts like watermelons."

He stood, motionless, as I faded around the corner of the building and ran for my horse.

Chapter 16

THE LAST branch of Beaver Creek turns off south from the main stream high up in the Wolf Mountains, above the Tongue. It is a wild, plunging little rush of water, bright and sparkling, but singing with loneliness.

Even the wind is quiet up there, and the bird calls muted.

Wi was a ball of copper-orange, low over the distant Big Horns, when I reached its headwaters. Facing the Shining Mountains, I began stepping the westward paces—ten, fifteen, twenty, twenty-five, thirty—then I saw it.

Ahead of me a faint trail, as thin and delicate as though chipped out by the Iktomi, the little Spider Men of Sioux fable, ran swiftly up to a tiny ledge pocketed on the face of a granite monolith which plunged in a sheer drop, fifteen hundred feet, to the Valley of the Tongue below.

Across the breast of this pocket spread a buffalo robe of whispering grass, supporting a tipi of three slim pines; and in its heart, quiet forever beneath the soft, brown needles, lay Star of the North.

No gruesome, carven stone, no staring, outflung cross, marked her resting place. At her feet a blanket of nodding grass, at her head, the softly talking pines. Above her the vaulting blue and cloud-puff white of the prairie sky, below, the warm, red earth and granite rock of the mountain. Beyond, for every hour till the last, the glistening snow-shield of the Big Horns; and daily, the final, warm flood of rose-light benediction of slowly descending Wi.

It was the Sioux way. God was everywhere. Who would dare mark a certain spot? Point a set direction?

I said my last farewell to Star in the Indian manner, without words. How long I lay there silently sharing her piney cover, I cannot remember. But the air was thin and cold and the sky grown black when Hussein, whickering inquiringly from below where I had tethered him, aroused me.

As we went cautiously down through the dark along Beaver Creek, a coyote call, high and lonesome, followed us from the shoulder of the monolith above.

"Good-bye, Star!" I whispered, and went forward more quickly through the growing blackness. . . .

One thousand miles: a thousand miles north, always bearing a little west. The way was long, the hunting bad, the trail dim.

In a grassy valley, two days' journey north of the line, Hussein and I parted trails for the last time. His feet were split and broken to the frog; cannon and hock so splintered he could hobble but a few steps at a time. His eyes, never right since I broke him down on the long run after Star, were gone.

I fed him hand-picked meadow grasses all the while crooning and clucking to him, gently rubbing his scarred back and rusty flanks with a handful of tough wire-grass. When he had fed, I led him to the stream. He nuzzled the cold water but would take none of it. I put my left arm around his neck, my cheek hard-pressed into the tattered mane. The ugly head swung around, eyes staring dimly, soft muzzle reaching for me.

He didn't feel the barrel of the Colt sliding in under his

flopped-ear. The shot echoed strangely flat and dull in the silent valley.

Wasiya, the Winter Giant, was breathing down the collar of my faded sergeant's jacket before I finally came into the mountain-ringed camp of Sitting Bull, far up the West Branch of the Canadian Red River. Standing on the trail, looking down on the lodges below, I had one thought: to see my son and deliver to him his mother's last bequest.

With darkness, I went into the valley, seeking out the familiar red and black tipi of Tatanka Yotanka.

Someone was stirring about inside but the chief's shield and pipe were not in their rack outside the flap and I knew he wasn't home. Presently a very healthy infant's lungs began to exercise themselves within, followed shortly by the grumbling exit of a withered old grandmother bearing an empty water-skin.

As soon as she was out of sight I slipped into the tipi. The baby was lying naked, after the Sioux manner, on a soft-tanned elk robe.

Now, I know nothing about babies but any fool could see at a glance that this one was a chief. He was straight of limb and strongly made, and could kick and scream like a buffalo calf with its head held down. And another thing: as soon as he quit bellowing, which was the instant I picked him up, he opened his eyes and I could see they were as green as jade. This was Star's son. No doubt of that.

I was still holding him, tight-clutched to my breast like any dry-dugged old squaw, when I heard the quick moccasin-step outside. "The old grandmother," I thought, stepping lightly to one side of the flap. "I'll just tap her once, just so, on the place where the braids part. No great harm to her and a peaceful exit for me."

The flap parted and the Colt barrel went up and back—and just as quickly fell back to my side.

"*Woyuonihan*," I said, perforce touching my forehead with the Colt barrel, since the other arm was full of the Hawk-That-Couldn't-Walk.

"*Hohahe*," grunted Tatanka Yotanka. Then, after a long, hard stare, "Sit down. Have you fed?"

"No."

"We will eat."

"Are you not afraid of ghosts?"

"There are no ghosts," he answered, his obsidian eyes boring at me. "I never believed you were burned. But I didn't think you lived, either. You will tell me the story."

"Shall we not have the food, first?" I requested. "I have not fed in three suns."

"*Wonunicun,*" grumbled Sitting Bull. "I apologize."

The grandmother came in then, roasting and serving us hump, tongue and ribs, to Sitting Bull's order. When we were full-fed, he belched very well, instructing the squaw, "Go outside and sit. Do not listen and let no one enter."

She was gone, and quickly I told him my story, ending with Crazy Horse's murder.

"He was the greatest Sioux," said Tatanka Yotanka. "He was the son of all our blood. I loved him."

I was amazed to see the glistening tear-track coursing the seamed gullies of his cheek. "Aye," he nodded, unashamed, "a tear. A tear for Tashunka Witko. A tear for the war chief. A tear for our people. They will never fight again."

"He gave me a message for the people, before he died. I said I would bring it to you."

"He said?"

"He said, 'Tell the people it is no use to depend on me any more now.'"

"Even as I told you"—the old man bobbed his head—"the Sioux will never fight again."

I thought it time to see what was in the wind. I knew the medicine-man viewpoint better than to suppose I was going to get away with ghost-walking into the middle of Sitting Bull's camp. "What of me, Uncle? Any dreams for me?"

He thought a long time, watching his pipe smoke drift. "You will have to go," he announced, finally. "I myself do not know if you are alive or dead. I thought Crazy Horse stole your body before he caused the pile to be burned. But I thought you were dead. Now I don't know. But the people know. The people know you are dead. You'll have to stay dead."

"Where will I go? The white man will not have me."

"Go north. Go far north, to the great water called the Slave. I have heard there are Indians there. They do not know the Sioux. They do not know you. Go and be happy, but you can't live with me. My people will not live with a ghost. You will have to go now. I have not seen you. They have not seen you. That's all."

"How about the grandmother?" I asked, hopefully. "She saw me!"

"She looks but does not see," he pronounced his words with flat finality. "She is blind."

"In the war camp on the Greasy Grass, his mother gave

me this." I locked the silver chain about the baby's neck as I spoke. Sitting Bull's eyes widened at the sight of the Aztec amulet.

"I believe you," he said at last. "But the people believe in ghosts."

"I am going," I answered.

"The baby sleeps." He nodded. "Go quietly."

"Wakan mani." I saluted him, rising.

"H'g-un," he said, simply.

Outside the tipi, the old squaw sat hunkered down under her blanket, crooning softly.

"Wakan mani, Grandmother." I smiled, patting her gray braids.

"It's a bad night," she complained. "Colder than a buffalo's tit in a snowbank."

No one saw me leave the village, and only the stars followed me as I plodded up the cascading course of the river, due northward through the night. The old grandmother had been right. It was cold. And dropping colder with the speed of a stone plummeting still water. A keening wind began to whistle down out of the north, humming its lonely song into my gritted teeth, bringing with it the ice-fresh smell of the snow which, hours before dawn, lay thigh-deep upon the trail.

I buttoned the lean cloth of the Seventh Cavalry coat higher about my throat, hunching my shoulders into the rising gale. The first stinging slivers of sleet began spitting at me out of the blackness. . . .

THE LAST entry in Colonel Clayton's journal is the one above, recounting his departure for the Slave Lake country from Sitting Bull's Canadian camp on the Red River.

The following spring (1878) a French-Canadian trapper, far south of the Great Slave, stumbled over a skeleton, still shredded with the tattered remains of an American soldier's jacket beneath which, carefully wrapped in oiled skins, rested the journal herein recounted.

The document was addressed to the Clayton family of La Grange, Georgia, and it was there duly delivered the summer of '78.

As these final words are appended and I look slowly at the faded pages before me, a picture of the bleak northland, driving snows, a wolf's dreary howl and a few, poor human bones, snagged with the faded blue of 7th Cavalry cloth, arises, and I think, indeed, "There were no survivors."

ABOUT THE AUTHOR

WILL HENRY was born and grew up in Missouri, where he attended Kansas City Junior College. Upon leaving school, he lived and worked throughout the Western states, acquiring the background of personal experience reflected later in the realism of his books. Currently residing in California, he writes for motion pictures, as well as continuing his research into frontier lore and legend, which are the basis for his unique blend of history and fiction. Ten of his novels have been purchased for motion picture production, and several have won top literary awards, including the Wrangler trophy of the National Cowboy Hall of Fame, the first Levi Strauss Golden Saddleman and five Western Writers of America Spurs. Mr. Henry is a recognized authority on America's frontier past, particularly that relating to the American horseback Indian of the High Plains. His books include *Chiricahua, The Bear Paw Horses, I, Tom Horn, From Where the Sun Now Stands,* and *The Squaw Killers.*